T0348981

THE INTERPRETER

ALSO BY DAVID K. SHIPLER

The Wind Is Invisible: And Other Poems

Freedom of Speech: Mightier Than the Sword

Rights at Risk:
The Limits of Liberty in Modern America

The Rights of the People:
How Our Search for Safety Invades Our Liberties

The Working Poor: Invisible in America

A Country of Strangers:
Blacks and Whites in America

Arab and Jew:
Wounded Spirits in a Promised Land

Russia: Broken Idols, Solemn Dreams

THE
INTERPRETER

a novel

David K. Shipler

GREEN CITY
BOOKS

Green City Books
©2025 by David K. Shipler Living Trust
For more information, contact Green City Books:
editors@greencitybooks.com
Published 2025
Published in the United States of America
ISBN: 978-1-963101-07-2

First Edition
designed by Isaac Peterson
cover art by Isaac Peterson
Library of Congress Cataloging-in-Publication Data has been applied for.

To those who interpret their countries'
wars for those who watch from safety.

AUTHOR'S NOTE

This is a work of fiction mixed with fragments of truth, inspired by a good friend and interpreter who was never free to write his own story. Yet all the main characters are invented, including the correspondent and his wife, who are not meant to resemble anyone real. Most episodes are entirely made up; a few are embellished from reality. Sadly, the scenes of torture actually occurred as described. Several minor players are modeled on real people of the same names, among them Vietcong Colonel Võ Đông Giang and US Ambassador Graham Martin. Likewise, the characters Mrs. Thương, Nguyễn Thị Hoà, and Võ Tấn Đức resemble people who endured the misfortunes recounted here. Captain Bud Traynor and Captain Tilford Harp are the real names of real heroes.

CHAPTER 1

Lanh thought he had earned his reputation for street smarts, yet here he was being street-dumb, allowing himself to be propelled by the witless American into the dicey checkerboard of rice paddies.

The correspondent for the *Tribune* was pressing forward, all on the word of the paunchy regional commander who over lunch in Diên Khánh had belched his assurances that yes, government forces had the area completely pacified. No mines lurked beneath the dusty, shell-pitted footpath, no menacing Vietcong hid among the brush lines that bordered the paddies. The refugee settlement beyond was as safe and still as the baking midday sun could make it. So said the slightly poetic regional commander—poetic because of the lyrical seasoning that Lanh enjoyed sprinkling into his translations to make his country into a land of metaphors.

The path was empty. Not a single child was using a stick to roll the bare rim of a bicycle wheel. No old man balanced a shoulder pole laden with baskets of rice. No young couple rode with a brace of ducks hung over their motorbike. There was no symphony of beckoning cackle-calls by women sitting cross-legged behind tarps spread with guavas and durians. Instead, absence ruled with silence.

"Too quiet," said Lanh, who stopped walking and squinted up at the long nose of the new boy in town, here to blind the countryside with his alabaster skin. *There is a reason we call them Long Noses.* Lanh kicked away the unkind thought, then said, "Pen, we need to turn around."

"Why?" asked Pen.

"Could be VC."

"What? It's relaxing after the scary chaos on the road. There's nobody around."

"Exactly."

"The commander said it was safe."

"Commanders always say it's safe."

"Let's keep going. I really need to talk to those villagers. See if the rumors are true."

Lanh was sure the rumors were true, that Vietcong at night were dropping grenades down the refugees' wells to suggest that they might better return to the VC-held villages they had fled.

"Why?" Pen had said when he'd first heard the report. "I thought they were trying to win hearts and minds."

That was you Americans who were trying to win hearts and minds. Then Lanh answered, in the weary patience of a teacher too familiar with the lesson: The VC want population. They have grabbed land since the so-called ceasefire, installed their blue and red and gold flags high on long bamboo poles to stake their claims. But the land is no good without people they can tax and recruit as fighters.

This still photograph of the war at present was where Lanh was careful to stay unless asked. Pen asked nothing further, so he did not hear about the past, the long sweep of the past that churned inside Lanh's meditations. Nor did he hear Lanh's prescient observation on the future: *The war is ending, so fear is rising.*

History begins the day you arrive in the country, Lanh realized once again. His previous charges in the *Tribune's* bureau, one after another, had not brought much with them either, except America's disillusionment and exhaustion and the whiff of tear gas from streets at home. But here on the ground, the logic of war evolved perpetually. This war of national liberation and national captivity, of anti-colonialism and anti-communism, of independence and subjugation—this war had shifted shapes through decades until now in 1973, in scruffy patches of hardship, it had cheapened into a struggle over land and over people, but not over whole people, not for their hearts and minds. Americans had counted dead bodies to measure success; the Vietcong counted live bodies, all commodities on the balance sheet. That was the real story. The grenades down wells? That would be a story for the daily paper, quickly read and then shredded by the shrapnel of events.

Lanh was trying hard not to see his newest boss as a cocksure veteran of three weeks in Nam, a poseur in his pressed khaki safari suit, a seeker of bang-bang, an evader of history, and a keen spotter of the momentary.

Pen insisted, so down the empty path the two hunters resumed their stride, each hunting in his own way. Lanh gave a sour gaze sideways as he wondered at the correspondent's focus, like a cheap lens that blurred the periphery where ambiguity could be found. Lanh was a photographer, too, and he knew about depth of field and artful composition. Such certainty, he thought. What would certainty feel like? Lanh hunted with doubts, like a gatherer of hints and questions. He noticed the slightest telltale movements in the brush, listened to the hush, took heed when locals fluttered away like birds before a storm. If he had been a Bedouin, he would have felt the presence of smugglers in the winding desert wadis. If he had been a fisherman in fog, he would have picked up the smell of unseen land that lay too close. Pen, at home a sailor in New England fog, should have sensed the parallel long before he finally did.

Nothing was happening on the path, which became a low dike through a stretch of neat paddies that ran as far inland as residents of Diên Khánh dared to go. Thin, green shoots of rice were plump with grain, almost ready for harvest, and the refugees, Lanh knew, would be afraid but eager to return to their own villages, not to miss the crop. The VC's timing was adroit.

Soon after the paddies disintegrated into fallow ground, the scattered tin-roofed bamboo shacks of refugees came into view. Not so much a camp as a rough cluster of makeshift shelters, the settlement suddenly enveloped them. Swarms of smiling children surrounded them, gazing curiously at Pen, demanding candy, begging Pen to take their picture with the Pentax hanging around his neck. A few ventured close enough to reach out and touch the hair on Pen's arms, a novelty. A little boy grabbed his hand and pulled him over to a well to see the stones collapsed in among themselves.

All the while, Lanh squatted and joked with the kids and watched adults who stood at a distance, intrigued and wary. He ambled over to them casually, motioned for Pen to stay away, chatted them up in musical Vietnamese, said something that made them all laugh, and when they were loose and the conversation fluid, Lanh gestured with a flick of his hand down at his side, for Pen to approach.

At least Pen had already learned to keep his notebook in his pocket at first. Lanh had given the little lecture early on: The "peasants" of South Vietnam, bruised, jailed, tortured, mangled, and terrified by both sides, were inclined to tell the visiting stranger what they thought he wanted to hear. At the edges of control, after all, they had to switch allegiances between day and night, as infiltrating VC fighters entered after dark, then at daybreak melted away to patrols of swaggering government soldiers. Even vocabulary shifted, Lanh said. Communists became liberators at sundown, and the government became the Saigon regime or the puppet administration. The words for *hamlet* and *village* and *province* were all different, derived from the separate lexicons that all civil wars devise.

Lanh liked that his Americans spoke no Vietnamese, so language could be his zone of freedom, his poetic license. He liked that he seemed magical in cutting through a farmer's ingratiating haze to reach some firmer core of truth. To get there again and again took time, though, more time than they turned out to have.

Lanh translated Pen's questions gently. The refugees answered gracefully.

Vietcong taxes? The old man in the conical hat, face calloused by the sun and the war, gazed far out for a moment, then said, "On a stalk of rice, you keep the grain at the top and the grain at the bottom. They get all the grains in between."

The sons? A woman quivered for an instant, then answered in a voice so high it sounded like a shriek. "They join because they have to."

"Or they want to," said another woman at her side.

"Hãi did not want to. He was swept away like chaff in the wind."

The wells? "We hear explosions in the night but are too afraid to go out. Ten of fourteen wells have been destroyed. Soon we will just dry up." She bent down, scooped up some earth, and let it filter through her fingers.

Never before having worked through an interpreter, Pen both wanted and hesitated to trust every word, Lanh figured. He had seen that puzzled expression on the faces of other newcomers who loved the quotes but doubted the eloquence of humble farmers, poor and uneducated. Poor in material goods and uneducated in classrooms, Lanh would say if asked, but rich and thoroughly schooled by warfare's demanding hardships and countryside politics. Besides, lyrical explanations could hint at something barely disguised, too risky for the teller to say but safe for the listener to infer.

By now Pen was scribbling furiously, getting names and ages as if he were still covering a fire in Boston, where fussy editors demanded every detail. Then, a man of middle age, his blue shirt unbuttoned casually halfway down his chest, came smiling and introduced himself as a village leader. His assessment was crisp and critical: "These people here don't want to live with the Communists. That's why they fled to the nationalist side. And now if the nationalists don't look into their situation and help them, where do they go?"

"Help them how?" Pen asked.

A volley of shots peppered the quiet and sent everyone scampering, kids out front, the elderly behind and moving with stiff quickness toward a large bunker of sandbags. Lanh thought he saw Pen's notebook shaking. More shots, but from where? They seemed stereophonic, a *rat-tat-tat* from all around. Lanh calmly pointed to the treeline, grabbed Pen's shivering elbow, and guided him to the bunker.

They were the last in, and stood just inside the doorway. An old woman, teeth stained red with betel, spotted Pen with alarm. "Mỹ! Mỹ!" [American! American!] she gasped. She pushed on his back and shoulder, trying to force him out to rid her shelter of this mortal risk to them all if the VC entered. She was too feeble. She couldn't budge him. He carried America's bigness, its inertia, its stolid anxiety. Lanh said something sharply to the woman, and she desisted. *How casually we endanger people*, Lanh thought. A trembling resentment rose to his throat.

The small-arms fire continued, on and on like strings of firecrackers. Pen shuddered and steadied himself against a row of sandbags. Lanh watched him and the others coolly, eyes darting into shadowy corners of the bunker, reading sounds. Then came a series of explosions at the perimeter of the settlement. "Mortars," Lanh said with a nod. It had taken a while, but the commander's regional force had deigned to resist, from a safe distance.

The shooting stopped, followed by soundlessness, this time as a respite not a warning. Villagers stepped tentatively out as if testing whether the ground would hold them, and gradually resumed their daytime lives. Pen moved gingerly from dimness into comforting sunlight. He rearranged the expression on his face. "Can we talk to a few more people?"

he asked Lanh, who answered simply, "I think we better get out of here."

Lanh had seen this before, a reporter trying to drown his boiling panic with cold professional duty.

"I'd just like to get that man's name." Pen nodded toward the village leader.

Lanh repeated, "We better go." And so they did, with Pen looking torn between fear and curiosity, glancing over his shoulder at the unrecorded details that would leave holes in his story.

As the two of them walked back along the dike which became a path, they saw coming toward them a contingent of the South Vietnamese regional unit in their baggy olive drab fatigues, led by the paunchy commander, whose look of surprise was hard to read. It was more complicated than relief, more conflicted than worry. "I thought you were dead," Lanh translated him as saying. And so did the residents of Diên Khánh, evidently, for scores of them turned out and lined the path to gawk at the surviving American ghost.

Probably half an hour had passed since the first shots and the appearance of the government soldiers. Pen asked Lanh to ask the commander what had taken so long and by the way, don't you guard the perimeter of this settlement? Lanh didn't fudge the question, and the self-indictment came back from the commander: "It was lunchtime. Our unit was on break." This answer, an omen, made Lanh smile thinly.

"The Lunch Hour War," Pen cracked, and got a dry laugh in return, a foreboding they would both remember a year and a half later as Saigon fell.

Riding back down the coastal highway in the bureau's dented Fiat, Lanh behind the wheel, they sat quietly for a while, Pen leafing through his notebook, redoing his scribbled handwriting so he could decipher it later. Lanh negotiated among the bikes laden with large tin boxes, bundles of firewood, baskets of brass shell casings, slabs from wooden ammo boxes, mangosteens, bananas, the newest harvest of rice, and whole families of children wedged between parents—the land's rich bounty mixed into the detritus of war, with nothing discarded and everything put to use.

This was the chaos Pen found scary, Lanh realized. An orderly man comes to Vietnam and does not see the order in the seeming disorder. Instead, he is soothed by the dangerous calm.

Lanh displayed no smugness about his accurate apprehensions of the day, and Pen offered no deference. They were both pros in their own ways, doing their jobs behind businesslike shields of purpose that betrayed no introspection. Lanh guessed that Pen felt vindicated, that he had pushed past Lanh's timidity, collected just enough for his story, avoided death or capture, and proved to himself that the uncertain countryside of Vietnam could be navigated with success. Lanh's summation: the American needed education.

These thoughts, barely formed, resided unspoken as the two men sat side by side. However, Pen's right hand shook as he tried to rewrite his notes. Lanh's hands were steady on the wheel.

In late afternoon they pulled over by a stand selling grilled shrimp on rice noodles. An ancient woman trudged along the side of the road, her gnarled hands clutching a long cloth wrapped around an entire wooden ammunition crate on her crooked back.

Lanh put down his bowl, walked to her, smiled a greeting, and began to chat. He spoke with his entire body like a dancer, never still. He bobbed on the balls of his feet, stroked the air with his hands, touched the crate delicately, cocked his head to listen, threw it back to laugh, concentrated his gaze in respect. Pen stayed where he was, busily picking out shrimp one at a time with his chopsticks. The woman put down the empty box as if her bones ached and sat on it. In a few moments, Lanh brought back her story. "She buys these crates from the ARVN artillery unit up the hill," he reported. "She pays three piasters and takes them to the refugees down there and sells them for four. They break them up to make houses."

"For one piaster profit? A true capitalist," Pen sniffed. "A real entrepreneur. Leave you folks alone and you'll build a new Taiwan."

Yes, which is why she is a bigger story than grenades down wells, Lanh wanted to say.

They sat on two other upturned crates and finished their bowls.

Nguyễn Văn Lanh took his motorbike from the Saigon bureau to the twisting alleys overhung with drying clothes and busy with scampering children, working his way into the labyrinth that wound to Lane 342, where his narrow house stood wedged among other narrow houses, all happily jammed with multiple generations and carelessly decaying with the passing years. He could have afforded better with his *Tribune* pay, but he chose to stay behind with the people.

The street boys who were called *bụi đời*, the "dust of life," drifted into his neighborhood at night to escape the police roundups that tried to keep the capital clean—clean of the human calamity that war created. Some boys were filtering into the alleys as he made his way home. At first light they would migrate to beg where foreigners were willing to dig into pockets and hand them a few piasters. The dust of life. He felt more like them than who he was.

His two little daughters, Linh and Hiền, ran to hug him as he bent to them. Thuận came drying her hands with a rag and embraced her restless spirit of a man. "So?"

"He's new," Lanh said. "Thinks he can read the country already. I have work to do." Out of the children's earshot, he told her briefly what had happened, and the dark shadow that he knew well passed through her eyes. It did not touch her smile, which Lanh valued as his people's mask of discomfort, much misread by Americans.

"What's the AP guy's name?" Her way of asking, once again, if he couldn't work for a correspondent seasoned by war.

"Mandell," Lanh said. "Yes, he's an old hand here, he knows the limits and the risks and can calculate them as well as I can. But they have Dinh, you know. They don't need me, and the *Tribune* does. And Rosie hired me there. Even though she's back in the States, I'd be letting her down if I left. Besides, the AP doesn't tell the human stories, the ones I look for. The ones I hope for."

It was an old discussion, so Thuận let it go and turned to dinner in their rudimentary kitchen. Great water bugs, like roaches on steroids, scuttled across the counters. Thuận and Lanh paid no attention.

Josiah Pennyman IV, a name that Pen detested, had the bureau's driver, Mr. Kỳ, take him to his villa just north of the cathedral, where his cook was ready with a meal. The house was a colonial artifact worth venerating, a stone and plaster structure of French refinement, somewhat renovated by its Vietnamese Francophile landlady, Madame Bian. She had blessed it with an air conditioner in a window of every bedroom, lazily turning ceiling fans in the humid living room, a sunny internal courtyard decorated with young palms and big glazed pots filled with flowering plants, and a long dining table where one *Tribune* correspondent after another had entertained cabinet ministers and ambassadors.

The house was the only thing that Julie liked about Saigon, so far. It fit her upbringing, an elegant escape down a short cul-de-sac away from the constant bee-like buzz of motor scooters that permeated the mind of the city. She thought of herself as the world's only thirty-year-old who pined for her adolescence, those teenage years as an ambassador's daughter in London. Here, she wore a slightly pinched expression of annoyance and apprehension.

She had not yet unpacked her acrylics and chalk pastels, her brushes and pens, her large tablets of acid-free paper. To become accomplished, in defiance of her parents' whining about her professional choice, she would have to mobilize herself. On the way to this place, propelled by eagerness from the gallery owner who'd sold her benign landscapes at good prices, she had been carried along by the promise of uneasy adventure, a kind of war reporting of her own. Now on the ground, her purpose felt thick and sluggish, her mission naïve and impractical. How was she to reflect on Vietnam with lines and colors?

She gave Pen a brittle hug as he came through the door, then scolded him fondly.

"You're late, my love. I was worried."

"Sorry, Jule. Wild traffic on Highway One, and a good story."

"At least call."

"No place to do it."

"From the bureau, when you got back?"

"Oh, yeah. Sorry. My head is too full. An exciting day."

"Well, I had an exciting day, too, circling around my supplies, not daring to pull them out, because when I do, they will sit there calling out to me to do something with them. I'm paralyzed. Am I failing here already?"

Her paralysis paralyzed him. Only tinny phrases of reassurance came to mind, and he didn't even believe them. "You've only been here three weeks. You'll find your way, you always do. If you get out into the city, you'll surely have some ideas."

"Saigon moves too fast for art. It needs to slow down. Or I need to speed up, but I can't. Paint has to dry. Ink has to dry. Seeing needs time. Everything in this city is a noisy blur. It makes me think I have no attention span." Pen said nothing more.

She had spent the day as always, late out of bed, reading from a collection of American poets who used words like light patterns, spiced by a romance novel with a racy cover, deadened by a sinking weight that made her legs too heavy to walk out of the villa into hot, disorienting streets. If emotions had colors, she realized, hers would be gray. Only in flashes did she feel anything—moments of anger at Pen and the war and the daunting city, sadness about herself. Mostly she felt nothing. Yes, paralysis.

What a comedy, she thought. *A shotgun wedding so you could avoid getting drafted for Vietnam, and now you're here anyway, by choice—your choice.* "Did you ever think about that, Pen, how we got married before we knew what the hell we wanted and then ended up in Vietnam even so?"

"I know. Irony abounds. But we knew what we wanted. We wanted each other."

"We wanted each other's bodies. My parents were concerned."

"Parents of girls are always concerned."

"How the fuck would you know, my dearest? You haven't wanted to have one."

"Not yet. We will. We'll know the time."

"Sorry. Sensitive subject. You don't need this now. Tell me what you saw today."

And when he did, she was worried for him, of course, but more intrigued by the old woman selling ammunition boxes.

"What did her face look like? Did you get a picture? You're writing a story about her, too, right?"

She knew the blank look. Pen had not noticed the woman's face, had not taken a picture, had not even remotely thought of doing a story. "I don't know, no, and no. One sad attempt to make a piaster here and a piaster there doesn't exactly justify space in a newspaper."

"But it would justify space in a tablet of art. What did her face look like?"

Pen thought a moment. "Wizened."

"Oh, what a graphic description!" And they both laughed and hugged and went to bed, lying quietly with their eyes open to the blank ceiling.

In the darkness of the bedroom, they could hear the low thunder of artillery, boom after boom. "Outgoing," Pen announced, as he did every night. But he had not yet learned to recognize the sound of every weapon in a war. Each had its audible fingerprint. The M16 rifle, the AK-47, the Thompson submachine gun, the Browning machine gun, the fragmentation grenade, the mortar, the bazooka, the 105-millimeter howitzer. Pen was not there to cover combat, and he would never hear the 500-pound bomb dropped from a B-52, not after the 1973 Paris peace agreement and the putative ceasefire six bloody months before his arrival.

"Outgoing," he would declare wisely, like an old hand. The word was supposed to be reassuring, but Julie shivered. She had heard the term "H and I," harassment and interdiction, fired randomly into the land surrounding the capital. "At least the guns are not aimed at us!" Pen would try to say it lightly.

"No," she would reply. "They are aimed indiscriminately at innocents who are just trying to live their lives." And soon they slept into dreams they would not remember. Except that Pen remembered his own shuddering that day, the small-arms fire rattling around him, the old woman in the bunker, his hand trembling over the notebook.

Every night cannons resound in the town
A street cleaner stops sweeping and listens

So the lyrics of Trịnh Công Sơn came into Lanh's hearing with the distant booms. Sơn was always in danger, he knew, too honest in his songs.

The cannons disturb a young child
At midnight a flare shines in the mountains

"Cannons like a chant without a prayer," he said the line aloud, and Thuận knew he was singing in his head the Lullaby of Cannons for the Night. She hummed part of the mournful tune.

Turning out the bare bulb hanging from their bedroom ceiling, he said, "Too bad it's not raining tonight. Rain makes you sleep better." Rain took him back to his grandfather's farm when the water purred and splashed outside, turning the earth into its sweet metallic smell. A safe place. *Too bad it's not raining tonight*, he thought again.

Too bad, because Lanh would remember his dream. Alone in a swirling monsoon on an empty path, he had to keep spinning around to turn away from the contorted faces. They appeared and disappeared like vapors. Their accusations were carried to him and then away by the hostile wind. They rose in volume and fell after bursts of words. The bus driver gave him a glare of honesty: "It's mined."

The sampan driver, brow creased with condemnation: "VC over there. I'm not taking you." The peddler woman, mouth open in horror: "They're always in that hamlet." The laughing boy on a bike, a malevolent grin, tossing his head: "Not safe." One after another grimaced in disdain. Then the unctuous colonel in green fatigues, fat cheeks glowing, mouth twisted by the lie: "Oh, go ahead. Tell the Long Nose the army has everything under control. He will tell Washington. We are winning. Go ahead and see for yourself." A gold tooth flashed in a challenge, a dare, a death sentence. The soldiers behind him laughed gruesomely. Lanh tried to run, but as in every dream, his legs would not move. He cried out. Thuận rolled to hold him and carry him back into some level of sleep where she hoped he would not remember.

CHAPTER 2

At the end of the alleyway, the pho man's charcoal brazier made the morning air pleasingly pungent, a signal of life. The man gave Lanh a crooked smile as he ladled out a large bowl of steaming noodles in a simmering broth of tripe, basil, and cilantro and handed him a slice of lime, a clutch of bean sprouts, and a shallow dish of nuoc mam.

Lanh suddenly made a private vow to take Pen to a place where they made nuoc mam, to see if Pen would be repelled, shocked, and sickened. Or would he be hit with stunned admiration at the process of producing the rotten-smelling fish sauce, the amber treasure of Vietnamese cuisine? Ah, add a few circular slices of red peppers when you're about to eat, pour it on your food or dip a slice of pork into it, and make every taste vibrant. Pen had been happily eating nuoc mam, but what a wicked test to show him the art of its creation. What a gleeful test before the hard schooling soon to come for both of them.

"Are you thinking?" asked the pho man. Yes, Lanh said, thinking about taking his boss on a nuoc mam tour. The pho man laughed, then whispered in a breath of conspiracy, "No, thinking about what I asked. About liberation, brother."

A time might come when Lanh felt comfortable enough with Pen, as he had with Rosie and most other reporters, to tell of his nagging worry. Someday, he'd predict, he'd meet a Vietcong guerrilla his age who had spent years subsisting and fighting in the jungle. Lanh would have to account for how he, Lanh, had spent those years: in urban comfort, working for the Americans, even as an interpreter at MACV, the American military command, where Rosie first found him. He would have to face that man, surely a wiry and spare figure of sacrifice and hardness, and take himself to account.

This was his haunting fear, which hovered in his self-appraisal like a line of poetry, real enough as allegory. And he had made the mistake, one morning over his breakfast of pho, of ruminating this way to the pho man, whose crinkly smile suddenly dissolved into a gaze of new interest in this neighbor who came daily as the roosters crowed.

A disjointed series of furtive conversations followed, day after day. A younger man whom Lanh had never seen in his quarter once appeared while Lanh was working noodles into his mouth with chopsticks.

He gave his name as Minh. They talked congenially for a while, and they both knew instantly from their pronunciations that they were originally from the North, for they had carried with them the *gi* and *d* spoken as *z*, not the Southern consonant *y*. Lanh's wanderlust had brought him South, where now, if he could choose, he would let the shifting winds of curiosity make him a footloose vagabond. He loved traveling the country to the cities bloated with refugees and the villages destitute from fighting. You must see a lot, Minh said. Lanh nodded as he ate. You must know the struggle for liberation.

Lanh gave him his sideways glance. Politics and treason were so closely intertwined here. "I see it, but I don't know it," Lanh answered. "To know it you have to transplant rice, then have to flee your village before harvest. You have to tread carefully among the mines in your own lands, pretend to support one side by day, the other by night. You have to teach your children not to pick up the grenades and rockets that lie around looking like toys. You have to—"

"Yes, yes," said Minh, who glanced quickly around. His voice was so low, nearly a hiss, Lanh could barely hear him. "Do you also have to love your freedom? Do you also have to help your country be free of the foreigner and his puppets? Do you have to help in the struggle, even in small ways?"

"I am not a fighter." Lanh looked down at this bowl.

"The gun is not the only weapon," said Minh. When Lanh looked up, he saw an enigmatic smile cross the face of this younger man. "Information can be sharpened, like a bayonet." Lanh said nothing. "You translate words. You can give your people whatever voice you wish the Americans to hear. But you put bitter words in their mouths, lies about grenades down wells."

"What! You read what the American writes?"

"We read what he hears you tell him. Remember, the people have many words hiding. Like birds camouflaged in the jungle. You can find the right ones and let them fly." Then Minh slid away like an apparition in the crowd of morning merchants.

The pho man watched as Lanh finished his bowl in unusual silence.

Pen rode to work on his clunky orange bike, with its balloon tires and single gear, which made him strain and pant and sweat in the morning heat while lithe young women in their graceful pastel *áo dàis* glided past. They barely pedaled, it seemed, and looked directly ahead, backs straight, as if propelled by some charm that guided them harmlessly through intersections cluttered with bicycles and motorbikes, cyclos with large foreigners cruising along in their ample front seats, battered Renault taxis left over from the French, corrugated Citroëns like recycled sardine cans, little three-wheeled Lambrettas packed in open cargo areas with people on hard benches, and the occasional white Mercedes of those who were profiting from the war.

Pen tried to stifle his panic by being mystified and fascinated by the capacity of the Vietnamese to avoid collisions without seeming to take notice of one another. The girls in the flowing *áo dàis* never turned their heads toward oncoming traffic, furtively shifting their eyes and varying their courses and speeds almost imperceptibly. No driver swerved or slowed suddenly, but merely threaded through the crawling confluence of traffic, as if to acknowledge the other would be to respect a humiliating obstacle. Pen began to think that this was how the Vietcong and North Vietnamese conducted warfare, as General Giáp prescribed: Attack where the enemy is weak, retreat where he is strong. Someday, Pen thought, somebody will write a doctoral thesis on the cultural traits revealed by how people drive. Meanwhile, when he misjudged the flow of intersecting vehicles and had to stop abruptly, he received looks of disdain.

Some mornings he went to the office by cyclo. He would walk to the end of his alley. He would pass the sumptuous villa and air-conditioned white Mercedes of the courtly Swiss gentleman who headed UNICEF in Saigon, a compensating privilege for the assistance that the man's burdensome paperwork conveyed to children starving, wounded, and orphaned. Pen would pass the shuttered, three-story home of the wealthy young Vietnamese couple whose gains—whether ill-gotten or deserved—elevated them enough in the country's rickety scaffolding to allow them to look down, which they did by mercilessly under-paying and exploiting with long hours the supply of hot and cold running servants who populated their household: this according to gossip that Julie had picked up from her and Pen's own cook and housekeeper. (Americans avoided the word *servants*, in a pseudo-egalitarian pose borne of their history.)

Pen reached the conclusion of the alley, which offered a traveler a quiet moment before bursting into the chaot-ic thicket of the broad avenue that led eventually toward the cathedral. More often than not, a cyclo and its driver were waiting there on the sidewalk, usually the same man. Dressed in khaki shorts and a greasy sleeveless undershirt, he wore a wispy goatee like Hồ Chí Minh's and eyed Pen hopefully. His vehicle seemed designed to minimize guilt, like a rickshaw but with the laboring driver pedaling from high on a seat behind his client, not in front where his ex-ertion could be seen by the relaxing passenger. Pen waved to the driver with a smile and settled himself in the forward bench. It was wide enough for two and had been lovingly upholstered in better days. Now the plastic covering was slightly torn, but that took nothing from the joy of coasting, coasting silently among the surrounding cacophony, residing in front with a full view and with all effort comfortably behind and out of sight, weaving and borne into and above Vietnam, part and apart, accomplice and observer. The cyclo, Pen decided, offered something as close to a metaphysical experience as possible in this land assaulted by guns and sandbags and soldiers and lame and begging children. The ride was therapeutic, his nervous distaste for unpredictable disarray fading block by block into an aloof acceptance. He felt totally relaxed by the time the driver wheeled him up onto the sidewalk in front of his office on Tự Do Street. Pen paid him well, much more than the going rate, and in return received a nod that was grateful, but not at all obsequious, before the man pedaled off to some lucrative intersection.

Always on that sidewalk those days a ravaged woman squatted with a lethargic infant in her arms, the baby's head pockmarked with sores that drew hungry flies. From near her side a skinny boy with a twisted leg crab-skittered up to every passing American, stretching out his hand. "Money?" he would say in English. "Food. Food," and point to the baby and his mother, who would utter something between a moan and a plea. A few, but only a few, would pass a folded 500-piaster bill to the boy, trying not to touch his filthy hand.

Pen passed them by, giving them a wide berth. Upstairs in his office he plunged into a dry story about rice being imported from Louisiana to stanch the wound of wartime harvest deficits in the country that once fed itself abundant-ly. He wondered if anyone would read it.

Late in the morning, when the sun was high and shad-ows shrank to insignificant spots on streets and sidewalks, Pen glanced down through his window and saw Julie step out of a cab. From the mouth of her large paisley shoulder bag stuck the edge of a drawing pad. She started for the office, then slowed and stopped before the woman and her children. She leaned toward the sick baby, fumbled in her bag, pulled out a bill, and placed it gently into the boy's outstretched hand. Then she disappeared into the building entrance and arrived moments later in the office, practically breathless.

"Did you see that poor mother, Pen? Her children are sick, she looks as if she hasn't eaten forever. Did you see her?"

"Yeah, she's there every day."

"I want to draw her. Could I ask Lanh to ask for me? And why don't you write about her? Her suffering must be a story for you."

"I'm busy with rice harvests and imports. Boring but necessary."

"Well, that mother down there is not boring and is also necessary. Look at her beautiful, tormented face. Did you ever see such a face?"

"I didn't notice her face."

"You didn't notice? How could you not notice? Her eyes burned through me."

Pen looked up into Julie's bright blue eyes.

"Like the old woman on the road whose face you didn't notice. So I finally reached into my supplies this morning.

They seemed heavy. Then I left the house and came looking. The woman down there on the street seems to be the only one in Saigon who is staying still enough to catch and put on paper."

Lanh, reading at his desk, said nothing, but he peered over his newspaper to regard Pen and Julie, as if for the first time.

Carried along in the long flow of his own history, Lanh often wondered if everyone wore masks and disguises, and how to see past them. He had his camouflage—his words, his camera, his talents as a fixer for foreigners—concealing the folktale about himself that he wanted to believe—no, that he truly believed. *We all have legends about ourselves*, he thought. *What is Julie's? What is Pen's? What is beneath his safari-suit disguise?*

"Well, go ahead," Pen said. "Lanh?"

"Come down with me and Lanh, please, Pen," said Julie. "Talk to her. Listen to her."

"I've got to finish this piece."

"Can't the piece wait?"

He glared up from his typewriter, then down through the window at the begging family. "Just let me finish this paragraph." He typed with an impatient clatter while Julie turned to Lanh.

"How about it, Lanh? Do you know anything about her?"

Nothing and everything, Lanh thought. *I do not know her name, but I know her as I know my country.*

"No, I don't."

They passed through the curtain of air conditioning that guarded the second-floor office, into the muggy stairwell, and down onto the raucous street. Lanh bent slightly over the fragile woman, smiling gently, speaking softly but cheerfully, and respectfully—always respectfully. His lilt had a rhythm like a song. He opened his hands to her as if he, not she, were the beggar. Since misery is often captivating to those who do not share it, the small ensemble quickly locked Pen into caring. As she spoke in Vietnamese and Lanh listened, into Pen's notebook went the haunted desperation on her face, the blank eyes of the baby, the torn and grimy clothes, the infected wounds, the rotted teeth. As Lanh's translations came, the notebook filled with details: names and ages, home village, scourges of war, her soldier husband's death, street living, scarce piasters, hunger, scavenged food, sickness. *How easy it would be to embellish her words*, Lanh thought, *and how unnecessary*. The mother's name was Mrs. Thương.

Lanh could feel Julie watching. She fingered and squeezed her paisley bag, as if itching to pull out the contents and begin. *Go slowly*, he thought.

The boy's name was Tài. He whispered to Lanh that his mother would send him blocks away and beat him if he came back without money. Older boys would sometimes steal the few bills stuffed in the tin can he held. Often, for scraps of cash, his mother carried buckets of water for fishmongers in the market and dumped it into tanks to keep their fish alive. In her absence, the baby girl lay on the hard concrete like a prop, a can in front of her, Tài behind with an outstretched hand.

Lanh took pictures. He asked, for Julie, if she could make a drawing. The mother said something rapidly.

"She wants to be paid," Lanh explained. "How much will you pay?"

Julie glanced at Pen, knowing the reporter's hard rule against paying people for their stories. "Look," he said. "If you want to pay her to draw her, that's fine. But then I can't write about her."

"Yes, yes, of course, that's the choice." Julie slumped a little. Her first outing thwarted.

"No matter, though," he said. "I'm sure there are plenty more stories like hers to report, a dime a dozen." Lanh glanced at him.

"No," Julie said. "It's more important that you write about her. Maybe I can draw her from Lanh's picture."

The photo the paper ran looked like a pietà, the mother cradling her infant daughter. Pen wrote sparely with compassion, understated as the *Tribune* demanded, just enough to require readers to travel toward the tale and complete the landscape themselves. He wove the story in only 600 words, and when it was published, his more hardened colleagues in the Saigon press corps ribbed him as "the new boy in town." To those who had walked past her again and again, the woman whose name they didn't know was a fixture on the street like a lamppost. They never thought to write about her; she seemed no more remarkable than the lingering humidity after dark in the teeming city at the edge of war.

"Hey, Pen, I've got a tip," confided Buckley, the *Post* guy. He was perched on the Continental Shelf, the worn old hotel's wide veranda. Pen walked by well before lunch, and Buckley was already crouched over a frosty Ba Mươi Ba, a wretched beer by his account, brewed under unfortunate French tutelage. Imagine, he often whined, if Vietnam had been colonized by the Germans instead. Maybe they'd also be able to win the fucking war. "So, Pennyman, here's a good story for you: On Nguyễn Huệ after dark, there's a one-legged whore who gets around with a crooked stick for a crutch." Buckley gave a raspy laugh.

"Oh, that's how you spend your evenings," Pen grinned. He beat the urge to blame Julie for pressing him into the story. Besides, Murphy had Telexed him a herogram for the "touching piece"—crusty old Murphy of the green visor and plaid suspenders, who actually knew the word *touching*, and who'd sent Pen off with instructions to write what the wires did not, what AP, Reuters, UPI, Agence France Presse were missing.

"We can always use the wires," the editor had said. "You'll be our own guy there. Look with fresh eyes, and tell us what we're not getting."

Fresh eyes. In fact, over their very first lunch after Pen had flown into Saigon, Lanh had jabbed his chopsticks into the air and offered the same advice he had tried on every correspondent: "Your first impressions will be the most accurate." Before getting into the quagmire of complexity and nuance, Lanh urged, write with innocence—not with ignorance but innocence. "There's a difference." Then he paused and picked up a prawn while he watched Pen's face to see if the mission was being accomplished.

Pen gave a very slight shake of his head and frowned. "I don't know, Lanh. You have to know what you're talking about before you write."

Lanh beckoned to the waiter for more tea. He fiddled with his chopsticks. He veered off at the oblique angle that hardly ever worked with Americans. A reporter came to Saigon, he remembered, who waited and waited until he knew enough to write and never did, so he never wrote anything but breaking news stories. His editors weren't happy.

"Who was that?" Pen asked.

"I don't want to say."

"Did that really happen?"

"I don't want to say." And they studied each other for a moment before Lanh's face started crinkling, the precursor to his teasing laugh.

"We had a wisecrack in the newsroom," Pen said. "Don't let the facts get in the way of a good story." He quickly added, "It was a joke. We were honest. But I don't want to make mistakes."

Now I'll talk directly, like an American, Lanh decided. "Did Rosie tell you anything useful before you came?"

"Lots. She told me I didn't know shit, so the human story would be as close to the truth as I was likely to get. 'You don't know the history or the culture, you don't have time or space to learn.' Something like that."

Lanh's entire face smiled in delight as he heard his own words to her coming back to him. She had acted as if she had figured out Vietnam, he told Pen, but she did her best work when she was writing about people who seemed small but carried the big issues on their backs.

"Yeah, but I didn't take that as gospel. I do have to learn the history and culture to do a good job."

Lanh took a moment to cock his head and look far away over Pen's shoulder. "Well, meanwhile," he said, "write the story that's in plain sight. You don't have to know every-thing to know a person's story."

"What do you think about her? Her indignant pas-sion—was that a bias? We talked a lot about it in the news-room. A bias toward what? Against what? Did she favor this side or that side? Did she want us to win the war or lose it?"

Lanh said nothing, so Pen went on. "You can't be bi-ased. You have to report things as they are, not as you wish them to be." Lanh's smile was long gone. "She warned me against doing what others did—sticking to what they called news. They put folks they met in their files, she said, and waited for 'context.'" He mimicked her air quotes with his fingers and copied her rolling eyes and disdainful look, enough to get a knowing nod from Lanh, who worked his chopsticks and sipped his tea and stared down at the dregs in his rice bowl.

"I've seen those correspondents," Lanh said finally. "They hope that time alone will give them x-ray vision through the surface of suffering. 'I'm saving string,' they tell themselves. I've heard it many times—until they can tie loose ends together into a whole—a whole that often cloaks the people."

There the conversation ended. Lanh did not go on to pronounce his misgivings about Rosie—even Rosie the compassionate. The Vietnamese were being collected one by one, artifacts in the display. His advice could lead Pen to do the same: to collect. *Unless he moves past seeing us as conve-nient to his work.*

The tea was cold, and the check lay beside Pen's elbow. They plunged back out to the sweltering din of Saigon, which had a way of suffocating elevated thoughts. Rosie's pleas were swallowed by the rush of war. Mostly Pen stayed in the groove of easy "news." It was orderly. The shifting patterns of fighting in the countryside, the pretend politics of the country, the flagging economy, and the dubious intelligence reports on combat victories and Communist atrocities made ready reporting and expected reading.

Yet something else had been awakened by Mrs. Thương and her emaciated children. *You missed the woman selling empty ammunition crates*, Pen imagined Lanh thinking. *Her story would have told more about Vietnam's economic prospects than all the data on rice imports.*

Lanh was not consulted, though. On politics and war and other front-page stories, Pen's went to Boston as caricatures, Lanh thought, as reality misshapen into the newspaper format. Their categories of winners and losers weren't hazy enough. The players did not evolve. The layers of ambiguity were opaque, the well of doubt was never plumbed. Lanh was never asked to read a piece before it was dispatched, his long perceptions were never mined. He was a machine, he realized, a translating, photographing, fixing, arranging, seducing machine—seducing his proud and pummeled countrymen to give up their inner torments to the Americans. To the press, yes, but still to the Americans. Somewhere he had read that the term for *interpreter* in some African language was "word changer." Sometimes he felt a raging vacuum inside himself.

Word changer. Should he be that? Should he do that? Did he do that by making a sentence sing? Would he be found out?

He had little idea what Pen noticed as they passed along shrapnel-pocked roads and paddies framed by broken dikes, through clustered villages armed with soldiers and sellers, barefoot children, motorbike mechanics, tinsmiths, fruit peddlers, squatting women stirring pots and spitting red betel juice into the dust. He did not know if Pen realized that every Vietnamese had a story to tell, if he would only make the time to stop. Lanh had not heard Julie tell Pen that Saigon moved too fast, that pauses were needed for the artist. Lanh did not know that she was finding what she called "human still life," holding people steady in her memory while she painted—and that Pen was watching her work. Collecting.

So Lanh went along at Pen's pace. They focused hard and reported efficiently and translated poetically and photographed artistically and took the measure of the faces etched by war. They calculated the affinities of the population, reduced the story to 700-word dispatches that began with where, what, and when. And sometimes why. Only sometimes.

"What do I do?" Lanh asked Thuận one night after their two little girls had departed into sleep. "I tried being like an American, talking directly, telling him to write what he sees. It hasn't worked."

"What does he think about the war?" she asked.

"What does that have to do with it? My problem is he sees us as props in his play. 'Good quotes,' he says. 'Good story.'"

"That answers the question."

"You mean he wants the Americans to win the war after they've given up and left?"

Thuận gave that dry despairing laugh that now drifted across much of the country. "Maybe he wants the Communists to lose."

"Yes, of course he does. He still thinks it's possible. He thinks the American War has been a good cause."

"So," she said, "that means he sees the people as prizes in the war, not as victims of the war. He wants to capture them by winning. He thinks capturing them will save them. Does that sound right?"

"I don't know. Maybe it does."

"And maybe he is right, Lanh. Maybe if he thinks that, he is right that it will save them—us. We don't want the Communists."

"We don't want any of them. Win. Lose. Victors. Victims. I'm exhausted by the dictionary that doesn't have any words to describe us."

"And you want to get him to see it your way?" She gave him a glance of amused admiration.

To this, Lanh embraced his wife with the adoring look he knew had made her love him since more than a decade past. "I am right!" he laughed so loudly she shushed him, not to wake the girls. "I feel like I'm fighting gravity. It's pulling us down into the neat boxes of this side and that side, and I'm trying to travel in a higher orbit. Yes, I'd like him to fly there with me. Or at least see me where I am. See me. Rosie did, eventually."

"Rosie!" Thuận's exasperation usually ended conversations. But she went on. "Maybe you shouldn't tell him what to think. Maybe you shouldn't be so straight. Go to him a little sideways."

"Lots of Americans go too fast," Lanh said as they sped up to Quảng Trị. But Lanh was the one driving! And he was talking about Pen, of course, scolding indirectly so the reprimand would ricochet precisely to its actual target. "They don't stop to see the people, to hear their stories." *Still, they better hurry. The war is ending. Fear is rising.* "They don't take their time to absorb the country. They're always in a rush. So they don't know us."

"I'm sure you're right," Pen said. Lanh wasn't sure he'd caught the ricochet. "That's how we got stuck in the quagmire," Pen added. *That bad quagmire metaphor,* Lanh thought. He'd read the book, too, with its superior tone and deficient skepticism. It questioned how the war was being fought, not whether it should be fought at all. Page after page, Lanh had waited for Halberstam to condemn the entire precept of America's purpose, and it never came. As he reached the end and snapped the book closed, he groaned to himself in distress. Now he wondered, *Are you that way too, Pen?*

Lanh had read another book as well, the one now driving them northward: Bernard Fall's *Street Without Joy.* Pen wanted to see the stretch of road famously named by French troops back in their own war. Lanh thought it an odd pilgrimage, war tourism. "It's abandoned," he'd told Pen. "Nothing there but bad memories. Everything obliterated in the seventy-two North Vietnamese offensive, you know."

"I know," Pen replied. "I need to go. And I need to go on July twenty-eighth." *Ah, the obsession with round numbers,* Lanh understood, the twentieth anniversary of the French assault on Viet Minh dug in along the road's villages, used to ambush French forces on nearby Highway One. Lanh sighed and shrugged, resigned to a day wasted just so Pen could say he'd been there. *Or are you trying to connect with history?*

As they headed north toward Quảng Trị, though, they were slowed behind a couple of army trucks whose open bays were crammed with children, women, and men jostling among wooden bed frames, tables, and bulging sacks overflowing with clothing and pots. Lanh was poised to pass them, then realized who they might be. Refugees, he had heard, were being helped to return to Hải Lăng, on the Street Without Joy. "We should follow them," he said. "Maybe they're going home."

Sure enough, the trucks soon swung laboriously off Highway One onto a narrower parallel strip of blacktop, Route 555. "This is the Street Without Joy," Lanh said triumphantly. "Did you will this coincidence?" he asked Pen. "Did you align the fates?"

"I wish. Luck smiles on us sometimes."

"Sometimes," Lanh answered with a slice of longing.

The trucks pulled over in a field of ruins that could have come from a forgotten culture. Concrete shells of houses stood precariously among chipped columns and fragments of walls. Rice paddies, smothered by wild weeds, were bordered by vague humps of earth, the faint memories of dikes. Down from the trucks into the desolation climbed the families, who busied themselves stretching tarps and arranging possessions. Among the goods unloaded, Pen jotted down, were heavy bags of rice marked "Crowley, Louisiana."

Can you love people you don't know? Lanh approached with practiced care. He spoke to them gleefully at first, then soberly, delicately, almost tearfully. His face, as supple as an actor's, carried the lightness or heaviness of every phrase in sweeping brushes of mood. Whenever he spoke or listened, his eyes glistened in playfulness or sympathy. *Words are insufficient, so I perform.*

Most of the adults were old enough to tell of the French War, of the armies that had passed back and forth across their exhausted lands, the French soldiers and Viet Minh fighters, and then the Americans and the Vietcong and the North Vietnamese. They told of the taxes and goods pried from their hands. The French troops simply took what they wanted without paying, one farmer said. The Americans were nicer. They paid. "I'm not saying that just because I am talking to an American," he insisted. Lanh translated without a note of skepticism. Pen wrote it down dutifully. But Lanh wondered how the words he cradled as he passed them on would chafe on that sly Minh at the pho stand. *And does Pen have faith in my faithfulness to truth?*

The only sounds were from chickens and ducks and crying children, no laughter. There were no smiles among the returning refugees, Lanh noticed, not in coming home to the Street Without Joy.

And so Lanh was quiet as they drove back south, to Danang. Pen also said nothing.

CHAPTER 3

Julie had finally stirred herself to sign up for tennis lessons at Cercle Sportif, the faded colonial club whose Vietnamese waiters in white still served gin and tonics under the colonnade by the pool. To think and plan, she needed to strain her body. Frustration had drilled its way into her days, and her bones felt restless, confined to the capital by the patches of fighting in the surrounding countryside. She needed faces to draw and paint. Portraits had become her desire, more urgent than the landscapes that brought her initial praise. She had earned accolades for her portraits of the sea, the palette of infinite colors contained in water of various moods, which she loved to spend hours studying beyond her easel. But faces challenged her to link eye to heart, a difficult connection.

"How about if I go along with you to Danang?" she had asked Pen. Or to Buôn Ma Thuột, she had asked another time. Or "down to Cần Thơ and the villages you're going to visit in the Delta?" He had slid his glance aside, a precursor to an awkward no, she knew.

"Too dangerous," he said.

"Oh, for heaven's sake, darling! I'm not some fragile flower. If you can risk it, so can I. We don't have kids yet to care about. Besides, with Lanh we're not going to get shot."

"Jule, I almost got shot on the central coast in that refugee settlement."

"But you didn't, sweetheart. Besides, I thought you were running away from your fear."

"What?" He gave her a cold look.

"From Roxbury, when you ran away from Charlie Barrett, lying with a gunshot wound in his leg. You were so ashamed. Aren't you trying to fight that off now? Pretend to be brave?"

"Don't be cruel, Julie. I'm not running away from anything, any more than you're running away from your privilege."

"Oh, but I am, darling. Don't you see? If Barbies had been invented, I would have had one that looked just like me, with the whole wardrobe."

"Well, you can't help being beautiful." And Pen reached out to cradle her face in his hands.

"Please, Pen. You know what I mean. We've talked about this. So much adulation, not seeing what was inside my head, only what was on the front. I started to resent my pretty face. Get it?"

"I guess so, it's a little weird."

"Oh, come on. So now I've come to a place where I can find faces, other faces, and through them try to get inside people, not just stop on the surface."

"Wow. Interesting."

"So, I need faces. Faces. This country is full of strong, eloquent faces."

"None in Saigon?"

"Yes, but I told you. Things move too fast. I think out in the country, in the villages, people might slow down, have time, be willing to sit for a few minutes at least to let me watch them, sketch them. I could even give them quick sketches of themselves or their kids. Do you think they would like that?"

"Lanh would know. He likes to soften people up before I interview them. Would it disrupt his style? We'll see what he says."

"And your style? Would it disrupt your style?"

"Do I have a style? What a grand word for what I do!"

"You have more style than you realize! Anyway, I need to get out. I feel stifled here. I wish I were a loner, but I'm not, it seems." She spent a moment figuring how to explain. "I'm—I'm, well, you could say I'm like one piece of a mobile that needs wires and other shapes to connect and balance. Do you see? I don't do well on my own. It's like I don't see any circles of friendships I fit with. There are circles of belonging that are also circles of exclusion. I can imagine them drawn on a page. You have to be a journalist or a diplomat or a contractor or a do-gooder trying to save humanity. So what am I? A wife. I'm only a wife. I'm not even a house-wife, because I don't have to take care of a house. It's all taken care of. I don't have a kid to mother. I'm an artist of sorts—"

"Of sorts? You're terrific!"

"—without a community of artists. I'm an ambassador's daughter, but can I slip easily into the culture of diplomats?"

"Of course not. The embassy thinks the press corps is the enemy."

"And you all are, because you cut through the years of government lying, which is so inconvenient for them. I'm tainted too, married to the enemy. Do you know what Sally Falmouth from the embassy told me?"

"No," said Pen softly. "Who is she?"

"She's a low-level consular officer about my age. I met her that day I offered to volunteer at the American school to teach art. And by the way, I can't get an answer from the school. When I call and ask what's the status, the polite secretary with the Southern accent says, 'Still pending.' Pending? I want to *volunteer*, for Chrissake. I'm not even asking to get paid. This is the pattern. I always hit like, like—" She rolled her eyes toward the ceiling, searching for the perfect phrase. "Like I hit a screen of slick courtesy and no traction of engagement. Like Buckley's wife, Anna, when we first met, says, 'Sorry, but we're leaving in a few months, so I don't need any new friends.'

"Anyway, Sally Falmouth was picking up her son. She seemed nice. When I suggested we have lunch, she was apologetically candid, very daring. She said something like, 'You have to understand. Martin is a difficult ambassador. Actually, he's quite paranoid. If your husband gets a story Martin doesn't like, he's going to want to know who's been talking. And if we'd had lunch or something? I'd be screwed.'

"That was the gist of it. I tried to lighten it up and asked whether she really knew deep, dark secrets. That hit some nerve, I guess, because it shut her up for a moment. She clenched her lips and gave a strained smile, and said it wouldn't matter: 'Guilt by association.'"

Pen was giving Julie a stare like an animal about to be shot. "I'm sorry I brought you here," he finally said. "Somehow I needed this after Roxbury."

"You didn't *bring* me here like some awkward piece of baggage!" Then, more quietly, "I *came* here with you, Pen. And Roxbury? I know. You feel guilty. You were. But don't think you can solve your guilt by taking risks here. That's over. This is a new blank canvas."

"I don't know the answer to this," he finally said.

"Because there is no answer, not to the friendship problem. It's not your fault, Pen. I just need to paint, the way you need to write." And she marched upstairs to change into her short white pleated tennis skirt and blouse.

She didn't need tennis lessons. She needed company. She needed her muscles to ache and her body to sweat. She hadn't slipped much since her days on the Wellesley tennis team, and it felt slightly good to put on the outfit and pull her honey blond hair back in a ponytail. At the end of the alley she found a dusty Renault taxi to Cercle Sportif and met her instructor, a willowy woman in white.

"I'm Hạnh," she said, stretching out her hand. Her eyes, with the tint of chocolate, seemed immediately curious, even searching.

On the court, Hạnh gave Julie pointers about her serve, which was accurate but slow. She was being too careful, Hạnh said in fluent English, too calculated. "Let loose, hit hard, take a chance." A good lesson, Julie thought. Hạnh was a little better, so she pulled Julie up subtly. And that's the way it went twice a week. As Julie improved, Hạnh ratcheted up her game another notch to stay just better enough to challenge but not demoralize. An endearing skill, Julie felt.

After their sessions, they began a practice of sitting for a while at an outside table to cool off with tall glasses of lemonade. And talk, and talk, and talk about family and profession and whatever futures they could imagine. Except that Julie did most of the talking.

In what they shared about themselves, shadows played. As on the court, Hạnh adjusted hers to Julie's. Their mothers were passive, their fathers domineering, disappointed in the men their daughters had married, in the work that wasted their skills. Julie felt diminished because of her vast unfulfilled potential in her father's eyes. "Me too!" cried Hạnh. "My father had big ideas, bigger than a tennis instructor! I am no good to my father."

"Oh, I'm sure that's not true," said Julie. "I wouldn't go that far about my father. But no good to him? No. He admires me. I think. I think he admires me, deep down. Maybe not overtly. He imagines me as a diplomat like him or a doctor—a doctor would be fine for him."

"My father, too—a doctor. That's what he wanted me to be. Lots of steady work in a war," she snorted her gallows humor.

"But my mother supports me. She's very into the arts, a real patron of museums and theater. She loves ballet. She encourages me. She didn't want me to come to Vietnam—of course."

"Why of course?"

"The war. The danger."

To this, Hạnh darkened a little. "Of course." Then, looking over Julie's shoulder into some unfocused place, she said, "The war is going to end, you know. That's why fear is rising. We are accustomed to war. We know how to live in it."

Danang was busy with jeeps and armored personnel carriers and soldiers in street-colored khaki. Official buildings were dramatically marked by low piles of sandbags manned by sleepy guards with M16s. Women in conical hats balancing shoulder poles of whatever harvests they'd been able to wrench from the mined and tattered fields and orchards, wove among the bikes and cyclos to the central market, whose wares thinned and swelled as an index of the shifting military control in the countryside.

They headed toward an interview with one of only two reputedly candid American diplomats. He was the consul general in a country where consuls general did much more than issue visas and help sick or imprisoned American citizens. The man was supposed to report on what was going on and was too good at his job to suit Ambassador Martin back in Saigon.

Lanh stopped at the door of the American consulate and said he'd wait for Pen over there, at a sidewalk table of that little café. "Okay," Pen said, then checked himself. "Wait. Come in with me. I've heard this guy has a lot to say. I'd like to know what you think. I'd like to know if you think he goes too fast past the people." He gave Lanh a winking grin.

Never before had a correspondent invited him into one of the enclaves of Americanism that pockmarked his country. "He won't want me there," Lanh said. "He'll kick me out."

Pen hesitated a beat. Would he lose the interview? That he didn't want. On the other hand—what the hell. "If he won't have you," Pen said, "we'll know how seriously to take him."

Lanh took off his sunglasses and peered at Pen. At the door, a Marine guard waved Pen through but gave Lanh a pat-down.

Pen took a few steps as if to walk on but then turned and said, "No. If you're going to search him, you're going to search me." This was another first for Lanh.

"Not necessary, sir," said the Marine.

"Yes, it's necessary. No discrimination."

The straight-backed Marine in crisp, clean camouflage too neat for the city, snapped a clear, "Yes, sir," and gave Pen the frisk. "You're free to proceed, sir."

Up the stairs to the second floor, another Marine guided them into a bare office with no trace of personality, no family pictures, no diplomas or awards, no kitsch or crafts except for an unpolished brass shell casing that some enterprising metalworker had fashioned into a fluted vase. The vase stood empty in a bookshelf next to a huge easel displaying a detailed map of I Corps adorned with pins of various colors.

Dan Gabriel rose from behind his scarred desk. "This is Nguyễn Văn Lanh," Pen said, "my assistant in the bureau." Gabriel shook his hand warmly. If he was startled having Lanh, he showed none of it. "Sit down, please," said Gabriel. Lanh perched on the edge of his chair, ready to be expelled, but it was not to be. "Tea? Coke?" Gabriel left his office for a moment and returned with a steaming mug for himself and a couple of frosty bottles for his guests. He said to Lanh, "I'm very pleased to meet you, finally, because Pen's predecessors have spoken highly of you. Rosie Everett was very proud of hiring you away from General Westmoreland."

Lanh gave a foxy smile of embarrassment. "The general wasn't too happy."

"I'm sure not," said Gabriel. "He wasn't happy about much of anything—when he was being realistic, that is." Lanh gave more of a laugh than Pen had heard before. "And he had good reason," Gabriel continued. "He'd have even more reason now. The ARVN are losing up here, relinquishing territory all over. Want the briefing? On background, though, no name, just 'a Western official.'"

"Of course," said Pen. And Gabriel was off and running, using a chewed pencil to tap on the map, detailing the dates and directions of NVA and VC advances, explaining the pins he'd inserted where units were located, where land was contested and control shifting, listing the respective strengths and losses of the forces on each side, and culminating in the grimmest assessment Pen had encountered from any American, even bleaker than what the notoriously pessimistic Australian military attaché in Saigon had offered after a visit up here.

Pen questioned him closely, and the consul revealed his doubts that ARVN would last outside the cities in I Corps much more than six months without intensive ground reinforcements and additional air power. He'd recommended as much, and it was being considered. But they had to move fast, he said, because the army was being hollowed out by dispiriting corruption.

"Have you heard that?" Gabriel asked Lanh. "What's your assessment? How bad is the corruption?" Lanh retreated into a series of quick mental calculations about this uneasy turnaround of questioning. His comfort lay in his middleman role, relaying words back and forth, standing outside looking in, but sometimes looking in at himself as a misfit alien to all the political categories imposed on his country. Whatever his own ideas, he kept them nearly shapeless, submerged far beneath the tides of war, and he did his job close to the surface of practiced excellence. Yet silence stifled thought, he remembered from the line Rosie had quoted as she tried to push him toward clarity. Yes, he recalled—from Forster, whom he'd never read: "How do I know what I think until I see what I say?"

Lanh squirmed in his seat. Then he said he didn't have a detailed picture of corruption in the army except for what he'd heard in scattered rumors from friends and cousins and sisters of soldiers. Nothing solid enough to, say, put in the paper.

"Like what?" asked Gabriel.

"Yeah, like what?" demanded Pen.

Lanh sat quietly.

"Well," Gabriel went on, "we have reports that artillery units want bribes from infantry units to provide them with covering fire. Do you think that's true?"

"I don't know if it's true, but I've heard the same."

"And we have reports that medevac crews won't fly in to evacuate the wounded without a payoff. Does that ring a bell?"

"Yes, a friend at Tansonnhut told me he'd heard pilots talking about it. But I don't know if it's true."

"I think it's true," said Gabriel. "We have our ways of checking." Since US troops had withdrawn, the army brass had grown demoralized and defeatist and terrified, he said. ARVN units sometimes staged spectacular assaults in places with hardly any NVA or VC. And if they were unfortunate enough to find some to fight, he remarked, the ARVN unit would leave an exit open for the enemy to escape. "No point getting cornered into a real battle."

"Oh!" Lanh said. "That's what happened when I worked in the Delta."

"When was that?"

"Nineteen sixty."

"Well," Gabriel sighed, "the past is never quite past. Now leadership in the field has evaporated in some cases, and some units up here, especially those close to NVA lines, have degenerated into a free-for-all, every man for himself."

The war is ending, Lanh thought again, *so fear is rising*.

"Jesus," said Pen. "I didn't know it was that bad. I've never heard anybody at the embassy say anything close to this."

"Look, between us, they're living in a dream world down there," Gabriel continued. "The ambassador never travels out of Saigon. He doesn't see anything of the country he's trying to defend." For a few beats, Gabriel hesitated as if considering his fate if Pen and Lanh proved untrustworthy. Then he gave a subtle shrug and plunged ahead. He'd dispatched his downbeat assessment to Ambassador Martin, who refused to relay it to Washington, Gabriel told them, so he'd bypassed the embassy and sent it directly to a State Department colleague, who put it in the middle of the next interagency war cabinet meeting "like a grenade on the table."

"That must have been amusing," Pen winked. "Your folks aren't quite used to that kind of thing, are they? You know what James Reston calls the State Department?" Gabriel shook his head. "The Fudge Factory."

Gabriel's mask of principled sincerity slipped just a touch, toward a mischievous grin. But no, he was sorry, he couldn't give his memo to Pen. "Classified, you know."

That evening, eating fish and shrimp and pork dishes at Lanh's favorite seaside restaurant, they talked over the interview, wondering where Gabriel's self-destructive honesty would take him. "He's on a roll of stunning candor—and insubordination," said Pen.

"But is he skeptical enough?" Lanh asked. "Does he question the war, or just how it's fought? What kind of war does he think it is? Not a war of independence. Not an anti-colonial war."

"Right," said Pen. "Is that really what it is? And by the way, how come you didn't tell me about the rumors of pay-offs in the army?"

"Because they're just rumors."

"Still, I want to know everything you know, Lanh."

No, you don't. And you can never know everything I know.

"No matter," Pen said, "from Gabriel we've got a great story." Lanh flinched. "Ah, well, that's the perverse nature of news, isn't it?" Pen apologized. "A bad story is a good story. I remember in Boston spending several days with the busiest fire house in the city to do a profile, and by chance nothing happened except a small trash fire in a vacant lot. The firemen were so disappointed that they had to resort to telling me stories about 'the good fire' they'd had the week before and 'the good fire' they'd had the week before that. And I finally said to them, 'You're kind of in the same line of work that I am. We say it's a good story when it's bad news.'"

"I don't know what's good and bad anymore in Vietnam," said Lanh. "Except for some things." He

47

nodded toward a nearby table where three portly, oily South Vietnamese colonels were gorging themselves. They oozed corruption. Lanh leaned across to Pen and lowered his voice. "I can't stand Vietnamese who have no sign of suffering on their faces."

CHAPTER 4

P en's little story about the desperate mother and her begging children got more than teasing from colleagues. Weeks later, from a thick manila envelope sent by Boston, out poured an assortment of letters. Some were handwritten, some neatly typed, one in a child's wobbly print. Some included checks made out to Pen, others asked how to help. Could they send her money?

The phone rang, and Tân, the office manager, conducted his interrogation of the caller, screening with unfailing courtesy. He was used to parrying sultry voices murmuring "Robert?"—one of Pen's predecessors. When he broke the news that Robert had left the country, apparently without a farewell, the woman's falling tones of dejection gave Tân an admiring smirk. Once he hung up, he always shook his head in amazement and revealed to the bureau: "Robert had many friends."

This time, though, he spoke in English and handed the phone to Pen, who heard a man announce himself briskly. "Erik Sendstad from Norway, in Saigon running a home for orphans and street kids." And, he went on, for those whose defeated parents could not afford to care for them. Perhaps he could help that mother get her children medical

49

treatment and healthy nourishment and give them a safe roof over their heads.

Faces flickered through Pen's thoughts, first of Julie, then the mother, finally her children scarred and sick. No story he'd ever told had benefited anyone. He told stories for himself. This he'd realized somewhere along his way, in his waning belief that sunlight cured maladies, that words alone raised consciences. Back in Boston, in his spare style of strong images, he'd described the sinning slumlords who didn't buy heating oil for apartments whose pipes froze and drove impoverished families to huddle around the toxic fumes of gas stoves, where gangs called in false fire alarms and then stole axes and crowbars off the firetrucks that roared to the address, and used the tools to break into vacant apartments and crash through walls to adjacent homes to steal whatever could be sold for drugs. He wrote, and nothing improved. Pen's affecting prose dropped into the city's vacuum of caring. He came to feel as if he were shouting into an empty room that answered with his own echoes.

And now, on the other side of the world, a little piece buried inside the paper, with a small photo of a skinny boy and his limp sister in the arms of a woman with dread in her eyes, was caressing a nerve of charity. Pen liked the solid warmth of Erik Sendstad's voice and arranged to visit the home with Julie. Finally, something for Julie, perhaps.

He took the office Fiat, with Mr. Kỳ behind the wheel, to Cercle Sportif to pick up Julie after her tennis lesson. She and Hạnh were drinking cool lemonade at a small round table, beneath a green umbrella.

"This is Hạnh," she said as Pen strode up. "Guess what! Her husband is an artist!"

"A political cartoonist," Hạnh corrected.

"An artist with the pen and the mind, too," Julie said. "We want to meet. He knows other artists." She was incandescent. Hạnh's silent smile, Pen thought, was enigmatic.

"Did you notice her odd look?" he asked Julie in the car.

"No, what do you mean?"

"I don't know. A glance of self-satisfaction, I thought. Didn't you see?"

"I was looking at you."

"You're the reader of faces. I wish you'd seen. It was peculiar."

The children's home stood behind a weedy patch of ground on a street that must have once been an upscale colonial quarter. It was lined with feathery green tamarind trees. Stolid mansions were garnished with vines of rose-flowering bougainvillea, remnants of elegance. Every house seemed to sport a brass plaque announcing the presence of an institution: a government ministry, an ambassador's residence, a nonprofit devoted to doing good. The children's home had no plaque, just a dusty front yard full of kids in shorts and T-shirts and sandals or bare feet kicking a scuffed soccer ball so deflated that it seemed soggy when it tried to bounce. The appearance of Julie's white tennis outfit suspended all movement like a freeze frame. Games halted mid-play, little faces stared. Pen could practically feel a vibration of embarrassment run up Julie's spine. Then the film began running again.

Erik Sendstad stood straight. A shock of blond hair fell casually across his tanned forehead. He looked slightly weathered, as if his blue eyes had seen a great deal of the world, enough to make a different sort of man weary and resigned. When he spoke in that cordial voice, he sounded calmly grounded like a steady rescue worker during a disaster. "Clear-eyed," is how Pen described him later to Julie. "A man who isn't fooled by his own zeal."

In fluent Vietnamese, Erik talked to kids and translated as he guided Pen and Julie through the cavernous house. He knew every child's name, and he got radiant grins from everyone. They were clean, their clothes were washed, and they looked well fed. Each room was stuffed with bunk beds, rattan sleeping mats rolled up in corners, and hooks hung with sparse wardrobes of shorts and shirts—no socks. The place smelled of disinfectant. Two women busily mopped and dusted while another, a gaunt cook in a white smock, worked over steaming pots in the big kitchen. He introduced a middle-aged woman named Thi as his head nurse, assistant director, and "head of the Department that Makes Everything Run with Gentle Firmness."

She sat with them as Erik got a tray of green tea and brought it to the large veranda under a slowly turning ceiling fan, the joyful shouts of children all around. "How are you spending your time here in Saigon?" Thi asked Julie, who glanced at Pen for solace.

"I'm still finding my place. Well, looking for my place. I paint. I draw. So actually I'm looking for faces."

"Maybe there can be a place for you here," Thi said. "And we have plenty of faces." She swept her hand across the carnival of scampering children.

Julie straightened. She had been slouching at the table as if hunkered against an unforgiving wind, which was exactly what she was feeling in this city of war. Posture is everything, her mother had lectured. You can read a mood and a level of breeding by how a woman carries herself. In the full-length mirror mounted on the door of her bedroom as a growing girl, she had practiced resentfully, turning this way and that, throwing her shoulders back, tucking her chin in, eyes level and engaging. So she never felt comfortable in her own body. The prying eyes of men and the envious eyes of women repelled her, and she usually looked away unless she wanted something from them. And Vietnam was no place to pose like a debutante. But now she gave Thi the engaged stare, as if to seal a contract on an offer only tentatively made. She peppered Thi and Erik with her curiosity. How did you begin? How long have you been doing this? Where do your funds come from? How do you find the children? What understandings do you have with their families?

These were the easy questions, and the two of them answered alternately like a tag team. Donations mostly from Europe. Started when the house came up for rent and a Vietnamese priest asked if he could shelter a few street boys, about three years ago. The children find the home more than the other way around. "The parents can return and take them at any time," Erik said, "and are encouraged to do so if they can get back on their feet."

"And can they?"

"Rarely, I'm afraid."

She turned to Thi.

"I work here because my husband is in the army," she said and put on an impish grin. "He doesn't make enough to feed us and our kids, so I need the money!" Then she and Erik laughed and laughed.

"Because," he explained, "I pay her hardly anything! She gives the children so much that she gets it back in love instead of piasters."

She could be my first portrait here: the dark eyes probing, the black hair cropped short like a boy's, the little crow's feet just beginning at the corners of the eyes. Her lips twitch before she speaks, as if they are telegraphing what she is about to say. How to capture that? A portrait would have her on the verge of speaking, lips parted slightly.

"I might want to start with you," Julie said.

"With me?"

"Yes, Thi, a portrait of you. Would you sit for me?"

"Do you mean sit still? I am always in motion." Julie sank a little. "But, yes, if you wish, I'd be honored. We'll try to find a time."

But I'll need to know where you came from, Julie thought. *You too, Erik.* Two dimensions on paper never satisfy, she once told Pen. "No art is simply momentary."

"And news?" Pen had asked. "Is there no news that is simply momentary?"

"None at all. Don't you have to know what led up to it?"

"Sure, but every sentence about the past is a sentence less you have room for about what just happened today. Editors are impatient with history. So I chase the news from moment to moment."

She had shaken her head. "I think you have to change the definition of news."

"And maybe we have to change the definition of people?"

"Huh?"

"The people we meet, Julie. The people we know, or think we know. You say you need to know the past of someone you paint, but how much do we know about the friends we think we know, where they came from? Do we ever sit down and have them trace their histories? How many of my friends know that I ran from a wounded photographer and didn't help him? Nobody here, that's for sure, and I'm not about to tell them. We all have secret compartments. You too. How much do you tell friends about your uncaring nannies? They made you distrustful.

"You know you sometimes have trouble connecting with people, Jule. I feel you holding back. Distrustful."

She blinked a few times, then grabbed his gaze and held it tightly. "I was not encouraged to open up. When I did at school, my roommate told everybody she could find who'd listen. So I decided it's none of anybody's damned business."

"And maybe what I try to get from people is none of my business," Pen said.

Julie began to collect Erik's story like the quick pencil strokes of a tentative sketch. Was he here alone? He looked startled and then laughed. "Hardly alone. Look at all these kids!"

"I meant your family."

"I knew what you meant. My wife died of cancer. We had no children. So I'm alone in that sense, but I don't feel it."

And what did he do before? "Before . . . there were many befores." He picked from his biography only the latest chapter, representing the Red Cross. "I was in Syria visiting prisoners and taking letters to and from their families. And in Lebanon. And then here, beginning in 1970."

"You learned Arabic? And Vietnamese here?"

"Yes, it's essential. You can't depend on interpreters when you're visiting prisoners. Interpreters are too easily corrupted." He looked at Pen as if expecting an objection.

"That's why you have to know your interpreter very well," Pen said, his voice as confident as he could manage. "You have to know and trust that he won't slant the words or censor the narrative."

Erik just nodded.

"Do you suppose the mother you wrote about will be willing to take my help?"

"I don't know," Pen said. "She might have a lucrative little business going, using her kids for sympathy."

"Yes, we see a lot of that. A lot of exploitation. May I go have a word with her?"

"I'm not in charge of that," Pen exclaimed. "I'm not her agent."

"Of course not. But you wrote the story, people have contacted you and me wanting to help. So you're involved."

Involved? Pen had never been "involved" with people he wrote about. He stood apart, a watcher and storyteller, no more. Once bad news was out on the table, it was up to others to act. Not him. He felt cleansed passing the buck. "You don't need my approval," Pen said. "We can introduce you to the mother, then it's up to you and her."

"Such detachment," Julie said under her breath. "Erik, do you ever think parents take advantage of you by giving you their kids? Do you help the parents get back to taking care of them?"

"Yes and no. Yes, some take advantage, and no, I have no way to help them, really. We roll with the thunder of the war, that's as much as we can do."

"That's a poetic way to put it," Julie said.

"It's a helpless way to put it," Erik answered.

The small rescue operation proposed by Erik got an uncertain reaction from Lanh when Pen told him. Lanh had cultivated a thousand looks to convey his despair and irony, his encrypted rage and enticing charm. He knew he was too young for his skin, which looked like comfortable leather. It creased and wrinkled on command in strategic corners of his eyes, across the bridge of his nose, around his mouth, across his forehead—all in accordance with his words, or others'. His face betrayed his thinking, he figured, or it fooled people into believing so. This time, though, he made sure Pen couldn't read it. His squint of contemplation was intentionally admiring or cynical, take your choice. He wasn't sure himself how he felt, but he did give a new inner smile for Pen, who had seen the story and had written it to touch readers. And now some form of help was coming— maybe not enough to save that mother on the street, but maybe enough to protect a child or two for a while.

"Is this how Americans ease their guilt for creating the family's crisis in the first place?" Lanh asked Thuận that night.

"Sure, yes, maybe," Thuận said. "But if so, at least they feel guilt."

Lanh sang Sơn's line in his thoughts: *In the future, even stones will need each other.*

From the office in the morning, Lanh went downstairs with the small, formidable delegation of Julie, Pen, and Erik, and listened to Erik speak gently to Mrs. Thương, who kept smiling uneasily through a mouth of gapped, red-stained teeth. In the end, she did not want to give Erik her son, whose lame scuttling along the sidewalk brought her profit, or her listless infant daughter, whose visible misery advertised her own. "What is her name?" Erik asked.

"Anh," the mother told him. "Well, she needs to see a doctor, don't you think? I know a doctor who could help."

The mother was unmoved, even by Lanh's tender coaxing, even by Erik's offer for Anh's health.

The silence of defeat settled on them all. Then Julie spoke, looking from Pen to Erik. "The money that's coming in," she proposed. "What if we paid Mrs. Thương if she agreed to keep the children off the streets?"

"Wait," Pen said. "Paying a mother to protect her children? Is that okay?"

Lanh cocked his head in doubt. "It makes you uncomfortable?"

"Sort of. It seems wrong. I can't put my finger on why. Like buying the children."

"Oh, no, darling. Not at all. Just helping her so she doesn't have to use them as beggars."

Mrs. Thương, excluded by language from the debate, sank from standing into her squat, still cradling her ailing baby. Erik remained erect. Julie maintained her mother's rule on posture. Pen gazed past them to the complicated traffic on Tự Do. So the foreigners conducted their discussion over Mrs. Thương's head, you could say. Only Lanh bent toward her from time to time. Then he straightened, looked from Pen to Julie and back to Pen, and said to him,

"I see your worry. Paying her not to have her children with her. It would be unusual."

"And if not, she will keep them on the street," Julie declared. "Sick. In danger." Mrs. Thương was staring at the passersby she could not approach for piasters while these strangers were hovering over her.

"We could just give her all the money that's coming in," said Erik.

"Yes, maybe," Lanh said. "But she might keep the children begging."

"If we give her what the kids would collect," Julie insisted, "she'd have the freedom to leave them in a safe place. Erik, what do you think?"

"I've never done anything like that, but let's see what she says."

"Let me," said Lanh. He crouched beside her and put the offer in such a musical lilt that Pen thought nobody could resist. She did, for a few moments. She asked something of Lanh, and he asked them all, "She wants to know how much."

"Well," Erik said, first in English, then in Vietnamese, "how about four thousand piasters a week?"

She nodded. It might just cover food. The deal was struck.

After her next tennis lesson, Julie wanted to tell Hạnh all about Erik's home. She guessed correctly what Hạnh would say: "That's great what he's doing!" And then she asked a question that propelled Julie ahead. "Will you help him there? What will you do?" Julie realized what was happening. She was filling the friendship vacuum.

"Please tell me all about it as you go along," Hạnh said, as she always did. Why did she begin painting? What was it like being an ambassador's daughter? How did she meet Pen? Why did they get married?

Julie had to explain the term "shotgun wedding," adding that she hadn't been pregnant, thank heavens. "Although looking back, I kind of wish I had been. We have no children. Pen doesn't want any, at least not yet. I do. No, we got married so Pen could avoid the draft: August 23, 1965, two days before President Johnson ended the marriage deferment. Our entire families thought I was going to have a baby. They pretended not to be scandalized. Then, wow! No baby!" Her laugh was not really a laugh. Hạnh reached for both her hands and whispered something so low that she couldn't quite make it out but decided it was "I'm sorry."

"So he didn't want to come fight in Vietnam?"

"Nobody thought about Vietnam then. We were hardly here, right?"

"Right. Mostly advisers. The first ground troops, just a few thousand, came five months before, in March."

The crisp accuracy of this footnote from a tennis teacher might have struck Julie, but she was still caught in her wedding. "All he cared about was not going into the army."

"He must have cared about you, too."

If Julie still smoked, as she had in high school, she would have lit a cigarette at this point, taken a long, dramatic puff, and flicked away an ash. She wished she could. That would have been easier than fighting to swallow her turmoil. She wanted to continue, needed to. But no. *Enough. Enough soul-baring for today.*

So she ventured questions about Hạnh's marriage, how they met, how they managed in the stress of war, whether they had arguments, how they resolved them. Hạnh's answers drew Julie into an illusion of intimacy, a soap opera poised for the next installment.

CHAPTER 5

Once the early sun rose enough to penetrate Lane 342, the shadows would evaporate and the dust would simmer. So Lanh walked to the pho man early, in the shade, nodding greetings to neighbors he barely knew, to smalltime sellers and traders gathering their wares on shoulder poles and motorbikes. A friend to all with whom he had never truly spoken, Lanh gave them cheerful good wishes, a gold tooth flashing in his smile, and admired the gradual filling of the alley with the earnest hustle of the coming day. It always revived him, this daily renewal, this cycle of new beginning. It softened him, worked on him like a massage of sore muscles, stirred his love of his tormented country.

The young man who called himself Minh, cradling a bowl of steaming pho, was waiting on an upturned wooden crate. "Good morning, brother." Lanh's cheer drained away. He gave him a diffident hello.

"Been traveling?" asked Minh.

"Always," Lanh said.

"Up north?"

Lanh tried to ignore the question and watched the pho man prepare his usual, dropping slivers of flank and tripe into the steaming broth.

"Danang?" Minh said, but it came as more of a statement than a question.

"What, are you following me?"

"We keep track of things that interest us. What did you learn?"

"What I learned you can read about in the *Tribune*."

Minh took a break from the interrogation and turned to the dregs of his pho, tipping up the bowl and letting the last noodles and liquid slide into his mouth. He wiped his face with the back of his hand.

"I don't mean to offend you," he told Lanh. "You have no cause to be nervous. Your powers of observation are much admired, and you are regarded as a patriot. So I am told."

Lanh gave his trademark sideways look at Minh and lowered his eyes to his bowl. He contemplated the ingredients—the floating bean sprouts, the tiny slices of red pepper, the fatty meat and noodles and bits of green herbs, and saw the intricacies of his history in this pho, whose parts made a whole but kept their own separateness, too. Integrity. The segments of his life interacted in a messy soup, jointly delicious but each holding to its isolation from the others. A recipe for painful yearning, he thought. It would be so much easier to simply belong, and lazier to slide into one prefabricated container or another. Just settle in comfortably in the pro-Saigon box, relying on the Americans and fooling yourself into believing that your country, the part of it where you now exist, is democratic and independent. Or live clandestinely in the pro-Communist box, where you can call yourself a liberator. Or travel on the margins of legitimacy as an idealistic Third Force opponent of both

Saigon and Hanoi, naïvely hoping for true democracy and a peaceful end to the war by reconciliation, not conquest. Or, perhaps more appealing, retreat into the countryside of idyllic times among your grandfather's fields, riding water buffalo to turn the fertile earth. "I am just a buffalo boy," Lanh liked to say. He announced it to each new correspondent.

"You entered the American consulate." Minh's declaration, spoken so quietly as he leaned forward, could not have been heard even by the pho man nearby. The sentence yanked Lanh by the throat, up and out of his wandering thoughts. He drilled a rare look of indignant terror at Minh, who gave nothing more than a sly smile. A real pro, Lanh thought.

"So, you have a tail on me?"

Minh shook his head in disdain. "We watch the consulate. Did you learn anything that might help your country, brother? That might assist the liberation?"

Lanh took a long look up and down his alley, as a man might survey an unfamiliar intersection before picking a direction. He felt propelled backward many years to that night in his hut in the steaming Delta, when Binh appeared with three behind him, their eyes bleak with fear, faces darkened in the lanterns' glow, whispering entreaties for safe passage into Cambodia, running from their folly in Saigon.

If they had managed the coup successfully, if higher officers had joined them, if Diem's palace guards had turned, if Diem had been deposed with a bullet in his forehead, then Binh and his comrades—and perhaps Lanh, too—would have been comfortably seated in some exalted thrones of influence where they could have decided whether to commit good or commit self-enrichment.

The choice that night did not seem like a choice. It had the force of gravity. Binh was too old a friend to deny, so Lanh stuffed his government pass in his pocket, the pass that got him through lines and checkpoints to issue some of the miserly aid to farmers that American advisers imagined would buy hearts and minds. They left the hut silently, got into Lanh's government-issued Jeep, and drove as close to the border as feasible. Binh and company escaped. Lanh was found out, of course. There were spies everywhere, on all sides.

He spent two years sleeping on a raised concrete platform with fifty other men and boys in Cần Thơ's stinking prison, full of mosquitos, sweat, and the smell of urine. He spent the following years remembering the meager bowls of cold rice crawling with tiny black things the size of pencil points. And the screams of boys being raped to the sound of laughter.

Minh interrupted his memories: "The Street Without Joy," he said to Lanh. "A man you decided to have lie that Americans were so nice because they paid for what they stole. Why do you choose such words?"

"I didn't choose them. They were his words."

"I hope someday you will understand that you chose them."

"I don't choose other people's words."

"Oh, really? They are all poets, speaking so beautifully?"

Lanh hesitated. Then, with the slightest quaver, "I translate what they say."

"Do you, now? Every word is so elevated?"

"Every word has meaning above itself. I give the words true meaning."

"True meaning? Not literal meaning? I think you are putting gold leaf on a pagoda to hide simplicity."

Lanh felt an unfamiliar churning inside his chest. Minh went on. "And since you are very proud as you decorate the words of your comrades, why not do it for the cause of liberation?"

"My translations are the truth."

"Not the truth. The meaning above truth—you admitted. Besides, do you think that man spoke the truth?"

Lanh was silent, then: "That's what he said. I am faithful to the words I hear."

"Faithful," Minh spat. "Not faithful to the words. Faithful to the *meaning* as you would like to imagine it. Which is faithful to nothing, it seems." His voice was nearly a whisper.

"Faithful to that man's truth," Lanh replied. He wanted to flee.

"So everyone has his so-called truth," Minh said, "and you accept them all until your mind is full of many truths. You must be suffering all the time from confusion."

To this, Lanh answered with a cold stare. He did not say anything more to Minh. Instead, he stood slowly, walked down the alley to his motorbike, and rode, dangerously distracted, to the office in Tự Do Street.

Every Saturday morning, in one of those oddities of war, a South Vietnamese army bus took foreign correspondents to hear from the enemy—at a Vietcong press conference in Camp Davis, named after the first American killed in Vietnam. It was a small enclave inside Saigon's Tansonnhut air base, turned over to a delegation of the National

Liberation Front, whose presence as part of the Joint Military Commission in Saigon to monitor the charade of peace, was mandated by the Paris accords.

When the bus pulled into the camp, the journalists were greeted cordially by unarmed Vietcong fighters in green fatigues and pith helmets, each emblazoned with a red star. Lore had memorialized a quip by a brash reporter from the Chicago *Daily News* who'd done a tour in Nam himself when Vietnamese friendly to American troops would point down jungle paths and warn, "*Beaucoup VC.*" As the bus pulled into Camp Davis for the first press conference and the correspondents looked out at all the red-starred helmets, the *Daily News* guy declared, "*Beaucoup VC.*" An explosion of mirth inside the bus got puzzled looks from the hosts.

Inside a Quonset hut, the reporters were seated at two long tables laden with bottles of water and sodas. In front stood an easel bearing a large, colorfully detailed map of South Vietnam on which pins had been placed. Presenting was either a paunchy major whose nom de guerre in Vietnamese meant "Direction South," or Colonel Võ Đông Giang, an ascetic as thin and taut as a wire. The colonel spoke French from his days in a colonial lycée and Spanish from his days at North Vietnam's embassy in Havana. Anyone who tried to debate him in one of those languages was in for a good-natured tussle. The colonel always emerged smiling in victory. Here, however, he spoke Vietnamese in his Northern accent about the reverses being delivered to the puppet regime in Saigon, translated into English by a young, fluent Vietcong soldier.

Pen enjoyed the reporter's license to move between sides in every dispute, traveling back and forth between contrasting truths—or clashing delusions in the case of this war. Finding nuggets of reality in the muck of propaganda challenged him to stay grounded. Yet after his briefing in Danang, he was more disposed to accept the colonel's flourishing account of battlefield wins. They had seemed no better than puffery before, so Pen skipped a good many VC press conferences. But now he listened more closely and tried to mesh the colonel's map with the one Dan Gabriel had shown him in the consulate. They coincided remarkably well, especially up north in I Corps. He didn't know about the Delta or the Highlands. So the colonel's military information appeared valid, while his more political accounts— of multitudes rising up for the liberation and running toward VC areas—had Pen rolling his eyes as he stopped taking notes. In any case, he was there for a different reason.

When Giang's formal presentation ended, Pen took him aside and said in broken French that he'd be interested in visiting the territory of the Front de Libération Nationale. It was something a few other correspondents had done, but surreptitiously to avoid being blocked by South Vietnamese authorities. Jamison of *Time*, who couldn't keep his mouth shut about his plans, tried twice and was twice intercepted by South Vietnamese police, making him the butt of derision among the foreign press corps. If Pen was trying to demonstrate bravery, it was against physical danger, not humiliation, whose prospect tightened him with tension. *Discretion*, he promised himself.

The colonel seemed welcoming and suggested that at next week's press conference, Pen might receive approval, along with instructions on when, where, and how to cross the invisible line somewhere in the countryside. This was exciting. It would repair his reputation. A step into the risky unknown, reporting from a VC village, would be a coup of sorts, an insight into life on the other side. To play it safe, he would say nothing even to Lanh and Tân. Only to Julie.

"Pen was in Danang," Julie said to Hạnh as they walked. "The American there thinks the war is being lost." The remark came like a tripping stone in the path that made Hạnh interrupt her step a beat.

"You should tell Dương. He'll be interested. He's more interested in politics than I am. He's always thinking about his next cartoon."

"I can't wait to see his work. This is a great idea, skipping out on our lesson to do this." Turning from a tamarind-lined boulevard, they entered a quietly confining street that muffled the city's buzz. At a raw wooden door beside a tiny restaurant, Hạnh produced a key and rattled it into the lock. The door opened with a creak of complaint. Up steep and narrow stairs, a loft spread out atop the entire restaurant. Cooking smells made the air close.

A stocky man hunched over a broad, scarred table in the middle of the room. In his left hand, he held a scratch pen poised over a small bottle of black ink. As they entered, he did not look up but raised his right hand in a stop signal, as if to call for silence. He dipped the pen in the ink, moved the tip to the paper, hovered for a moment, then touched it delicately to the surface and drew it smoothly once, twice, three times in what Julie could barely see were parallel curves. He went on in this fashion, back and forth between the ink well and the paper, for only a minute or so by the clock, but by the measure of her curiosity, for an age.

Hạnh motioned for her to take a seat in the corner, but Julie remained on her feet to survey the studio. Two easels stood askew, each bearing a large cartoon, one seemingly finished, the other still a sketch of an idea. Against a wall, a cabinet with wide drawers must have held hundreds of drawings, Julie thought. She had a file like that herself at home. On several wicker and bamboo tables, piles of drawings rose precariously, ready to be toppled and scattered. The light in the loft was not good. Long fluorescent bulbs hissed and flickered.

At last, Dương put down his pen, walked to embrace Hạnh, and shook hands formally with Julie. "He does not speak English," Hạnh apologized. "I'll translate if you wish." She said something in Vietnamese to him, he brightened, and replied. "I told him about the American in Danang, Julie. He wants to know what he said. 'Our news is so full of propaganda,' Dương says, 'we don't really know what's going on in the country.'"

"Oh, well, I don't know it all, but he had a map and showed Pen where the Communists were gaining ground, and he sent his pessimistic report straight to Washington because the ambassador wouldn't allow such a downbeat assessment. That is simply outrageous. When my father was ambassador, he would never have censored his own people. Reporting accurately is a key obligation of an embassy. Martin is blind to reality. All the correspondents think so, except the guy from the LA *Times*, who's in his pocket. Do you know that before he came, the CIA station chief did a weekly briefing for American journalists, but now he's not allowed to do it? How stupid. And the embassy won't answer questions or give information. They've cut themselves off. Idiotic."

After the translation, Dương smiled thinly, shook his head in an imitation of disgust at the Americans' horrendous behavior, and said, according to Hạnh, that he wondered how the Danang guy had managed to get all this negative information. Julie shrugged. She had no idea, but they must have lots of people reporting to them from the field.

"And is your husband going to write about this?"

"Of course. I suppose he'll have to avoid using the American's name. But the ambassador will probably know all the same."

"I'll be interested to read his story." Hạnh was speaking, but was she merely translating? Julie couldn't tell, and wasn't sure whether she was talking to Hạnh or to Dương. Did he speak a little English, or was Hạnh the one carrying on the conversation, just pretending to be an interpreter? It felt slippery.

"Okay," Julie offered, "I'll bring you a copy when it's done. Can you see the *Tribune* anywhere?"

"No. Sometimes their articles are reprinted in *Stars and Stripes*, which I get at a kiosk on Lê Lợi."

"But let's get on to seeing his cartoons if you don't mind."

No smile can compete with the radiance of an artist flattered by interest in his work. Beaming, Dương led them to his table, to the piece whose ink still glistened. He did not try to explain what he had drawn, nor in the following hours and following visits did he translate his images into words. Sometimes Julie would have to ask, for the meanings were often obscure to her. He would then offer brief tutorials on the political figures pictured, drawn as grotesque caricatures in heavily lined crosshatches. Yet in the end, he would always insist that the meaning was hers to decide. He was not trying to tell her or anyone what to think. "Although perhaps I would like you to be as sad when you look as I am when I draw."

Kissinger stared out from the nearly completed cartoon on the table. His mouth was a keyhole. His nose was the size and shape of an elephant's trunk. Each lens in his eyeglasses reflected a different image: a hammer and sickle on the left, the stars and stripes on the right. "So Kissinger is two-faced?" Julie suggested. Hạnh smiled indulgently, knowing what Dương's answer would be, and translated.

"Do you think so?" Dương replied.

And so it went whenever Julie would seek illumination until she finally said, "Okay, I get it. I'm also an artist. I don't like to explain everything. I figure if the viewers don't understand, then either they have failed or I have failed." Dương gave a great laugh of appreciation, and shook Julie's hand as if they had just settled a contract.

He guided her around the room, opened drawers, pulled out sheets of drawings: Nixon as a villainous doctor wielded a menacing hypodermic needle filled with a dose of dollars. Leonid Brezhnev with an evil grin reached to shake hands while, poking out of his sleeve, a miniature North Vietnamese soldier thrust a rifle with a fixed bayonet. Mao stood on legs decorated with the American flag. A huge, voracious dragon named Corruption opened its mouth to devour a hapless peasant defending himself by brandishing only a hoe. Under the title "After the Victory," a skeleton with chopsticks squatted over a bowl of bullets. A peasant was nailed with American and Russian missiles to a cross in the shape of Vietnam. The noses of Nixon and Kissinger were frequently drawn as B-52 bombers.

"No President Thiệu?" Julie asked. Hạnh didn't have to translate, for Dương understood immediately, made a cutting gesture across his throat, and slid open a lower drawer. Leafing down among the folios, he pulled out a small eight-by-ten sheet, placed it gently on top of the chest, and stood back. Hạnh giggled. In meticulous strokes of his pen and its tips of various widths, Dương had drawn a rat holding a fishing pole. On the hook at the end was an enormous elephant.

Julie frowned. "The elephant?" she asked. "The Republican Party?" Again, Dương understood without translation, smiled broadly, and nodded. "But the rat? I don't get the rat."

Hạnh answered in nearly a whisper, "Thiệu was born in the Year of the Rat." Julie guffawed. Hạnh continued: "My husband never sent this one to a newspaper. The censors would not have allowed it. He is very skilled at weaving through censorship." She translated for Dương what she had just said, and he replied with a wry grin, "like a maker of this rattan furniture who intertwines the reeds so they are tight and perfect."

"So the cartoons are tight and perfect, with no compromises?" Hạnh translated to Dương.

"I don't think of them as compromises," he answered. "They are evasive maneuvers, like the army in the jungle. We live in a political jungle."

"Still, you seem to get away with a lot," said Julie. "Most of what you do is published?"

"In three different newspapers. I have made friends in the press and elsewhere." He pointed upward. "And my wife knows people." He pointed upward again. Hạnh looked startled at the words she had just spoken, as if her momentum as an interpreter had made her mouth move faster than her brain. A shadow of worry and reproach touched her eyes, which fixed Dương with a quick glare like a glancing blow.

"Tea or Coca-Cola?" Hạnh asked abruptly.

Erik Sendstad was proper and slightly aloof with Julie as she went about volunteering with the children in his home. He looked like a Norse god, she thought, and his remoteness, mixed with kindliness for the kids, qualified him for a portrait that would have to capture those crosscurrents. She was not sure she could pull it off.

Her "place," as Thi had suggested, could be counted as many places, all small and insignificant, she felt. Thi guided her warmly to one enclave of duty after another: playing with the children, tracking grants for Erik, recording sparse information on the whereabouts of parents who might return at any moment. Being with the children comforted her and churned up turbulence. They needed but eluded her full emotional embrace. They drew her into a soothing, troubled region of desire and disappointment. Pen came periodically to visit, to be relieved by her discovery of a purpose here. She seemed happier at home, less jealous of his adventures. She found herself more interested in hearing about his work, perhaps because she knew that Hạnh would be fascinated, giving them reason to linger longer after lessons.

"I have something to tell you," Pen said over dinner once Nghi the cook had left.

"Oh? Big news?"

"Maybe. I've asked to go into VC territory."

Julie's face was encoded. A slender smile, a jab of fear in her eyes and—what, envy? She interrogated him. Why? Where? When? "My darling, how do you know it will be safe? Is it worth the risk?"

Pen was not a man of absolutes, she knew, and so she watched him parse each variable as it came to him with a scalpel as clean as a dissection could be. Each question he answered with precision: to get a good story, albeit controlled, since they won't let him see all there is to see or hear from villagers all there is to tell. Where is up to them—they'll set it up. Maybe in the next ten days or so, after word at the next VC press conference. And it will probably be as safe as going anywhere else in the country, he tried to rationalize, since the VC wouldn't want anything to happen to an American correspondent under their protection. Still, there's a risk, but it's probably worth it.

Lots of buts, she thought. *Depends on what you get to see. It could be a fantastic story.*

"Don't tell anyone," he cautioned. "I haven't even told Lanh or Tân or anyone else in the office. The police or the army will try to stop me if they know. Like Jamison."

"Who would I tell, anyway?" said Julie. And then she flushed, because she knew exactly who she would tell—or would not, in this case. *Anyway, would it be terrible if you were stopped from risking your life?*

CHAPTER 6

The war has ended but has not ended. The boy sees it. "Lanh," his father says, "Japan has surrendered. Now we will be free." But not all of Japan has surrendered, Lanh soon learns. His friends whisper to him that Japanese soldiers still lurk in the honeycombed alleys of old Hanoi, rifles at the ready. They have not given up. They will fight to the death. Lanh is not sure whether to be afraid or excited. He is just nine, that age when fear and adventure begin to mix joyfully.

He soon understands that his father is wrong. That is something new and unwelcome. His father has never been mistaken in all of Lanh's boyhood. His father guides infallibly. Riding their bicycles side by side, Lanh and his father go to the temple and then carry home the fruits of the season from the market. Lanh's favorite journey is with his father—and his mother and sister—back to Hà Đông to his grandparents' rice paddies and, best of all, their water buffalo. Lanh can smell the earth after a rain, the soil of his ancestors. Why did his father move the family to the city? Why huddle over papers in a crowded office for the French, the French who worked for the Japanese in the war?

"We need to eat," his father explains again and again when Lanh's question comes to the surface. "You need a good school."

The Japanese troops are disappearing from the streets. "The Viet Minh are here," says his father. "Hồ Chí Minh is now our president. The Chinese soldiers have come to help us, just for a while. We are free." The streets have changed their names from French conquerors to Annamite heroes, from Rue Mirabel to Đường Trần Nhân Tôn, from Boulevard Henri Rivière to Phan Bội Châu. But the Chinese are looting, and Hanoi is becoming a place of new tensions. Months are passing like clouds of alternating sun and shade. Chinese uniforms finally disappear, and the city seems to hover in the air like a dancing kite, waiting for the right time to be pulled back to earth. Then another language is heard. "The French," says Lanh's father. "The French again."

"That cannot be right," says Lanh. "We are free now. You said so."

"Someday," answers his father. "Someday."

Lanh's neighborhood friend, Liêm, who is two years older, tells him a secret as they walk home from school. "Do you hear the gunshots at night?" Liêm asks.

"Yes. Or are they firecrackers?"

"Gunshots. The Japanese soldiers are trying to kill the French. That is good."

"Good? So the war can go on?"

"So the French cannot come back. We were a colony. We want to be free!"

"Someday," says Lanh in the serious voice of his father.

"Not someday," answers Liêm. "Now. Now. Tomorrow. Today."

Then Liêm tells Lanh the secret. He has organized boys to help the Japanese soldiers, after dark. The Japanese do not know the back alleys of the Old Quarter, the special ways to get close to the French, shoot one of them, then melt back into the night. Boys show them. "Will you join us?"

"How will I get out of the house?"

"Sneak out after everyone is asleep. We do this very late, at midnight or beyond."

Beyond, Lanh thinks. So, he lies nearly awake on his mat until he hears his father snoring deeply. His mother and sister are silent. He rises like a spirit, crosses to the door in his bare feet, carries his sandals outside, slips them on, and glides to the corner.

Liêm points wordlessly, and they walk quickly straight, then right until they can make out dimly in the darkness a clutch of boys Lanh doesn't know. Liêm is taller than the rest. He gestures a silent introduction of Lanh, then tilts his head toward the Old Quarter, and they follow.

A rat scurries along the curb. The slight light of a lantern glows from behind a dusty window. The air is cool, a beautiful time, Lanh thinks. They stop deep within the refuge of the alleyways and gather around Liêm.

"From here we each are paired with a sniper," he whispers to the boys.

"What's a sniper?" Lanh asks, and the boys snicker.

"Don't laugh," scolds Liêm. "None of you knew either, two weeks ago. A sniper is a soldier so perfect with a rifle that he can shoot a man in the head or the heart at one hundred meters—in the dark."

"What do we do?" asked Lanh.

"They know what to do. Tonight you come with me. I'll show you." Liêm gives each one an address, and they scatter like black cats into the darkness. "Let's go," he says to Lanh.

Across what the boys call the Street of Copper, where all coppersmiths before the war sold pans and bowls and shiny sheets of metal, down the Street of Wood, along the street once bursting with butcher shops and hanging meat, into a narrow alley and through a tiny courtyard, the two boys run as swiftly as fish swim in the rain-swollen Red River. Then up worn stairs to the roof and into a ramshackle shed perched precariously on the edge, and face-to-face with a big man in a frayed olive uniform, looking more hunted than hunter.

With no words in common, Liêm and the Japanese soldier just shake hands, Liêm gestures an introduction to Lanh, and the soldier frowns in worry. He holds his open hand down just above his waist, as if to say, "This boy is too small, too young."

"Okay. Okay," Liêm reassures him in a fragment of English, which the soldier seems to understand. And then they set off down the stairs, along the alley, back through twisting ways that Lanh knows well from days and days of playing and running with his pals and hiding, jumping out, and shooting them with scraps of wood. How different it all looks at night, invisible and thinly lit by a moon through filtering clouds. The days are not scary. The night, Lanh realizes, is going to bring faces appearing and vanishing before he can tell who they are. They are going to try to talk to him, but he will not be able to make out what they are saying.

And if he tries to talk back, they will evaporate, perhaps in wails of laughter.

Soon the boys and their sniper are through a rotten door with peeled green paint and into a crumbling entranceway, up crooked stairs. Liêm pushes open a door into a room, or rooms, once a home, perhaps, now cluttered with cobwebs and dust that smell like the mold in the small abandoned shoe factory where Lanh and his friends have made a fortress. Liêm guides the sniper to a window. Lanh looks. Down through an intersection, on a larger street, three French soldiers smoke casually. One flicks his lighted butt so it traces a little arc through the air.

Liêm pulls Lanh back to give the sniper space. The man stands a few feet away from the window and studies the scene. Then he reaches into a pouch around his waist, pulls out a clip of bullets, and jams it into his rifle with a click.

"Lanh," Liêm whispers. "Get ready to run. As soon as he shoots, the French will try to find him—us. We have to guide him at a run back to safety."

It's like a game, Lanh thinks. He can outrun any French. What if they shoot? He can dodge and disappear into doorways, find old ruins. He is dressed in black, as Liêm told him to be, so this is a thrill. Only the ghosts worry him. But he can be brave for his country.

The Japanese soldier brings the gun to his shoulder, squints through the sights for a moment that lasts and lasts—then a single bang and a kick of the rifle against the sniper's shoulder. Liêm grabs Lanh by the arm, and they run with the man behind them down the stairs, out through the door, back into the alleys, twisting and turning as beastly French shouts echo in their wake and lamps are lit in windows. And when the ugly sounds finally grow distant and die away, the boys and the soldier stop in a corner of deep shadows, breathing hard.

"Did he hit him?" Lanh asks Liêm.

"I don't know." Liêm looks at the sniper quizzically, gives him a thumbs up, then a thumbs down, as a question. The man answers with a thumbs up and a smile that Lanh thinks looks like a ghost's.

He is assigned the next night to the same sniper, but alone this time. So after school, he meanders home by a long way, watching for places where the French put their soldiers—not too many, Liêm has said, just two or three, a small guard or patrol.

When Lanh sneaks out of the house and slips on his sandals, his heart beats fast, and he nearly runs to the gathering of boys, who stand like the men at corners in the mornings hoping for work. Liêm gives them instructions, whispers Lanh's into his ear, and pats him on the shoulder.

Lanh knows how to get there, but he stops at every turn and watches and listens. Not for the French. For the spirits. When he crosses the courtyard and climbs the stairs and emerges on the rooftop, he goes to the shack and finds nothing. It is empty. He whirls around and scans the roof. Then a shadow moves at the edge, and the soldier appears, buttoning the fly of his olive trousers.

"Okay?" asks Lanh.

"Okay," the sniper answers. And they descend, Lanh in the lead, down the stairs, across the courtyard, through the labyrinth of alleys to a dirt lot behind a crumbling wall, a hideout Lanh has found within view of a building across a street. In and out of the building's front door, French soldiers come and go in the partial light, even at this late hour. And even now, the street is not empty. Occasional bicycles and small trucks pass between the sniper and the French. Everything is moving—the targets and the obstacles.

The sniper stares, aims, then lowers his rifle. He waits. Lanh wonders if this is a good place. "Okay?" he asks.

"No okay," says the sniper, and shrugs. But he keeps on looking, staring, brings his rifle to his shoulder, holds it for a very long time, then puts it down. Again and again he goes through the motion, aiming and waiting for an opening between the sparse traffic and whatever French soldier might be at the doorway at the moment.

This is like trying to kick a goal, Lanh thinks. And much later in his life, it will trouble his memory, because of the risks and opportunities of probability and chance.

CRACK! goes the rifle, and they run away from the sound of a crash, a horn, hollering, then gunfire. Away through the maze into the safety of darkness.

When they finally stop in the deserted alley where the sniper hides, Lanh imitates Liêm from the night before and holds his thumb up, then down, in a question. Did he get him? The sniper shrugs. He doesn't know.

CHAPTER 7

Every Thursday in the late morning, Võ Tấn Đức pedaled his cyclo to the Cộng Hoà hospital, parked in front, and went in to sell a liter of blood for 200 piasters. The extra weekly cash helped his wife buy rice and portions of fish for their two daughters. He had a lean look of strength about him, but a bony face shrunken by worry.

On this particular Thursday, after filling the bottle bright red and being unhooked from the tube, Mr. Đức patted the small bandage in the crook of his left elbow and walked unsteadily out into the glaring sun. He stopped short at the clinic door and stared at the curb beyond, stunned. His cyclo was gone. He looked frantically up and down the block. Nothing. A thief had taken his livelihood. His howl could be heard even above the midday buzz of motorbikes.

Through the long afternoon, he wandered about Saigon looking for his cyclo. "All the money from my blood has been stolen," he told his wife that night. "All my blood has been stolen."

The next afternoon, he took his cheap wristwatch to a pawnbroker, and with the money treated his two daughters, Kim and Hoa, to a movie, a rare pleasure. Then, to escape the heat of the day, they walked into the cool shade of the cathedral. "Stay inside," he told them. "I'll be back soon."

The brick cathedral had no stained glass anymore, shattered during World War II. Its two high square towers did not reach gracefully toward God but stood cut off from divine aspirations, anchored to the earth. In front, a stained white Madonna looked down at the sinners who passed, her palms turned up in a gesture of absolution and solace.

The father returned carrying a box of matches and a plastic bag filled with a liquid. "I am surrendering," he said. "You obey your mother. If she gives you rice, eat rice. If she gives you salt, eat salt. Don't be difficult."

"No!" Kim shouted. "Why leave us? Don't leave us alone in this world!" She held her little sister by the hand and followed their father into the park across the street, crying for help. "Stop my daddy! He's trying to kill himself." People bustled past. The girls saw him kneel, open the plastic bag, and pour the liquid over his head and shoulders and chest.

Kim ran to him screaming, lunged for the box of matches, and knocked it away, scattering them on the grass. He shoved her hard.

"Get away!" he yelled. "Get away! It's going to be hot as hell!" He grabbed the matches, pushed her to the ground, took some steps to distance himself, and burst into a fiery torch. The little girls both tumbled back, away, their faces forever scarred by horror.

Pen and Lanh were being driven past the square by Mr. Kỳ when they saw smoke rising from a crowd. They told Mr. Kỳ to stop, and they both darted into the park, pushing through the crush of people who were circling a contorted figure that looked like charred wood. He was moving, moaning. Pen could not take his eyes off him. A siren pierced the traffic. The girls were tear-streaked but talking, and Lanh bent over them gently, almost embracing them, speaking with softness and translating simultaneously while Pen wrote and wrote in his notebook, sentences he could later barely read.

Lanh got the man's name, and Pen insisted that they follow the ambulance to the hospital. "But the girls?" said Lanh.

"Let's take them," Pen answered, and they piled into the back of the office Fiat, Lanh beside them, Pen in front, and Mr. Kỳ plunged headway through the snarling lines of bikes and motorbikes and army trucks and automobiles, racing in the open wake created behind the ambulance.

Into the emergency room they ran as the medics ahead easily carried Mr. Đức on a stretcher. Nurses, jaded by the daily plague of injuries, registered no shock. One swept her hand toward an inner door, and the medics kept moving, following her gesture until the patient had disappeared and his moans had grown muffled. "At least he's still alive," said Pen, and he bent to comfort the girls. "He's alive," he said again, and beckoned Lanh to translate.

Lanh did so, but he knew better. He had seen burns before. From kerosene lanterns capsized from tables, from napalm that sprayed fiery gel across villages. He had visited the Quakers' hospital in Quảng Ngãi. He had learned that survival from burns so extensive is only temporary. "Survival is not permanent," he said to Pen, who looked puzzled. *Survival lasts only as long as luck and chance,* Lanh thought to himself.

They stayed with the girls until their mother arrived, sheltered them in her arms, and led them, with Lanh and Pen following, through the corridors crowded with families who knew to bring baskets of food to hospitals that did not feed patients.

In a room with six men and the stench of rot, Mr. Đức lay bandaged with little showing but his eyes and mouth. He told his wife of his despair, of his sorrow, his sorrow for what he did in that helpless moment. "I felt so weak," he said to her. Lanh whispered translations into Pen's ear.

The little girls had hollow looks, and Kim stood stooped staring at her father, her mouth slightly open as if she were trying to catch her breath.

Pen, too, had a sunken gaze, Lanh noticed. He had stopped writing in his notebook and was shifting his stare from the daughters to the father to the mother and back. Lanh collected names, the family's address, the details he knew that Pen would need to follow up.

But Pen could not write anything that day. He went to the office and watched the blank sheet of paper in his typewriter to see if something would appear. He went to the window above the raucous traffic of Tự Do Street. He checked the AP ticker to see if anything had happened that would normally be defined as "news," and then went home.

"What's wrong?" Julie asked before he'd said a word. He told her about the look of charred wood and hugged her and wept. She held him for a long, long time, longer than they had done in many months.

They sat in their living room and had their housekeeper bring tea, and he told her again, "He looked like charred wood, still smoking." And over dinner, "charred wood. The daughter tried to stop him." And Julie listened over and over and reached for his hand across the table.

He and Lanh visited the family the next morning in their tiny, neat house down one of Saigon's narrow alleys. They drove the family to visit Mr. Đức, who lay conscious, bandaged and bound like a mummy. Then Pen went to the office to write his story in clean and simple prose. Context, he thought. It needs a paragraph of context. So when he was done relating what had happened near the cathedral, he inserted context, the "cosmic graf."

"Mr. Đức fought to stay afloat in a riotous economy of prices that had been driven up by the flood of American spending during the long war," he wrote. "Since the tide of American customers has receded after the Paris accords, all of Saigon has been struggling." He wondered if it was too much, too explanatory in a purely human story. But he typed it into the Telex machine anyway, dialed the number, and ran the perforated tape through as his sentences clattered out, on their way to Boston.

When his 600 words were published, his cosmic graf had been deleted, he saw when the paper came in the mail two weeks later. He didn't mind, though he queried the desk out of curiosity. "We thought it unnecessary," Murphy messaged him, "and didn't fit in your powerful piece." The little article ran obscurely at the top of page six. Pen, focused on news when he read the paper and oblivious to ads, did not notice that down the lefthand column, Filene's Basement touted its "mighty superdress," and below, Jordan Marsh announced its "Spring Sale."

By then, Mr. Đức was failing. Too much of his skin had been burned off, his doctor explained. Perhaps if Vietnam had the capacity to do skin grafts . . . but no, he was dying slowly, with his weeping wife and daughters surrounding his bed every day to watch him descend.

"Can't we do something?" Julie asked Lanh. When she visited, she hugged the girls and put her arm softly around their mother, but her jaw was set in anger. "Can we get him skin grafts? Can we get him to the States? My father was an ambassador. Maybe he can help."

Lanh would ask, knowing the answer. He translated for the doctor, a patient man with gray at his temples, who shook his head sadly. Mr. Đức could not travel now, the doctor said. Nothing could be done but ease his pain and wait. "Ease his pain and wait," Lanh translated. "Ease his pain and wait," he said again. A prescription for his country.

The Foreign Desk messaged Pen to say that readers were calling and writing, asking how to help the family. The mail began bringing checks and cash, hundreds of dollars that built into a couple of thousand. Pen deposited the checks in his account, withdrew the cash in piasters, and went again and again with Lanh and Julie to Mr. Đức's modest house to present the bounty to his startled wife. Her meager job was selling lottery tickets, and now she'd hit the lottery herself, just because an American happened to be driving by at that terrible moment. *Luck and chance*, Lanh thought. *Luck and chance. Survival, for a time.*

The hospital had plenty of morphine, thanks to the Americans, so Mr. Đức was lowered gradually into peaceful painlessness. And then his breathing ebbed and stopped, and his wife became a widow. Lanh got a call in the office and passed the word to Pen, who slammed his fist on his desk. "Shit! This fucking war!"

"He's getting to be like Rosie," Lanh told Thuận that night.

"There's nothing better you could say about him."

"He's starting to see people, not just problems. And he writes beautifully. He might turn out to be good."

"And what about his street smarts?"

"Hmm. That's still a work in progress."

"Officers always say it's safe," Lanh told Pen. They were driving south to Cần Thơ, Mr. Kỳ at the wheel, Lanh in the front seat half turning to talk to Pen and Julie in the back. On her lap she cradled her sketch pad and a little case of pens and pencils, poised to record as quickly as she could, then refine at home, like Pen fleshing out his sparse notes later on the typewriter. She was reluctantly adjusting to perpetual motion.

"I'd rather hear from bus drivers, truck drivers," continued Lanh, the patient instructor. "The guy on a bike, in a sampan. I like to ask the farmer, the woman selling vegetables or pho. They know which roads are mined, where the VC are. They won't pretend the government's got everything under control. I didn't do that near Diên Khánh, because we were in a hurry. I hoped to find somebody there on the path to ask."

"Yes, but it all worked out, didn't it? What if people had said don't go? We wouldn't have gone, and we would have missed that story. Isn't it a balancing act?"

"We say the basket at each end of the shoulder pole must weigh the same, or you will stumble."

"So what should we have done?"

"That's up to you. You're the boss."

Julie scolded: "You should listen to Lanh." Lanh shifted awkwardly in his seat.

"I might be the boss," Pen went on, "but I'm not the expert."

"*Expert* is not a word I would use about myself or anyone in war," Lanh said to the passing countryside.

"What word, then?"

"Listener. Listen to those on the ground. We have an old proverb: If you know, speak forth. If you do not, lean against a post and listen." *I cannot be too oblique. The Americans don't get it. Not like Linh and Hiền, who understand when I criticize another child's misbehavior.*

"Look," Pen said testily, "I did not come here to get killed." He glanced at Julie. "I was relieved to be assigned after the Paris agreement, because I figured that Americans—and editors—wouldn't care about combat coverage after our troops withdrew. And that's what happened. It's callous to say, but Americans don't care as much when Vietnamese are the ones fighting and dying. You know that."

"Yes, I do." A weariness crept into Lanh's voice. *But a bullet does not know the difference between a Vietnamese and an American.* He turned and examined Pen's gaze and thought, *We intersect at sadness, even though we begin from different places.*

They rode quietly for a while. Was the lesson over, Lanh wondered? Was it futile?

A dark, oblong shape appeared in the middle of the road, then took on meaning as they approached. Now fins could be seen. Even Pen could recognize an unexploded mortar. He grabbed Julie's hand. Lanh stiffened, Mr. Kỳ kept driving at speed, Pen opened his mouth to yell, Lanh reached for Mr. Kỳ's arm and began to speak, and then the mortar round was under the car, all their muscles locked as they drove over it, and Lanh spun around to watch it recede through the back window. Since it hadn't blown up under them, he was still in one piece, his fury intact, and he could shout at Mr. Kỳ, who was shocked by the tone but replied calmly. Lanh shouted again. So did Pen: "What the fuck were you thinking?" Mr. Kỳ answered firmly, and Lanh, his entire body contorted in disbelief, translated: "He says nothing could have happened because Americans were in the car."

Lanh looked from Mr. Kỳ to the road and back again as if he were shaking his head in a surrender to superstition. "If this were nothing more than one man's crazy belief in some spell cast by an American riding along a road . . ." Lanh mused, then didn't finish.

"It's more than that?" Pen asked. "Is this what we've done to you?"

Years later, the story became satire as Pen told it at dinner parties, laughing at how Americans were thought responsible for everything good and everything bad that happened in Vietnam. For Lanh it was something else, and he didn't mention it ever again. Not until his interrogation.

"I'm not easily scared," Pen declared. "I covered riots in Roxbury where cops were shooting shotguns blindly down dark streets." He did not say what he had not done in Roxbury. He did not explore the shadows of shame. When Julie put her lips close to his ear and whispered very softly, "Shouldn't you tell Lanh?" he shook his head and continued: "I've interviewed drug dealers and gang bangers."

"I know," Lanh said. "I read the paper."

"I wasn't foolhardy, and I took advice. One dealer told me to walk with both hands in my back pockets to pull back my jacket so everybody could see I didn't have a gun and wasn't a cop—or another pusher. So I did. An old street reporter showed me how to fold and bend a copy of the newspaper so it would be as hard as a club when I went home late at night."

"Hmph," said Lanh.

"What does that mean?"

"Nothing. It means I'm thinking. About where fear lives inside people."

"For me, it's not where but when. It comes afterwards, not at the time. It comes after the riots and after getting off the streets full of junkies and pushers, and after crouching in that bunker—that's when I feel fear. After the fact. Isn't that strange?" Julie was studying him. Was it with loving discovery? He wasn't sure. *Is there something wrong with me?* he asked himself, not for the first time.

Lanh didn't react right away. Then quietly, almost to himself: "Fear plays its game with all of us." He gave a half turn toward Pen in back. "Diên Khánh worked out, right, but the commander did nothing for half an hour. We were lucky—lucky that their lunch break ended!" They laughed and laughed, but Mr. Kỳ did not, because he spoke no English. Lanh told him in Vietnamese, and he threw back his head in such long delight that he swerved and nearly hit a chicken. That took them all into laughter again. Julie, too, but thinly.

"If it's a game—fear, that is, do I need to know the rules?" she asked. "Do I need to have felt fear to paint the people who have? Lanh, how can I get in behind their eyes?"

Lanh stared ahead at the blacktop road caressed along each side by startling green. Then he looked back at Julie, at Pen, at Julie again. "That's exactly the question," he said, "but you might not like the answer. You can't get behind their eyes. You can only paint what your own eyes see. Some will think you are taking something from them and giving nothing in return. Their faces, their stories." He twisted around in his seat and told Pen that he knew how to tell stories, so they should go find them by watching and listening closely and trying to see "through the warfare that flashes like a specter across our path."

Lanh the poet, Pen thought. He should be much more than he is.

Cần Thơ was jammed with carts on wooden wheels, Lambrettas piled with burlap sacks of rice, swarms of bicycles and buzzing motorbikes carrying braces of ducks, bloody sides of pork, stacks of engine parts, baskets of fruits of every color, and entire families clinging on with little kids sandwiched between the grownups fore and aft. Pen felt the scary chaos becoming picturesque. It gave him a new pulse of joy.

"The gateway to the Mekong Delta," Lanh announced with jovial fanfare.

Mr. Kỳ crawled through the jumble. Lanh scrutinized Pen for a moment to see if any of his tutorial had sunk in. "I hope you might be discovering our Vietnamese secret."

"What's that?"

"The secret is, there are no secrets. Every Vietnamese carries a jewel—his life, which is illuminating if you hold it up to the light and examine every facet. All you have to do is ask, and the jewel will be offered for your inspection."

"Yes, I'm getting that. But you have to ask in the right way."

"In the right way. That's my job. To help you ask in the right way. It also means we don't really have to risk our lives for stories. Especially now, with the Americans gone. The stories are everywhere, strewn across every farm, clustered in every village. The jewels are just waiting for you to pick them up. And by the way, most correspondents don't know that."

Their hotel was seedy. The beds in Pen and Julie's room sagged when they dropped their duffels on them. The bathroom tile was scarred and cracked, the mirror was missing a chunk in the corner, and rusty water dribbled out of the faucet. Nevertheless, Pen was scaling down his hotel standards to three criteria: "I'm fine if there's enough hot water for a passable shower, there are no bedbugs, and nobody's shooting at me." The first two, Lanh would reply, might be arranged. Julie girded herself to be a good sport, leaned out the window, and began sketching the crowded street scene below, trying to freeze time.

"You know, Jule, I wouldn't say this to anyone else, but I'm beginning to sympathize with our troops who couldn't tell friend from foe. Which village was for them and which against? Which women and even kids had grenades in their baskets? No wonder they shot civilians. I mean, of course they shouldn't have, but how could they know who wasn't dangerous?"

Her withering stare was a dark rainbow of revulsion. *That's what he took from Lanh's lesson?* She said, "My Lai."

"Of course," Pen replied too blandly. "Sure, that was an atrocity. Terrible. Criminal. But I understand it a little more now. I think I get it."

"There are some things that you should never understand." Her gaze did not waver.

"I know, I know. But fear. It was about fear. Maybe not My Lai. That was pure revenge, unfocused revenge. But there must be other places, other cases, ones we've heard about only in hints and assumptions. I'm just trying to get inside people's minds and figure out why they do what they do. You know, behind their eyes."

"And not judge them?"

"The more you understand their motives, the less you judge them."

"Why would that be true? Were segregationists not to be judged because you understood their bigotry and fear? Were Nazis not to be judged because you understood the history of Germany's humiliation? Come on, my dear. People are not only victims of circumstance. They also have responsibility for their choices."

"Yeah, sure. But sometimes choices don't seem like choices. Or they have to be made too quickly. Or—"

"Or cruel people dehumanize others."

"So American soldiers were cruel?"

"Some. Others were made cruel by war," she said.

"So you agree that they were victims of circumstance."

"I said not *only* victims of circumstance. We are all shaped, and we all shape. I'm not willing to let American GIs off the hook for killing civilians. Period."

She did not understand, he thought, and worse, did not understand him. She was not fascinated by ambiguity. *This is a place of intoxicating riddles. Why not get drunk on the confusion below the obvious?* She was still staring at him. Then she turned away. "I've got an appointment," he said.

Pen had not yet traveled among the flooded rice paddies of the Delta. He had not yet abandoned solid ground for the uncertain waterways that meandered among farms and hamlets. Vietnamese called the main branches of the Mekong the Nine Dragons. The river rose from trickling webs in the 16,000-foot Tanggula Mountains of China's Ginghai Province, gathered crystal substance through Tibet, divided and connected into and out of branches and tributaries of various names in various languages, formed the borders between Burma and Laos, then between Thailand and Laos, graced Vientiane, coursed into Cambodia and adorned Phnom Penh before flowing muddily into South Vietnam, spreading into a thousand fingers of lifeblood for farmers and fishermen as it slowed and languidly deposited its treasure of silt in a fan of fertility. Its canals were so vulnerable to warfare that they were once patrolled by American navy swift boats. Now, Pen had heard, the South Vietnamese navy was in a crouch, leaving most of the Delta to North Vietnamese regulars who had moved in from Cambodia.

As expected, a very different picture was painted by the bald, beefy American who received Pen in the consulate. Lanh did not even try to go in with him this time; he had a friend to visit, an old buddy he'd helped escape after the attempted coup, a man who had not slept on a cell's raised concrete floor, who had not eaten the infested rice. When

Julie heard of his plan, she invited herself along. "Would he let me do his portrait?" Lanh shrugged but liked her curious eye.

"We're in good shape," said the American to Pen, unrolling a huge map of the Delta on a conference table. "ARVN here"—he pointed—"repelled the NVA unit that had infiltrated through here. Artillery and air strikes drove them back across the border. And here and here the Navy is active, denying VC the use of this area here. They're on the offensive—I mean the ARVN is on the offensive—because the rice harvest is on, and they want the peasants to get to their fields."

"Any sign of a ceasefire?" Pen knew the answer. The ceasefire had disintegrated months ago, but he liked to ask dumb questions. They pierced the uptightness of officials who preferred reporters uninformed.

The American relaxed and laughed from his beer belly. "I wish!" he said. "Well, actually, I don't wish, because if everybody stopped fighting, the situation would be frozen in place and the Commies would hold too much of the Delta. Shit, they're everywhere. Bad scenes here and there. So, what I said before? Might be a bit of an exaggeration. Certain spots aren't in such great shape. The Commies are good at what they do, the fuckers. NVA regulars know how to fight a war. We need to drive 'em the fuck outta here. And we will. We will."

"What makes you think so?"

A long pause, a stroke of the chin, and finally, "Because I'm supposed to think so. That's my job."

"We're planning to go down there, to Long Tien, for a story on how you harvest rice in the middle of a war. Who controls the village and the ways to it?" Again, Pen knew the answer—or the official answer according to Lanh's tutorial.

"There?" the American put a stubby finger on the map. "Oh, sure, that's fine. No sweat. All under ARVN control. They drove the NVA Fifth Division back into Cambodia. Very secure. You'll pay a gook with a sampan enough, and he'll take you." The man stopped. "That's off the record— the gook part. We're not supposed to say that. I was here with the First Cav, you understand. Well, not right here. In An Khe. Seems like a long fucking time ago. Picked up some slang. Actually, this is all off the record. Embassy isn't delighted to have us talking to the press."

"Fine," Pen said, thanked him, shook his hand, and headed for the door.

"Keep your head down," said the American with a grin.

At first light, Mr. Kỳ drove them out of town on a road already pitted with neglect by the absent American contractors and construction troops. Lanh had seemed distracted over their dinner the evening before. He did not pay much attention to what he had ordered, the crispy yellow pancakes enveloping shrimp, minced meat, and vegetables; pork rolls; huge grilled snails with pepper and fermented tofu; fatty chunks of duck and rice noodles cooked in a broth.

"How was your friend?" Pen asked, then to Julie: "Did you get a portrait?"

Sullenly, she shook her head.

"He thinks he's still being hunted," Lanh said. "Maybe he is, I don't know. Maybe the Special Branch has a long memory. I've told him about prison. He's not eager for the experience." And then he laughed, his leathery face crinkling at every point where skin could bend. "Me, I'm always eager for the new experience!" But his eyes did not dance.

He suggested an early start to make it a daylight trip. Along the country roads, he said smiling, "The night cloaks the VC."

With a frayed army map on his lap, Lanh peppered Mr. Kỳ with directions in Vietnamese. The sun climbed, the light brightened. The wind blowing through the open windows grew hotter. The road wound through hamlets, then along green rice fields pregnant with the sweet and pungent smell of wet earth. A woman herding a line of ducks with a long, thin stick stopped traffic. A water buffalo lumbered beside the road, a boy on top.

"That was me!" Lanh shouted. "That was me. I loved that. So high, riding a powerful beast. Nobody has as much control as a buffalo boy." He stuck his head out the window into the wind and inhaled deeply and waved as they flew past the buffalo boy. The boy waved back.

Down a dead-end dirt lane, Mr. Kỳ pulled over beneath the shade of palms by the muddy water. Lanh got out. "Stay here a minute," he told Pen and Julie.

Three sampans were pulled halfway up the bank. Nets were drying in the sun. A trio of men lounged nearby, smoking and laughing. Lanh suspected this might be a hard bargain, and he walked up casually, his arms spread outward as if he had just touched down accidentally in this idyllic place.

He squatted next to them, fingered some stems and leaves on the ground, gazed around without saying anything at first, then asked, "How's the fishing?"

When you ask a man about his profession, especially when it relies on skill and luck, you will get tales in a torrent of pride and pity, and that is what happened under those palms a few kilometers down the waterway from Long Tien. Pretty good, said one man. Not as good as it used to be, said another. Off and on, said the third.

"The government shells, scares the fish, which hide in the grasses."

"What are you catching?"

"Black carp, catfish, pike, trout—but not so many now."

"I had a good day yesterday."

"But before the Communists came, much better."

"Are the Communists here?" asked Lanh.

"Here and there, night and day." The man pointed, probably in the direction of Long Tien.

"The government shells the flags."

"The Communists' flags?"

"The Communists' flags. On tall poles. The government doesn't want the flags. The Communists shoot back. We have to be brave to fish."

"And to harvest rice?" Lanh asked.

"To harvest rice, too. My brother stepped on a mine." The man waved a hand in some far-off direction. "Now he has no foot and cannot plow or plant."

"Whose mine?"

"Ha. Who knows? The Front's or the nationalists', who can say?"

"So who does your brother blame?"

"What does it matter? A mine blows off the foot that steps on it."

Lanh wished Pen could hear this conversation, but a task was in order.

"I have Americans in the car," he said. There was not even a glimmer of surprise. Who else would be coming here in a white Fiat? "They want to go to Long Tien."

The fishermen must have figured out what was coming, because they all looked hard at Lanh, then across the water to the clusters of reeds, then at the ground. They said nothing.

"What do you think?" Lanh prompted.

"I think the Americans are crazy," said the oldest fisherman, who had just the wisp of thin, long whiskers on his chin. They all laughed, including Lanh.

"Yes, all Americans are at least a little crazy," said Lanh.

"A little?" said the youngest, who looked like a boy. "A little! Right, a little!" And they all laughed again.

The lilt of the laughter reached Pen and Julie in the car. "Lanh has a knack for softening up suspicious locals," Pen said.

Lanh watched the fishermen in silence, hoping one would offer some opening. Finally, the oldest spoke. "Long Tien is okay. Getting there is not. The Vietcong hide in the day along the banks and in the brush and come out at night. Maybe they wouldn't attack, maybe they would."

What followed was an intricate discussion of routes and times and probabilities as Lanh led the fishermen through their own preferences, where they cast their nets and lines, how they did the calculations as the patterns of safety shifted day after day. When he had enough information, he put the question.

"What if we go that long way around, on the way to Cai Rang?"

"It would take a while."

"How long?

"Almost half a day."

"If we left now? Would we be back by dark?"

"You better be!" And they all roared as the kid flicked his cigarette into the water.

"How about taking us for three thousand?" Lanh proposed. He knew this was about a day's catch, maybe a little more.

The men gestured for him to step away while they consulted, and Lanh went back to brief Pen. The oldest beckoned to Lanh. "Eight thousand," he said. Lanh pretended to be stunned by practically tripping backward in shock.

"How high can I go?" he asked Pen.

"As high as you need to."

"Six thousand," said Lanh, and the men smiled at one another. It was the kid who drew the job, patted on the shoulder by the older two as if they were giving him a gift.

"Do they think it's safe?" Pen asked. So maybe the tutorial had stuck after all.

"Relatively, the way we're going."

Pen began taking notes. The sampan was long and narrow, made of boards of varied faded paints, salvaged no doubt from the scraps of ruined houses. At the stern was a large outboard motor with a shaft angled at about forty-five degrees to give it forward thrust without too deep a draft, Pen figured. However, it had no cover over the huge fly wheel, which spun dangerously.

"You know what happens sometimes?" Lanh asked Pen. "Girls get their long hair caught in those wheels and it's pulled out by the roots. I saw some at the Quaker hospital. The girls never look the same."

The fisherman's name was Chi. He said he was seventeen. He pushed the sampan into the water and motioned for Lanh and Pen and Julie to get in. She had said nothing, but she was watching, fingering pencils. The boy wound a rope around the fly wheel, gave it a hard pull, and the motor coughed to life. They were off, through meandering curves in the Delta waterways, as complicated as an old city's streets.

Around a bend, they glided through a small village, passing a woman in a long sampan. She was dressed in a yellow shirt and salmon-colored pants and rowed standing with two long crisscrossed oars. Along the banks stood houses on pilings that held them just above the water. They were painted in pastel yellows and blues. Julie made a quick sketch, and labeled it with the names of colors. Then she turned to the boy, drawing him with a brevity devoid of detail but suggestive enough of his good looks to present to him when they put ashore. Pen figured this was her method of taking notes, engraving his features in her memory until she was home behind her easel. He tossed her a smile while she worked.

The motor clanged too loudly for conversation. Pen watched Lanh, who seemed captivated by the passing rice paddies and occasional hamlets. Was he on guard, or pining for simplicity, elemental and elusive? Two black shadows appeared in the gray-green water ahead. Logs, perhaps, requiring just the slightest course correction. As the sampan cruised by, its slender wake rolled them and turned blue bloated faces to the sky. Black-clad arms and legs floated askew. The boy took no notice. Julie stared as if recording for the sake of recall. "VC!" Lanh shouted over the noise.

The first dead bodies I've ever seen, thought Pen. He tried to spot their eyes and turned and stared back until a bend in the waterway left the decay behind. *And we eat the fish that eat them*, Pen almost said aloud.

When the sun was high, the bamboo houses and thatched roofs of Long Tien came into view around a crescent curve. Chi put the sampan into the bank, and a welcoming squad of children came running barefoot, eyes bright with joyful curiosity. Lanh pulled out his camera, and the kids beamed up at his lens, crowded around, pointed laughingly at Pen's nose. They reached out to touch the hair on Pen's arms, then beckoned Lanh to follow them into the hamlet.

A cascade of villagers invited them into their minimal houses, flooding them with stories and laments. In the sea of rich green paddies, there were booby traps made of grenades and trip wires. Their field work was punctuated by army artillery and VC gunfire. Yet they had to eat. Pen jotted down the words of a farmer squinting out across the lush land: "If every time you hear the noise you go home, you will be home all the year."

The dirt road through the hamlet was cratered where mines had exploded, but villagers on bikes, motorbikes, and Lambrettas were zigzagging along, oblivious to the risk that fighting might erupt. Pen and Lanh strolled with the gaggle of children bouncing around them. Beyond the cluster of houses, the sweep of countryside was painfully pretty for a war.

They reached an army post, just a thatched roof on poles, a sleepy place. Then the crack of an exploding artillery round broke the quiet. A puff of smoke burst in a treeline across a clearing. High on a bamboo pole attached to one of the tallest trees, a large flag fluttered: a broad red stripe on the top, a broad blue stripe on the bottom, a big gold star in the middle.

"We have a man who shoots down flags," said a soldier at the post. "He's good. He shoots them with that," and pointed to a long, sinister barrel on a low tripod. Pen had never seen one before.

"A fifty-seven-millimeter recoilless rifle," Lanh said. "They waste ammunition on flags."

"Ah," said Pen lightly. "It's safer than shooting at the VC or NVA. They'll shoot back." Lanh gave him a nod.

The cluster of welcoming children, some chewing on sticks of sugarcane, stood off to the side listening.

The soldier offered Lanh and Pen rice wine from an old man's bottle. From under his conical straw hat, the man explained his theory of wartime economics: The fighting could be good for those who knew how to thread through the canals and rivers. He made his hand weave like a fish. Farms were mined or shelled, farmers driven from their lands into the swollen sanctuary of Cần Thơ. So the price of rice was high, he said. His solution: He bought low and kept a stash and sold high. He flashed a toothless grin of victory. "Now, it's a calmer time. When the flags first went up a year ago, there would be planes dropping bombs, artillery fire all the night, and the gunfire was like the winter rain." Lanh half-smiled at the metaphor.

"Do you have children?" Pen asked. When Lanh translated, a shadow crossed the man's face.

"One son with the Communists, one son with the nationalists. For all I know they are out there shooting at each other," and he waved his hand in a wish to brush away the tangle of the war. Those were the words Pen heard from Lanh and entered into his notebook, along with all the other resilience and fear he gathered that day in Long Tien.

Julie's pencil moved briskly as Lanh watched closely. "You must have to imagine the lines on the paper before you draw them," he said. Her eyes widened at the notion. She'd never thought of it that way, she confessed, but yes, perhaps. Then she tore out the page and handed it to the old man, who saluted her happily.

Chi the sampan boy seemed jumpy on the way back. He gunned his outboard, took the curves fast, and crouched low as they raced along, the wake jostling the reeds and grasses along the banks. Pen noticed that Lanh had set his mouth in a thin line of tension; his eyes darted ahead and beside their track.

The afternoon was waning. The tall ferns, whose shadows had been stubs in the overhead sun, now cast dark angles across the edges of the canals, a feathery green sputtered in the softening light. Lanh watched for movement along the shore. Chi kept his focus on his pathway through the brown water. Pen felt all his muscles tighten, as if he were heeling close-hauled in a vicious wind. Julie continued on her drawing of the boy, filling in shadings, transforming him from a cutout character into three dimensions, or so she thought—an illusion of three dimensions. She caught his eyes, alertly narrowed.

Then, nothing happened. The canal opened into wider water, Lanh let out a laughing sigh, and soon they could see their Fiat and Mr. Kỳ stretched out beneath a palm, his hat over his face.

Dusk came on the road back to Cần Thơ, however, and Mr. Kỳ drove quickly through the wafts of cooking smoke along the way. The dull glow of hanging lanterns, appearing and disappearing as they fled by, made Pen think of fireflies. In the last hint of day, they crossed the bridge and saw, stretched out below, the dark shapes of sampans and boathouses crammed together, a refugee city within a city, the yellow spots of lanterns bobbing helplessly.

At home the following night, lying in wait for sleep, Lanh said to Thuận: "Imagine if I had translated according to the bidding of one side or another: 'My sons are both with the Front to fight for our liberation and to make their father proud.' Or, 'My sons are both with the nationalists to fight against the Communists and make their father proud.'"

"But you would never do that," she said.

"No. Reality is more interesting. But I am transplanting tender rice shoots. I am pulling up people's lives, showing them to Pen, and putting them back in the ground so they will either flourish or die." Thuận had no reply.

Julie had a lot to tell Hạnh, but their unwritten rule required the tennis lesson first, so she danced and muscled through the hour on the court, so obviously preoccupied that Hạnh asked after a bungled serve, "What's wrong? Something on your mind?"

"Later," she called back.

The cyclo driver had died, she said over their lemonade. She put the sweating glass to her forehead, but sips felt only sour and dried her mouth. Money for the family was coming in. The older daughter still stared vacantly.

"Helplessness," Julie said. "That's what this war is all about, isn't it? Helplessness. You can't help even where you can reach out and touch people. You can't really help. Whatever you do is like throwing water against the wind."

"The money will help," said Hạnh.

"Only temporarily. Then it will run out. Readers will turn to the next tragedy. The mother will sink, maybe send her kids out to beg. Maybe have to give them to Erik Sendstad."

In a taxi to Dương's, where Julie wanted to watch him draw, Hạnh began a soft interrogation. "Tell me what else Pen is working on," she asked. This peculiar line of interest kept distracting the eye like a wayward brushstroke.

"He and I went down to the Delta, to a village where they're trying to grow rice in the middle of fighting."

"Was there fighting?"

"Not when we were there. But the army was shelling VC flags, and control shifts from day to night. Those poor farmers. All they seem to want is to be left alone. Right?"

"How did you know it was going to be safe when you were there?"

"Pen's in good hands with his interpreter. A savvy guy. But next he's going—" She stopped just short of the secret, and the cab pulled up to the little restaurant below Dương's studio.

Hạnh tried to continue as they walked upstairs. "Going where?" Julie didn't answer.

The light in Dương's studio seemed gray, and he sat on a stool doing nothing. Well, not nothing, he explained through his wife when she challenged him. "I am thinking. I spend more time thinking than drawing. Do you, Julie?"

"Maybe. I haven't timed it."

"Some artists create from the ends of their fingers," Dương said. "They don't know what they're making until their pens and brushes touch the paper. I'm not that way. I need to see it in my head. And you?"

"I need to see it with my eyes," said Julie. "I don't have enough imagination to just conjure up an image in my head."

"Conjure?" Hạnh asked for translation's sake.

"Invent, imagine, think up something that's not real. I need reality. Although these days, with everything moving so fast, I try to remember what I've seen and then do it from recollection. When I do a portrait that way, I'm sure it's not faithful to the face. Sometimes I think I see myself looking back at me, which bothers me."

"Why does it bother you?" Dương asked. "Doesn't it free you to mix yourself and what you remember with your interpretation, like mixing colors? Can't you change the character of the person as you paint? I do that!" He gave a huge guffaw and pointed to a drawing of Nixon bearing a nose like a B-52.

Hạnh said something in Vietnamese, Dương replied, Hạnh said something else, and Dương's answer came in agitated rhythm, his hand gestured in dismissal as if flicking away a fly. Hạnh tried again, Dương replied in a brusque word, and Hạnh turned to Julie.

"He's interested in your husband's work. You started to say where he was going. Dương would like to know." She coughed in discomfort. "Maybe what your husband is seeing would give him some ideas for cartoons."

Julie's bullshit alarm went off, and a gust of cold stirred the air between them. She watched Hạnh's eyes, which widened in a show of sincerity before sliding toward the distant window. *You forget. I can read faces.* Dương, for his part, had grown fascinated by the sketch on the paper before him.

"What does Dương want to know?" Julie asked.

"He wants to know—"

"Aren't you going to translate the question?"

"But I already know what he'll say." She spoke to Dương, he shook his head and shrugged.

"Well," Hạnh said, "just what Pen is planning or finding out to give Dương some ideas. Where is he going next?"

"Oh, I don't know. I can't say. He's got so many plans and ideas, and things come up here and there, some riskier than others, I suppose."

"Why can't you say?"

"He told me not to. I mean, you know, competition."

"Competition?"

"From other correspondents." Her neck turned red when she lied.

"I'm not the competition."

"No, of course not, but I'm here to watch Dương work, if I may."

Dương, who had not followed the jousting in English between Hạnh and Julie, held up his hand for calm and quiet, motioned Julie to a stool behind him, and let her look over his shoulder at the quick, confident strokes of his dark pencil. A dove took shape rapidly, Kissinger riding on its back like a cowboy with bombs in holsters and an eagle's fierceness in his eyes. On top, Dương wrote *Hòa Bình*. Peace, Hạnh translated.

Julie settled into a cyclo for a decompressing ride to Erik's home where her regular duties as a playmate with the children took her to a place of comfort within herself, one rarely visited in her art. In fact, Lanh had troubled her as he watched her sketch the old man and the sampan boy. He asked if seeing outside herself all the time blinded her to seeing inside herself. It was an intimate question, one that got her thinking. She didn't give an answer. But it seemed to her, and Pen later thought she was right, that Lanh was asking it about himself. His mission, his work of handling others' words, did not open gateways into his own reflections, they concluded. He was always gazing outward, never inward.

Lanh might have laughed sardonically and wished it to be true. The altitude of the disengaged observer could be an easy place. Just ask Pen, Lanh might have said: the consummate traveler who glides above the hardships he's describing. Or so it seems.

Julie managed to get Thi to sit still a few times for an ink drawing that caught more than her placid allure. Even as her eyes darted at every wail or laugh from a child outside, they were fixed on paper as wells of worry. No matter her blithe efficiency, some unsteadiness was recorded on the page, so affecting that Julie wanted to keep the portrait, not give it up as she planned, as a gift to Thi. She took it home and taped it to the wall above her dresser.

"I would not even want to sell it," she told Pen. "I don't know why."

"Are you collecting? Capturing?"

"That sounds selfish. Hell, I'll give it to her. I should."
And she did, with a pang, and with a strange look from Thi
as she inspected how Julie saw her.

"Very nice," Thi said coolly. "Thank you."

"Don't you like it?"

"Oh, yes, Julie. I like it very much. It will make me
think—not only of myself, but of you."

Julie gradually realized that she was being drawn to
Erik's less by the chance to practice her art or to give tokens
of assistance than by a tiny treasure named Mai, who seemed
as fragile as a bird and just as quick around the yard. Her
eyes were too wide for her little face, her black bangs cut
unevenly, her oversized black pants and white shirt flopping
around her as she ran barefoot with the boys.

The yard was strewn with little prizes from the streets:
broken bits of brick, marbles and stones, coins, corncobs
and sticks, sandals and rubber bands, bottle caps and cans—
all props in inventive games. Julie watched and watched and
couldn't figure out the rules, and without the language she
couldn't ask the kids. Thi wasn't around.

"Erik, what are they playing?"

"Honestly I don't know how it all works."

"Can you ask them?"

"No time now, sorry," and off he went to send his cook
for food, or pay his bills, or consult with the doctor who
never asked for payment, or meet with a desperate mother—or whatever he did in his long and busy hours.

Julie was left squatting as she'd learned to do, getting
down to the children's level. All right, sometime she would
bring Lanh—and maybe Pen. Faces could not tell stories she

did not know. She needed words. *Damn!* Sketches would be superficial, or wrong, or just little trophies.

The boys were ignoring Mai, who pirouetted around them trying to break in. A boy skimmed a sandal just above the surface of the ground into a pile of rubber bands that had been carefully assembled, scattering them. He whooped in victory, scampered across the yard, scooped them up, and stuffed them in his pocket. Two other boys assembled another pile, and the next took his turn with the sandal. Mai picked up a sandal. The boys yelled at her. She dropped it.

"Mai," called Julie, and the girl came, looking down at the ground. "Show me," Julie said, opened both her hands in a gesture that she hoped meant, What game do you play? Mai beamed, darted to a corner of the yard, picked up a handful of chopsticks and a rubber ball, and ran to the sidewalk, beckoning to Julie.

Mai squatted, threw the ball into the air with her right hand, let it bounce once, and caught it with her left. Then she tossed the ball with her left hand, and while it was in the air, coming down for a bounce, she held the chopsticks in a bunch and flipped them over twice with both her hands. And caught the ball.

"Jacks!" Julie exclaimed. Mai looked blank.

She threw the ball again, tossed the chopsticks on the ground, picked up two with her left hand, and caught the ball with her right. The next time the ball lifted into the air, she slapped the chopsticks twice against her right palm and caught the ball. The next time, she tapped them twice on the sidewalk, then threw them down, picked up two with her left hand, put them under her arm, and caught the ball. She never missed.

Each time the ball flew and then bounced again, she performed a new trick, tossing the ball higher and higher and doing each move in threes, then fours, fives, sixes as the chopsticks clicked and clicked. A few boys stopped their game and watched, mouths open.

CHAPTER 8

L anh's father is getting suspicious. "Did you go out last
  night?" he asks.

"What do you mean?"

"I didn't sleep well. I thought I heard you go to the
door."

Lanh does not answer. He never lies, except that all his
nights for two weeks have been the lie of a hidden life.

"I woke up, too," he tells his father. Nothing more is
said. The silent moment speaks as it does after a monsoon
rain has stopped beating on a tin roof. Later, much later,
Lanh will think back on the quiet end of this conversation
as the unspoken eloquence after a harsh wind vanishes, gunfire dies, lovemaking finishes. Everybody knows everything.

By his seventeenth night guiding the Japanese soldier
through the rainy alleyways, Lanh has learned to combine
the clearest views of French targets with the most confusing
routes of escape. He dresses in his black trousers, his black
shirt, and the black beret he has pilfered from a roadside
stand. He climbs the stairs to the shack on the roof, greets
the soldier with a bow that he has learned, and leads the way
down, out, and through twisting labyrinths.

The cobblestones are slick. The soldier slips and catches
himself before his rifle clatters to the ground. Lanh motions

him into a dark doorway in case anyone has heard. But the city sleeps.

The courtyard Lanh has found that afternoon after school is small, abandoned, and marked by a wall whose top is protected by shards of green and yellow glass. An old ladder with bamboo rungs lies on the ground, probably a remnant of a gardener's care or a mason's work. Not more than thirty or forty meters on the other side of the wall, a khaki guard shack stands in plain view. In the rain, three or four French try to crowd inside, but they are much too large to fit, and Lanh laughs at them inside his thoughts. One or two are always at the door or just outside. It is the same later, in the dark when the Japanese soldier leans the ladder against the wall, climbs, and peers through the jagged pieces of glass onto his targets.

It is not as easy a place as Lanh has thought, and the soldier is unsure. He has to release his hands from the ladder, take the rifle off his back, lift it to his shoulder, aim carefully, and not be seen. He hesitates, then climbs down. He runs a hand along the wall, at the height of his eyes, to try to find a hole by feel, perhaps one that can be made big enough to sight a rifle through. Lanh does the same, reaching high over his head. Now and then a hand stops. Fingers scrape at the concrete between the stones, and then move on.

Impatiently, the Japanese soldier slides his hand along the wall down to the corner. Nothing. Lanh is shrugging an apology. The soldier gives him an unfriendly smile but not a glare, because they are comrades in the night, Lanh believes. The soldier climbs the ladder again, one hand holding on, the other gripping the rifle. Leaning forward onto the stonework for balance, he pokes his head above the glass, raises the gun, lays it between shards, and looks along the sight.

Suddenly, a shout from across the street. Voices of alarm in French. A shot shatters glass, and the Japanese slaps his eye with his hand. He wobbles on the ladder, tips, and tumbles in a yelp of pain. More shots whine and ricochet off the wall. Lanh rushes to the warrior lying curled, holding his bloody left leg, a splintery bone sticking out in a sharp point below his knee.

Lanh tries to lift the man, but he is heavier than a sack of rice. Lanh grabs the rifle, planning to shoot the French voices, which are gathering momentum. "*Non!*" says the soldier, one of the few words they have in common. He gestures with the back of his hand for Lanh to go, to run, to save himself. Courage, Lanh thinks. Terror, he feels. Indecision freezes him, and the Japanese soldier, his comrade in the night, contorts his body enough to reach out and push Lanh toward the exit, and barks something in Japanese that sounds like a frightening order.

So Lanh puts the rifle in the soldier's arms, turns and runs, and looks back from the darkness just in time to see a French head at the top of the wall. He hears a shot as he races away along the slippery cobblestones, through abandoned courtyards and the remains of the daytime market, sliding and sliding and putting a bloody hole in the knee of his trousers, and finally, soaking and trembling, gaining the safety of his doorway and his house.

His father is standing staring at him. He says nothing but, "Come, let me wash that knee and get you dry clothes."

CHAPTER 9

After Colonel Giang's briefing for the press at Camp Davis, his deputy, Major Direction South, asked Pen to step into an adjacent Quonset hut before getting on the army bus back into town. It would have to be a quick conversation to avoid alerting colleagues. Competition annoyed him and thrilled him. He hated scrambling all the time to avoid getting scooped, but it would sure be delightful to beat the *Post* or the *Times*. And he wouldn't mind seeing his star rise in the Boston newsroom.

"Please listen carefully," the major said through the young interpreter. "Two weeks from next Tuesday, go to Bình Long. Take a bus, not a taxi. While you are on the bus, tie a white handkerchief around a camera strap or backpack strap over your left chest. One kilometer after Bình Long, you will see a dirt road to the right at a small shop with a few wooden tables outside. Ask the driver to let you off there. Have a cup of tea at the shop until ten minutes after the bus has left. Then walk back two hundred meters the way the bus came. A narrow path goes to the right from the road through some trees into jungle."

Pen was writing as fast as he could.

"In about one hundred meters, the path divides into a fork. Follow the righthand fork slowly. Soon a pretty girl in a blue hat will pass you on a bicycle. She will be riding slowly enough for you to follow her. As you walk, a man will appear wearing a white rag tied around his neck. He will give his name as Khải. It means triumph." They both smiled.

"He is your contact. He will lead you to our district. Now, this is very important. If you are followed, please stop and turn around. Do not lead the Saigon puppets to us. Please."

Someone shouted that the press bus was leaving. Pen shook hands with Direction South, thanked him, and dashed away.

Pen circled around the trip in his mind, trying to find the safest route—not to travel but to tell Julie that his adventure had been scheduled.

Once Nghi had left that evening, closing the door with a click, Pen waited. Julie was too joyful. She seemed cloudless for the first time in a long while.

"Do you know what she did? She tried to play a game with the boys—they were tossing sandals at a pile of rubber bands—and they shooed her away. So she showed me her version of jacks—a ball, a half dozen pairs of chopsticks, tossing them down, picking them up, clicking them on the ground, all kinds of tricks while the ball was in the air. Just like I used to play with jacks except much cleverer. Mai is so adorable. She had those mean boys all standing around watching her in awe. Oh, Pen, you should have been there."

"I wish. What other games were they playing?"

"I didn't understand them. They looked intricate, and I can't talk to them so I couldn't ask. Erik was too busy to interpret." She gazed down at her plate as a thought flashed, then extinguished itself. She could ask Hạnh to the home to talk with the kids. But no, she was neatly compartmental-ized now. Don't break down partitions.

"Maybe Lanh can come someday. And you. Maybe it's a story for you."

"Could be. It would be fun to watch. I've noticed kids in the streets with cans and bricks and all kinds of trash that they make into toys." There was a pause, a breath of oppor-tunity. So he told her. "Jule, I'm going into VC territory. It's all arranged."

"Oh, shit. I mean, oh, great!" A grimace. "When?"

"About two weeks. Remember, not a word to anyone."

"Okay, I know, darling. But—"

"But what?"

"But nothing."

"Did you tell someone this was in the works?"

"No, no, I don't think so."

"What do you mean you don't think so?"

"Well, I mentioned to Hạnh—"

"Hạnh?"

"She was asking about your work, dear, and I said something about how I couldn't say, and then she pushed. She pretended Dương was interested, though I'm sure he couldn't care less."

"And?"

"And I didn't go any further, I don't think. Really. They can't have guessed."

"Oh, brother. You sound a little out of touch with your-self, not like you."

"Don't worry. I told her you didn't want the competition to know what stories you were working on."

"Did that satisfy her?"

"Well, she said she wasn't the competition. But that was it. Relax, my darling, she's just a tennis teacher."

"Just a tennis teacher," Pen repeated, "whose husband manages to get away with political cartooning."

"She's a friend, Pen. At least I think she's a friend. I like her, the part of her I see. We see in parts, don't we? There are parts invisible, too—unreachable. I can make them up when I do portraits, that's what Dương said. A pretty deep fellow, makes you think. Hạnh, on the other hand, is mostly small talk."

"I'd appreciate it if your small talk didn't include my work."

"It doesn't, usually. Well, sometimes. She seems extremely interested."

"Interested," Pen snorted. "Well, I hope she doesn't screw me. I have a lot at stake on this trip."

"Proving yourself?"

"Not in the way you mean. Proving that I can be a foreign correspondent and take initiative and find stories without the desk giving me assignments every day. It's really a different line of work, being alone here, and I have to show I can do it."

She put her hands softly on his shoulders.

Mai ran up and wrapped her arms around Julie's legs in such a strong and desperate hug that Julie couldn't move. Lanh squatted down and in a minute had the sketches of her story. Her mother was sick. Her father was a soldier somewhere.

Her oldest brother was in jail for something. Her older sister tried to earn money, but her younger brother was too little to work. Mai was in "Erik's house" until her mother could get well and come for her. Maybe her younger brother could come here, too. She would like that. She missed them.

The look on Julie's face took Lanh back to Danang years before, when Rosie had met a dusty little street girl and just wanted to pick her up and take her along to a place of love and safety. Rosie the romantic, the idealist, the skeptic, the pragmatist, the outraged purveyor of all the injustice and agony that she could pack into 700 words day after day. She had to leave the little girl where she was, of course, after going to an orphanage to tell the nuns about her, and hoping they would do something—something kind, not cruel.

So Lanh had seen that face before, and it concerned him. *This little girl has a family!* Pen watched his wife in surprise, Lanh saw. From questions to answers, Lanh shifted his glance back and forth between Pen and Julie, comparing two translations of the same text.

Mai demonstrated her game of jacks with chopsticks. Lanh took pictures, Pen took notes. A boy nicknamed Robber and his pals explained their games. First, one called *dánh bi lõ*. They dug a hole with their fingers, cleared out the pebbles, and smoothed the dirt. Robber took a green marble, cradled it in his forefinger and thumb, and shot. It rolled, skidded a little off course, then swerved back perfectly into the hole. So Robber had the first turn at hitting another marble. And for that he pulled out his favorite, red woven with a white stripe.

"If I hit his three times, I can pick his up." And he flicked his champion marble at Xuân's blue and yellow one a few feet away. *Click.* Then again, *click.* Then a third time, *click.* A marksman. Xuân looked on sadly as Robber dropped it in his pocket.

"Do girls play this?" Pen asked.

The boys all hooted in hysterics. "They couldn't hit a hole ten meters wide!" one shouted. Mai put on a stormy look.

Xuân showed off another game, called *năm lỗ*, which Lanh translated as "five holes." With their fingers they dug five little holes in the dirt. Xuân shot his marble into the first hole, then into the second, then into the third, and straightened up to explain. "Whoever shoots into the fifth hole gets to hit the other kids' marbles."

Lanh tried it. "I used to be good," he told the boys. He descended gracefully into a squat, his arms limber and his fingers splayed in a dramatic flourish of showmanship. A couple of kids stood over him with their arms crossed in disdain. He took a marble and rolled it precisely into the first hole. "Ha!" he crowed and stood in victory.

"You've got to keep going," the chorus of kids chanted.

"I'll quit while I'm ahead," said Lanh. "I'm out of practice. I used to do this in Hanoi, too many years ago."

"Me too," Pen told the kids. "Well, not in Hanoi, in the US. We had bags of marbles that we won and lost. We'd draw a circle on the ground, put marbles in it, and try to hit them out."

"We have that!" Robber said. He led them to the sidewalk, took a stone to scratch a triangle on concrete, and they all contributed marbles until there were nine, arranged like billiards. Each boy picked a marble from his pocket, crouched down, and shot it at the cluster to try to knock one or two out of the triangle. "It's called *dánh mọt*," Robber said, which brought Lanh a glint of nostalgia.

"I remember this," he told Pen. "But *mọt* is pronounced 'maw' because it's not a Vietnamese word. It's an imitation of *mort* in French. So the game means dead marble. A little pocket of life where somebody wins. Nobody ever wins this war, but here, somebody always wins. The game ends, instead of going on and on."

Marbles aside, the common denominator of most contests involved sandal-tossing. Sandals were flung, flipped, and sailed at any leftovers the streets could yield: cans, bottle caps, towers of stones, broken bits of brick, plastic jugs, rubber bands, the higher the piles the more cheerful the contest. And they threw sandals at each other, naturally, dodging the missiles amid screeches of delight.

Pen thought he had enough and stopped writing in his notebook, but Lanh was having fun. He kept crouching and asking and gesturing and making his hands follow the lines of the boys' explanations. The kids loved his curiosity, and when he straightened and finally seemed ready to go, they wouldn't let him.

Robber stood a can inside a circle drawn in the dust. A boy named Binh, who was It, stood beside the can, knees bent slightly in readiness. Robber explained: He would throw his sandal at the can to knock it as far out of the circle as possible. Binh would run to get the can and return it to the circle before Robber could get to his sandal. If Binh won, Robber was It. The name of the game? *Tạt lon*, "throw can."

Robber skimmed his sandal, struck the can with a twang, and dashed as Binh raced for the can, grabbed it like a fish from a pond, and got it back into the circle just as Robber reached his sandal.

"I beat you!" yelled Robber.

"No you didn't!"

"I did so!" He turned to Lanh. "Didn't I?" Lanh managed a magnificent shrug that said, Are you kidding me? I'm not getting into the middle of this.

"What about racers with spools?" Lanh asked. Oh yes, said the boys. When they were out on the streets, they collected empty thread spools, put sticks through the holes, attached rubber bands to the sticks and wound them tightly around the spools, then set them down to run in races as far as the unwinding rubber bands would take them.

"But we don't have any spools," said Xuân. "Can you get us some?"

"I'll look around," Lanh said but didn't promise. Lanh never made a promise, even to his daughters, especially to his daughters. Even if you were sure that you could keep it, a promise had a way of evaporating in the heat.

"We used to play war on Công Lý," Xuân recalled. Armed with corncobs and stones, he and his friends lined up in teams across the street from each other, one side the Vietcong and the other South Vietnam. One day after school, the boys were hurling corncobs as grenades. Corncobs were valuable weapons, not as common as you might think, and the warriors needed all they could collect from the gutter. So after Xuân threw one that landed short, a good pal of his ran into the road to recover it.

"A car hit him. He died. Then we didn't play the game much anymore."

On Tự Do Street, Lanh noticed Mrs. Thương on her usual corner, but now she had her children with her again. She had lasted only a couple of weeks, no surprise, really. She had probably tried to follow the deal with Erik and had simply failed. A woman alone with a wounded gaze and her hand stretched out had grown too common to shock anyone into pulling piasters out of pockets.

She spotted Lanh and quickly turned away. She picked her half-naked baby off the grimy pavement, shouted to Tài in a piercing shriek, and gestured him away down the street. She strode as quickly as she could from Lanh.

But he was faster. He tried to be kind. He asked whether she was eating enough, had enough for the children. She gave him curt answers. Finally he went up to the office and told Pen.

"She's broken the bargain. Maybe we should call Erik. He keeps giving her money."

It happened to be payday, so to speak, so when Erik arrived, Mrs. Thương stepped toward him, then stopped as she saw Lanh come out of the office. She stood wildly paralyzed, poised to flee, anchored to her ground.

As Lanh listened, Erik talked to her for a very long time, offering to take the children in—just for a while, to get them clean and fed and dressed in something besides their filthy rags. And checked out by a doctor. Mrs. Thương kept shaking her head, pointing toward Tài as her source of sustenance.

"Then I can't keep giving you four thousand piasters a week," Erik said as kindly as he could. A crosscurrent of doubt played with Lanh. *Is that okay?* Pen had asked when the deal was first proposed. Now Erik was going to pay her for giving him her kids?

"You said you would keep your children off the street," Erik said.

"I did. I did. I gave them to my neighbor. But now she has work. I have no place to leave them." She left unsaid what Lanh figured she was thinking: Their obvious wretchedness brought compassion from strangers.

Again Erik urged her to let him take them for a while. Again she shook her head and spat betel juice into the gutter.

"I'm not giving up," Erik told Lanh as they parted. "I'll be back tomorrow."

Lanh slept well, because it rained. That freshened the morning air in Lane 342. He wanted an early start, and the pho man was just lighting his fire. His few tables were empty, and he shrugged an apology as Lanh approached.

"Too soon. Why so early?"

Is this an innocent question? The answer is true and therefore innocent, a rare coincidence. But we all have safe spaces behind veils of mutual suspicion. Is he trying to penetrate mine?

"I want to catch a lady in the market. She made a deal and broke it."

"Oh! She owes you money?"

"No. She took money from a Norwegian and promised to keep her kids from begging in the street."

"So what if her kids beg in the street? Everybody's kids beg in the street."

"These kids are sick. The boy is lame and gets beaten if he doesn't bring money. The girl is a starving baby with legs like the matches you use to light your fire."

The pho man shrugged again. "Lanh, you never accept things as they are. You always think they should be better than they can be. Come down to earth. We are at war. We are poor. We need every tool we have, and our kids are some of our tools."

"No," Lanh said. How differently Thuận had answered him. "Save them if you can," she had said. "I know you will do it as if they were your own. Your heart is bigger than our history."

"Our hearts are bigger than our history," he told the pho man, who snorted a laugh and tended to his pot, now boiling.

"We are the victims of history," the pho man said, and ladled out Lanh's regular bowl.

At least that seducer Minh wasn't around at dawn. Lanh slurped down his noodles and his broth, put some ravaged bills on the table, and saluted a goodbye to the pho man.

His motorbike carved an easy path this early to the office, but he didn't stop there. He passed along Tự Do Street, cruised to Hai Bà Trưng Street, turned into side streets, and didn't see Mrs. Thương until he got to the market, which was coming to life as stalls were opened. There she was, carrying a plastic yellow bucket of water for the fishmongers. Tài was a few steps behind her, holding Anh with one arm and a rusty can with a pleading hand.

Lanh zipped back to the office building on Tự Do, where Erik was already waiting. "Hop on," said Lanh, and together they wove through the thickening currents of motorbikes and coughing taxis and graceful girls in their colorful *áo dài* biking with perfect posture.

They wheeled up to Mrs. Thương so suddenly that she nearly spilled her water. Lanh and Erik were polite, Mrs. Thương less so, but she slowed her walk to listen. Erik promised—he could promise, Lanh thought with envy. He promised to get a doctor to see Anh. He promised to feed the children and clothe them. The mother was unmoved. Lanh joined in. "In a few weeks, their faces will no longer look hollow," he told her. He was trying his hand at promising. *Is it okay?* "Anh's legs will be thicker than matchsticks. Then you can come back for them." He looked at Erik, who nodded a definite yes.

A crowd began to gather around them, a gnarled old man with rotted teeth, a few women old enough to have children of their own, a curious cyclo driver. They listened, and then they began to talk to Mrs. Thương like a windstorm, Lanh thought, the way the gusts came before a monsoon rain in beats of insistence.

"Clean beds!" a woman said.

"Clean clothes!" cried another.

"Good food. A doctor!" the cyclo driver declared.

The old man had been quiet, and now he spoke, in a voice resonant with authority. "You have to take advantage of this wonderful offer. You have to take advantage!"

She couldn't have escaped with her bucket of water unless she pushed roughly through the throng that encircled her. A fishmonger in the crowd, a familiar face, said loudly that her boy never laughed. Her girl would never survive on the street. "This man is opening a door," she said. "Walk through it."

"Please," said Lanh. And he said it with a softness that finally broke Mrs. Thương the way a stick, dry and brittle, can snap in a child's hand. She kept her tears inside, but Lanh could see them clearly enough.

He and Erik led the torn family to Tự Do Street, where he had parked. They crammed themselves into Erik's tin-can Citroën and jostled off to the home, which made Mrs. Thương's eyes widen. Boys and girls ran out to greet them as novelties, as they had other children many times.

"They will be fine here," said Lanh.

"Come often to see them, please," said Erik. "And when you get better work, come to take them back. Where do you live?"

In a narrow crevice between two buildings near the river, she said, under a tarp she had taken from the Americans and strung up to keep out rainfall. And then she wrapped her arms around her children. Tài clung to her. Anh cried and cried, and Mrs. Thương seemed on the edge of changing her mind. But then she was gone, promising to be back soon. Promising.

She has her homelessness, I have mine, Lanh thought. *I could learn more about her if she had not become our cause, if I were embracing her with questions. She would tell her own story without having to run. We all have our own stories. What is hers? I am too entangled to listen.*

He stayed for a while. Thi smothered the children in cooing and caring so unfamiliar that they seemed slightly afraid. She had to scrub them and scrub them. She cleaned and bandaged a deep cut in Tài's foot that would require stitches. Anh's ears discharged yellow pus. Through a stethoscope, her lungs sounded as if they were under water. Erik called the doctor, who would be coming that evening.

Lanh slumped into the cushioned seat of a cyclo for the ride back to the office. It should have been soothing, gliding along without effort, but every muscle was stiff. What was the point of that? She'll never be able to take them back to a healthy life. She'll never have enough money. She'll never live anywhere but in an unwanted slice of vacancy between decrepit buildings. She'll have to make them beg. Or she'll leave them there and they'll be lost to her. What are we doing, trying to help when help cannot grow in barren soil?

Pen reacted happily once Lanh told him: "Such a good result from a little story on page eleven."

Mischievously, Lanh figured that it was time for his test. Why not take a quiet day and drive to the coast, he proposed, to a village famous for its nuoc mam? "You can see how it's made."

"Maybe Julie would like to come. Is it safe?"

"Safe from the fighting, mostly on Highway One. But maybe not safe for her stomach. She might never want nuoc mam again!"

Pen and Julie had been happily dipping their *chả giò* in shallow dishes of the thin amber sauce, pouring it over their rice noodles, wetting their chopstick bites of pork and beef. For Pen, it had become as indispensable as ketchup to a kid. Yet the education of innocents is rarely painless, and Lanh, unfolding the miseries of his shattered land, took some pride in provoking guilt among the decent Americans who, through his voice, heard his country's cries. This nuoc mam discovery was something else. Divorced from war, it carried no shame. Cuisine was surviving, even with the depletion of rice—rice, the essence. The language contained a different word for rice at each step of its existence: ripening, harvesting, husking, preparing. Yet rice had been dishonored by the mined fields and sweeping rushes of combat, which forced South Vietnam into the humiliation of importing nourishment in bags stenciled with the magnanimous announcement of its origin as "The People of the United States."

We are begging for our soul, Lanh told himself.

Still, the *chả giò* wrapped in greens and dipped in nuoc mam, the *bún* dashed with nuoc mam, the inventive substitutes for spices gone scarce in the fighting, the enormous snails, the slices of tender beef with lemongrass, the *chả cá*—hunks of fish arranged in a donut-shaped pot around a core of glowing charcoal. The war could be won or lost, no matter, as long as the clean, fresh tastes of creative cooks lived on in every kitchen.

And nuoc mam, indispensable nuoc mam, with its tang and bite and faint hint of rot. So valued that everyone knew of the episode a decade before: A shipment of precious nuoc mam was delivered to a Vietcong unit. Then North Vietnamese troops seized it from their comrades-in-arms, and in despair and protest, a Vietcong fighter defected to the South. What a hero! A man of good taste, a true patriot!

Julie, excited to be getting out of Saigon again, turned her face into the hot wind through the Fiat's window and examined every woman trudging under heavy loads, every child carried on a back, every family jammed onto motorbikes, every man squatting with engine parts laid out as enticements to call on him for repairs, recording their faces in her memory.

The village was humble and sad by its look, but the smell in the pitted street beside the factory was alive and bracing.

Inside, the fishy assault slammed Pen and Julie like a putrid storm of ancient decay.

"Oh, god!" Julie brought her hand over her nose.

"Wow. Pretty strong," Pen said, and blinked his stinging eyes.

"I'm not sure I can stay here," Julie said softly enough that she hoped Lanh hadn't heard. He pretended not to, and forced down a smile.

Aside from the odor, the visitors found a sweet welcome. The owner greeted Lanh like an old friend and presented his daughter, who shook hands as if she were in charge. They walked them proudly through the process.

Four great wooden vats sat atop a platform. From each, a peg-like tiny spout hung over a wooden barrel covered with a circular piece of plywood open with a small slice directly below the little pipe. The stench made Pen's eyes water and kept Julie's hand over her nose and mouth.

The father and daughter gave the tour like partners in a duet, interweaving their sentences so that Lanh's translations had no source but the responding melodies of the mingled voices. First, fish were mashed and put into the upper vats, they explained. Small sardines were preferred, but when the US Navy was here, firing on fishing boats they thought were smuggling weapons for the VC, it had been difficult to get fish from the sea. Using freshwater fish required added salt.

The mash of fish and salt fermented in the upper vats for several months, about six months ideally. Julie felt like retching. Pen began to get interested. Then the little spouts were opened and the liquid drained down into the lower barrels. That liquid was then poured back into the upper vats and allowed to sit for three months more. Then drained again. Then poured back. The best nuoc mam would take a year, the daughter said with a charming smile. Lanh was watching his Americans.

Julie had to leave, get outside, find some healthy air. Pen was scribbling notes now, thinking of a story. "Amazing!" he said. "Fabulous! Something so delicious from all that rotten fish! Who could imagine?"

When Lanh translated, the father and daughter smiled and bowed in appreciation for the appreciation. "The passage of time seasons all of life," the father said—according to Lanh. Pen wondered again how it was that all Vietnamese spoke in poetry.

So what? Lanh makes the quotes delicious.

In the street outside, the daughter tried to present them with a gift, a large bottle of nuoc mam the vibrant color of seasoned life, but Pen wanted to know from Lanh if he could pay for it, please, not to take a piece of their livelihood. Lanh put the question to the father with a certain intensity that spelled insistence. The father shrugged with pleasure and accepted a few piasters.

Shaken hands and broad smiles all around, a slight bow by the father from a more traditional era, and they were off with Mr. Kỳ behind the wheel, Julie's window wide open to clear out everything down to her lungs.

Nobody said anything for long enough that Lanh eventually had to ask what they thought.

"Now I'll eat nuoc mam with new admiration," Pen said. "It's pretty disgusting when you know how it's made—when you first think about it. But then you realize the artistry of it, how creative an idea it is. Amazing. Impressive."

Pen looked at Julie, who said nothing, and she didn't have to. Lanh was quite sure that she would never eat nuoc mam again. So, one pass and one fail.

CHAPTER 10

T he day before the Tuesday of Pen's Vietcong ren-
dezvous, he told Lanh and the office manager, Tân,
that he would be reporting and writing at home
most of the week, and hopefully kick a cold that was coming
on. Tân, a congenial fellow whose main flaw Pen thought
was believing people unreasonably, registered no suspicion.
Lanh, however, wondered.

Tân had organized the bureau with an efficiency envied
in the Saigon press corps. The pride of his achievements
was the telephone and Telex service he was able to maintain
when others' kept collapsing. He got a phone installed in
Pen's villa within a day. And when the office phones went
down or the Telex line failed, Tân called his trusty phone
repairman—never the communications agency still known
by its French initials PTT.

Within hours the lines were back up, and the repairman would stop by the office, a little sheepishly, where
Tân would reach into his bottom drawer and hand him
a bottle of Johnnie Walker Red purchased by Pen (and his
predecessors) from the PX. Pen did not seem to know that
Tân knew, and that the repairman surely knew that Tân
knew, that the lines would go down whenever that bottle approached empty and needed replenishment. When

Pen marveled at the repairman's quick responses, Tân said through a canny grin, "We understand each other."

So whatever Tân knew or thought he knew about Pen's days at home brought only a secret smile. And Lanh smiled not at all. Instead, he worried.

Hạnh did not know either, and anyone writing a transcript of her conversation with Julie that day before the Tuesday could not have found a hint of betrayal, even inadvertent. Over their customary lemonade, Hạnh inquired as usual about Pen's ongoing work, and when Julie reacted with a puzzled frown, Hạnh explained simply that the partisan Vietnamese press could not satisfy her and Dương's interest in what was happening in their country. Nor could the Voice of America, which their portable shortwave radio picked up at night. Hạnh lamented her ignorance. Pen's stories sometimes ran in the *International Herald Tribune*, which Hạnh bought most days at the rickety newsstand run by a tooth-gapped woman across from the Continental. But the paper was too full of other news, she told Julie, stuff she didn't care about from the States, Russia, Europe.

"I am hungry!" she declared. "I want to know what's going on." What was Pen seeing in his travels? What did he think about how ARVN was fighting? Would the economy get worse? "Should we leave?" she asked. "I sometimes think we should leave, go to France or somewhere. Get out of here before it's too late."

That one struck Julie like a fist. *No*, she thought. *You're my best friend here. You can't leave me.*

Hạnh asked her again. "Should I leave?" Julie hovered in that twilight between selfishness and empathy, a familiar, uncomfortable place. She wondered what Lanh would do, Lanh the iconoclastic patriot.

"That would seem rash," she finally replied. "Things aren't collapsing. You have good work teaching tennis. Dương is able to draw and publish. Besides, don't you love your country?" Instantly she realized that she had gone too far. Hạnh gave a look Julie had not seen.

"I'm not even going to answer that."

"Oh, I didn't mean—"

"Never mind. Pen would know better than you anyway. Why won't you tell me more about what he's learning?"

"Mending Wall," she said.

"What?"

"It's a poem by Robert Frost. It can be interpreted in many ways, but it's about walls, boundaries, their pluses and minuses."

"What does that have to do with anything?"

Julie regarded her with an exasperated gaze. "Look, his work is his work. It's separate. Which reminds me. Can I have an extra lesson or two this week? Pen is going away tomorrow."

"I have an hour tomorrow at three. Maybe Thursday, too."

"And don't ask me where he's going."

Hạnh gave her warm laugh. "Okay, where is he going?"

"Secret!" she whispered with a smile.

"For how long?"

"A few days at least."

In Vietnam, two and two hardly ever equaled precisely four. It was said that even what you saw with your own eyes was a rumor. So how did Hạnh do this calculation? She relaxed back in her chair the way a woman does after a gratifying meal.

Pen left at dawn, when Julie was tensely awake. He remembered to stuff a white handkerchief in his pocket, put his camera and extra film in his backpack with a few changes of clothes, and take extra notebooks. The parting goodbye did not feel loving but onerous, like a mutual reprimand that neither dared give a voice.

His usual cyclo driver was not at the end of the lane, so he hailed a little blue and yellow taxi, pulled out a piece of paper written with the Vietnamese words for bus depot, and spoke them with tones as careful as he could manage. Once, he'd muddled the tones of his own street name and ended up in Cholon.

But the driver understood and dropped him in the middle of morning chaos. Entire markets were boarding buses: women laboring with heavy mesh baskets of vegetables, burlap sacks of rice, slaughtered chickens tied in bundles around their legs, men heaving rusted machine parts to sell somewhere. Little kids were being herded aboard when the driver screamed and blocked a man who carried an overflowing sack of liter jugs filled with something the color of urine. Pen caught the whiff of gasoline, which was scarce in the countryside. He'd seen bottles lined up along the road for sale at many times the price in Saigon, a worthy enterprise thwarted now by a stiff arm from the driver, thankfully.

The crowded bus lurched away into the crazy streets, maneuvering around khaki-colored APCs, threading among the biking girls who blossomed in bright *áo dàis* like princesses. In front of government buildings, piles of sandbags slipped past. Soldiers at guard posts lounged lazily as if their day had already oppressed them with boredom.

Pen dozed in the swaying as if he were on a gentle sea. Off and on he awoke enough to peer through his grimy window at the passing fields rising into hills, the blur of conical hats along the road, the occasional water buffalo. Again and again the bus pulled over to a halt, children and families poured off with their wares, others piled on with theirs. A woman carried a wicker cage with two live ducks inside. The heat climbed. Three hours passed. The twilight of sleep seemed a no man's land between fear and the exhilaration of danger, like the jostling bus in Boston he used to take from his night shift on rewrite along the neighborhood boundary between comfort and poverty, security and crime. The risk had stirred him into an alertness that made him feel street wise. He had slid his gaze over every face, sifting through the passengers for the mugger. He had shifted his wallet into his front pocket and kept his hand there. Once safely home, he would open a beer and relax into satisfaction with himself.

"Bình Long!" the driver shouted, and Pen snapped awake. Now he had to estimate one kilometer. He remembered to pull out his handkerchief, bend down, and discreetly tie it around the lefthand shoulder strap of his backpack at his feet. A young man across the aisle glanced at him, then pretended not to.

He had chosen a seat on the right, just a few rows behind the driver, so he could spot the turnoff and the café, and when the dirt road and the square wooden tables came into view, he stood and gestured, the bus pulled over, the front door opened, and he stepped down onto unfamiliar ground. He tried to seem casual. He picked a chair and table in the shade, sat, and checked his watch as the bus rattled off.

A bent man ambled out with a handwritten menu, but Pen just smiled, said *trà*, and looked around as he waited for his tea. Was he being followed? Not that he could tell. People were looking at him curiously, an American without a Vietnamese companion, but he noticed no sign of stealth.

His tea glass empty and the ten minutes expired, Pen rose, shouldered his backpack, and ambled slowly back along the road until he saw the footpath to the right. He paused, pretending to be patiently undecided, then turned and followed Direction South's instructions, walking while waiting for the girl in the blue hat. He took the righthand fork after about a hundred meters. No girl passed him on a bike. A young woman rode the other way, but bare-headed.

He walked farther than he'd expected to. No girl, no man called Khải with a white rag tied around his neck. The path soon grew deserted, that signal Lanh typically took as an alert. Pen stopped and pulled his T-shirt up to wipe the sweat off his face. And suddenly his arms were pinned behind him. Two young men in white shirts and black pants were talking to him in Vietnamese, their faces angry.

"What the hell?" Pen shouted and half laughed. "This is your hospitality? This is the way you greet a visitor?"

The men clearly did not understand. One whipped out a pair of stainless handcuffs, clicked Pen's wrists behind his back, whirled him around, and frog-marched him back along the path to the main road, where a small police van with a blue light on top was parked. They pushed him into the back.

"Oh, shit," Pen said.

If the two handcuffed men already inside were jaded by hard experience, they did not show it. Their astonishment gave Pen a sour sense of notoriety. They exchanged looks and words that Pen could grasp even without the language. They were intrigued and afraid, and they smiled at him in that way that Pen had learned to read as discomfort.

Damn, Pen thought. *Why didn't I study Vietnamese before I came? These guys might make a story.*

It is the privilege of a journalist, Pen had always known, to harvest profit from every encounter, no matter how unpleasant. And how unpleasant would this be?

A narrow wooden bench ran the length of the van on each side, enough for a dozen prisoners crammed together. With his hands cuffed behind him, Pen had trouble scooting back enough on the bench to stay there easily as the van wobbled along. In a town he thought must be Bình Long, the back door was opened by a uniformed cop, who gestured them out. One of the other men stumbled as he stepped down to the ground, and fell. The cop laughed and kicked him in the ribs.

But Pen was greeted by a pallid man in plainclothes who unlocked his cuffs, shook his hand, and said in English, "Sorry, Mr. Pennyman, but we had to do this. Come with me, please." While the others were pushed through one door, Pen was led graciously to another, and into a bare office with only a metal desk, two chairs, and a buzzing fluorescent light.

The man introduced himself as Bảo and sat down across the desk. "You are not very good at keeping secrets," he began.

"I thought I was," said Pen.

"So you admit you were trying to keep a secret."

"Not really. You know very well who I am and what I do. Everything I learn I write, and you can know it too by reading my newspaper."

"I am familiar with what you write. We read it before it is in your newspaper!" Bảo smiled and showed his tobacco-stained teeth. He pulled a pack of Marlboros out of his shirt pocket and offered one to Pen, who shook his head. Bảo lit up and blew a fog of smoke in Pen's direction.

"So, what's your problem?" Pen asked, knowing the answer.

"Our problem is that you American reporters love the VC and want to show how noble they are, so you go into villages they have imprisoned and see what they want you to see and write what they want you to write."

Pen's brain was telling him to stop talking. But caution, or fear, was not in its usual place in the pit of his stomach. It was in his head, trying to make him calculate. *They are not going to do anything serious to me. They depend on us, still.* So when his gut began to boil in resentment, he let it out. "I am not so easily fooled, Mr. Bảo, if that's your name." Bảo took another drag on his cigarette.

"Oh, is that so? And what did you hope they would let you uncover?"

"I had no idea. I think my readers would be interested in knowing something about life under the VC. Wouldn't you? Aren't you interested?"

"My interests are not the subject."

"They should be. You're fighting a war against an enemy you hardly understand. You're trying to win over peasants whose true opinions are hidden from you. You—"

"I hardly understand? I will tell you what we understand. We understand that when the VC assassinate someone pro-government, they pin an indictment on the body convicting him of something like 'treacherous activities against the people.' I understand that they force twelve-year-olds to join them, ripping them from their families. Wait a minute. I'll be right back with something that even you might understand."

Bảo slammed out of the room. Mosquitoes whined around Pen's head. In minutes Bảo was back with a document typed in Vietnamese. "This is a directive from the Central Committee of the Quảng Nam Provincial People's Revolutionary party dated February 7, 1972," he said, waving it at Pen's nose. "Do you read Vietnamese? Of course not, but you think you can understand our country. I'll translate: 'The following categories are to be placed under immediate and ongoing investigation: the formerly French-affiliated; hard-core elements among Buddhists, Roman Catholics, Cao Dais, and Christian and Buddhist youth groups; Chinese nationals and their wives and children; wives of foreign nationals or half-breed Vietnamese; persons whose relatives work for enemy agencies; and persons who travel freely between the enemy's and our own controlled areas for unknown reasons.'"

"Chilling," said Pen. "So you have a captured document. That would be very useful if you let me go into VC territory and question them about this kind of thing. Will you? If you want Americans to have a picture of oppression under the VC—"

"You'll never get that picture by being treated as an honored guest by the VC. And we can't expect anything from

Americans. You have already betrayed us. Now you are trying to subvert us with Communist propaganda. When the Special Branch can stop you, we will. I have beaten you today, my small contribution to the cause."

Båo threw his butt on the floor and stamped on it, stood, and started to leave.

"You haven't beaten me." Pen tried to mask his churning distress. "You've just given me a different story to write. About the way South Vietnam treats American correspondents. It might even get more attention than whatever I could have written from VC territory."

Båo narrowed his eyes and leaned over the desk until his face was a foot away from Pen's. "You don't care. You come, you go, you drift through the country arrogantly assuming knowledge while you bathe yourselves in ignorance."

"Where did you learn such good English?"

"I had good teachers."

"In school?"

"In school and what you call the Agency. They also taught me how to get confessions—at the Farm, Camp Peary."

"No kidding. I didn't know the CIA trained foreign agents there."

"No kidding," Båo echoed. "You're ignorant and curious at the same time—a rare combination."

"I'll admit to both—ignorance and curiosity. I'm a journalist. I have a license to be curious."

"Not in this room you don't."

"What led you to study English?"

"Why should I answer you? What difference does it make to you?"

Pen said nothing, a technique he'd learned from Delaney back in the newsroom, who'd told him, "People's favorite subject is themselves. Don't fill the silences. Let them talk, even if they don't seem to want to. They will, eventually." So Pen stared at Bảo as the seconds ticked along.

Bảo finally said, "First, it was a way to touch the outside world. Then it was a way to get ahead with the Americans, who were running the country. Now it's because you need to know the language of your enemy."

"Wow. You think we're your enemy? We spent fifty thousand lives and treasure trying to defend you."

"And we spent two million lives while you dicked around in the South, never invading the North, never putting the squeeze on the Chinese or the Russians. You could be sitting in Hanoi right now."

"Come on."

"And you never cared about us. You cared only about yourselves, to stop the Communist spread because you thought it threatened you. And it does. But you have no courage. You have no will. You have left us to face the Communists alone. Doesn't that make you our enemy?"

Pen wished he had his notebook to write all this down, but his backpack had disappeared.

"That's sad, what you just said. And interesting. Mind if I quote you?"

Bảo straightened and glared. "You are trying to interview me? I ask the questions here."

"Sorry, but my job is to ask questions, too. Please sit down. Let's talk more."

"Bullshit," Bảo spat. "You've told me all I need."

"But you haven't told me all that *I* need. You said we were ignorant. Okay, so help me become less ignorant."

The interrogator, now the interrogated, hesitated on the brink of acquiescence. He lit another Marlboro. He blew the smoke, away from Pen this time. He seemed about to resume his seat but said nothing. So Pen went on.

"I don't think most Americans have any idea that people like you feel so much hatred toward us. I haven't found that anywhere else here. If anything, it's the opposite. Mostly people seem to have too much faith that America will come to the rescue. They think America pulls strings behind the scenes, that whatever happens is somehow controlled by the US. Our driver went over a mortar round in the middle of the road without even slowing down, because he said nothing bad could happen as long as an American was in the car."

Båo took a deep drag on his cigarette. "Look," he said. "Your driver is a superstitious man. There is too much superstition among us. But I can't be drawn into this discussion. I have a job to do, and it's a good one in the Special Branch. No, you may not quote me. It would be the end, and I have a wife and four kids."

"How about if I just say 'an official' without your name?"

"It would be known who the official was. You must think we're stupid."

"Speaking of knowing, how did you know I was going into VC territory?"

Båo smiled his stained smile. "Wouldn't you like to know."

"Yes, I would. I didn't tell anybody but my wife."

"Oh." That stopped him for a beat. "We have sources. We try to follow what's going on."

"You followed me?"

"No comment." And then they both laughed, as if near the end of a tense and friendly game.

"I actually enjoyed meeting you," said Pen.

"I enjoyed meeting you, too, because since I had you intercepted, I get a commendation."

"What now?"

"Now we give you a free ride back to Saigon. No handcuffs, though. You can ride with my sergeant in his Jeep. Luckily for him, he doesn't speak English."

Pen had never learned how to be openly angry, especially when the target was blurry and the cause undefined. His father had been too angry, his mother too timid. Pen had strained toward a middle ground, to "temper my temper," as he liked to put it, to neither suppress nor explode but reshape his fury until it came out in reasonable form.

So a lump of rage sat inside him all the way home. He had no idea where to hurl it. By the time he walked through the door and met Julie's startled questions about his early return, he had grabbed it and squeezed it down into a mass of resentment, humiliation, and dejection. A prized opportunity lost, a feather in his cap floating away. He had nobody to blame. He had no story to write but his own, and that would be little more than 400 or 500 words inside the paper. He couldn't even quote Bảo, though the man's bitterness would now season Pen's sense of the country. No Vietnamese he had met had been so direct; Bảo must have been trying to be like the Americans he'd worked with. How to tease this distaste into the open during interviews? Lanh would have some thoughts, and Pen would listen differently. *Thank you, Bảo.*

"You're the only one I told," he said to Julie. "They must have me under surveillance. Or they hear everything the VC says at Camp Davis. You didn't tell anybody, did you? No, of course you wouldn't. You think your tennis teacher guessed? But how could she? You didn't say anything. I am really pissed." This he said in such moderate tones that their maid, who spoke no English, did not even look up from her dusting.

Consumed by his own questions, Pen failed to see the nape of Julie's neck turn crimson. He did not notice that she looked away as she rewound the tapes of Hạnh's undue interest and her evasive answers. But when she didn't eat much of Nghi's beef and lemongrass, one of her favorites, he asked, "Jule, are you feeling all right?"

"Not quite. I think I'll go up to bed. So sorry about your trip, darling." She didn't sound very sincere until she added, "I'm glad you're home safe."

Lanh listened the next day to the story of Pen's abortive venture into VC territory, shook his head in sympathy, and thought: First, the VC must have known that he was compromised, because their people didn't meet him. They would have been arrested, too. Second, the Special Branch must have known in advance when he was going, and maybe where, because they don't have the manpower or the interest to follow every American correspondent all the time. So somebody told them, or told them enough so they could pick him up at the bus station or at Bình Long. Third, the agent Bảo was not just spouting off. He was sending a message, surely under instructions. The secret police don't get a chance very often for a sit-down conversation with a reporter.

"When he told you not to quote him, he probably hoped you would quote him."

"Huh?"

"He wouldn't know your rules. He'd expect you to agree and then break the agreement. They had this chance to shoot their hostility at American audiences."

"Who is 'they'?"

"The Special Branch. While the government is sitting in air conditioned offices being polite with the Americans, the Bảos are wading through the muck of rice fields in the real world. They know what's happening, like the consul up in Danang. They've got to be worried. They must want to sound an alarm."

"All right, fair enough," Pen said. "But how real is that resentment? Is it typical? Can we get ordinary Vietnamese to say those things?"

Lanh did not travel in a universe of categories, so he couldn't say whether distrusting America was "real" or "typical" or concealed by a survival instinct to say the expected. In the shifting uncertainties of this war, he explained to Pen, even your own belief was like dust in your hand. Who knew what people really thought, and maybe they didn't either. The Communists were the true nationalists or the invading threat, the Americans were the true friends or the bumbling traitors. Fear, infatuation, regard, hatred all came in different mixtures on different days in different places. Who knew how they added up? "When I worked in the Delta, most farmers just wanted to be left alone to grow their rice. You saw that when we went there."

"So how do we get into those fears and hatreds? How do we get people to talk honestly about them?"

"We can't, because most people can't afford to be honest with themselves. But we can ask them to talk about their own experiences—and listen closely."

Since the Vietcong press briefing on Saturday would bring Pen mortification, he would skip it. Colonel Giang and Direction South would disparage him. His only true defense would be defensiveness, protesting his innocence, asserting his scrupulous secrecy. "Are your quarters here bugged?" he might ask. But this in the presence of his press corps colleagues would generate the same snickering that he had joined when Jamison was intercepted. No, he'd wait a week or two before riding the bus out to Camp Davis.

CHAPTER 11

I n the first hint of dawn, Lanh lay between sleep and waking, that daily moment of clarity.

We are lucky to have the Americans. Next to them, Vietnamese are canny. Next to them, Vietnamese are resilient. They make us patriots. They make us treasure our land. We are never so smart and steadfast as when we are next to the Americans. We are the opposite of arrogance, of greed, of brutality in our hearts, but only when we look at ourselves against the mirror of the Americans. What will we be when the Americans are gone? The war is ending, so fear is rising.

He was halfway through his morning pho when Minh sidled up, took a seat at a little table close to him, and frowned.

"Did you ever try to help someone who repaid you by putting you at risk?"

Lanh concentrated on his pho.

"Lucky our people saw what was happening."

With unerring focus, Lanh picked out a slice of gray tripe with his chopsticks, dipped it in dark sauce, and deposited it dramatically in his mouth.

"Your boss was careless."

Lanh cradled his chopsticks across the bowl. "This used to be a place of calm," he told Minh. "I love coming here to eat my pho in the peaceful moments before the day becomes intense. It's like meditation, which as you know, requires a complete absence of distractions."

"Would you like to know who sold him out?"

"*He* might like to. I'm just an interpreter and photographer, that's all. Actually, I'm a buffalo boy."

Minh let out a mean laugh between his teeth. "Maybe you used to be a buffalo boy. Now you are something else. And I am inviting you to be something else again."

Lanh answered, "As the clouds move their shadows across the canals and fields and hamlets, every Vietnamese becomes something else. *Almost* every Vietnamese. The struggle is to be steadier than the shadow of a cloud."

"Exactly," said Minh. "If the steadiness is for a purpose. What is your purpose?"

Lanh wondered at Minh's marksmanship. It was the question he asked himself and could not answer. So instead he asked, "Who sold him out?"

"Oh, you want to know after all? The lowly interpreter and photographer wants the bigger picture?"

Lanh spat at the ground and got up to walk away.

"Don't leave in anger. I'm not trying to taunt you. Just get you to think. If you want to know, try what the Americans call a smoke operation."

"What's that?"

"An old intelligence trick to smoke out a spy—you must know the expression in English." Lanh shook his head. "If you have a suspect, you feed him false information and see if anything results. If it does, you've got him."

"It's not my business."

"Okay, Lanh, then here's something that might be your business. It's what journalists call a good story, because it's such a bad story." Minh stopped to watch Lanh closely.

"I'm listening."

"In Cộng Hoà hospital, a woman named Nguyễn Thị Hoà is shackled to a bed. She is a prisoner and was horribly tortured." Then, as the slanting sunlight began to warm and brighten the alley, Minh faded into the growing crowds.

Lanh suggested to Pen that they visit the hospital in the late evening, after most staff was gone. Dusk had died into darkness by the time they entered the barren courtyard in front of the pockmarked building, a remnant the French had left behind. Lanh spoke softly to a sleepy attendant at a tiny desk. She flipped open a ledger, whispered something back, and Lanh beckoned.

"Two thirty-two," he said.

They moved swiftly but not enough to spark suspicion, up broad stone stairs and into a hallway dimly lit, where relatives were gathering to leave after delivering their dinners. The room contained several beds, but when Lanh asked aloud, "Nguyễn Thị Hoà?" he had to look down. The young woman who answered was not on a bed. She lay handcuffed to an olive-drab stretcher on the floor, as if a casualty of combat.

Her legs were covered with a blanket. She looked spent. But she smiled in relief when she saw Pen. "Thank you," she said. "I thought nobody knew."

It was always Lanh's policy to say clearly that he and Pen were journalists for the *Tribune*, writing an article, never allowing people to assume otherwise. So if this precarious woman imagined that Pen was an authority with the power of rescue, Lanh never let her hope take flight. She nodded as if she already knew who Pen was and expected nothing more than publicity, which might at least make the Saigon regime take care. When she said, "Saigon regime," Lanh knew which side she was on.

Speaking as softly as possible, Lanh collected the scattered fragments of her story. She was twenty-six. In the market one morning, a woman she didn't know came to her, spoke nicely with her for a moment, then walked off. Minutes later, four men in plainclothes grabbed her, shoved her into a police van, and took her to an interrogation center in Khiên Cường.

Two male policemen led her to a bare room with a metal desk in the corner and several chairs. They told her to get undressed. She refused, so they pulled off her shirt and trousers. They took off her shoes. One beat her with a stick, stinging blows on her chest, back, and stomach. When she cried out, one covered her mouth with his hand. When she started to fall, he yanked her upright by her hair.

They attached electrodes to the ends of her two index fingers and led the wires from an old cranking telephone. They moved the electrodes, one to her nipple, one to her vulva. Pen did not know it at the time, but American soldiers who used this method had called it the Bell Telephone Hour.

The interrogators shouted, "Confess!" When she did not, they cranked. The shock and pain rippled like a burn through her entire body. When she continued to resist, they covered her mouth and nose with a handkerchief and poured bucket after bucket of soapy water onto it. When her belly swelled from the water, they kicked her in the stomach. With their hands under her rib cage, they picked her up and dropped her. They tied her legs apart and kicked between them, she told Lanh and Pen without a flicker of embarrassment. They put a live meter-long eel up her vagina. As she said this, she winced as if it were being done again. She bled for ten days straight. They kept taking her back and forth between the hospital and the interrogation room. Now she could barely walk.

Pen noticed something. Lanh's voice wavered as he translated, this time without his usual poetry. There was no metaphor in what he had Hoà saying, just a spare account, as if she had crossed some barrier and left terror behind. She seemed, through Lanh, to be looking at herself from the outside. Pen felt a pang of envy at her detachment. He glanced from his notebook to the handcuffs that shackled her right wrist to the bar of the stretcher and saw engraved in the shiny metal, "Made in USA."

When her mother entered the room, Hoà's steadiness ended. Tears flowed and her whole body shook as her mother bent to hold her as thoroughly as the stretcher and cuffs would allow. Pen stood aside. But he had more questions of the kind he didn't want to ask, to let her affirm or deny her affinity for "the other side."

Why did she think the police tortured her?

"Partly for fun," she said.

"What are your political views?"

"Before, nothing. Now?" Her mother shot her a glance of warning, and Hoà said, "Now, I can't say." Minh was in Lanh's head, editing, and Lanh was pushing him away.

Then, just inside the door to the room, a man with a worried face appeared. He looked too clean, Pen thought, in a sparkling white shirt and dark trousers, like Bảo of the Special Branch. "You are not allowed to question a prisoner," he said to Pen. "Please come with me," and as he led Pen into the dim hallway, Lanh deftly slipped away in the opposite direction.

"What did she tell you?" the man asked.

"Nothing interesting."

"Will you write something?"

"I don't know."

"Please don't. I'll get in trouble with my superiors." And after smiling the classic smile of discomfort, he let Pen go down the staircase and out the front door into the darkness. But where was Lanh? Pen crossed the courtyard to the street, looking up and down the block beneath the graceful tamarind trees and the clouds of insects vibrating around every outdoor light. No Lanh. Pen strolled slowly up the street one way, back the other way, back and forth, back and forth.

Suddenly Lanh materialized. "Let's go," he said in the clipped edge he'd used in the bunker after the VC attack.

They walked quickly to the office car and slipped in, closing the doors as soundlessly as possible. "Special Branch picked me up," said Lanh. "Checked my ID, wrote down some things."

"Shit. What will happen?"

"I don't know. Maybe nothing. I hope nothing. I told him she had nothing to say."

"That's what I said, too."

But Pen had never seen Lanh so tense. He seemed about to speak again, then hesitated, as if balanced at the edge of candor.

"Did he warn you, threaten you?" Pen asked.

Lanh did not reply. Silence, that refuge of deception, Pen thought. "Come on, Lanh, I need to know if you're in danger."

Lanh fixed his eyes tightly on the road. "He told me that I had an obligation as a patriotic citizen to translate appropriately."

"What does that mean?"

"Everybody is trying to get me to reshape words."

"Who's everybody?"

"Don't worry."

"I'll try not to. But do you worry?"

"I don't worry. I resist."

"You'll let me know, won't you, if somebody pressures you to distort translations?" He wanted to ask about the metaphors but didn't want to know.

Now Lanh took his eyes off the road and turned squarely toward Pen. "It doesn't matter, because I say exactly what the people say, no more, no less, no tilt this way or that. You are hearing what I am hearing."

"And they're so poetic!" Pen said. Lanh gave his sideways look, the dark lights of the Saigon night playing on his grin.

Nguyễn Thị Hoà made a story all by herself, Pen knew, yet was also part of a larger story. Maybe that would be the better approach. The brush with the secret police troubled him, not for himself but for Lanh. And he had long since passed through the period of first impressions that Lanh had told him were the most accurate. Every vivid tale was a symptom, only a symptom.

"Maybe I should wrap this young woman into the inevitable story of war," Pen said. "It's the story of

David K. Shipler

disillusionment. What begins as a noble purpose decays. If you get close enough, you can smell it."

"What do you mean?"

"I think I should hold this story," Pen said.

"Why? Not on my account," said Lanh.

"Partly but not entirely. She has to be one of many, don't you think? Wouldn't it be more important to do a whole long piece, maybe a series, on political prisoners? Show Americans what our troops have won here?"

Lanh took his eyes off the road and looked at Pen carefully. "Sure, but she also needs the publicity to save her."

"I wonder about that," Pen said. "The Special Branch knows we were there. She's in the spotlight. You got the mother's name and address, right?" Lanh nodded. "So we can keep track of Hoà through her. If anything worse happens, we can write it right away. What do you think?"

Lanh was not accustomed to being asked his advice on how a story should be written. He nearly answered, "That's above my pay grade," the sardonic evasion taught by Americans, adopted by Vietnamese officials who deserved a sneer. He kept quiet, though, rubbed raw by his ill-fitting country.

When they pulled up on Tự Do Street outside the office so Lanh could jump on his motorbike and head for home, Pen said, "I'll need to find someone else to interpret on this story, Lanh. A foreigner, probably. Somebody who won't be in jeopardy."

Lanh opened his mouth to protest. From time to time, he had often thought, everyone has to drink from a well of sadness down inside, as if to cool whatever joy dwells above. He wanted to insist falsely that he would be safe if he stayed

159

steadfast to his love of Vietnam. He wanted, needed, to know the darkest parts of it, to turn sorrow into the open. Yet from somewhere in his childhood there came to him the Buddha's teaching that sorrow is the product of craving, and craving is for things that are impermanent, as all things are, even life.

So he peered through the open car window at Pen's caring, heaved his shoulders in a sigh of resignation, and said, "I don't like it, but thank you. And remember when you meet people who have been arrested briefly and released, or never arrested but allowed to oppose the government gently, political dissidents here are just ornaments. They are shiny things to tease you Americans into thinking that we are free."

As Lanh climbed onto his scooter and buzzed into the night, Pen knew that he was doing the right thing. He did not know that protecting Lanh today meant endangering him tomorrow.

Julie considered confronting Hạnh. She wanted to accuse her. Hạnh would deny it. Her innocence either real or false, Julie would not be able to tell. So they sat over their lemonades talking about little of importance. Hạnh asked nothing about Pen's work, which only fed Julie's misgivings. Yet she did ask about her art, what she was drawing and painting, whether she would bring work to show Dương.

She had cracked Julie open and invited in more of her than most friends, and none in Saigon. Today, though, Julie's answers were brisk and efficient. The two did not linger at the table, and Julie felt an odd taste when they said goodbye. *I wonder how I can nail it down. Why do I need to know? To take the measure of the friendship? Or to thank her for protecting my husband?* The subversive thought made her practically laugh aloud as she walked from Cercle Sportif toward the street.

Coming the other way, Sally Falmouth looked perky in her tennis outfit. They stopped together for one of their customary chats, which Julie knew would go about as deep as polish on a fingernail. Hi. Hi, how are things? What's going on? Adjusting to Saigon? What are you up to? Erik's? Oh, yes, I've heard great things about him. How's life in the embassy these days? If I could tell you I would, and it wouldn't be pretty, but you know I can't. I was just making conversation. I know, but conversation around here can get people in trouble. That's right, said Julie, and an idea struck her.

"Look, this is a question you probably won't want to answer, but—"

"Then better not ask it."

"The worst that can happen is that you'll say you can't say. You know my father was an ambassador. He sometimes talked, maybe out of turn, about tradecraft."

Sally stiffened. "You're already in a no-go zone."

"Wait. Hear me out. Somebody ratted on my husband when he tried to go into VC territory."

"I know. I heard they stopped him."

"I want to know who. Or, more precisely, I want to rule out someone." Sally said nothing. "Is there a way? Do you have a technique?"

Sally looked down for an escape hatch.

"Did you ever hear your father mention a smoke operation?"

The term took her back to the dinner table one evening, into conversation she wasn't supposed to be old enough to grasp. Her agitated father was musing about a spy in the embassy. Maybe we'll run a smoke operation, he told her mother—give him something phony, smoke him out.

"No," Julie told Sally. "Never heard the term." That was Pen's method. Pretend you know less than you do to get more than you knew.

"That's all I can say. Sorry." And Sally was off with her racquet under her arm, not as jauntily as before.

In the cyclo for the short ride to Erik's house, Julie drifted into wondering. *How could I pull a caper like that alone?*

She found an unexpected tableau in the courtyard. Pen and Erik stood together talking earnestly, immobile over the whirling kids around them.

"I would help you if I could," Erik was saying, "but it might jeopardize my visa, and I can't afford that, as I'm sure you understand."

"What's this about?" Julie asked.

"After the woman in the hospital last night, I've decided I want to do a series on political prisoners, and I can't use Lanh—or any Vietnamese who would be vulnerable. I need a fluent foreigner."

Julie worked hard to suppress her sneaky thought: They could ask Hạnh, Vietnamese or no, to see if she would sensibly decline or suspiciously jump at the chance. What better opportunity for a snitch! Right on an inside track with a reporter contacting political dissidents! If she's a spy, she'd be delighted to sign on. If she's scared, then she must be an ordinary citizen, levelheaded with anxiety.

162

"I know a French woman who works with the Quakers here as a medical assistant," said Erik. "She speaks English and good Vietnamese, and might be willing."

"Great. How do I reach her?"

"Let me," Erik said. "I'll sound her out and let you know."

Julie's secluded scheming kept scratching at her, though, like a game she itched to play. She had needs. The need for purpose. The need for trusting friendship. The need to test that friendship. The need to suffocate doubts. Seething Saigon. How could such a busy city be so lonely?

"Look," she said to Pen that night. "I want to find out whether Hạnh snitched on you. Maybe from what I said she deduced that you were going into VC territory. Although I never told her that, didn't even hint at it."

"So why do you suspect her?"

"She's just too interested in your work, asking questions all the time. I want to test her."

"How?"

"Ask if she'll be your interpreter for the prisoner story."

"Oh, terrific. If she's a government informer, she'll tell them right off and they'll put a tail on me. No thanks. It's not worth it. I've already lost one good story. I don't want to lose another."

Julie clenched her lips. "It's worth it to me to know whether my friend is really a friend. I like her, Pen. I don't want this shadow. If she accepts the offer, we'll know she's a spy eager to report on the people you interview, and that will be the end of her as far as I'm concerned. If she's afraid to say yes, we'll know she's a normal person who wants to stay out of trouble. And if she does say yes, you can turn her down and say you've found someone else. It's important to me to know. Please." *I could go ahead anyway, without his permission.*

"No, Jule, sorry. It could put people at risk."

She felt like taking the darks and the lights of secrecy and trust and smearing them together into a shade of gray that would feel just right.

Two evenings later, as they sat reading after dinner, a slender silhouette appeared outside a large front window. "*Bonsoir*," a voice called softly. "*Bonsoir*."

Julie opened the door to find a woman in her twenties or early thirties, with straight black hair to her shoulders, skin the alluring color of coffee with a dash of cream, and a lively look of expectation. "I am Michelle Allard," she said, sticking out her hand. "Erik sent me."

Mindful of the pitfalls of biased translation, Pen (and especially Julie) subjected Michelle to challenging skepticism and questions perhaps too personal about politics, motivations, ideals, and even family. She replied with equanimity, even volunteering that they probably wondered why she was "Black, as you say in America." They did not say they wondered, although they did, and she answered anyway, in a lilting soliloquy.

"My mother is from Côte d'Ivoire. My father was the son of a French planter there. My grandfather supported the Vichy government during World War II, by the way. Not that I'm proud of it. My mother's father and mother worked on the plantation, and my parents met there when they were just teenagers. My father rejected his father's life and beliefs. It's like a romantic fairy tale of love conquering politics and class. When the war ended, they moved to France, and I was born in a little town called Tournus, in Burgundy. Great wine country."

"Quite a story," said Pen. "Does it influence your thoughts about the war here?"

"Absolutely. I am the product of colonialism and its downfall. I am a mixture of privilege and poverty. I know what France did there—and here, too—and I see America doing the same, almost the same. The war is essentially an anti-colonial war. The Vietnamese are fighting to get out from under the foreign boot."

Pen looked enchanted. Julie scowled. "You don't sound very objective," she said.

"I'm not."

"Then how can you interpret objectively?" asked Pen.

Michelle tossed her hair and gave him an open look of pride eloquent enough to suffice for an answer. "I can translate the words that are spoken, no matter what is said, whether they fit or don't fit what I might believe. I value honest journalism, and from what I've heard and read, you are honest."

Julie rolled her eyes as if to say, complimenting my husband on his reporting is the way to his heart. And it was. Pen nodded gladly.

Michelle went on to explain that she wasn't pressing him for the job. She had enough to do at the clinic and would be able to work only evenings. But she had heard patients' stories about torture, and so might make a contribution by helping Pen. If, on the other hand, those stories turned out to be wrong or exaggerated, she was willing to help him determine that, too. "Let the chips fall where they may. Isn't that an American expression from Las Vegas?"

"You might lose your visa," Julie warned.

"They haven't been kicking out foreigners, and there are lots of us with sympathy for the antiwar movement."

"But you can't be sure." Julie was watching Pen and pressing the point. "You could even be arrested."

Michelle smirked. "Like Pen was arrested for—what?—five hours? I'm not worried. Anyway, I'm scheduled to leave in three months, back to Paris. So an early departure wouldn't be a tragedy."

Pen hired her on the spot without consulting in private with Julie, who gave Michelle a cold goodbye and said nothing to Pen.

In the weeks that followed, Pen worked normally by day with Lanh and abnormally by night with Michelle. She knew people who knew people.

The snowballing effect of one source leading to others, and the others opening doors to more, carried him into a semi-underground universe of malcontents, union leaders, student activists, Buddhist monks, writers who couldn't be published, newspaper editors who looked over their shoulders, political oppositionists excluded from politics, and on and on until Pen was laboring under such piles of notes that he wondered how he would ever wrestle them into a coherent whole.

From time to time, after an evening interview, he would drive Michelle home and go up to her place for a beer and debriefing, organizing in his mind what he had heard and what they were accumulating. She was sharp and perceptive, and devoted to unfailing accuracy, discounting some stories as inconsistent and embracing others as credible. He noticed her long, graceful fingers as she gestured to punctuate her words.

He made no secret in the office of his project. Tân was irreverent enough to approve, he figured. And Lanh was morose about missing out on it. But that agent Bảo had tipped Pen off—"I am familiar with what you write. We read it before it is in your newspaper!" So Pen had to keep it from the government. He didn't want to be tailed, didn't want to expose the former prisoners unless they were willing to take the risk—their calculation, not his. He would pigeon out his communications with Boston. He typed a message in cablese:

```
murphy expennyman saigon: fyi
onworking long takeout political
prisoners so will submerge
periodically in coming weeks.
please do not rpt not message
me about this in saigon. utmost
discretion needed. cheers.
```

Mandell was going off to Bangkok for R&R, so Pen drove up to the AP office. He pulled Mandell aside and handed him the message to be Telexed from there. Mandell, that veteran of journalistic propriety, said, "Roger," and didn't read it.

Pen might have put away his curiosity about the informer who got him arrested, but Julie had not. She would go ahead with her little caper in the clandestine arts, and if Hạnh said sure, she'd love to be Pen's interpreter on a story about political prisoners, she would know. And she could just come back to her later and say, well, too late, Pen already found someone. And then she would lose her only friend in Saigon.

The day was steamy during tennis, and sweat had soaked her headband by the time they sat down with their lemonades. She put the frosty glass to her cheek and forehead, took a sip, leaned forward a little toward Hạnh, and embarked on her quest as if she were trying that expert slope at Stowe again, terrifying and thrilling and foolhardy. She had dislocated her shoulder in a rough swirl of crystal snow.

"Hạnh," she began and heard a tremble in her voice. "Pen needs an interpreter. It's for a sensitive story, so Lanh can't do it. Your English is good. Would you be willing?"

Hạnh looked through her into her thoughts, making her want to squirm away. She studied Hạnh in return, imagining little gears spinning inside her brain, figuring. They both took swallows of their lemonade. Hạnh said nothing.

"So, what do you think?" Julie asked.

Now Hạnh looked away toward the court they had played on, already busy with another pair. "Why me? What's the story?"

"You because I know you. The story—this is confidential, now—is about prisoners who have been tortured."

Hạnh jerked away as if she herself had been jolted through electrodes. She tipped her chair back, as if to gain distance from Julie, or perspective. She stared at Julie acutely.

"Look," Julie said. "If you don't want to, I understand. If you think it would be unsafe for you, that's okay. That's understandable. It could be dangerous."

Another few seconds of pause. Another glance toward the courts. Then a strange smile. "Not *could*," Hạnh said.

"Would. Any Vietnamese who consorts with those people, not to mention helps a journalist do it, would get to experience what they have gone through."

If Hạnh was puzzled by Julie's bright look of relief, she gave no sign. Julie relaxed in her chair and exonerated Hạnh with a wave of her hand through the humid air as if dismissing a pesky insect, no longer a bother. "Fine. No problem. Understood."

Pen and Michelle spent long, dark evenings in tiny flats, out-of-the-way restaurants, Buddhist temples, and lonely parks, Pen scribbling frantically in notebooks now stacked on his desk at home. Although they always looked behind them as they traveled to their meetings, they noticed no tail until one night when they left his car outside a quarter of narrow alleys leading to the flat of a recently released lawyer.

A woman turned a corner after they did. When they stopped as a precaution, she lingered in place, some fifty meters back. When they walked again, she waited a few beats, then came along as well. "We're being followed," Pen whispered. Michelle nodded. They broke off and found a little restaurant still open, went in, and shared a plate of stale *chả giò* and a bottle of lukewarm beer.

The woman was gone when they emerged. The street was empty. They walked in a circuitous route, and if they picked up another tail, they didn't notice. A young man buzzed by on a motorbike. A stooping man walked the other way. They took a chance and found the ex-prisoner's building, climbed narrow stairs, and talked with him for an hour or more while his wife served tea. Michelle insisted on telling him what had happened, but he answered casually with a Russian proverb he'd heard from a cellmate who'd been trained in a camp near Moscow: "If you're already wet, rain isn't frightening."

And so it usually went when they were followed: no great anxiety from most of these brave folks. But not always. Michelle began getting messages from within her dissident network that the wrong people knew of Pen's project. A few former prisoners changed their minds and said no to interviews; some decided against letting their names be published, diluting the credibility of the reporting. Several passed word that they'd been visited by cleanly dressed men and clearly warned. "Damn! What the hell's going on?" Pen exclaimed. "I thought we were being so careful."

"Somebody—what's the word? Starts with *s*."

"Snitched," he said. "No, I can't think who. Maybe I've been under surveillance since the VC trip. Damn. This series will be weaker without some of these people."

Yet fear is not a fault, Pen observed. Nor is its opposite a measure of virtue. "Nobody should be blamed for being afraid," he said with more conviction than he felt. He and Michelle wondered together as they rode to her place one evening after interviews how much courage they could manage if facing the same dangers. They decided together what they would like to believe about themselves, and admitted together that they had no idea what they would actually be willing to do. No idea what they were really made of.

"How principled are you?" she once asked him.

"Less than you, I imagine."

"I don't know. Your principle is getting the truth out. Mine is, well, maybe revolution."

"But would you be willing to be tortured for your revolution?"

"It's not yes or no, black or white," she said. "Listen to these people we've been meeting. They are not reckless. They step carefully, testing their footing before putting their weight down, trying to gauge the degree of risk without compromising too much. It's fascinating, and it takes brains."

"And they don't break, at least that's what they tell us."

"They don't break. They don't give the Special Branch names of others. They don't confess falsely to being Communists."

"But some do. We just haven't met them. I've heard the military courts are full of people from the countryside who've confessed under torture."

She pushed her hair away from her brow with her long fingers. "So would you confess to something you didn't do?"

"Would you?" he asked.

"I'd like to say no."

"Of course I'd like to say no, too," he repeated with an echo of doubt.

"But what about your family?" Michelle pressed on. "Your friends? Remember Nhâm, who was forced to watch the torture of three friends."

"Nhâm? Oh, yeah, the student, the emaciated guy who looked like he hadn't eaten in months. Yeah, he wouldn't say he was a Communist. He was brave enough to withstand the torture—of his friends!"

"You're a cynic deep down!" she laughed.

"How about something less hypothetical? What about a more likely test, like being in the middle of the fighting somewhere, maybe here in Saigon? Then what? I ask myself this all the time," he said, "and I just don't know. Should I carry a gun? I don't. I won't. I'm not a combatant. Would I freeze? Would I get excited? Would I play the hero and try to rescue somebody, or would I cower? Or run away? It kind of happened up near the central coast, and I did okay, I guess. But it was fighting lite, combat with a small *c*. All we had to do was crouch in a bunker—cower, you could say. I was shaking afterwards."

Michelle was looking at him differently, the way Julie used to. "I read somewhere that cowardice is actually NOT being able to express fear," she said warmly.

Roxbury. Glass shatters in crystal melodies, fires lick the dingy blocks and flash on the faces of looters and cops with shiny helmets. A burly officer raises his shotgun and fires down a dark street at no one, at everyone. Screams pitched high descend into wails. Or are they sirens? The whine of ricochets close by to the right, and then a cry from Barrett, who is down, holding his leg, his camera lying broken on the pavement. He is bleeding hard, his gaze up at Pen, pleading.

"I was afraid in Roxbury," Pen confessed to Michelle. "Since I know it, I guess that makes me brave."

"Roxbury?"

"Long story. Humiliating story." He almost went on, stopped himself, then pushed ahead, surprised at the quaver in his voice. Why did he need to tell her? Trust is an odd commodity, he thought, visible in the eyes, audible in the gentle lilt of acceptance. She had both. She listened closely to his primer on race in America or, more precisely, the 1967 riots in Boston's Black neighborhood of Roxbury. A peaceful demonstration by mothers against inadequate welfare services had failed for three days to draw the welfare director to come for a conversation. So they chained the doors of the welfare office closed, locked the workers and several cops inside, and finally provoked an appearance by the director—who refused to talk with them. Standing in the street among the demonstrators, Pen and a veteran photographer for the paper, Charlie Barrett, a pro who kept his cool, were suddenly surrounded by a melee of angry cops wielding long, black billy clubs and shouting "Kill 'em!"

"What?" said Michelle.

"Yes, 'kill 'em.'" Crowds flocked to the scene and fought back into the night along Blue Hill Avenue. Pen found a pay phone and dictated his story breathlessly to a rewrite man back in the office, proud that he could compose coherently from just his scribbled notes. Barrett handed rolls of film to a copy boy who had been dispatched to take them back to the newsroom. Running youths smashed windows and threw every brick and bottle they could find at the cops. They charged the cops again and again. The cops seemed scared, which made Pen scared, so he and Barrett stayed with the demonstrators, afraid of getting nailed by a brick or a bottle. But finally the cops—there were probably a thousand of them by then—pulled out shotguns and started firing, first into the air but then leveling their barrels down the street. Pen remembered one big cop in particular, furiously red-faced, aiming in their direction. He could still see the face, he told Michelle. Pen ducked, tried to find shelter. But Barrett stood erect as if invincible, shooting pictures until he fell in a scream of pain. His leg was hit. Pen panicked, yelled that he was going to get help, and raced away to a pay phone to call, and to save himself.

Michelle said nothing, but her soft stare seemed more compassionate than judgmental. Something in her look allowed Pen to say, "It might be that courage isn't something you have, it's something that comes upon you, that suddenly finds you when you're in a situation that demands it. Or it passes you by. Yes, it can pass you by. Maybe it's not your achievement, or your fault."

On days without compelling news, Pen stayed home and typed up notes and labeled them by penciling a letter in the margin beside each passage, each letter standing for a particular subject. He hoped for some semblance of organization when he got around to writing.

He had taken pictures of the prisoners who would allow it, and while he dared not have the film developed in country, he reconstructed their faces in his memory with cues from his notebooks, the way Julie was doing portraits. He tried to see them clearly, he tried to know them as he assembled their stories into a mosaic.

Professional torturers, he learned, are good at leaving no scars—except sometimes in the eyes. Occasionally Pen could see a deadness. Or, in some, a remaining glint of terror beneath the shield of a steady gaze and strained control. The height of fear, some said, came not in beatings or shocks or near drowning but in long anticipation, especially at night when the bell rang on the block and the guard's step fell and the key rattled in the lock.

Under a bare bulb in his room, stripped of books and papers by the police, a philosophy teacher who ran and lost for the National Assembly took a pen and paper and sketched the arrangement of cells in the Saigon police headquarters. He and others told Pen of a sign on desks and walls: "If he is not guilty, beat him until he renounces. If he does not renounce, beat him until he dies."

It was here, the teacher said, tapping his pen on the diagram, that he saw the head of the bank workers union succumb, and not by hanging himself, as officially reported. When the man was dragged dead from his cell, his arm had swollen and blackened like putrid meat. The flesh along his ribs had been pounded raw.

The philosophy teacher had run on the platform, "Fight the Americans and Save the Country." It was a North Vietnamese slogan, although he insisted he was not a Communist. Every day of his campaign, he was arrested in the morning, held for several hours, and let go—then after the election, imprisoned for two years. For his idealistic belief in the democracy that was being championed and subverted by America, he subjected his family to cascading arrests—his teenage son for protesting his father's imprisonment, his daughter for possessing tapes of antiwar music.

Through Michelle, the tales were told efficiently, like the rapid pop of small arms fire that spoke without elaboration. And without the eloquence of poetry that sang in Lanh's translations. Not because of the interpreter, Pen assured himself, but because of the trauma, whose language had to be stripped down in the telling. He could ask Michelle what she thought. He could ask Lanh, even confront him. No, he could ride the graceful flow of Lanh's fluent artistry, which made the stories in the paper so musical. He was being praised.

At home in his little office, made frigid with air conditioning, Pen punched the typewriter keys hard and strung the accounts together relentlessly, as if on a rescue mission. Yet when he told Julie what he was hearing, she asked whether he needed to be so graphic. "That Michelle, she's okay telling all these horrors? Women especially will find the sexual torture hard to read."

Pen's notebook was insistent nonetheless. He feared that whatever tales he didn't write would stay with him, plaguing him like secrets:

The student beaten on the soles of his feet, the cold interrogators who casually attached wires from his nipples and genitals to a hand-cranked telephone. Who poured soapy water into a cloth held tightly over his nose and mouth. Who jabbed pins under his fingernails and bent them back and forth by running a ruler across them. His fingers were still swollen.

The union leader, one of a score rounded up after clerical workers staged an illegal strike for higher pay, who was blindfolded during interrogation, wrists handcuffed behind him, soapy water forced into his mouth and nose until he couldn't breathe. "Who gave the order for this strike?" the interrogator asked again and again. The leader claimed he never told.

Nhâm the student activist, tied to a chair sometimes, blindfolded sometimes, beaten every day, and shocked by a cranked phone. When he didn't confess falsely to being a Communist, the police brought his friends in one at a time and made him watch. One friend, a young woman, they tied to a chair by the ankles, bound her stomach with a rope, and wrapped a filthy cloth tightly around her eyes. A man twice her size slapped a long rubber truncheon with a deathly thud against one kneecap after another. Two policemen thrust their hands under her ribs and pulled them out. They used the soap-and-water method.

Nhâm, feverish with rage, confessed to nothing.

So the interrogators proceeded with more intimate methods. She never pleaded with him to confess. She just yelled a question at her torturers: How could they be such savages?

Michelle, though frazzled with fury, translated smoothly as the student described the interrogators, some in uniform, some bare-chested, as "very professional."

"Are you sure of that word?" Pen asked.

"Yes," said Michelle, and went on. "He said they did their jobs very coolly, without hatred, drinking Coke and smoking and speaking among themselves in tones so soft they seemed only to be performing a routine task, neither elated nor repelled."

"Unbelievable," said Pen, and held his head in his left hand as he wrote with his right.

A lawyer they met had been jailed because his son, now fourteen, had joined the Vietcong at the age of twelve. Pen thought to mention it to Lanh. "Do you know the line in the Bible about how the sins of the fathers shouldn't be visited upon the sons, or the other way around?" Pen asked.

Lanh gave one of his wise smiles and said, "I know about it very well."

Pen gave Lanh *Pink Hearts*, a book of short stories secretly published by a circle of antiwar student writers who were arrested for the offense. In one tale, a peasant who battled with the Viet Minh against the French is tormented by the fear that his two sons, one fighting on each side in this war, will kill each other. He becomes an opponent of both sides, floating untethered to any allegiance except a transcendent patriotism. Like the man they'd met in the Delta.

"Yes, I know this book," Lanh said. "It is a yearning. These students understand more than their elders."

Pen wrote in bursts, silently composing each sentence in his mind, then typing quickly so it wouldn't disappear, then pausing in search of just the right word, typing, and pulling the carriage back to obliterate a phrase with *x*'s, retyping to catch the mood and the rhythm of terrible detail.

Then he had to interlace the stories with the view from 30,000 feet, as he thought of it: the broad landscape. Enough dissenters were tolerated to make a complicated set of contradictions, he believed—"ornaments," as Lanh had said. The press was varied and not entirely unfree, though enough editors had been arrested and enough issues confiscated to induce a culture of wary self-censorship. Writers could write irreverently, to a point. Unions could organize as long as they resisted infiltration by Communists. Monks could speak of peace individually but not assemble into a movement that might gain a critical mass. And all these permissions and limits were fluid and unpredictable. Police dossiers were the fruits of rumor, coincidence, and the accidents of distant family relationships.

As a result, Pen concluded, arrests were no deterrent. They were as random and arbitrary as storms, nothing people could avoid by tailoring their behavior. So they were pointless. They served no purpose, and citizens were treating the risk of imprisonment as one more inevitable feature of a world at war.

Michelle did not like these conclusions. In their late-night debriefings in her tiny flat, she fought against them. The arrests were a pattern of oppression, a method of colonialism, carefully constructed to crush all possible movement toward Liberation. She pronounced Liberation with a capital *L*. The disagreement left them slightly disappointed in each other.

The reporting could have been stronger. Those who'd backed out left unsourced tales and pockets of generalizations in the series of long pieces. No Pulitzer for this, Pen figured. Still, Americans would see something of what they'd been supporting, he told himself. When he had finished writing, he and Julie were due for R&R in Singapore, then on to a beach in Malaysia. So he tucked the precious typescript and his rolls of film in a small backpack that he would never allow to be separated from his body, boarded the Air Vietnam plane at Tansonnhut, looked out the window as they climbed to see if he could spot Camp Davis and all the VC running around in their olive green pith helmets, and settled back to sleep more deeply than he had in quite a while.

In Singapore, at the Reuters office, he handed the pages to a clerk for transmission to Boston. The next morning, he found an envelope that had been slipped under the door of his hotel room. Inside was a message:

propennyman exmurphy prisoners received.

CHAPTER 12

Instead of going to school, Lanh takes a different turn a few blocks from his house, hops on a rickety bus with some change that he's saved up, and heads out from Hanoi among convoys of ungainly French military trucks until tight rows of houses give way to fields and forests. Nearly everything motorized thins to bicycles and wood-wheeled carts pulled by languid buffalos.

He's heading toward his grandparents' village, Hà Đông. But he doesn't get off where he and his father normally do. He holds his breath and stays in the seat whose dry, cracked leather chafes his bare thighs. The village ends. The unfamiliar road becomes unpaved and bumpy, the signs of commerce fade. Boys with long bamboo poles fish in scattered ponds, women in conical hats bend in the paddies. Rice! He'd heard the sorrowful anger in his grandfather's voice telling his parents that the foreigners had made him grow cotton and jute, nothing to eat. Soldiers would come steal what food they could conserve. The only difference through years of war was the soldiers' language: Japanese, then French.

But here, through the bus window, Lanh sees waves of green shoots of rice, like a soothing sea. So, this is what liberated land looks like. The bus stops at a neglected cluster of thatched huts. The end of the line, the driver shouts. Lanh is one of three passengers left, and as he steps down getting a quizzical glance from the man at the wheel, he feels the same way as when he walks into his classroom for a test on lessons he hasn't learned. He will have this moment as a nagging dream for decades hence.

He has been firmly instructed not to write down the directions, so he has committed them to memory and sets out with his sack of food and clothes, through a struggling hamlet and then beyond, through another tiny settlement whose name his grandparents would not know, where the country road dwindles to a path.

The sun is high and hot, so Lanh sits and leans against the rough trunk of a *cây vải* beneath a clump of bright red lychees, sheltered by a lush umbrella of green spilling down around him. He looks up into the comforting shade at the leaves, long and shiny with veins like maps his teacher has shown of the Red River and its tributaries. He pulls from his sack a few rolled balls of rice and brown strips of dried fish, and a canvas-covered canteen that he stole last summer from a dead French soldier. He should sleep now and travel farther much later, in the soft security of darkness, but his heart is too keyed up. So he finishes eating and moves on.

It is a long way to the camp, along broken earthen dikes and then through the muck of flooded fields onto a winding trail into stands of teak and milk fruit, banyan and cannonball trees. Dusk comes subtly through the forest canopy, announced with slants of waning light and new calls of life to herald the night. Lanh stops again to sit and eat his meager fare, slaps away a platoon of biting ants, and rises again.

A moon has appeared, luckily. Its pale glow descends in spires just enough to turn the path slightly lighter than the dark green that crowds in along each side, reaching for his ankles. The moon seems high by the time he smells wood smoke and hears murmuring ahead. He presses on until he sees the orange of a fire through the vines and ferns, quickens his pace, and calls out the word he has been given: "*Quốc! Quốc!*" [Patriot!]

Dark figures turn their faces toward him. Several rise with their rifles. Lanh steps into a small clearing, calls, "*Quốc!*" again, and the men reply with the same word in a chorus. Two come to embrace him and lead him toward the others. Around the fire stand lean-tos of tattered canvas and burlap propped up in front by gnarled sticks, anchored in back by stones. He can see the ground inside each one covered with cut fronds strewn like careless carpets. Nearby he can hear the chortle of a stream.

They have cooked a wild boar, flavoring the jungle with a rich incense of roasting. They are laying slices into bowls of rice and nuoc mam and something green and diced small. A bowl is passed to Lanh, he is handed a pair of chopsticks, and he sits cross-legged with the rest and eats.

Nobody questions him, which feels odd, as if his coming were as natural and expected as dawn. Instead, their conversation continues among themselves about things he cannot quite follow: military terms, letters and numbers, places and dates, plans that sound coded and obscure. Family, too. Daughters, wives, brothers, mothers ... all left behind somewhere in some place of nostalgia. Lanh feels as if he has entered a secret circle of purpose.

One man finally asks his name. He gives it. They ask where he lives. He tells them. There is a whistle of admiration. All that way? When did you leave? This morning? They hail him. "Brave, strong boy!"

"I want to join you," he says, and they react as if he has told them nothing outside their own field of vision, as if he has shared his discovery that the jungle is dark. They simply nod and say nothing more.

"Tonight, you will sleep," says one man who is taller than the rest and seems older in his eyes. Some are barely more than boys, like Lanh. "And tomorrow, Brother Quốc will come to camp, and you will meet him."

"Who is Brother Quốc?"

All the men together give a laugh as sudden as the burst of green branches in a papaya tree. He is supposed to know of Brother Quốc.

"You will see," says the older man.

Dawn comes with stealth. It holds its breath while the cacophony of night noises dies first, replaced by bird calls that Lanh has never heard. From the lean-to that he shares with the older man and two others, he can see in the half-light two shadows with rifles shouldered across their backs move silently out of camp. Others have lit the fire whose white smoke rises straight like a pure offering in the windless twilight.

A pot is on, boiling. A man is throwing in handfuls of greens, unknown parts of the boar, rice noodles. Bowls are filled and passed around. A kind of pho, Lanh thinks, but thinner than he knows from home. A couple of men talk to him. Who is his father? What does he do? Does he have family who are peasants? Lanh is not quite sure about the word *peasants*.

"My grandparents grow rice," he explains. "They used to grow rice until the foreigners made them grow things you can't eat."

"Where?"

"Hà Đông."

As shafts of sunlight catch wisps of smoke from the dying fire, more men materialize at the edge of the camp as if they have been imagined. They come without announcement, without a sound, Lanh notices. Everyone looks at an older man, gray-haired, gaunt with a wisp of beard on his chin, not muscular like the others. He has a kind, wise face, Lanh thinks, creased and weathered. One after another, the men who have been in camp stand and say, "Brother Quốc." Two teeth are missing near the front of the smile he gives to them, and then to Lanh.

"Brother Lanh," he says. "Welcome. You came a long way to find us."

They sit cross-legged around the embers. Strong tea is poured into dented tin cups. Nothing is said until Brother Quốc begins.

"We will talk about operations in a moment," he tells the fighters. "But first we must talk to Lanh. And everybody must listen."

Lanh is sure that everybody is listening—to his wild heart thumping.

"Why did you come?"

"To join the Viet Minh," Lanh says.

"And why do you want to join with us?"

"To fight for freedom."

"Do your parents know you're here?"

"They do now. I left them a note at home."

"How old are you?

"Twelve."

The men lean forward, intent on this dialogue as if it were a lesson from a master to a pupil. Perhaps they know what is coming.

Brother Quốc gazes out and up into the jungle green as if taking inspiration from the vibration of color at a special part of the spectrum. So Lanh turns his eyes to the jungle too, and feels the lush harmony.

Brother Quốc puts his arm around Lanh's shoulders the way a man holds a man, but with a longing look that the boy will forever remember as love.

"Do you want to help your country?" Quốc asks.

"Yes!" Lanh practically shouts.

"Then," says Brother Quốc, "go back and finish school."

CHAPTER 13

“ I am sorry, Mr. Pen. Your lease, in July no more.”
The war is ending, so fear is rising.

February 1975. Madame Bian, the villa's business-like owner, who spoke better French than English, carried a large woven bag when she met him at the branch of the First National City Bank on the first of every month. Pen placed a withdrawal slip on the teller's counter, and in return, the teller began to pile up 500-piaster notes in bundles tied tightly with frayed white string. Counting the cash meant counting the bundles only, trusting that the bank had included the correct number of bills, each now worth a pittance.

Usually, satisfied that the rent had been paid, Madame Bian would look around nervously, then scoop the bundles into her bag, walk to the door to survey the street before exiting, and disappear down the block and into her black Peugeot.

That was the normal routine. This time, though, she gave Pen the bad news. When the lease was up, it would not be renewed. Why, she would not say directly, no matter how strongly Pen objected and pressured. She fished for the right words that would reveal the minimum needed to be understood.

"Situation," she finally said. "Situation bad."

Pen tried to look puzzled, shrugged and shook his head in a pretense of ignorance, and seemed ready to prevent her from leaving with her bag of cash until he got her answer. He suspected the answer and disliked it intensely. Evasion, a frequent practice in the face of a reporter's curiosity, often provoked little more than resignation. He was used to it. But this time was personal and annoying. He pressed her. She deflected. He insisted. She was impervious. So he tried to be menacing, as quietly as he could and still be understood. "Have you paid taxes on this money you've been getting?" He nodded toward her bag.

She started as if he had slapped her and spat out her reply. "You *Americains*," she said with perfect French pronunciation, "you torture everybody."

Then she motioned him angrily to a corner of the bank lobby, far from other customers, and lowered her gaze as if speaking to the floor.

"Communists come," she said. "*Americains*," she added. And she drew a finger across her throat.

"The canary in the coal mine," Pen told Julie that night. "She doesn't want to be associated with Americans when it all goes down."

"And is it all going down?"

"At some point." He reminded her that, nearly a month ago, the NVA took Phước Bình, the province capital, just seventy-five miles from them—only a village, really, but a symbol. "They're on the offensive in the Central Highlands." Julie sighed and rolled her eyes at Pen's newspaper-lecturing mode, his incurable habit. Her loving annoyance made it a family joke like a little vaudeville routine that got them both laughing—except at dinner parties where she had to behave. Then on the drive home she could needle him for holding forth so. And he would counter that the conversation would have been dull otherwise.

"The ARVN is corrupt and terrified," he continued. "Lanh says soldiers can't live on their pay cuts. They're robbing people and looting. The militias are breaking and running. There's an electricity of dread in the air. Don't you feel it?"

"Not really. The Cercle Sportif is as much of an oasis as ever. Nobody seems nervous. Erik's kids are healthy and happy, though more are coming in, so the place is getting crowded. How much time?"

"I don't know. Not past July, I guess, if Madame Bian's right."

"And, darling, what are you going to do as it all collapses?"

Pen had no answer, so he said nothing except, "Report on it."

"Watch the North Vietnamese tanks roll in?" she asked.

"We'll fall off that bridge when we come to it." His grandmother's favorite malapropism.

Julie didn't laugh.

The next morning, he and Lanh arrived at the bureau dressed in more presentable fashion than usual, climbed into the office Fiat with Mr. Kỳ, and rode to the interview that Pen had finally nabbed with the Foreign Minister. His press secretary, a Mr. Thảo, had made a point of requesting that Pen bring an interpreter despite the minister's passable English, an old tactic to blame the interpreter for any gaff, and to give more time during translation to consider the question.

Waiting in an outer office, Lanh pulled uncomfortably at his pressed trousers. He fidgeted with the buttons on his shirt. *Hey, buffalo boy,* Pen wanted to say. *Don't want to be here?* He caught Lanh's eye and gave him a sympathetic smile. And Lanh's line about the corruption-oozing colonels in the Danang restaurant came back: "I can't stand Vietnamese who have no sign of suffering on their faces."

Mr. Thảo walked in, shook hands, bid them to sit again, and said the minister would be with them shortly.

"I read your articles," he told Pen. "The prisoners." He waited for Pen to reply.

"Oh?"

"Yes." Mr. Thảo was smiling, oddly. "These articles might hurt us. I have a brother in the army." He kept smiling. "I am worried that as the Americans cut aid, we won't have enough fuel, and my brother's unit might not be able to fly by helicopter. They might have to go on foot, and they could be ambushed." The unrelenting smile.

Then Mr. Thảo added, "But I love the way you write."

A bloodless attack, Pen thought. *I hardly felt the blade.*

The Foreign Minister did not mention the prisoners series. Too bad in a way, for Pen was poised to tell him that his editors had held the pieces while they jostled with him over his graphic descriptions, toned them down, insisted on a sidebar detailing North Vietnam's oppression—not at all the topic of the series on *South* Vietnam—and actually spared readers one obscene detail of torture. The sentence reporting a live eel being inserted into the shackled woman's vagina, and the same form of rape used on others, had been muffled. It came out in the paper as "live eels were put in contact with their bodies." Pen had slammed his fist down on the page, then dove on his typewriter and banged out a withering attack on his cowardly, biased editors, a message that he wisely put in his drawer to let cool until the following day, when its futility became apparent. And so, he thought, translations of the truth by interpreters were interpreted by reporters and filtered by editors into acceptable forms. How close to reality can readers get?

He sometimes chewed over his own cowardice, not about war but about editors. Editors who mangled his copy, unwrote his prose when he tried to make it sing, or cut off the perfect kicker at the end of a story—that affecting quote or sculpted phrase that would leave the reader with a poignant taste of tragedy. He was known on the desk as more amenable and polite than he ever felt, probably his childhood instinct for self-preservation against his father's explosive wrath. Pen postured as a mensch who avoided the typical rants by the prima donnas who were resented for their bylines, which conferred undeserved celebrity above the anonymous copyeditors wielding sharp pencils over missing or misplaced commas, misstated or misspelled words, senseless sentences that cascaded in from around the globe. Pen wished he had the guts to go back at them. But the paper was already ten days old or more when copies finally reached Saigon, and nobody in Boston had memory long enough to reconstruct a rationale for an act of demolition a decade of days ago. Pen, on the other hand, had the misfortune of memory. He instantly spotted every change in what he had written so forcefully. *Deterrence*, he sometimes thought. *If I blasted them, maybe next time they'd be gentler*

with the words. He never did, and they never were, much to
his credit in the eyes of the editors.

Lanh felt the electricity more than most, because his spirit
was attuned to vibrations of change and fear and possibility.
A twang of tension ran along Lane 342 like a lute string that
was too taut. The neighborhood was in a hurry. Tiny houses were being crammed with cuts of pork and racks of fish,
with cooking fuel and baskets of papayas, with huge bags
of rice labeled "Gift from the People of the USA," as if the
American War hadn't been responsible for turning Vietnam
into a beggar instead of a rice grower, as if the combat in the
countryside, the mining of the fields, the uprooting of the
farmers, and the deaths of their sons and daughters had not
eroded their fruitful future.

The pho man's anxiety betrayed an edgy thrill, though.
"It's coming, brother. It's coming," he said, leaning into
Lanh's face as he handed him his bowl.

"And what will 'it' be?" Lanh answered. "Liberation or
subjugation? Peace or a new kind of silent war for the soul
of the nation?" The pho man spat on the ground and walked
away.

Minh appeared at a nearby table. He watched Lanh but
said nothing to him as they both shoveled in their noodles
and tripe and bean sprouts. Minh loaded his pho with circular slices of red pepper and swigged from a huge glass of
water.

So much unsaid lay buried in this war, Lanh thought.
*This man and I have stories to tell each other. Why not? Why
not? Because we are afraid of each other and of ourselves, what
we might reveal. What if he knew I tried to join the Viet Minh*

*and then just went back to school? What if I told him I helped
the Japanese shoot the French and got a Japanese killed? Or
helped my comrades escape after they tried a coup on Diệm, but
never tried myself? Or worked for Westmoreland? He knows
only how I've exposed my country to Americans reading at
home in comfort day after day.*

Rosie had called him from Washington the night before. "Lanh," she had said breathlessly, "the end is coming,
or the beginning it might be better to say. How are you doing? How is Thuận? How are Linh and Hiền?" She was not
waiting for his answers. "Do you think it would be good for
you to go out to the countryside, out of Saigon? Or can you
make contact with—" and she stopped herself, perhaps wary
of other listeners on the line. "How will you ride the wave
that's going to flow over you?"

Lanh had no good answers for her, but her voice of
concern connected him to far-off, alien ground, at least by a
slender thread of compassion. *Ride the wave. Yes. How?*

"We are fine," he told Rosie. "Thuận is teaching her first-
grade class. The girls have lots of friends. They just made a
whole family of dolls out of old rags and scraps of wood.
They're more creative than if they had lots of toys. I'm busy.
Pen is learning. He's not bad."

"Not bad?" Rosie shouted. "He's terrific! That prisoner
series has the peace movement mobilized all over again to
make sure we don't keep trying to save an oppressive regime!
Did you work on that? You did good."

Lanh's silence was his answer.

"Look," Rosie said. "Keep in touch. Let me know what's
happening with you. If I can help, if I can do anything."

Make the Communists humane when they come, Lanh wanted to say. But he just laughed a dismissive laugh Rosie must have recognized. They said goodbye in an air of melancholy.

"Did she have any advice?" Thuận asked.

"Nothing realistic. She cares. That's enough for now."

"What was unrealistic?"

"She asked if I thought we should go to the countryside."

"Well, if there's fighting in Saigon."

"If there's fighting in Saigon we'll be safer here on Lane 342. No tanks can even fit in here!" He stretched his arms wide as if measuring. Playfulness touched every part of his face except his eyes.

"I'm nervous, Lanh. And so are my kids in class, picking it up from their parents. They're unruly. It's hard to get them to stay still. They want to bounce around all the time. A couple of girls asked me what was going to happen. I told them everything will be all right. We are all Vietnamese, all part of the same country. A father came in the next day after school and told me I was lying to them, making propaganda. I answered, 'I'm just trying to calm them down.'"

She was saying the same reassuring things to Linh and Hiền, Lanh knew, and maybe they believed her, or maybe they were getting old enough to see the shades of gray in the twilight between sun and gloom.

"You're not wrong," Lanh said. "They've been in the jungle and the mountains fighting, but they are all Vietnamese."

"They are a different sort of Vietnamese from us. Do you know that Phượng's mother is burying diplomas behind her house so they don't look too educated? And photos of relatives in uniform."

"We are a country of secrets," Lanh replied. "We know how to bury them, then dig them up when it suits us."

"What about *our* secrets?"

"Like your father?"

"Like my father, pictures of him in the army," Thuận said. "And your father, the bureaucrat for the French."

"A long time ago," Lanh said.

"Well, I'm hiding my family pictures somewhere. Where? What about behind that broken board in the back closet? We can put things there."

"Or burn them," Lanh said. It was bitter sarcasm, and Thuận did not take it well.

"I am not going to destroy my memories. Just hide them for a time."

"For a time," said Lanh. "That's the optimist in you. For a time." He added, "Rosie wondered if I had any contact with the Communists."

"She said that on the phone?" Thuận spoke in an octave of alarm.

"No. She started to, then caught herself."

"And do you?"

"What a question. Of course not. Well, there's that fellow Minh who hangs around the pho place, but I wouldn't call that contact."

"Maybe you should get to know him."

Thuận was stirring at Lanh's defiance and belonging, two ingredients that in all his years he couldn't make into a blend. So he just shook his head and went to wrap his arms around her as if she were a sturdy trunk holding him against a torrent. She tipped his head back and wiped her fingers across his wet cheeks.

He then climbed the wooden ladder to the precarious loft where he kept a messy desk, and reached into a lower drawer for his old flute from boyhood. From the seasoned bamboo came a weathered tune of mourning and longing. He listened to the words inside his head:

I want to love you, to love Vietnam
In the storm I whispered your name
A Vietnamese name.

As Minh sat in silence the next morning and ate his pho slowly between glances Lanh's way, and Lanh spooned the last of the liquid out of his bowl, they both lingered, each waiting for the other to start. Lanh gave in. He moved to Minh's table.

"I'm being the reporter now," he cautioned Minh. "What's the situation in the field?"

Minh made his colorless face into a patronizing smile. "Very good," he said.

"How much time?" Lanh asked.

"That doesn't depend on us. It depends on you. If you fight, it will take longer. If you run, it won't be long."

"You? Who is you?"

"You, the Saigon regime, the American puppets."

"I have no part of them." Lanh's cheeks burned. He had hardly seen Minh laugh, but now the man opened his mouth and threw back his head in such a gleeful howl of contempt that the pho man started, stared, then looked quickly away once Minh caught his eye. Lanh fingered at his ankle for his knife, always strapped there. *This man is not my friend. If I deal with him now, nobody will mind. A few weeks from now will be different.*

Lanh tried a smirk instead. He leaned forward so that Minh could hear a voice that carried a low note of conviction and a pretense of warning. "You are not a good spy if you know so little about me," Lanh began. "You must be very lowly, not trusted with many facts. How does it feel to be a little tool in the hands of masters who depend on your small ignorance? Liberation will not liberate you. You are destined to remain a minor functionary while a new world is built around you, a new world that will tower over you."

A flicker of doubt might have blinked through Minh's eyes, Lanh hoped. He left Minh sitting as he rose into a controlled posture of confidence, mounted his motorbike, and rode casually out of the alley toward work, trembling all the way.

"I have to leave," said Hạnh. "I—we, Dương and I—cannot be here when the Communists come."

"Will it really be that bad?" Julie touched her hand across the table. "Could you just avoid the fighting and then resurface? Well, no more tennis lessons, I suppose. No more political cartooning."

Hạnh's eyes darted away, back and forth. The corner of her mouth twitched. "I really have to get away."

"Is there a place you can go that's safe? Some village? Then come back when everything has settled down? What about your family? Your mother, your sisters?"

"Them, too, but me especially. I've got to get out of the country. I, we—Dương was in the army. He'll be arrested, or worse."

"Huge numbers were in the army, Hạnh. They can't arrest everybody."

"Can you help us leave?" she asked in a plea—no, an insistence. A challenge. "You've seen his cartoons. Not flattering to the Communists."

"Not flattering to the government either. Won't the Communists take that into account?"

Hạnh practically spat exasperation across the table. "You have no idea," she said with a bite in a new voice, one Julie had never heard. "You have to help us."

"I don't see how. How?" A hollow weakness hit her.

"A plane ticket. A US visa. Say he and I helped the Americans." It was practically a command, which made Julie feel frail. *This must be what the end of every war is like.*

"Please." Hạnh said the word so tenderly that Julie could hardly speak until she found a blade of fact and logic to slice up the problem. A plane ticket, yes—well, she would have to ask Pen. But the hostile embassy? No chance. They hated reporters; they'd never grant the visa. Maybe Sally Falmouth, but she was wary. Her father? Long retired, no more contacts at State. And wouldn't Hạnh and Dương have to get exit visas from the government? Men of his age were considered military assets, how could he do that?

"I could get those," Hạnh said with odd certainty.

Julie gave a weary shake of her head, wanted to say that she valued their friendship, but even sincerity would seem empty now. She had to hold her honesty, give no hope and no promise, not even to pledge that she would ask Sally, which she would. And she would get the inevitable answer.

They were entering a strenuous time of fragile favors, so Julie made a reckless call to Sally's office. "May we meet?"

Julie asked. "I have something to tell you." Tell, not request, to tease her curiosity.

The next day they shared a table at Cercle Sportif on an off-lesson day for them both, and Julie prefaced the problem with apologies alongside compliments for Sally's presumed humaneness, and an offering of tantalizing intelligence: The war was going badly, the jittery Saigonese were preparing for the worst, indicated by their landlady's termination of their lease. Pen had told her that Lanh's little quarter was stocking up on rice and kerosene, and so on. Sally shrugged. None of that was news. Only Ambassador Martin was in denial, she said. "He never travels the country. We know what's going on."

Then, the tennis coach and her husband. "So that's what this is about," said Sally. "What did they do for us?"

"He was in the army."

"Oh, please. Everybody was in the army. The only visas we're issuing now are for certain kinds of people who would be especially vulnerable. And Martin doesn't know we're doing it. He still thinks we're going to win. This is just between us."

"Okay, I get it." Julie had done her duty, and she could tell Hạnh that she had tried. But that's all she could tell her—nothing about special visas for special people. Yet maybe Hạnh was that certain kind of person, her agitation was so high. All this overthinking had revived the old suspicion, crushed so well before.

"Jule, you need to leave," Pen told her.

"No."

"Yes." South Vietnamese deserters were swaggering drunk in Saigon's streets, swinging their M16s around, beginning to break into shops. Roads into Saigon were choked with civilians pouring in from the Highlands. "It's the apocalypse," he said. "The thin veneer of order is cracking. Like Roxbury, how easily civility fractures."

"That sounds melodramatic."

"Look, people think we've betrayed them. Lanh says we should be more afraid of the South Vietnamese than the North Vietnamese or the Vietcong. They could turn on any American they see. I'll have Tân get you a flight to Bangkok."

Her long stare straight at Pen meant helpless resignation. "Just a couple of days," she demanded. "I have goodbyes to say. There's Erik. There's Mai. Oh, Pen, can't we take her? She needs rescuing."

"Everybody needs rescuing. What about her mother?"

"I don't know anything about her mother. I need to go to Erik's."

"I'll get Mr. Kỳ to drive you. It's safer than a cyclo or cab."

The dirt yard at Erik's swarmed with kids as usual, but not only kids. Adults, too, many mothers coming for their children, swooping them up in their arms to whisk them off to an imagined space of safety.

Erik, frantic, quickly gave Julie some news. Mrs. Thương had taken her boy Tài back into the streets. She'd left little Anh, whose damaged heart and hearing would need medical care available only in Europe or the States.

A strong hug came around her knees: Mai, smiling, reaching up. Julie hoisted her, heavier now, and hugged her and kissed her and wet her face with tears, a face with a puzzled look.

"Erik, I want to take Mai, rescue her from this place, give her a beautiful life. Can we find her mother to get permission? Do we need permission?"

He took a step back to eye her closely. "Yes, you need a stack of permissions. You have to go through a bureaucratic maze to adopt a kid. I'm not even sure where her mother is."

"Do you have her name? Maybe Lanh can find her."

"Whatever we know Thi has in the files." This he delivered in a breath of coldness.

"What will you do?"

"I might stay. I need to care for the kids who are left. We'll see. Every minute there's a different answer to a different question. Be safe, Julie. And thank you. Thank you for everything."

She could hardly see through her stinging eyes as she dashed out to the office Fiat and practically shouted, "Cercle Sportif!" which propelled Mr. Kỳ through streets already descending. She thought of the pained and struggling crowds in a Bruegel painting. She ran into the clubhouse, asked for Hạnh, nobody knew. She searched the courts. She wasn't playing. Nobody was. She combed the grounds, strangely isolated from the growing wilderness outside. She needed the final farewell, so sat at their usual table.

She had never seen Hạnh except in whites, but there she was, a lithe woman in dark slacks, light-blue shirt, walking toward her with her gym bag at her side, an uncertain stride as if wondering.

They hugged long and deep as Julie mumbled her Bangkok plans. Maybe you'll get out, Julie said, which made

Hạnh grimace and ask, "Could you wait a moment? I've got something to give you," and she charged into the clubhouse, then ran back with a large, thick folder under her arm. "I figured I'd see you again, so I brought these. Would you mind taking them? Dương's best, the ones he's most proud of. We're burning the rest, or burying them."

"Burning? No! Whatever for?"

"Oh, Julie, do you really not understand what's going to happen here? People are burying and burning their family photographs, their army commendations, their diplomas. If we do leave someday, or find ourselves in better years, we'll ask you for these back. Keep them, please, my friend."

That was their farewell, and Julie fled down the front path to the car, where she sat rattled by the early gusts of panic sweeping by.

She had just two days to do something about Mai.

Julie's plea came in a torrent that overwhelmed Pen's resistance. Okay, he relented, the niceties of procedure be damned. Mai was precious and should be saved. And everything was breaking down. Bureaucratic rules must be crumbling as well.

Even outside observers who live in a miasma of corruption have to breathe, and as they take in the tainted air, they grow accustomed to it. So it was with Pen. He asked Tân, whose skill at petty bribery had kept the office running smoothly. Tân seemed intrigued, dubious, and troubled all at once, Pen thought. But he said he would do something.

What he did first was to ask Lanh if he knew some magic that could get Mai out. Who is the right official? Did he know? Lanh could not keep a secret from his face, and the shadow that fell looked like grief.

"I don't know," he said, then stole time, while Pen was writing, to ride his motorbike too fast to Erik's house. He found Thi in the office.

"Hello, Thi." She gave him a surprised smile. "You know the little girl Mai? Do you have her mother's address?" To her questioning look, he explained with a hasty lie—that Julie wanted to give the family money. The file that emerged from the cabinet had only one slender page, mostly blank, with a name and an address not far from Lanh's own house.

He sped there, found the crumbling stucco structure, banged on one door inside, then another, calling the mother's name and getting no reply, climbing stairs, feeling the rise of hopelessness. Finally a voice came faintly from behind a door, it opened a crack, and Lanh repeated the name.

"No," an old woman whispered. "She and her children come and go. I haven't seen them for two days."

"When you see her," Lanh said, his entire body acting out his plea, his sentences carrying the tune of desperation, "tell her to go right away to Erik's house and get her daughter Mai. The Americans might be trying to take her away."

The woman opened the door to show her terror and her shock. "Why? Why would they do that?"

"Because they love her," said Lanh. "And they do not love Vietnam."

The woman frowned, puzzled. "I don't understand."

"It is hard to understand, I know," said Lanh. "Just please, if you see her, tell her to go right away and get Mai before it's too late." He wrote down his name and his address on nearby Lane 342. "She can come to my house any night if she wants to ask me about it. But she should not wait. She should not wait unless she wants Mai to go to America."

The woman opened her mouth as if she were going to say something, perhaps, *What is so bad about going to America?* But she stopped, nodded, thanked Lanh for caring, and closed her door softly, sadly.

Well-meaning Americans, Lanh thought. He did not like himself as a cynic, but how they held themselves in high regard! How much injury their virtue had caused, all in the name of some imagined good. He remembered too vividly from age eighteen his final days in Hanoi, during the long-sought French evacuation. Hollows in the surface of order had opened like whirlpools. Chinese were said to have raped village girls. Buses were breaking down in mysterious flurries of acrid soot, as if their engines were dying of thirst for oil. Viet Minh coming north by ship to Haiphong were told in a supposed Viet Minh leaflet to bring warm clothes, fueling fear that they were being sent on to China to labor on railroads.

He could still see the printing on another leaflet, ostensibly signed by the Viet Minh, announcing property seizures and currency reform. In two days, the value of the wadded bills he had carefully collected fell by half. He felt the chill of disillusionment with the Viet Minh, not knowing that both leaflets had been forged by the Americans to spark financial panic. He did not know that the buses' oil had been doctored by a contaminant poured by agents of the United States who nearly succumbed themselves to the toxic fumes. He did not know that the tale of Chinese rapes was a fabrication by the Saigon Military Mission of US Colonel Edward G. Lansdale.

He would read about all this only seventeen years later in the Pentagon Papers, courtesy of *The New York Times*, whose correspondents, along with those of the Associated Press and the New York *Herald Tribune*, were thanked in the documents for being "warm friends" of Lansdale's operation by providing helpful analysis, "a valuable service for their country."

Julie worked intensely on her final portrait, hoping to finish before her evening flight to Bangkok. She had begun with a photograph that Pen had taken, a close-up in a moment of warm and thoughtful contemplation. Beginning with pencils, she had then filled in with chalk pastels, breaking the narrow rectangles of chalk in the closest colors, stroking the paper with their edges, rubbing the lines they left with her finger to blur them, and finally going over them with a tiny, damp brush to blend and smooth the hues of skin and hair and eyes. A few finishing touches this morning, and she met her deadline.

She stood back from the completed work, pronounced it satisfactory, folded brown paper around it, and dashed out to where Mr. Kỳ was waiting to take her to the office. There, she placed it in Lanh's hands in solemn, joyful celebration. "It's for you," she said. "Open it, please."

He laid it on a desk, removed the paper, and stared at himself. Tân looked over his shoulder and nodded. Lanh said nothing for a long while. He soaked in his lopsided smile, his head cocked—was it jauntily or reflectively?

"I look serious and happy at the same time," he said. "You make me look as if I have some wisdom that I am about to share, or have just shared. Is that really how you see me?"

"Exactly. It is how Pen sees you, too, and how I suspect everyone who knows you sees you, understands you. Thank you, Lanh, for all you have done for us. And for your country."

Pen, oscillating between the streets and his typewriter, spent hardly any time at home after Julie flew out. The villa seemed cavernous without her. The nights no longer seduced him. The booms of outgoing artillery died away to save ammunition. The racket of helicopters disappeared. The darkness sat poised constantly on the edge of dawn. So between his few hours of shallow sleep, he and Lanh prowled Saigon, which looked like a film running at double speed. Kids to school, mothers to markets, vendors to stalls, all the normal bustle at a sprint. Despite the government's constant voice of optimism and resolve and the US Embassy's stoic fantasies, the Saigonese sensed peril, like sea birds fleeing inland, Pen thought.

"We have a proverb like that," Lanh told him. "When dragonflies fly in the autumn wind, storms are coming."

Demonstrations against the government for every possible reason coalesced and dissolved, their leaders were arrested, whole issues of newspapers were seized, editors and reporters jailed. Truth vanished, so rumors flourished. One held that the ever-powerful Americans had cut a deal with the North Vietnamese to give up swaths of the country. Luckily for Pen's career, he scoffed at conspiracy theories. But he could see, via Lanh's x-ray vision, that beneath the city's tight drumhead of anti-Communist fear, anger seethed.

Retreat from the Central Highlands unleashed a flash flood of humiliation and alarm that flowed down escape routes toward the coast and the capital. Ranking officers wearing insignia of northern units materialized in the city, Lanh noticed, a signal of abandonment.

"It's not like a building that falls because a foundation gives way," he told Pen. "This building is collapsing from the top." Indeed, the officers were followed by deserters from the rank and file, privates and corporals who roamed the Saigon bars at nightfall, infiltrating the avenues and plazas with drunken loudness and thieving desires. Passersby gave them wide berth, and Americans noticed their glares. "They will be the real danger," Lanh repeated. "More than the North Vietnamese troops."

Pen liked Lanh's building metaphor and used it in a story. The Saigonese were not pulling together, as far as Lanh could tell, and through Lanh's eyes Pen could see it too. They were not helping one another. They were not volunteering. They were not donating blood. They were jacking up prices to impossible heights, even as soldiers' diminished pay put food for their families out of reach. They were not assisting civilians now flooding into the city, their fellow citizens whose hunger in the countryside had them eating cactus, leaves, roots, and banana bulbs from trees. Civilization seemed like a windshield spidering into filigrees of cracks before shattering completely.

The lowliest of entrepreneurs were adapting in struggles to survive. Their inventories were mutating on panchos spread across sidewalks. The usual wares—stolen American hi-fi parts, flak jackets, belts, helmets, and cartons of cigarettes—were giving way to shards of broken households:

tattered clothing, pens, dark glasses, fragments of costume jewelry, necklaces of fading blossoms.

Lanh pressed Pen to have a look outside of town. Pen, with a queasy premonition, resisted a little—a role reversal from the days when Lanh had to be the one to impose caution. How strange an awakening, Pen thought.

Where did bravery end and foolishness begin? Or was there ever bravery in the drive to step onto untested ground? No, ignorance. Knowledge weakens, like Adam's bite from the apple.

Driving the road north, they pushed against gravity. Mr. Kỳ honked his way through tangles of olive-drab Jeeps, their canvas tops open at the sides, packed with officers. Then trucks and miniature buses swaying under crowds of soldiers and their families hanging from roofs, hoods, and door handles. Droves of the newest refugees followed, flowing south on foot under shoulder poles balanced with clumsy bundles of possessions, piled onto bikes and motorbikes loaded with every child and grandmother who would fit, crammed into decrepit French trucks and cars from a bygone war.

Pen saw a wild river. Lanh saw, in the deserting officers, the rats that had run from a house fire up at the end of Lane 342 some months before, trailed by the human residents, the innocents escaping from their own homes.

Lanh said nothing, his words waiting somewhere. He stared through the windshield, then swiveled from side to side to surround himself in the lamentation, which embraced and pleaded and tried to seduce. He wanted to belong here, but the passing eyes, the glares. *Look at the eyes!* They saw through him into his privilege. No camouflage would make him invisible, no flak jacket would shield him, no jocular banter would soften the rage of terror in their eyes.

Farmers stooped under bags of precious rice, women under the woven conical hats of the fields, the ragged children tearful with hunger, the men in filthy bandages, the soldiers lost and frightened casing the weary lines of despairing countrymen to pilfer and rob. Lanh fastened on the remnants of existence tied optimistically to motorbikes and hand-drawn carts: cooking pots, sewing machines, electric fans. Pen sat in back, silently scribbling in his notebook.

People started banging on the car, beseeching them to turn around and take them to Saigon. Men gestured pathetically at their ravaged children, their broken elders. One pointed to his bloody feet and cried that he had lost his sandals while diving from a North Vietnamese barrage. The column of refugees, looted by their own soldiers and then shelled by the enemy, looked shipwrecked. Lanh lowered his window and found his words, but only the words that formed questions, none that formed cogent answers.

Pen, though, had no words for questions, only the ones for answers, which he wrote and wrote as legibly as he could through his quivering hand, fragments from Lanh's translations. Officers running. Soldiers in disarray. Families scattered. Mothers with two of seven children. If the others were alive, where? Husbands without wives. Brothers and sisters without each other.

Brothers and sisters, Lanh thought. *We are all supposed to be brothers and sisters.*

The car could barely move. But Mr. Kỳ was traveling quickly into his own jittery state that Lanh knew he would not survive. From behind the wheel, his voice an edgy pitch, he said the engine was overheating, code for fear. All right, Lanh said without translating for Pen. We'll turn around in a minute.

CHAPTER 14

Lanh's dead father leaves a vacuum in Hanoi that his mother and sister cannot fill. The way south is opening before partition hardens, and eighteen is always the age of motion, of flight. His mother lets him go through a screen of tears as if seeing him pass into an afterworld. He takes the crumpled cash he's earned by selling military detritus he's scavenged after school—dented helmets and bandoliers of rusty ammunition, webbed belts stained by souls' last draining, brass shells to hammer and melt into implements of life.

The journey is slow, complex, and full of exhilarating risk. He thinks first to find the Viet Minh unit from years back, knowing the futility of the search—except to reconnect with an old and nobler impulse. The motorbike driver leaves him at a village where the battered buses pass. The bus route takes him past the village of his absent grandparents and their confiscated fields. Then a three-wheeled trucker invites him to squeeze into the open bed in back like a piece of cargo. And when he gets to the hamlet whose name his grandparents never knew, Lanh raps on the tinny cab and jumps out, looking for the path he once followed.

Paths once followed grow over quickly, even in strife, and he finds only a hint, a slight trace of foliage less thick, the faintest echo of a memory. Without a machete, it is a memory that he cannot penetrate. Foiled, he shrugs off his detour to the withered recollection. He will leave his moment of childhood pride there by the side of the road and hitch a ride on a wheezing truck back the way he came.

The driver, taciturn at first, soon detects that he has a listener sitting beside him. He does this route in daylight only, because he has a wife and five children in Hanoi. Once he grew rice, because it was safer than carrying a gun. Now the Viet Minh and the French leave him alone to drive his truck, because they know he is needed. He wants to love his country, but it is hard to find it, he explains.

And you? He asks Lanh. The driver's last comment echoes. "It is hard to find it." So Lanh says he is looking, looking for his country, heading to the South, not to flee but to find.

An old teacher who had grown up in the South had given the class a proverb from the Mekong Delta: "Go out one day and come back with a basket of knowledge." But he is not coming back. He is going out, only out.

The driver nods in sympathy. Lanh admits he tried to join the Viet Minh but was turned away. The driver laughs dryly. Because you are just a boy, he says to Lanh, and don't know any better.

Because Lanh talks to everyone he meets about their destinations, real and imagined, and since people are surprised that they want to say so much about themselves, they never want to part with the lanky boy and his curious gaze. So when the truck arrives at the dusty crossroad where one direction points to Hanoi and the other southward, the driver nudges him to stay aboard some kilometers more.

But the load of clanking scrap metal is destined for a family factory in Hanoi, a real destination desired by neither Lanh nor, it seems, the driver. As Lanh hops down, the driver tries to hide his regret behind a casual wave goodbye, and leaves a billow of exhaust behind.

Lanh shoulders the cloth sack tied with twine. It contains all his temporal possessions, including the tawny bamboo flute his parents bought him from the old Chinese proprietor who hastily emptied his shop while sinking in the muck of war—that other war, long gone now. Lanh's seven-year-old fingers could barely reach the holes, his breath could barely sustain a note. But he found rooftops or shabby parks and played alone like a shepherd. Walkers paused to listen. In years he hasn't blown a tune. Only the smooth bamboo, as hard as aged acacia, soothes him in its touch.

He stands at the crossroad for a little while and lets the clear sky sing. He looks north along the road he's traveled and thinks of the smoky air of Hanoi's intrigues, rumors, and decline.

A million northerners are fleeing south, moving by sea, by trail, by foot, by whatever vehicles are willing. As all refugees everywhere in every time, they are pushed by fear and pulled by hope.

"I am not fleeing," he tells anyone who will hear him. "I am on a journey to learn." This he says to the drivers of ox carts and Lambrettas, to the burdened civil servants who have crushed children and belongings into buses and trucks. He gets indulgent smiles, or people simply look away.

Is it disaffection or wanderlust that drives him? He decides on the latter, a restless ache. Every southbound step he takes along a road, each hamlet he passes slowly in the ox cart where he's blessed with space among the farmland's thinning yields, every hectare and kilometer his course line meets, Lanh possesses simply by his presence. He is acquiring his country. Across the fraught parallel of Seventeen Degrees North and into the empire of Bảo Đại, river by river, mountain by mountain, plantation by plantation, one Vietnamese at a time in brief but deep connection, the weary land is becoming his.

No goal looms in any plan. He journeys into infinity, content to give himself to perpetual motion without a resting place. Hills rise into the Trường Sơn Mountains, then descend toward the sea. From the back of a bicycle pedaled generously by a man little older than himself, Lanh's vision is captured, across the flat green of fields and scattered trees, by the slant of red tile roofs: the citadel at Huế. Roads in are rutted, lined by houses crippled by blown walls that still support thatched roofs somehow. Yet at the center, in dignity, the Imperial City embraces him. The Perfume River, meandering just as he does, passes serenely among stone works fashioned into temples, dragons, gates, pagodas, and tombs. Sampans idle quietly, their half-round cabins of woven fronds concealing mysteries. The Thiên Mụ makes him smile, with its seven stories of diminishing size trying to fool him into seeing it as taller than it can be.

Huế is magic to him, from his books. Huế is ancient to him, from his teachers. The Chinese, the Cham, the Nguyễn dynasty, a knotted legacy, now his. He has to touch the unreality with his hands, to feel the rough stones of the wall that once guarded the citadel, and will again.

This is not a place to leave so quickly, if ever. He pauses here for part of his life.

CHAPTER 15

"We could try to fly to Huế," Lanh said. Mr. Kỳ had managed his U-turn. They were taking a fleeing farmer and his wife, their children stacked on top of each other in the Fiat. Lanh revived his charming curiosity, Pen put a hundred questions before they entered Saigon together and the family bowed and clasped their hands and gave gracious thanks as they folded themselves into the capricious currents of the city.

"Do you think we can get on an Air America flight to Huế?" Lanh's chest burned, a tart longing. "We should see what's going on there."

The unraveling was loosening Pen's fabric. The urge to witness and to write pulled against the common sense of worry. He did not want to be drunk on misery like Mandell, or drawn to violence like the photographer Stone, who had no clue when to be scared. They were hearing of mobbed aircraft in Huế, vigilante soldiers trampling women and children to get aboard, an entire ancient capital bleeding until it would lie sapped, a cadaver dead to everything except its history.

The Telex clattered out a message from Bangkok, the Siam Intercontinental:

HOW LONG WILL YOU STAY? ALL MY LOVE JULIE

The question stood apart, far outside his calculations.
He knew she had taken a ground-floor room whose sliding doors opened to the patio around the pool. They had
stayed there at times. He could picture her dining alone in
the hotel's seafood restaurant, served by white-coated waiters in artificial coolness, writing out a message to him on
hotel stationery and dropping it at the front desk with her
winning smile and a few baht to reward the clerk. Maybe
he let her sit down at the Telex keyboard to have a brittle
conversation.

A WHILE LONGER. NO URGENCY YET. LOVE PEN

CAN YOU GET HANH OUT? ALL MY LOVE JULIE

What was she thinking?

NO IDEA HOW. LOVE PEN

AND MAI?

That made him glance toward Tân, who had given him
no report on progress, if any.

HOW ABOUT THE BUFE?

He laughed aloud and got a look from Tân. "She wants
the buffee!"

"Oh, maybe I can get it packed and shipped to Boston," Tân said seriously.

"Are you kidding? Well, thank you, Tân. You are truly eagerly efficient in every way. But the last thing you need to worry about now is a Bloody Useless Fucking Elephant." Pen then startled himself with a thought that perhaps Vietnamese, proud of their ceramic industry, did not share the disparaging mirth of US troops in the logistics units who had bestowed the nickname on the thousands and thousands of weighty, two-foot-high ceramic elephants that GIs were persuaded to buy for a song and send home at tax-payers' expense. Rosie liked to say that there were two kinds of Americans: those who had been to Vietnam and those who had not. BUFE, pronounced *buffee,* had entered the lexicon of Nam like a secret handshake, an instant password among the soldiers, diplomats, journalists, and do-gooding humanitarian workers who could tell at once that for all their differences in opinions and perspectives, they shared the essential qualification that set them apart from the mass-es of their countrymen: They had been in Vietnam. They knew.

"But ours is really nice," Pen added hastily for Tân. Indeed it was, a charming piece in white and green and gold gracing the doorway into their villa's living room. And he liked it because he could say "buffee," preceding it with a redundant adjective when it nearly tripped him up, which was often.

"I love it!" Julie had declared when it was placed on the villa's tile floor. She would never see it again, Pen thought with sour satisfaction.

The flight to Huế was bumpy. The CIA plane, occupied only by the certifiably insane—reporters, photographers, and a few Americans of indeterminate affiliation—taxied to a distant corner of the airfield, far enough from crowds surging against the terminal's chain-link fence. A gray, unmarked bus took them around the building, depositing them in a lot where several cyclo and cab drivers still jostled to make a few final piasters from the foreigners.

"Let's go to Vinh's, see if he's still there. Maybe get a meal." Lanh was floating, briefly. "He had a street stall when we met twenty years ago. It might have been the first place I ate in Huế. Then a small restaurant, then a bigger one. Foreigner and Vietnamese, all mixed together like tripe and noodles in pho."

"Ha," Pen chuckled. "Who was the tripe?"

"I *like* tripe!" Lanh laughed. And so they hired a driver named Hải for the day, and off they went into spooky streets already abandoned.

"The Communists will do what they did in Tết," Hải declared. A bloodbath. Two thousand? Three thousand? They could not be counted in the mass graves discovered later. To hell with Minh's voice in his head, editing, censoring. History was real. Fear was true.

Lanh was dreaming of food, knowing it was a dream. The rice cakes and dried shrimps and crispy pork skin of *bánh bèo*. The baby mussels of *cơm hến*. The steamy round noodles of *bún bò Huế* topped with pigs' blood. The grilled pork in pancakes of steamed rice. "You have to taste them, Pen. Vinh makes the best. With mint, basil, cinnamon leaves. That is the real Vietnam." *Is there a real Vietnam?*

The driver's grating tone continued. "What's he saying, Lanh?"

"Still about Tết in sixty-eight. That's why the city has emptied out. People are on the highway trying to get to Danang, or at the airport here."

"Why hasn't he left?"

Lanh translated, and the man shook his head. "I have a big family. My mother is too old to go. My sisters, brothers, children. We belong in Huế. You know what we say. After the monsoon, the rice grows." Lanh nodded and touched the driver's shoulder lightly as if he were a brother.

"In Huế, I learned English," Lanh told Pen, "from a British teacher at Quốc Học High School. He gave me books, wonderful books, forced me to speak English when I got good enough. I taught there for a while too. Math. Their math teacher was killed in the French war. After lunch we'll go by and see if anybody's there. Do you know about Quốc Học? Diệm went there. Also," and he glanced at the driver, who seemed safe enough, "General Giáp. And Hồ Chí Minh." At this, Hải snapped his head toward Lanh, whose quick explanation in Vietnamese made the driver smile—a proud smile.

Down this street, turn right there, left here, two blocks more, and they braked to a halt in front of a big sign in English, "Perfume Restaurant." Lanh bounded out to see a pair of windows as blank as a corpse's open eyes. He pressed against the glass, peering like a hunter for a sign of movement. Tables were still arranged. The bar still had shelves of bottles. He tried the wooden door. Locked. He banged on it. Silence. "Vinh!" he cried. "Vinh! Vinh! It's Lanh! Lanh!" His voice broke as it cascaded over his own name. Now Pen was out of the taxi, nearly touching Lanh's shoulder like a brother.

Lanh stood at the window until his eyes adjusted to the inside darkness. Motion disturbed shadows way in the back. Then again. A figure, bending and straightening, bending and straightening, as if selecting and packing. "Vinh?" he shouted again and rapped on the glass. The figure turned, halted, then leaned forward and walked toward the window until daylight sketched a frown stiff with dread. The sudden shock of joy that burst across the face would prowl among Lanh's memories.

Vinh opened the door, beckoned them both in, shut and locked it quickly, and led them to a table well out of view. Lanh did not bother to translate; Pen did not bother to ask him. The friends embraced in a flurry of words, quick phrases back and forth like table tennis. Vinh was leaving, trying for Danang. The road was jammed and dangerous, Lanh told him. But he couldn't stay, Vinh replied. His wife, his three children, his future. If he could get to Danang, he could get on a ship to Saigon, he'd heard. No, the ships were overflowing, Lanh said. Crowds were waiting on the piers. But I can pay, said Vinh. I have some money, and he waved a hand around the empty restaurant. No matter, Lanh said. Those who got aboard barges and made it to ships were pressed together so tightly on decks that they were dying. They had no food. They were sick. Soldiers were stealing everything, killing those who resisted. Bodies were being thrown overboard. "I know from journalists reporting from there," Lanh insisted.

The volleys of words fell away. A veil of defeat curtained over Vinh.

"Why don't you stay here?" Lanh asked. "Even Communists need to eat!"

Vinh nearly laughed, but not quite. "I am a capitalist. I have a business. Do you really think they will just leave me alone?"

"They left you alone in sixty-eight."

"We fled to my parents' village. When we came back two friends had been executed. The restaurant was a shambles, looted."

"And now?"

"And now, you know better than I, Lanh, the North Vietnamese are marching toward the city. There is no countryside that is safe."

Lanh rubbed his hand all the way down his face, from forehead to chin, to help him think his way out of an impossible riddle.

Pen recognized the gesture. "What?" he asked.

"Vinh wants to leave," said Lanh. "He wants to go to Danang and try to get on a ship. It's crazy. Can't be done now."

"It sure can't. Not safely."

"He won't stay here, which would be the best thing. He's scared. You know, Tết."

"And?"

"And what if we tried to get him and his family on the plane back to Saigon? Do you think we could? Would Air America take them?"

Pen, not a savior by impulse or profession, tried to shift his gaze from Vinh's sorrow of surrender. He tried to look at some rational spot of objective computation. *You taught math, Lanh. Work out the probabilities. Also, we have*

*reporting to do. We are observers here, not participants. Well,
at least I am the observer. And I am scared. How callous am I?*

"Okay, Lanh, we'll give it a try. Have them meet us at
the airport at three, not in the terminal, in that lot where
they took us."

"Vinh, you cannot take anything," Lanh said. "Nothing
you can't put in a little sack or tie inside your clothes." Vinh
nodded, took Pen's hand in both of his, and they said their
uncertain farewells. "*Au revoir,*" said Vinh with a thin and
hopeful smile.

They were hungry, but there was no food in the lovely
vacancy of Huế, no *bánh bèo,* no *cơm hến.* "After the war,"
Lanh promised, "Vinh will have the best restaurant in
Saigon." The Perfume River was all the more alluring without the bobbing sampans, which must have been navigated
upstream to safer waters. The monuments and tombs were
all the more majestic in the calm. Their stonework, pockmarked still from the offensives in 1968 and 1972, reminded Pen of dying trees in an ancient forest, still standing but
harboring the miniscule life of decay and perhaps rebirth.
Lanh had to stop again at the wall, get out, and touch both
hands to the stone.

They encountered so few people that Pen's notebook
had many empty pages. Hardly anyone was left to tell their
stories. They thought of driving to the outskirts, to the road
toward Danang, but Hải sensibly refused, insisting that
refugees would hijack his taxi for themselves. So by three
o'clock they were back in the airport lot, where Pen handed Hải a wad of bills, wished him and his family well, and
looked around for Vinh.

He came in his own car, and out spilled his frolicking little boy, an older girl, and a somber teenage daughter. His wife, erect and draped in stately sadness, introduced herself with thank-yous.

The small bus came. A jittery American wearing a Hawaiian shirt and a pistol on his hip surveyed the waiting cluster of Americans and several Vietnamese. Vinh's were the only children. "Who are you?"

"Friends," said Pen. "Very *important* friends." He tipped his head toward Vinh and freighted the word *important* with encrypted meaning. Lanh clenched his teeth to avoid a smile. The guard raised his eyebrows, gave a knowing nod, and waved them all aboard.

But around the terminal the tarmac was swarming. Crowds had overcome the chain-link fence; Vietnamese soldiers wielding M16s were mingling among civilians. A helicopter hovered, then set down gently at the end of a taxiway and kept the rotors turning. Soldiers broke into a run and pushed past families bearing babies, dragging toddlers, and supporting the limping elderly. In the face of the advance, the pilot gunned the engine and lifted off, circling the field before disappearing.

"Shit!" Pen said. "This will be impossible."

"We'll do it," the American replied, and looked at Vinh, his "very important" asset. The bus rumbled away from the terminal. A cry went up from the crowd, which raced behind. The bus ran down a taxiway, across a weedy strip to a far runway, then parked near the end. The Air America plane drifted out of the sun, sank toward the distant beginning of the runway, and touched down with puffs of smoke from its wheels.

The American was on his cumbersome field radio to the pilot. "Better hurry down here, buddy," they heard him say. "Lots of company coming."

Shots like firecrackers came from across the field. Soldiers had their backs turned, firing over the heads of the refugees. *Their own families must be in that crowd*, Lanh thought. Then a bullet whined off the concrete beside the bus. The plane loomed larger, coming fast down the runway. The reversing engines screamed.

"Out now, folks," shouted the guard. And they piled onto the steaming pavement. Lanh noticed the sun locked in place, high and hot.

The South Vietnamese troops, a mass of olive drab, were almost on them by the time the plane lowered its steps. "Americans first!" yelled an Air America crewman, rifle held diagonally across his chest. He brought it down and aimed at the running, pushing soldiers, which slowed them for a beat, but only a beat.

Pen let others go ahead. He lingered with Lanh and Vinh and family. The crewman shouted at him to get the fuck on the plane. He was on the steps, Lanh at the bottom, Vinh pressing his wife and kids toward the stairway, when a soldier pushed in front, elbowing Vinh out of the way. Vinh took a swing at him. The soldier hit him in the belly with the butt of his rifle and turned to stomp on him as he fell.

Before the soldier could bring his foot down, Lanh crouched, reached to his right ankle and whipped out his knife. Its gleaming blade entered beneath the soldier's lower left rib in an upward thrust that must have hit squarely on his heart. A firehose of blood pumped out. Lanh waved his red-streaked blade in the soldiers' faces and shoved forward to reach for Vinh. Another soldier slammed him back, Lanh slashed his arm. A third then brought his boot down on Vinh's skull with a crack. The shrieks from his wife and children came from some dark and terrible place.

"Get aboard or we're leaving you behind! Now!" The crewman's face was red. Lanh looked winded, as if he had been stomped himself. He made no move, so Pen grabbed his wrist and yanked him halfway up the ladder. Lanh was jolted out of his trance. He blinked down at his lifeless friend on the tarmac, then up at the refuge above, and climbed weeping on hands and knees into the dark doorway of salvation. The plane began to move with the stairway still extended.

Two crewmen hammered away a soldier clinging to the ramp, and up it came. Through a window they could see Vinh's wife and children kneeling over him, around his head a spreading pool of blood.

Soldiers were firing wildly above and around the plane.

The flight to Saigon did not take long enough. They could not catch their breaths. The plane vibrated strangely, and the pilot came on the intercom to explain. "I think I have a couple of people hanging onto the landing gear. We can't retract it. They won't survive the landing, I'm afraid. And we're taking the coastal route to avoid NVA gunners inland. We're following Highway One."

Lanh stared vacantly ahead, but Pen gazed down along the road to Danang, clotted like an artery preparing for death. Miniature vehicles and people, tormented in remote silence, seemed to be going nowhere. He said this to Lanh.

"We have always been going nowhere," Lanh replied.

CHAPTER 16

Among the many events in Saigon after the fall of Huế, two held special significance, both occurring in near secrecy.

At Camp Davis, Vietcong Colonel Võ Đông Giang ordered his men to take boards and knives and dig bunkers for the approaching time when his forces would begin shelling Tansonnhut airport. "We will dig trenches and hold on," he messaged his superiors. "Do not worry about us."

And at an American diplomat's unauthorized dinner party for correspondents, evacuation was the sole topic of conversation. It violated Ambassador Martin's bizarre faith in South Vietnam's survival, which made him rant madly when anyone tried to coax him into reality. Departures would sap Saigon's morale, embolden the Communists, enter history as a pernicious self-fulfilling prophecy, he insisted. So, reporters were told at the dinner, clandestine arrangements were being made by the ambassador's subordinates, CIA agents, and military officers. There would be signals, times, and meeting places.

"What about our Vietnamese staff?" Pen asked.

"Yes, to the extent possible," said the diplomat.

"And their families?" asked Mandell.

"Immediate families, not extended."

224

After Huế, Pen tasted paralysis at times. His body heavy, every limb an impossible weight, he longed for the sanctuary of unending sleep in his air-conditioned room. But he forced himself to keep writing, two stories a day, sometimes three, updating as Boston's deadlines loomed, twelve hours behind Saigon's time.

Lanh, stricken, wept in Thuận's arms for Vinh, which frightened her. His daughters watched him in alarm. But he pushed into his work, his way to love his country. He and Pen scoured the streets, listened to the outpourings of retreating soldiers, pieced together the jigsaw puzzle of conquest and despair checkering the countryside.

Pen circled around Huế, then gave up his reticence. It was terrible about Vinh, he finally told Lanh. "I should have said no on the flight. Maybe they'd have had a chance over land and sea." Lanh could not summarize guilt so concisely. And Pen could not tolerate silence so easily. "Fucking soldiers," Pen went on. "But a knife, Lanh? Jesus."

"Buddha," Lanh countered with his sideways look. "Karma."

Danang fell. The embassy decided to help children leave, at last, and orphanages began putting them on flights that some official wordsmith dubbed the Babylift.

"We are going in four days," Erik told Pen on the phone.

"With how many children?"

"All of them."

"But what about their mothers? Are they all cleared for adoption?"

Silence.

"Come around when you get a chance, Pen."

So he and Lanh went in an hour. Kids were playing in the yard, as always. Little Mai ran up to him. Lanh sank inside. The mother hadn't come.

"Julie? Julie?" she asked.

Pen made a gesture like a plane flying away. "Gone," he said. She crumpled and looked down, hugged him around the knees, and shuffled away like a veteran of loss.

"Please understand," Erik explained, "these kids, especially the ones fathered by Americans, will be better off in Europe or the States. The Communists will persecute the Amerasians—or the society will. We can't wait for all the papers."

"But the mothers, won't they come looking for them?" Lanh asked.

"If they haven't by now, it's almost too late. Little Anh is still here, her mother hasn't come, and anyway she needs serious medical attention."

"And Mai?" asked Pen.

"Mai's mother I haven't seen in months. I don't know."

"Are you taking her?"

"Yes, unless her mother shows up very soon."

"Julie loves her. She'll want to adopt her."

Erik jotted down the names of two adoption agencies. "We'll be in touch with them when we land in the States. You can reach me through them. I'm sure they'll work it out."

TALKED TO ERIK. MAI COMING OUT FRIDAY. WE CAN PROBABLY ADOPT HER IF THATS WHAT YOU WANT. LOVE PEN

OH DARLING. YES YES YES. AND ARE YOU LEAVING?
TERRIBLY WORRIED ABOUT YOU. ALL MY LOVE JULIE

NOT YET. ARRANGEMENTS BEING MADE. LOVE PEN

HOW ABOUT HANH? PLEASE PLEASE HELP HANH AND
DUONG. PLEASE. LEMME KNOW DARLING.
ALL MY LOVE JULIE

Pen didn't send an answer.

Lanh ended the day in a detour to the address Thi had given him for Mai's mother. He rapped on the door of the old woman who had opened it suspiciously before. Again she opened it a crack, and brightened when she saw him. But she had no news. She had not seen the mother, although she confessed that with all that was happening, she had kept mostly to her rooms. She stepped out now onto the dusty landing and pointed a bony finger at a door near the bottom of the stairs. That was where the mother sometimes stayed.

Lanh descended and knocked, and knocked again, and called her name. Another neighbor emerged, shook his head, said something about illness, and retreated inside.

I am sentenced to betrayal, Lanh realized. *I can betray Pen or betray Mai—or betray the blood of my country.*

"Thuận," he asked that evening, "can we take that little girl? Keep her just until her mother reappears?"

"If she reappears," said Thuận. "Mothers are disappearing. Fathers, too. Who knows if she is even still alive? Wouldn't she have gone to the home for the girl? What about the father?"

"A soldier, I think."

"Dead or alive?"

"I don't know."

"So you want to stop Pen and Julie from giving this girl a safe home in America."

"It's her parents' decision!" His near shout made Thuận blink. Then, a whisper so his girls couldn't hear: "How would you feel if somebody took Linh and Hiền to America, no matter how rich a place it is?"

"I would be torn into sorrow," she finally whispered. "But if I could not give them a good life here, I would want them to have a good life there." Her sigh, a loving sigh, enveloped him, comforted him, steadied him. Yet he also heard it as a sigh of distress for what he might choose for them all.

A mother had to think of her children's lives more than her own happiness, Thuận went on. Then she reached to him. "I love you for knowing that it's wrong. But keeping her here without knowing about her mother is also wrong. There are two wrongs. Which one is less wrong?"

"We are always balancing wrongs." Could he balance the wrong he had done to Vinh?

Lanh climbed to his loft and pulled out his bamboo flute. The tune he played, by Trịnh Công Sơn, sang the words inside his thoughts, and Thuận heard them too.

The bird boards on the bamboo branch
The fish boards in a crevice of spring water
I myself am a boarder in this world
In one hundred years I'll return to the edge of the sky

The phone call came at home late in the sleepless night. Pen recognized the diplomat's voice, low and fast, saying

listen carefully, brief your staff, they will have two hours' notice, say nothing to others, bring nothing but what they can
carry in pockets and hide in their clothing, we will call your
office in the daytime or your home at night to tell you when
and where.

Pen phoned Tân and got a drowsy voice. "Tân, sorry to
wake you. Please have Lanh and Kỳ meet me at the bureau
at eight a.m., okay?" Tân, the canny truster of people, felt a
lightness in his chest for the first time since the fall of Phước
Bình.

Lanh felt the opposite and shook Thuận gently awake.
"I think Pen is arranging to get the staff out," he whispered.
Her face blossomed like jasmine, then dulled. Dread pound-
ed him.

"And the families?"

"I assume. Nobody would leave without their family.
We're meeting in the morning. He'll tell us."

She wrapped him tightly, as if she could clutch and carry
him as she flew away. She swallowed the question that would
have to be put between them. When they finally eased into
sleep, they both dreamt of standing at the brink of a broad
jungle ravine, calling to each other as loudly as they could
but not able to make out each other's words, which fell into
the wind. Thuận saw the children next to Lanh on the other
side. Lanh saw the children next to Thuận on the other side.

Lanh did not dare skip his morning routine, it would
only make the pho man suspicious. Where was that guy
Minh? He wondered and didn't ask. The pho man was
chary anyway as Lanh shoveled and slurped with hardly a
word. To a dubious look and a mundane question about the

family, Lanh gave a routine answer, said work was frantic, and putted off on his scooter into the steaming sunlight.

The eight o'clock meeting did not go well. Pen had little information except that the embassy would try to get them and their immediate families out on short notice, secretly. Tân and Kỳ peppered him with urgent pleas for mothers, fathers, uncles, brothers, cousins. And for at least one small bag each for valuables and cherished heirlooms small enough to carry. Lanh did not join the chorus, but he thought about his flute.

"I probably need numbers," said Pen. "How many in your families?" Tân and Kỳ ticked off their wives, their children. Lanh watched the floor.

"Lanh? Four of you, right? Thuận, Linh, and Hiền?" Lanh just nodded as if he had been asked to confess to a crime.

The phone at Lanh's home rang that night. Rosie's insistent voice, torn by static: "You won't leave, will you?" It was not a question. "You will be rootless!"

"What?" He hadn't caught the word.

"Rootless! Without roots. Without ties to what you love! You will be in exile!"

Thuận was listening to his end, so he couldn't answer aloud. "Who?" she asked. He mouthed Rosie's name, which made Thuận fold her arms across her chest.

"Lanh? Lanh? Are you there?" The crackly voice had a pitch of hysteria.

"I hear you," he replied at last.

"What are you going to do? Vietnam will finally be free."

He exhaled into the phone while Thuận watched him like a falcon.

"Don't worry about us," he said. "We'll be fine. You know I'm a buffalo boy."

He hung up, angry tears filled Thuận's eyes. *Lucky the girls are asleep. Now is the time.*

The conversation, if that's what it could be called, scarcely needed words. They came only in fragments of life, future, children, hope, possibility, danger, gambling into the unknown. Roots—yes, roots.

Rosie had told him what he already suffered, adding a word—*exile*—that had not occurred before in his agony of choice. It crystallized loss. Thuận held him in a devastated embrace. They grasped at each other as if to touch every part of their years, those before this instant and those coming after.

Early in the morning, still in bed before the girls awoke, she tried to get practical. What would he do for work in Saigon? Translate as before, teach English. What if he was arrested? For what?

"Do you really think you can travel outside the neat boxes you detest once the Communists rule?"

That snuffed out his strength to answer.

"I love you for that," Thuận went on. She loved him for his resistance, she told him, for never accepting the categories imposed on them all. "But there won't be any choice of categories. There will be only one category." Lanh shook his head so slightly that his disagreement looked unsure.

"What would I do in America?" he asked. "Be a waiter in a Chinese restaurant?"

"America has opportunity."

"America does not have the opportunity to be Vietnamese, to taste the perfume of our rice, to eat our mangos, to roam our mountains, to hear our language and our music all around us. Now is mango season. Do they have mango season in Boston?"

"What if they won't let me be a teacher anymore?" she answered. And her question soothed Lanh's stare of worry: the nightmare of Thuận across the jungled ravine. She would stay with him, whether here or there.

She saw him ease, and she spoke a clear answer to the unasked question. "Of course I will be with you. I will never leave you. But shouldn't we both agree? If we go, someday we could return, if. If."

"If," he said. "Yes, if. If what? If they decide to let us back after we gave up on our country? And by then would Linh and Hiền give up materialistic America?"

This was not the level where the true roads intersected. That they both understood. "We are thinking instead of feeling," Lanh said. "This is not about the head. It's about the heart. Our bodies can leave. Our hearts will stay behind. Better to keep them together."

He might have named her mother, her brothers, her sister, their nieces and nephews, all their lifelong friendships that would be thrown away like scattered chaff. But he could see her resignation. She slumped her shoulders in retreat, then had to get the kids up and leave hastily for her waning days of teaching. He nearly said aloud, *What kind of victory have I won?*

Rumors stalked the Saigon streets. An American shrimp boat captain was charging in gold to take corrupt

Vietnamese officials to US ships standing offshore. Pilots, for a fee, were making room for BUFEs. American contractors were collecting bribes to claim Vietnamese bar girls as their wives to get them past airport guards onto US military flights; the contractors would then peel off, return to the city, and pick up the next women packaged in net stockings and skin-tight miniskirts. An American doctor at the Seventh Day Adventist Hospital disguised his Vietnamese girlfriend as a nun escorting a planeload of children in the Babylift. All "good stories," none checkable or reportable in the mêlée of collapse.

A more significant story at the airport did not generate a single rumor. Working in a frenzy against an unknown deadline, a maintenance crew cannibalized parts from locks on the rear pressure door of a giant Air Force C-5A Galaxy to use on other aircraft. When a mechanic reinstalled the locks, he reversed a cam and committed other unseen errors, discovered during a pre-flight check that found only two of seven locks in working order. The plane was grounded.

But it was scheduled to fly hundreds of supposed orphans and adult escorts to Clark Air Base in the Philippines on Friday, including all left by their mothers in Erik's home. Pressed to get the plane cleared, another maintenance crew made a hasty inspection and overlooked the locks.

Pen did not know any of this. Nor did any other correspondent. Nor did Erik, who shepherded his charges into buses for the ride to Tansonnhut.

Nor did Lanh know that the old woman had finally spotted Mai's mother, who entered the front door with a gaunt man in khakis, a bloody bandage on his arm. Hearing what the old woman had to say brought alarm to them both, and a rush out into the alley and away.

The parents found the dusty yard in front of Erik's house strewn with toys: the soggy soccer ball, the tin cans and bits of broken brick, dried corn cobs, even a stray marble here and there. The gigantic house was empty. Their calls of "Mai! Mai!" echoed without response. Neatly perched on the edge of the veranda were several pairs of yellowed chopsticks and a brown rubber ball.

Lanh and Pen spent most of the day buttonholing civilians who had toiled their way down from the Central Highlands and Danang. Their children were unlike other children. They did not flock to the American. They did not crowd around giggling to touch his hairy arms. They did not pester Lanh gleefully to take their pictures, and did not make funny faces into the camera he aimed at them. They seemed to have blinkered senses. Their dark eyes were opaque pools, their mouths set in straight lines, spiritless.

In mid-afternoon, a story occurred to Pen the way a lightbulb turns on over a cartoon character's head: juxtapose the children staying and the children leaving. He and Lanh would go from the desolate kids in Saigon's streets to the airport, to the kids on the cusp of rescue. Lanh winced. *Rescue from their own country?*

"It will be heartbreaking and heartening all at once," Pen said.

"It will be heartbreaking and heartbreaking all at once," Lanh countered.

"What do you mean?"

"Children suffering here and children about to suffer there. They will be—what's the word?—uprooted. From their land, their people, their culture."

"Oh," Pen said. A second passed. "This is a wage of war."

"This is a curse of Vietnam, when abandonment is salvation. The Americans abandoned Vietnam. The Communists and the government have abandoned Vietnam's honor. And now Vietnam's children—the so-called lucky children—are being forced to abandon their heritage."

Pen let out a short hum of pain. "I see. Maybe I see. You know we are adopting Mai, right? So are we forcing her to abandon her heritage? She will grow a new heritage, an American heritage, which contains roots from all over the world, Lanh. She can also keep her Vietnamese heritage, we'll see to it. You, too, when you get to the States." Lanh looked away.

"You'll see," Pen went on bravely across the breach. "We don't force people to forget where they came from, and many hold onto their customs and languages. Well, some want to forget. Some feel forced, that's true, because the society can be unkind. They don't want to stand out, they want to assimilate and blend in and become just American. They want to put the past away and move on. The US is full of people who left their origins behind because they were driven from home by persecution or deprivation or fear. Or war."

"These are little kids!" Lanh shot back sharply. "They will forget Vietnam. They are not deciding anything. They are completely powerless."

"Okay, good point," Pen stumbled. "Yes, yes. They are. True. I wish I could quote you, Lanh. Maybe we can find somebody to say that so I can get it into the story."

"Nobody will say that. It is too wise!"

"Quite right, Lanh. Most of what you say is too wise to get into the paper."

The guard detail at Tansonnhut airport was tight and strict. Soldiers of the regular South Vietnamese army stopped every vehicle, checked every occupant's documents, and turned away almost everybody who had no proof of passage on a flight. Pen's and Lanh's press cards got them through, and they entered the teeming terminal.

Children of all sizes jammed every inch of space, serious adults towered over them. The hall echoed with raucous cries and chatter, grown-ups bounced babies in their arms, handed snacks to toddlers, changed diapers on benches, checked their watches, tried to be cheerful. A few quick conversations through Lanh with older kids about their futures and fears and families filled Pen's notebook with enough. He spotted Erik, a blond tower rising from a cluster of brown skin and black hair.

The rescuers were mostly white, the rescued were Asians. The rescued were being saved from the maelstrom created by the rescuers, who were devout believers in their superiority. If the saviors had a collective thought, Pen realized, it would be: *We are taking them not just from war but from a lower world.*

"This is exhilarating," Pen exclaimed nonetheless. "Uplifting. A bright spot." Lanh winced. Pen stopped, read Lanh's face for a moment, gazed across the tangle of children, and then added, "But let's see if anybody has misgivings." He began interviewing adults, asking the provocative question planted in his doubts by Lanh, getting glares of puzzled resentment and no useful quotes. He watched for a glance of respect from Lanh.

There was Mai, visible at moments through the milling crowd. She didn't see him. She was crying.

Should I go tell her that we hope she can come live with us, be part of our family? It would be too close to a promise. A little girl would cling to a promise, and promises are only misty intentions, he had learned from Lanh. But he was hungry for a hug, so he pushed and waded through the low tangle of children until she caught sight of him and stretched up her arms and he picked her up high above the landscape for a long, long time, her wet cheeks against his.

Erik's group was called first. They moved eagerly out onto the tarmac, where the C-5A Galaxy stood like a great ark, its huge rear loading ramp open to receive the saved. Toddlers holding hands with older kids, infants in the arms of volunteers from orphanages and charities, uniformed Air Force flight crewmen, medics and nurses, teachers from the embassy school, and whoever else had been able to wangle a place streamed in a broad swath across the scorching cement, up the ramp, and into the cavernous darkness of the aircraft.

Pen and Lanh stood watching for a while. With hundreds inside, the rear door swung up slowly like a drawbridge, the four mammoth engines started with a roar, and the plane lumbered to the runway. When Pen and Lanh looked at each other as if to ask if they should get back to the office, Pen saw fragility in Lanh for the first time.

"I wouldn't mind something to eat," said Pen. Upstairs they found a willing fellow behind the counter in the snack bar ready with a scant Chinese menu. The corn and crab soup came diluted and without crabmeat, a fitting comment on the enervating day. Lanh gave a resentful look, and they said nothing as they ate. Pen flipped through his notebook, penciling in lines and brackets to highlight quotes and color for his story. Then he suddenly told Lanh, in a half whisper, that watching the children on the tarmac made him keep seeing Vinh's children on the tarmac. Lanh closed his eyes and looked upward and seemed to hold his breath forever. Then he asked, "Which ones are saved?" Pen did not answer.

As the first aboard, Erik and his scores of children were given seats in the cargo bay, and as more kids and escorts flowed in and filled that lower deck, others flooded up into the second level. With some difficulty, the crew closed the aft pressure door, whose reversed cam lit the indicator showing it secured. Through the terminal windows, Pen watched the plane wheel down the runway and lift off effortlessly. It climbed and turned eastward toward the South China Sea and out of sight.

In the cockpit, the arrows on the altimeter spun clockwise until they pointed to 23,000 feet, where a callous rule of physics took over. With the cabin pressure at the equivalent of 8,000 feet, its pressure exceeded the air pressure outside by just too much for the two working locks on the rear pressure door. The door blew, the plane lurched as if slapped by a great hand. Shards cut through the center cargo door, part of the loading ramp, the rudder cables, an elevator, and several crewmen inside. A howling hole of wild wind and terrible sunlight lashed the cave of the aircraft, whipping pens and eyeglasses around like shrapnel.

In the cockpit, Captain Bud Traynor and his co-pilot, Captain Tilford Harp, strapped on yellow masks and fought at the controls, which made nothing happen, nothing at all. They had no rudder. Harp tried his pitch control. No response. Nothing. Suddenly some old advice of Bud's pilot father flashed back to him: more power. So he pushed the throttles forward, more on the two starboard engines to turn the plane back toward Tansonnhut. The elevators, stuck in a trim position for 260 knots, would keep the plane level as long as they maintained that speed: faster, they would climb, slower, they would dive. As Traynor banked left and began to descend, the plane accelerated, the nose rose steeply, the speed dropped close to a stall. He turned right, pulled back on the throttles, the aircraft dove, the speed rose again. And so Bud Traynor and Tilford Harp maneuvered by trial and error, like commanders in an unfamiliar war, back over land and toward the airport.

The wind was colder than any child had ever felt, the roar louder than any sound they'd ever heard. Below, the entire back of the plane opened to the startling blue of the sea, then an edge of bright white sand, then the green of land. Crying, screaming kids outnumbered the oxygen masks, so medics and crewmen moved masks from one to another, bundled and padded children, reassured them through their own hysteria, and strapped everyone in for a crash landing.

Pen and Lanh finished their unsatisfying soup, rose slowly to leave, and were caught by the rise of sirens. *An attack? Run or stay and watch?* The chronic dilemma of the newsman. It was odd. No rumble of artillery, no tearing sound of NVA rockets, no pop of small arms fire. Then a growl of diesel engines and, through the windows, flashing lights of fire trucks racing toward a runway.

Pen and Lanh ran but not to safety, down to the ground floor, out onto the tarmac, which swarmed with chaos. Lanh shot rapid questions at one airport worker after another but got shrugs until a uniformed official appeared with the news: emergency landing. Everybody back inside.

What happened? Which plane? How serious? The Babylift? Lanh put Pen's questions to the man, who walked him away from the eavesdroppers. Lanh returned like a mourner.

"It's the Babylift plane. There's serious damage."

Using only his engines, Bud Traynor lined up with the runway and lowered the landing gear. Everything looked good. Then the gear increased the drag, pulling the airspeed too low to keep the plane aloft. The runway lay two miles ahead, too far to reach. Yelling to each other over the whoosh of wind, the pilots shoved the throttles all the way full to bring the nose up, and then, just before hitting the ground, cut all power to zero.

The plane was going fast. It skidded through a rice paddy, then bounced into the air again, flew across the Saigon River, and banged down in a marshy paddy that ripped through its underbelly, broke the fuselage into four parts, and demolished the lower deck. Fires erupted.

From the terminal, Lanh and Pen heard the awful distant thumps and crunches and saw the black smoke rising in a plume. Fire trucks stopped at the edge of the field, unable to advance. Pen gave a long, low wail. Lanh touched his shoulder like a brother.

Not a sound emerged from the remnants of the lower deck. Annihilation is voiceless. Adults on the upper level began to stir, unstrap themselves, lift children and carry them through the twisted sheets of metal out and away from the flames.

The old reporter's reflex kicked in: Write down the time. It was 4:45 p.m. on Friday, April 4, 1975. Get the numbers from the Air Force sergeant standing there shocked. "Okay," he looked at his clipboard. "I don't have children's names, but we counted two hundred forty-three kids and sixty-two adults."

The minutes hovered. Across the expanse of the airport, nothing moved. Then, the flapping noise of helicopter rotors chopped the air into pieces and scattered them across the war. Pen fixed on the plume of smoke. He could not look away. The helicopters entered his field of vision and one by one, like dragonflies, disappeared at the base of the black tower.

"There's no way to get there," Lanh said softly. "It's all mud. We can't drive. We could walk, but it would take until dark. We would have only the moonlight and the flames to guide us. Moonlight and flames."

Staying busy usually kept exhaustion and tumult at bay— and fear, too, fear that only sneaked in afterwards, under the cover of silence. This was different. It was not coming from outside, not to be repelled and walled off. This infiltrated and took up residence. Pen imagined it like a virus, lodged in every cell. In Roxbury, it had passed through him swiftly, in and out like a fleeting chill. But just long enough. Just too long.

Before retreating to his bed, which is what his body craved, he answered Julie's frantic question. Yes, he Telexed, it was that plane. No, I don't know who survived. He sent Lanh and Tân to canvass hospitals and gather names of the anonymous children still alive. "Look at their faces," he instructed Lanh. "You'll recognize Mai . . ." He badgered the embassy and the Air Force for names of adults, dead and alive. They wouldn't give him the dead before notifying next of kin. But they released the list of survivors. The name Erik Sendstad was not among them. This he Telexed to Julie with all that it implied about Mai. He was glad he wasn't with her to hear her all-night weeping.

Pen withdrew into the cocoon of his air-conditioned bedroom. He called the office, told Tân he would not be in and to message Boston to use the wires. He thought he was shivering with fever. His daylight dreams were bizarrely knotted with serpents. All his muscles wanted a year's rest.

How many hours or days he was not sure. Nghi came and went, left him meals. "Nghi," he remembered to ask her. They spoke only broken French together. "Nghi, do you want to leave—*partir*? *Avec famille? Partir de Vietnam?*" She took a string of seconds to grasp the meaning, nodded a nervous yes. When the call came, he tried to explain, she would gather her husband and children in a certain place, carrying nothing. Tell no one. He put his finger to his lips.

Tân kept phoning him to read agitated messages from Boston, from Julie, from colleagues. Was he okay? *No, I'm damned well not okay.* "Yes, Tân, I'm feeling better. I'll be in." A cyclo would be slow and dangerous, making him a target. So would his orange bike. A taxi might be driven by a

VC sympathizer or an ordinary man appropriately pissed at Americans. "Can you have Mr. Kỳ pick me up in an hour?"

In the cool oasis of the office, the buzzing of motorbikes on Tự Do Street was muffled by the noisy air conditioner and the constant clacking of the AP and Reuters teletypes. Tân and Mr. Kỳ were fidgety. Lanh relaxed, reading a newspaper that he'd bought just before the copies were confiscated by police. The latest Telex from Julie, still on the machine, asked again about Hạnh, urgently.

The phone rang and sent electric tension through the room. "For you," Tân said, and handed it to Pen.

"At two fifteen at the northwest corner of Hai Bà Trưng and Gia Long. Got it?"

"Got it. Thanks."

He told them. The meeting place gave Lanh a wan smile. Tân and Mr. Kỳ jumped for the phone, one after another, practically shouting to their wives in rapid-fire Vietnamese. Tân, tear-eyed, embraced Pen and bombarded him with thanks. Mr. Kỳ shook his hand and half bowed. Pen mumbled well wishes, and they were out the door. Lanh didn't move, didn't call.

"I'm not going," he said. "Thuận and I are staying. This is our home. You probably guessed."

"I guessed," Pen said. But even what you expect can surprise you when it happens, Pen thought, as when the sun rises in a blaze at dawn or the rain ends in freshness. Or the gathering storm finally comes. "I guessed, but are you sure? To give up the chance to leave is a momentous decision."

"Either way it's a momentous decision. It is fate. Even the meeting place. Hai Bà Trưng Street, the two Trưng sisters who drove out the Chinese forty years after your Jesus?

And Gia Long Street! The unifier of Vietnam, the first emperor of the Nguyễn dynasty. If Americans had paid attention to how we name our streets, they would have understood. It is an omen."

"Lanh, think hard about this. What does Thuận say? A door is opening to you. Don't let it slam shut."

"I think with my head. I act with my heart. Thuận understands."

Much later, Pen's regrets echoed with arguments he might have made, promises he had no way of keeping, warnings he had no cause to give. They wouldn't have uprooted Lanh, he knew, but he might have tried. Now, he stood down. He said he understood, although he did not, entirely. He said he was saddened by the parting of a friendship. "Come back and visit!" cried Lanh with such confidence.

"Please call Nghi," Pen asked. But there was no answer at Pen's house, and none at hers.

"Please keep trying. She wants to get out. I'm staying for a while, and we still have work to do. But before I leave I'll make sure you have dollars, and my Pentax and the telephoto lens. You have the combination to the safe? I'll write it down. Everything in the office is yours—typewriters, phones, furniture, whatever you can sell if you need to." Lanh did not react, not visibly. Inside, gratitude and humiliation played a clashing chord.

Pen walked the few blocks to the First National City Bank and emptied the office account, taking all the cash in green, some $5,000. The teller didn't flinch. She must have grown numb as the undoing paraded across her life hour after hour. Pen hurried to the office, spun the black knob on the old steel French safe in the back of a closet, pulled down the large brass lever, and placed the thick envelope of bills on the shelf. He added his camera from his desk drawer.

"Thank you," Lanh said quietly.

Pen waved away his thanks. "How about Nghi?"

"Can't locate her."

CHAPTER 17

E arly thunder rumbled ahead of the monsoons, due about six weeks away in June. Anyone attuned to the signature sounds of weapons—which meant everyone—could tell that the North Vietnamese had not yet begun shelling the airport to the northwest. The thunder heralded the "mango rains" of sweeping squalls when mangoes ripened and appeared in market bins and sidewalk stalls, stacked invitingly by women from the countryside. Miraculously, mangoes adorned the markets still, but at desperate prices for whatever slivers of cash sellers could collect before their world crashed down.

Vietnamese never give up, Lanh thought.

He also knew to amend his pride. He started seeing olive-drab shirts, belts, boots, and helmets strewn along sidewalks and alleyways, even discarded rifles tossed by soldiers eager to shed any military trace. No passersby were stealing them. As much corrosion as Lanh had sensed, the collapse was rolling toward him with more velocity than he'd imagined.

And as much hollowness as Pen had witnessed in South Vietnamese forces, he'd reported too little on it. His newspaper had trained him never to use the future tense, a wise rule against predictions. But with his writing trapped in the present and the past, that was what he was able to see. Yes, writing set his field of vision, not the other way around.

Outside the capital, the North Vietnamese met virtually no resistance. Refugees from Nha Trang, on the coast, described mass flight, but well before the NVA was even close. The only impediment to their advance was the maximum speed of their tanks. Pen thought of Cornelius Ryan's line in *A Bridge Too Far*: They were losing the war faster than the enemy could win it.

The Telex kept rattling with Julie's pleas for Hạnh, and for Pen to leave.

MY PRECIOUS DARLING, ALL MY LOVE.

The words struck a false note in the city's disharmony of desperation. There was no love here any longer, nothing precious. Each message contained a beat of panic—hers amplifying his. But fear would have to wait. It wasn't terror that had reduced him to his bed. It was the fever of sorrow, he realized. *Later, I will have the luxury of fear. This will not be Roxbury.*

He and Lanh chased around the city. They muscled into crowds of frightened families crammed on the river wharves pushing onto tugs, barges, fishing boats. As a barge wallowing with refugees cast off its thick ropes, a man tossed a baby from the dock into the crowd aboard. Two men reached and caught the infant, its tiny arms flailing like a rag doll. Lanh's photo would become an icon of defeat. The father leapt toward the barge, nearly made it, grabbed the rusty gunwale, slipped, and fell with an unheard splash into the oily water.

He did not come up. A woman on the wharf wailed, another siren of grief singing in the city.

At the embassy, Pen and Lanh watched throngs thicken outside the walls as choppers touched down inside. Lanh tried to catch a few phrases from frantic men with wives and children in tow, who waved ID cards and papers in the faces of stoic US Marines. The observer's contortions, twisting into a crowd, offered no distance to him, no paces back. He was jostled by an American with a sand-colored crew cut, tattoos running down below the short sleeves of his tight muscle shirt. Lanh was sure he heard the man mutter "fucking gooks" as he pushed and elbowed women, tossed children aside, threw a punch at a Vietnamese blocking the gate, and managed to slip through as a Marine cracked it open.

"This is how we leave?" said Pen. "Climbing over the backs of our Vietnamese friends?"

"We have strong backs."

"I do not want to leave that way."

"Have you thought of staying? I hear Mandell will."

Pen shook his head. "Boston told me no. I didn't even ask."

"Boston has lawyers."

"I have a wife."

"I'm not trying to persuade you. But it would be what you call a good story—after the fall, liberation." Pen said nothing. *What redemption after Roxbury! They'd be amazed.*

Lanh drove them to Tansonnhut through neighborhoods clutched in busy hesitation, not far from his own alleyway. His neighbors' rapid preparations were carried out close to home, tentatively, easily suspended at a stroke of alarm. He pictured Thuận wrapping family photographs and treasured letters in torn cloth tied with twine, and prying boards loose from the back of a cluttered closet as a hiding place. Lanh had tried to mock her lightly, but she'd answered with a dark look.

At the airport checkpoint, thick envelopes were being thrust from car windows into the hands of a police sergeant with an M1 carbine slung over his shoulder in menacing nonchalance. Inside, the terminal pulsated with the sweat of fear, its customs counters empty of inspectors, its waiting areas jammed with favored or canny Vietnamese cleared to board the planes that were streaking in and out along the runways. One man Lanh recognized as the maître d' of the Indochine restaurant in Nha Trang. He looked remarkably pressed and sterile, as if he were about to escort diners to a table.

"Fine French and Vietnamese," Lanh told Pen. "Too bad we never got there."

Snatches of conversation passed through Lanh and landed in Pen's notebook as disjointed scribblings. Whenever a flight number was called, a clump of refugees surged forward as the rest moaned with disappointed apprehension. Through the window, studying a stairway ramp filled with boarding passengers, Pen was hit by a pang of desire to climb aboard right then. Jamison had done it, telling him, "Hell, we're a weekly. The NVA will miss our deadline!" He'd laughed alone at his own joke.

"What do you think?" Pen asked.

"Do you mean when you should leave," said Lanh, "or whether you should stay?"

"No, about Jamison. Should he be considered a coward, or does it take courage to leave behind the best story of your career?"

"It would take me courage to leave," said Lanh. "Courage I don't have."

"You have the courage to stay."

"I have no interest in courage—or cowardice. There has been too much of both, and see what they've done to us."

Back on Tự Do Street, the buzz and whine of motorbikes was dampening somewhat. If you can't become a refugee in the common way, you become a refugee in your own way, in your own rooms behind your own windows. The country had seen cascades of futile refugees: Danang from Huế, the coast from the Highlands, Saigon from everywhere else, and now—from Saigon—to the innermost shelter of home and family. Pen pulled from his notes and wrote as fast as he could, quick and dirty prose that editors would have to clean up. Some things he used to care about didn't matter today.

The office phone gave a few rings. Lanh answered, handed it to Pen, who listened to a woman's voice. "This is Sally Falmouth from the embassy. I'm a friend of your wife's—well, an acquaintance. I'm calling with evacuation information. Please don't repeat it if anyone is with you who can hear it. Ready?"

"Yes."

"I am going to list thirteen assembly points. Please choose the one closest to you and go there when the signal is given. The signal will be when the American radio station plays 'I'm Dreaming of a White Christmas' and the announcer says, 'The temperature in Saigon is 105 degrees and rising.' Understand?"

"Are you shitting me?"

She snickered but said, "No. If you want to be evacuated, be there."

He hung up and told Lanh, and they gave each other the deepest laugh they'd had in weeks. "Only the Americans," said Pen.

Barely two hours later, after he'd filed his piece, a young Vietnamese man passing him on the street started humming "I'm Dreaming . . ." then smiled with a sneer. The next morning, as he parked and walked to the bureau, a woman selling mangoes said in English, "White Christmas." There were no secrets anymore in Saigon, if there ever had been.

Pen figured he would get ready. He would cram what would fit in his favorite airline handbag, white with red letters spelling "Air Cambodge." It was already a keepsake of an ancient era, obliterated by Khmer Rouge nihilism in the ten days since they took Phnom Penh. The North Vietnamese would not execute the present with such madness, he was certain. The main insanities in town were Ambassador Martin's, still expecting survival, and his minions', predicting a Communist bloodbath. Lanh didn't expect it, so neither did Pen. Perhaps he should stay to see for himself. He would pack just in case, to keep his options open: his passport, notebooks, dopp kit, dollars, a change of clothes, and a small carving of a graceful apsara dancer he'd picked up in Cambodia. Julie had taken out her thick portfolio of art, thank goodness. The bag he would now keep with him at all times. Just to keep his options open. No point slamming a door.

His kitchen had gone out of business. Its shelves were emptying. Nghi had not come to work for several days. Maybe she'd gone to her parents in the Delta after missing the evacuation. Maybe she decided, like Madame Bian, not to associate with an American. Maybe she was in the crowds on the river wharf. Or were she and her husband and children crushing frantically against the embassy walls? He called her number. No answer. Rice noodles, boiling water, a little pork still in the fridge. Not the Indochine in Nha Trang, apparently, but sustaining.

About 7:30, as he was finishing his new job of washing dishes, a menacing boom rattled the windows, followed by another explosion, then another, then another. He ran outside. The blasts seemed to come from the northeast. Long Bình, he thought, the huge ammunition depot. He jogged to the end of his alley, into the street. A few people had the same idea, and one was pointing to a malicious glow far past rooftops and tamarind trees. He drove the office car to the bureau, leapt up the stairs, and scanned the AP and Reuters wires. Yes, probably Long Bình. He called the Defense Attaché's office, and the duty officer generously told him almost nothing, as usual, except exactly what he wanted to know: "Sorry, I'm busy with the attack on Long Bình. Can't talk."

A good reporter writes down times, sequences, small details, Pen knew, to give a story verisimilitude, a word he loved. But the turbulence was mangling his equilibrium. He was off balance, careening from sensation to emotion, fascinated and driven and sickened by his voyeurism—a spectator at risk, a participant apart. He wrote and wrote the way a unicyclist rides and rides to keep from falling. The words he sent skyward were merely entertaining; none would tear away the pall of the approaching "end." The end of what? The end of freedom? It was only a mirage, easily evaporating in the heat of inquisition. Ask the political prisoners. The end of prosperity? It was a stage set propped up by American dollars. The end of bucolic family comfort among the fields and orchards? It was strafed and mined. The end of war?

"Yes, the end of war," Lanh said, listening to Pen's thoughts. "So why should we be in such dread?"

"The unknown," Pen offered. "Even war became a known, like a bad habit. Its absence is unpredictable."

"You have learned something," Lanh conceded.

With their little knives and broken boards, Colonel Giang's men at Camp Davis had finished digging out a bunker just large enough for their small contingent, and after his crackling radio received a coded message, he ordered them inside. Tansonnhut would be a target. Sinewy from years laboring north to south and back along the Hồ Chí Minh Trail, calloused by living cramped in the Củ Chi tunnels, Giang had gained a reputation among his troops for charming ruthlessness. They obeyed.

Rockets started hissing into the airport. Sometimes they sounded like ripping canvas. A couple of bombs cratered a runway—dropped by South Vietnamese pilots infuriated by the evacuation who then flew off to U-Tapao air base in Thailand, or so the theory went. NVA artillery shells blew holes in taxiways, spraying hot shrapnel into aircraft parked nearby, etching them into monuments of war. The moment was coming, Pen felt. The crossroads.

He looked up from his typewriter at a slender woman at the office door. The face contained all of Vietnam's grief, terror, suffering, and privilege at once, haughty and scared, utterly dependent and completely entitled. "I am Hạnh, remember?" said the woman, the eyes hard, wary, and pleading.

"Oh." Pen's word sank with the falling tone of finality that tries to end conversation.

"I need to leave."

"So does everybody, or so they believe."

"Look, I really need to leave. I'll be shot. Maybe my husband will too."

Pen felt weariness rise like water in a sinking boat. Julie. Hạnh. For a flicker of an instant, he thought that if he could, he might help. "But I can't help. I have no way now. If you have connections with the embassy—"

"I can't get near the embassy. Maybe you can?"

"I would be torn into many small pieces if I tried. I'm sorry. No can do."

"I will be killed."

Now Pen was getting curious. He stood to face the woman, squinted at her, and tried to look like one of the interrogators he'd heard so much about. "Why do you think so? Who are you, anyway? Not just a tennis teacher?"

"I can't say more. I just know."

"An agent? An official? An informer? What?"

Hạnh was good. Even the mighty ocean ripples in a breeze, but this woman's expression fluttered not a bit. She watched Pen for a few long seconds, perhaps to see what flaws might appear in his resolve, then backed away, toward the door.

"Please give my warm wishes to Julie," and then she was gone. If Pen had been standing on the sidewalk instead of the tile floor of his office, he would have spat.

The phone again. A British accent, Byron of the *Times,* the self-appointed evacuation marshal. "I'd sing 'I'm Dreaming of a White Christmas,'" he said dryly, "but I can't carry a tune. It's time, Pen, with a slight change. Meet in one hour at eighty-seven Nguyễn Đình Chiểu."

"Isn't that where Air America pilots live?"

"Right-o, mate. They're going to take us off the roof in a chopper. Great fun. See you there."

The conveyor belt was moving steadily in one direction only. He could jump off if he had the stamina and the nerve. And he would test the thread holding him to Julie. *Selfish! You wanted to prove yourself, risk yourself at my expense!* That might be her true voice behind whatever sugary welcome she would give him. And her true voice would be almost right.

"You've decided," said Lanh.

"It's been decided. I don't feel like I'm making choices."

"Choices have been scarce in Vietnam."

"So I've seen. The safe's combination. You have it, right?"

"Yes. Thanks. I'll try to be in touch."

"And I'll try to come back."

"Sure. We'll go to the Indochine." A wistful smile between them.

Pen typed out a quick Telex:

MURPHY EXPEN DEPARTING SAIGON DESTINATION UNKNOWN. PLEASE ADVISE JULIE SIAM INTERCON. CHEERS.

"I'll drive you," Lanh said. Pen left his helmet and flak jacket hanging on a peg inside the office door, tools of the trade he hoped never to need anywhere again.

A small cluster of foreigners milled about in front of number 87. Lanh got out ceremoniously and stood by Pen. For men of fluency, these two had none. Their words were lost in a whirlpool that dragged them down to a strong handshake, an unprecedented hug, averted eyes, and a separation without looking back.

Choppers were ferrying Americans and Vietnamese to the Seventh Fleet offshore, but this Huey took them from the rooftop to the airport, flying fast and high enough to avoid the small-arms fire from South Vietnamese soldiers peppering the air—an angry farewell by a bunch of lousy shots, the amused pilot observed. Orange tracers passed in wide arcs. "Thank God we fucked up their training," he shouted over his shoulder. In a whirl of dust, the chopper landed at a makeshift pad near the DAO building, where flagpoles and trees had been taken down to make room for the climax.

Awful pillars of smoke rose from flames and explosions across the airfield. Inside the building, the newest evacuees were funneled through corridors, told to sit on the floor with their backs to the wall, and commanded by a Marine corporal to turn over any weapons. He passed down the line, holding out a box that rapidly filled with an astonishing assortment of handguns yanked from waistbands and knapsacks. Pen gawked. *Should I have been armed all this time?*

They waited. The air conditioning gave out. The vending machines emptied of snacks and drinks. Stupidly, neither Pen nor most of the others had brought anything to read. They had only themselves, a few US Air Force guys ready to turn out the lights, and whatever war stories they could think up.

There was the one about the guy from CBS who stood on a safe road somewhere to report on a battle, and began, "On a road just like this one . . ." There was the mercenary pilot in Vientiane who kept a grenade in his room at the Lan Xang so he never had to pay the hotel. There was the NBC reporter who started doing a standup on camera, then dove for a ditch as if to dodge an incoming round. Then he climbed out of the ditch and complained, "That wasn't good enough. Let's do it again." He repeated his dive, and maybe a third time got it right. His office screwed up and air-freighted the whole roll of film to Hong Kong for transmission to network headquarters, where they were not amused. Oops.

They talked about Jamison, unable to keep his mouth shut about his trip to VC territory. And they looked at Pen for his take on his own interception. "I told nobody except my wife, so it's a mystery. I have a theory, though."

"You think they bugged your house?"

"Maybe, but that's not my theory." Their expectation made him pause to weigh the consequences. *I owe the woman nothing. I should resent her if she's guilty, but you never know who's listening.* "I don't want to speculate. The person is still here and could be at risk. Not Lanh, of course. You all know Lanh. Absolutely not Lanh. Another character, possibly."

Quickly Pen moved to stories about Lanh, his canny street smarts, his poetic translations, his patriotism transcending the warring sides, and then the time with the swaggering soldiers on the coastal road. The office car, tooling along perfectly, suddenly died. Mr. Kỳ coasted to the side, got out, flipped up the hood, fussed around, and scratched his head. Lanh picked out a couple of coconuts from a middle-aged fellow who neatly sliced off the tops with a machete, injected a straw in each, and handed them over for a few piasters.

"I always thought I wouldn't like coconut milk if it came out of a box in the fridge," Pen said, "but warm and straight from a coconut on a hot day—nothing more refreshing except a Ba Mươi Ba." Meanwhile, Mr. Kỳ was chatting up a guy nearby who told him of a mechanic back down the road a klick. He could use his bike to go get him. So Mr. Kỳ climbed on the bike and pedaled away while Pen and Lanh finished sucking out the coconut milk.

"That's the story?" Byron said.

"No, that's the beginning of the story. While we sat in the shade waiting for Mr. Kỳ, two ARVN strutted around us looking very clean and haughty in their combat-free camouflage. They were staring at me and fingering their M16s. Grenades hung from their belts, and their chests were crossed with bandoliers of ammunition. Lanh caught their eyes and whispered, 'I think they want your camera,' which was around my neck.

"He told me to stay where I was and walked over to them. He had a way of joking around with people, putting them at ease, but in this case only he was smiling. They were looking surly. In a few minutes, their expressions changed and they wandered off. I asked what happened.

"'I recognized their patches,' Lanh said, 'from a division near Quảng Trị. Being way down here, they must be deserters, and I told them that I knew Colonel Chi, their commander, and please give him my regards.'"

"Oh, nice," said Byron. "Everybody needs a Lanh."

"And the car?" somebody asked. The long boredom made every detail fascinating.

"Mr. Kỳ rode up with another guy on the back of the bike—the mechanic. He took the distributor apart, I think, and asked if anybody around had a pack of cigarettes. Somebody offered him a smoke, but the mechanic said, no, he just needed a piece of the foil inside the pack. He tore it and folded it and shaped it and stuck it into some contact and presto! The circuit was complete, the car turned over and caught, and we were on our way."

There followed a muttered consensus of awe for Vietnamese inventiveness in the face of deprivation, punctuated by wonder at the ARVN's inability to apply the ingenuity to fighting the war. "Because they were taught by us," said Pen, "and we forgot what we learned fighting the Redcoats in the Revolution," to which there arose a chorus of agreement, even from Byron.

More hopefuls crowded into the DAO lobby, suffocating with nervous cigarette smoke: Americans, Brits, Australians, an assortment of correspondents, military men, civilian contractors, a smattering of women and small children, and several Vietnamese men scrutinizing faces. From across at the airfield, every hiss and crack of a rocket, every hollow rush of an artillery round ratcheted up the tension index. Pen pictured a jagged upward graph. There was no point asking the corporal or his sergeant when they'd get a plane, because their jumpy stares were blank with ignorance.

Pen guessed that runways were getting damaged. The reporters asked one another how much longer fixed-wing aircraft could manage. Finally the corporal, holding a field telephone to his ear, nodded to nobody and climbed up on a chair. He shouted for attention. "Your C-47 is about to land and will taxi as close as he can. He can't stay on the ground for long, so go out this door here and wait, and when you see him, run as fast as you can and get on board before the mobs over there or the ARVN beat you to it." He shook his head in disgust.

And there it was, an ungainly gray-green tube, nose tilted upward as if it didn't want to be here, racing toward them on the ground, its two props flustering the air behind, braking to a halt about 200 meters away, the passengers dashing over and around tumbles of abandoned luggage, five ARVN soldiers racing on foot from ninety degrees to the right, followed by a throng of Vietnamese men in civilian clothes. The plane door swung open, and two beefy Americans in the lead put their shoulders to the rolling stairway, jamming it into the doorway in time for the evacuees to start clambering up in discords of aluminum clatter. Pen got just inside the door when the five soldiers reached the bottom of the ramp and blocked it. They lifted their M16s and aimed at the remaining passengers on the ground. From the doorway, two Air Force crewmen drew their .45s and screamed at them together, "You mothafuckas!" The pilot, with silver captain's bars on his collar, pushed his way to the door, where he tried to look like a drill sergeant who could just stand there and scare you into submission.

"Who speaks English and Vietnamese?" he called to his passengers. A Vietnamese man already aboard stepped forward. In his sparkling white shirt and black trousers, his black hair combed too neatly, he stood in a practiced posture of easy authority. "Tell these ARVN that they can come if they let the rest of my passengers on. And keep that other bunch off."

The other bunch was a scrum of civilians not far behind the troops. The authoritative man shouted his translation, the five soldiers turned and looked straight into the .45s leveled at their heads. A rifle swung toward the doorway. A crewman's shot rang cleanly through the soldier's forehead, snapping his head back in a cloud of red-gray mush. He crumpled like a scarecrow, the passengers hit the ground like combat veterans. The Vietnamese interpreter shouted something. The four soldiers took the crewman's offer, kicked the body aside, parted, and gestured to the last passengers, who climbed with their tear-streaked children into the cabin.

By now the desperate civilians were at the ramp, faced by the four remaining ARVN troops aiming directly at them. One fired over their heads. Another shot whined into the tarmac at their feet with a puff of concrete dust. Pen stared at the panicked faces and tried in flashes to imagine them as whole people with families and hopes. The gunfire forced the crowd to fall back a few steps, enough for the four soldiers to climb in. As the crew tried to push away the ramp, two men on the ground made a leap for it, grabbed the handrail, climbed, and got hands on the hatch coaming as the plane began to move—faster and faster, heading for the damaged runway with the men still holding on, their bodies swinging and jostling, the two crewmen trying to reach them without falling through the open doorway. One man then slid away, rolling like a bloody sack along the ground. The other managed a hand to a crewman's wrist, an ARVN soldier caught his other wrist, yanked until they got arms under armpits, and pulled him in like a flopping fish. He lay on his belly, heaving for breath.

A cheer went up from the cramped cabin, where every two seats had five passengers. The door swung closed, the pilot swerved among craters and shrapnel, across a grassy median through a ruined landscape of burned-out planes and planes on fire, helicopter corpses, scattered chunks of metal. A burning C-130 forced the plane to turn tightly alongside the terminal building, gutted from explosions and looting, and through a maze of wrecked bikes, vehicles, and scattered suitcases that lay open, their guts of clothing spilling across the field.

Finally the pilot found a stretch of runway and lifted off to yet another surge of cheers. He flew the opposite of a falling leaf approach, the method of descending in tight circles over a safe donut hole around enemy territory. He rose in a close corkscrew to avoid North Vietnamese gunners and their Soviet SA-7 missiles. Then he came onto the PA system.

"You probably thought you'd booked a flight to Brunei," he said. "Sorry about that. We only have five hundred gallons of gas, not enough to make it. We'll give you a refund." Chuckles and groans. "The good news is that we can fly to Thailand, land of beautiful pagodas and beautiful women. The Thais don't actually want us, probably won't let us land in Bangkok. But I'm going to talk to our air base at U-Tapao. They're nice folks, and I'm sure they'll give us all a cold beer when we get there. It will take a little longer than usual, because I'd like to avoid giving the Reds an easy target. They've got the Delta and Cambodia, so we'll take the scenic route. Relax and enjoy the flight."

"This guy should be a Pan Am pilot," Pen said to all ten people within four feet of him. "What a thrill flying into Chicago with his commentary on air controllers herding thick swarms of planes all around."

But the pilot wasn't done. He came on again with the detailed itinerary. "We're heading to the coast, then we'll follow the shoreline for a while. Isn't it beautiful up here? Clear blue skies, amazing. You'd hardly know there's a war down there . . . Now we've got to take a deep breath and cut inland across the Delta, which the Reds have, as you know. Sorry about that, but at eighty-five hundred feet we'll probably go unnoticed, and it's only eighty miles across to the ocean beyond . . . So that went well. Now we're off the south coast of Cambodia, which you can see off the starboard side. Just imagine the hell going on below. No real danger up here over international waters. Next stop, Thai airspace. I think we're home free. Thanks for listening."

The US Air Force base at U-Tapao looked more like a Vietnamese base. Pen thought half the South Vietnamese Air Force had escaped there. He stopped counting when he got up to seventy fighters, transports, and gunships.

"Shit," he heard an American civilian say. "We trained these bastards, gave them the planes, and they didn't do shit to protect their country. They just ran. Fuckers."

The captain was right. The beer at U-Tapao was frosty cold, but it was Budweiser, imported to the PX. As every GI who'd been in Thailand knew very well, Singha was smoother, richer, just a lot better. Budweiser and Wonder Bread, the standard fare of every post exchange the world over. Pen did not want to be here on an air base that stank of spilled fuel and ruined pride.

And he was not there for very long, just enough time to handwrite his story of the end—his end, at least—which he tried and failed to dictate from an office phone on the base. The line was quirky; he couldn't reach Boston or the London bureau or even Hong Kong, and his colleagues were waiting behind him, tapping their notebooks without charity.

How to get to Bangkok? Air Force personnel just shrugged for several hours. Off his unicycle, his circus act complete, Pen finally had the luxury of fear. Tension drained through an escape valve of relief and exhaustion, replaced by a tremble in his hands. He snuffed back sobs. He thought of Lanh, of Nghi, of Tân and Kỳ—where were they now? He thought of Erik and Mai and all the nameless children. He closed his eyes, stretched out on a hard bench, and tried to grab onto sleep like the soldier gripping the coaming, falling and rolling, rolling, rolling.

Byron's jolly lilt brought Pen back. "Our heroic captain has been rudely told to vacate the ramp because they need the space," he said, "so he's getting gassed up and flying to Bangkok. Want to hitch a ride?"

"Of course." Over Bangkok, he looked down with odd trepidation as the sprawling monster unfolded, packed with unjust peace and undeserved fortune. A low yearning for

Saigon crept up like a seductive aftertaste. He was already missing the jammed, unruly streets, once scary, then picturesque, and finally invigorating. *I will never be gone from there.*

On the way to the Siam Intercontinental, the taxi driver offered Pen a girl for an hour or two or the entire night—or would he like two girls? "No thanks," said Pen. And when the driver pressed him, Pen finally shut him up by saying, "I'm going to meet my wife."

"Okay, maybe next time," and the driver flipped his card into the back seat. It had an ink drawing of a slender woman in sexy pose and scanty dress.

Julie had no idea. He couldn't reach her from U-Tapao and besides, what a great surprise it would be. Dusty, sweaty, and drawn, he got looks as he passed through the pristine lobby with only his white and red Air Cambodge bag slung over his shoulder. His knock on her door produced nothing at first. He knocked again. She opened it and gave a startled cry of delight, flung her arms around him, and together they wept and wept and wept, for different reasons.

In the morning, Julie opened her larger suitcase, fumbled down through the clothes, and extracted a thick folder. She opened the flap, fingered through the papers, and meticulously slid out an ink drawing as fine as an etching—of a little girl with uneven bangs and wondering eyes too wide for her tiny face. She propped it up on the dresser, and sat on the bed next to Pen to weep with him again.

That afternoon, after a long soak in the hotel pool, Pen returned to find a Telex that had been slid under the door of the room:

PROPENNYMAN EXBARRETT CONGRATS ON BRILLIANT
COVERAGE. YOU ARE A BRAVE SOUL AFTER ALL BUT AM
GLAD YOU HAD THE SENSE TO LEAVE. BY THE WAY, THE
BULLET STILL IN MY LEG FORGIVES YOU FOR RUNNING
AWAY IN ROXBURY, YOU LOUSY SOB. MY LIMP ENTITLES
ME TO SEND YOU THIS HEROGRAM. CHEERS.

Pen read it again, his mouth open. He held it briefly to
his chest, then folded it away and didn't show it to Julie, not
just then, because he knew what she would say: "Very nice.
A generous man. More than you deserve."

CHAPTER 18

Adrift without a writer, Lanh wandered into work in a looser form. He spun the dial on the old French safe—clockwise, counter-clockwise, clockwise, and stop—wrenched the heavy handle down and swung the thick door open. He took out the Pentax and the telephoto lens, put in a fresh roll of Tri-X, tucked another roll in his pocket, and closed the safe. Then he headed into the streets, shielding the camera under his shirt.

An unenforced twenty-four-hour curfew thinned traffic but did not deter all defiance. Lanh buzzed along boulevards unimpeded. The barbed wire atop the embassy's ten-foot wall bore shreds of bloody clothing, remnants of the toil out. He snapped photos surreptitiously, mostly with the camera at his waist: the litter across the embassy grounds; the ghostly, looted building; the final Americans silhouetted on the roof; the stolen embassy vehicles, stripped and abandoned at crazy angles wherever they had run out of gas.

Outside apartment houses where Americans had lived, looters crouched beside their booty—books, chairs, couches, food, toilets, sinks—waiting to be picked up with the spoils of war. One yelled an obscenity when Lanh took his picture but could not give chase without losing his treasures. Lanh replied with a wave and a smile.

Dropping his film at AP for processing, he left a note for their lab guy to please print a few good shots and wire them to Boston. Then he swung his motorbike to the office, where he slid the camera and the lens securely into the safe. Home now, but first a detour for a treat. He rode all the way into the narrow passageways of the central market, not daring to leave his scooter on the lawless street. Listless in the waning day, an array of stalls emptying of jittery vendors packing leftovers, the market seemed on the verge of long retirement. A woman putting away unsold mangoes spat red betel juice into the dust.

Lanh did a chatty negotiation with her, asked about her family, her village. She was in a hurry. "Two hundred for six," she told him. She was throwing her prices into the trash, too eager to disappear, too scared of rot.

"No," Lanh said pleasantly, and before he could continue, she came back at him.

"One hundred for eight."

"You're giving them away," he scolded. "It's usually five hundred for six. That's what I'll give you." He pulled out a bill and held it out. She furrowed her brow, suspicious that somewhere in this reversed bargaining lay a trick. "I mean it," said Lanh. "Take it, and give me your best six."

At last the woman cackled lightly, reached into her bag, and laid an array of mangoes on a bench. Every one contained all the beauty of the fertile earth and the love of possibility, the smooth skin's yellow fading into orange and red like a painter's palette. Lanh caressed each one with the tips of his fingers, picked the six, and put them in a small plastic sack she offered. As he left, she asked hopefully, "Are you a Communist?" Lanh shook his head and thought, *Not yet*.

At home, Hiền hugged her father happily, but Linh had a frown with questions. Will the Communists come? Will the war end? Will they kill people? Will we still be able to go to school? Can we still see our friends? Can we stay living here? To each one Lanh said yes, and Thuận's hooded expression spoke her silent qualms.

"Look what I have," Lanh said.

The kids jumped up and down. "What? What?"

He pulled out the mangoes, lined them up along the table, and got a knife. He carefully cut straight down next to the pit of the first until a thick, oval slice fell away. He did the same on the other side of the pit, and then to each of the other mangoes. He placed each oval slice skin-down on the table so the gleaming orange flesh of the fruit faced upward. Then with the tip of his blade he made crosshatches in the firm softness and handed a slice to little Hiền.

"Show us how to do it," he told her. So she took it in both hands, skin down, and bent the piece into a convex shape toward her mouth until the hatch marks widened and the squares of fruit separated, pushing upward like misaligned teeth, begging to be bitten off and devoured, which Hiền did with dispatch. Juice and pulp smeared around her smile.

"Did you hide the pictures?" Lanh asked after the kids had gone to bed.

"Yes, as well as I could."

"I doubt that you needed to."

"I hope you're right, but I doubt that you are."

Cradled by the distant booms, they descended only partway into fitful sleep, the kind that pulls and pushes at once, back and forth across a new frontier, seeking and retreating. Lanh scuffled against dreaming. He got up for some water. He took a piss. He climbed the ladder to his loft desk and moved old newspaper clippings around aimlessly. Back in bed, he began to lose the fight and surrendered to exhaustion.

Pen grabbed his arm so hard it hurt and yanked him through the open door of the chopper so suddenly it wrenched his shoulder. A US Marine shoved him forward into the cabin, but there was Rosie, screaming at him to get out, get out, get out, where's Thuận, where's your family, where's your home? He couldn't see them. They were not with him. The engine started, the great shadows of the rotors made the light flutter outside, the chopper lifted off in fogs of sacred earth, Vietnam grew smaller, then tiny, then insignificant until it vanished from all memory.

His shout woke the children. Thuận wrapped him, held him, told the kids it was just Daddy dreaming, go back to sleep.

The pho man served up a broad, proud smile of delight along with his steaming soup. "Aren't you nervous?" he asked Lanh. "Why didn't you run away like others who worked for the Long Noses?"

Why do I come here every morning? Not for the barbs of this annoying man. If only his pho were not so good . . .

"Did you ever hear of patriotism?" Lanh answered, locking eyes with him. "I am a *true* Vietnamese." He paused for a beat, the pho man fixed on him like a cobra, gaze unwavering. "Are you?" Lanh continued.

The pho man broke his stare and turned away. He said a few low words, nearly unheard. Lanh tried to imagine them, then tried again and again as the following months went on.

The eerie pause of Saigon brought memories of Hanoi in 1945, when the whole city held its breath. The chatter and thump of helicopters had died away, American and Vietnamese choppers fleeing to the Seventh Fleet. Windows in the office building facing Tự Do Street were smashed or open, gaps where air conditioners had perched. Lanh dashed up the broad staircase to the second floor. The door stood ajar. Inside, the bureau seemed in order but with vacant spaces as if everyone who'd left had taken something. He stood in the middle of the room, rotating slowly to conduct inventory. On each surface assigned to a typewriter, there was no typewriter. Where the two telephones had been detailed, there were no phones. On Pen's desk, where he had left his tape recorder, there was only a rectangle of clean wood surrounded by dust. Along the wall with the AP and Reuters teletype machines, there was now room for a sofa. The cracked leather couch that had rested along the opposite wall, for many more years than the tour of any correspondent, had been liberated.

Untouched by tangibles, Lanh felt only detachment. The humid heat gave the office an untried familiarity, as if Vietnam had finally conquered the air-conditioned loftiness. Then, a rush of relief about the safe. How clever of Pen to put the money in the antique relic of the colonial French, a useless chunk of metal so pretentious that some bureau chief before his time had banished it to the back of the supply closet stacked with notebooks, blank newsprint, carbon paper, typewriter ribbons, and dusty files. No looter would have had the knack to crack the safe.

He went to the closet. The absence hit him like a fist to the chest. He backed away, fell into a squat, covered his face with his palms, slammed a hand on the tile, rampaged through the chaos of the supplies, dredged into every corner, and found only four holes through the floor and bolts with ragged cuts of splintery steel. He wanted to breathe. He wanted to keep from crying, and from crying out. He wanted to say, *All right. All right. Now I am back where I belong, a buffalo boy.*

A voice called his name from the doorway and asked if he was there, if anybody was there. Not an American accent, nor Vietnamese. Japanese? The ring of an old childhood Hanoi sound, dread and purpose. The man was short, a little stout, and dressed neatly in the safari-suit costume of the day.

"Ah, Mr. Lanh? Riku Watanabe, NHK Television." He pulled a calling card from his breast pocket and presented it formally, Japanese on one side, English on the other. *In the middle of a war? At the ending of a war? Rosie should be here for this. Pen, too. Pen for sure.*

Lanh might have felt the tickle of a chuckle had it not been for the suffocating loss of cash and camera, security stolen. Instead, luckily, he stood composed in a hovering balance and obtained his first employment of the new era. Together in the doorway, the two evaded non-essential conversation. The denouement, as Pen had called it, was stampeding toward them. Watanabe's explanation was direct: He would be pleased to avail himself of Lanh's skill as an interpreter and arranger, now that the *Tribune* bureau was closed. The correspondent gave a sympathetic gaze over Lanh's shoulder at the sparse remains. An offer was made of pay, quite generous, and a guarantee for as long as NHK was allowed to stay in the country. They began immediately, a Japanese cameraman in tow. Across the road before the presidential palace, NHK filmed the banners, which Lanh translated: "No Negotiation! No Communists in the South! No Land to the Communists!"

"This," said Watanabe, "is like a cartoon of denial, isn't it?" Lanh gave him a glance of appreciation.

They raced from place to place in Watanabe's car, catching footage like fragments of a mosaic. Tense clusters of people formed here and there, some in front of the National Assembly, where the cameraman panned slowly across the scene. The camera, on his shoulder, followed a lone police officer as he walked; halted before the enormous, ugly bronze monument to soldiers; pulled out his pistol; raised it to his temple, and—*crack!*—collapsed like a doll in a splat of bloody gray. The cameraman, steady as a pillar, looked at his correspondent, then at Lanh, all seemingly unsure whether to celebrate or lament this rare achievement in television journalism.

At the river, crowds were still piling on to the few remaining fishing boats. On Lê Lợi Street, a restaurant's door was open.

"What is that song?" asked Watanabe. The music wafted like perfume from inside.

Lanh cocked his head, listened dreamily for a moment. "Trịnh Công Sơn."

"Ah, yes. The antiwar composer. Can you translate the lyrics?"

"Tomorrow you leave
The sea remembers your name and calls you back . . ."

Watanabe had his cameraman record, for the ambient sound of melancholy.

The whistle of rockets tore through the heavy air, punctuated by thuds somewhere. A few pops of rifle fire replied.

Sounds. That was what the end of war was all about, Lanh thought. *I am all images and words, not sounds. But sounds are the text now.* "Yes, get the sounds," he said to Watanabe. The man nodded knowingly, like the sniper in Hanoi.

No truck could make the engine roars that entered Saigon in mid-morning. The reverberations invaded before the troops, great, deep growls that made the streets tremble. The grumble shifted chords into a metallic thunder of steel on pavement as tank treads crawled laboriously into victory. Watanabe stood before his camera, microphone at the ready, speaking rapid Japanese while tanks moved untroubled behind him, troops in leather head gear or olive pith helmets sitting erect on gun turrets, eyes wide with wonder, white teeth flashing in amazed smiles. A few tanks still wore palm fronds for jungle camouflage. From swaying whip antennas flew the gold star in the middle of the flag of the National Liberation Front, a broad red bar atop a broad blue bar.

In the NHK Tokyo studio much later, once the victors allowed airfreight to resume, producers screening the film would see a lanky man in the foreground, white shirt and black pants, his back to the camera, staring at the slow convoy of tanks. The camera then moved toward the road and panned back across a growing crowd of Saigonese gravitating silently to the curb, anxious curiosity in their eyes. The man's face drifted into the frame. It appeared enthralled, as if by a parade of dignitaries. The producers had no way of knowing that the man was Lanh. Behind him and off to his left, another man was watching—not the parade, but Lanh, and with a narrow squint of malice. His expression was noticed by one of the producers, but of course they did not know his name either.

"The presidential palace!" Lanh said. "That's where they're going!" Racing through a web of back streets, Watanabe pulled up a block away. They jumped out and ran, the cameraman puffing behind under his weight of gear. They arrived just as a dozen rumbling tanks belching blue-white exhaust drove almost serenely across Công Lý Boulevard toward the ornate grillwork gate of the palace. For some reason, Lanh noticed the white numerals painted on the turret of the lead tank: 843. It smashed into the gate, rose as if to climb the steel latticework, then as the gate collapsed and the tank fell forward, clattered across the courtyard to the steps of the palace. Other tanks followed, gouging the lawn as they took up positions, some with huge guns facing toward the palace and others toward the surrounding streets.

A soldier grabbed the flag from his tank, dashed up the steps, and appeared on a balcony above, waving the flag back and forth with fierce delight. Trucks full of troops swarmed onto the grounds. A flag rose on the rooftop flagpole. Shots were heard in celebration. Lanh thought his heart had not beaten so fast since he was twelve, entering the jungle camp of the Viet Minh.

Watanabe was doing a standup in Japanese, long sentences, whole paragraphs really, rapid excitement in his voice. Lanh wondered what was left for him to do. Interviews? Hardly the time, but then Watanabe asked to talk to bystanders. They tried. They received the survivor's evasion, smooth gratitude for "liberation" without edges or corners. They traveled the city. Liberation flags were appearing in windows.

"Ha!" laughed Lanh. "How did they make them so fast? And where did they get the blue cloth? Blue cloth was banned from import, just for this reason!"

The revolutionary soldiers, *bộ đội*, were young with shy smiles, climbing off their trucks, fanning out, greeting the growing crowds as liberated, not conquered. Watanabe wanted to talk to some, but that sent a pulse of worry through Lanh. "It's probably not a good idea for you to be that visible to them. They might shut you down, kick you out. Let's wait a day or so and test the waters."

"Waters?"

"Sorry, an American expression. Let's see what happens, how things develop."

As evening came and the day cooled slightly, the soldiers set up camps in parks and plazas, lit little fires, and immersed downtown in the homey smoke of cooking.

Lane 342 was redolent with burning charcoal, rotting fish, and pungent diesel fuel when Lanh turned in and putted to a stop.

Thuận ran to him when he walked in, held him tightly. His girls had tear streaks on their cheeks, reddened eyes. "I was so worried about you. Is everything all right? Has there been killing in the city? Are they rounding people up?"

CHAPTER 19

Whatever Liberation promised to be in the following weeks, it was not liberating. Whatever Communism aspired to be, it did not forge Saigon into communal solidarity. Since Lanh had cherished no expectations, he was not disappointed. In the absence of the predicted bloodbath, which he had never anticipated, he found the newcomers somewhat efficient and upstanding compared with the bribe-taking, randomly oppressive "puppet regime" under the Americans. But he was left still wandering. In his recurring dream, he walked through an alley like his own, crowded with wary destitution, pounding on door after door in search of a place of belonging. People watched him suspiciously. Doors refused to open, or when they did, they were quickly slammed. Even in a green village of thatched roofs and slow water buffalos, farmers turned their backs on him. They would not let him climb up and ride. He ran to his mother, who cloaked him in a clammy embrace. When he cried out, Thuận would hold him and wet his shoulder with her tears.

His girls were hearing things at home they had to keep secret at school. During the war there had been wisps of hidden tales, told in euphemisms that Linh and Hiển could not easily repeat but, Lanh hoped, might register in some back file of their memories. He wanted them to know but not reveal. So they were sensing furtiveness in their father. The searching thoughts and searing stories he had brought home flew slightly above their reach, beyond what they could tell their friends or teachers. They had not understood why he would not trust a commander about the safety of a road, why a girl was shackled to a stretcher, what he meant by not liking "Vietnamese who have no sign of suffering on their faces."

"Isn't suffering bad?" Linh had asked.

"Yes, but not suffering is worse, because our country has always suffered." The answer deliberately left her in confusion. But he expected—this he *did* expect—that his maverick notions would come to life as his children grew.

Now the end of the war meant the end of indirectness. He could not depend on oblique approaches, no matter how culturally comfortable. "I have to sit them down and be clear," he told Thuận late one night. Then he delayed the chore until delay itself loomed into risk. He could not remember what evening it was, how many twilights after Saigon fell, how many after Saigonese yielded to calling their city by the name of Hồ Chí Minh, at least outside the sheltering walls of their homes. He could not remember whether it was before or after the pho man closed his stand and transformed himself into a snooping block captain enforcing vague norms of correctness. Yes, now he remembered: It was after, right after the pho man had started prowling down the lane prying into people's lives in search of incriminating photos and certificates. Lanh had barred the door.

"Go back to making pho! That's what you're good at. And—" Lanh added his disarming charm, "—I miss your pho. It's hard to start my day without your pho." Of course the pho man, exalted by his elevated position, had no trouble reading through Lanh's smile. He turned on his heel, and Lanh knew that was not the end.

So, yes, it was after that but before he encountered Minh, and just as well, for the specter of the unseen Minh was haunting him every time he walked past the shuttered stand and longed for pho.

The girls were already bringing home lessons on the beneficence of the late Uncle Hồ, the crimes of the Americans, the new days dawning, the new patriotic tunes long banned.

"Listen," Lanh said, sitting them down and bending forward to speak softly as if leading them through a dangerous jungle labyrinth. "Everything that happens in our house is a secret. When we talk about things, all those words stay right here, inside, like birds in a cage." The girls' heads swiveled toward the intricate wicker cage in the corner. "Some of your teachers wouldn't understand and might get wrong ideas about us. Your friends, too, and their parents. You know the whispering game we play?" The girls giggled at how the sentence, whispered again and again around the circle, came out all mixed up and silly by the end. "That's what can happen," Lanh went on. "People who don't know us well can get all mixed up and silly about us."

He stopped to look closely at Linh, then at Hiền, to study them. Did they understand? They nodded a little. So he gave examples. When he talks to Mom about his days, say, working for the Japanese television man, they should not mention it in school. Or the office safe that was stolen with all that money in it, and a camera. They must say nothing. Where he goes with the Japanese man, what he sees, what he hears. Like the Liberation soldiers who were walking down the middle of the street next to a long line of men, most in army camouflage, taking them somewhere. "Or what I say about the reeducation camps, where Phương's father was taken. Just because you had to be in the army shouldn't mean you should be locked away. We have all been prisoners in one way or another. I'd like to tell you all about it, but it stays locked in our house, together with us." Their eyes were widening and looking a little scared.

"Don't be scared," Thuận told them. "Your father is not trying to scare you. It's just that we don't know enough yet about your new teachers and the people who run the government."

Linh was not fooled. "You are scared," she said. "And now we have to pretend. They are going to tell us one thing in school, and you are going to tell us another thing at home. Can we tell you what they tell us in school?"

Lanh put his arm sadly around her shoulder. "Yes, you can. We are free thinkers in this house. The old Vietnam did not like free thinkers very much. The new Vietnam might not either. But I want you to grow up as free thinkers, even if you have to pretend not to be when you leave this house. Someday, I believe, we will all be able to find our places."

Hiền seemed not to be following. Thuận hugged her off in the corner to look at the pair of startling green parakeets, and spoke quietly, trying to explain. "Just keep our little birds in their cage," Lanh heard her say, happy that she liked his metaphor, as she liked all his metaphors, which was why they were in love.

He delighted in his work, which kept his life in motion like a flywheel, spinning reliably from the before into the after. He started to prefer television, because it cultivated his eye. Watanabe had keen vision, and from dawn into every early dusk the need for film played to Lanh's notion of Vietnam as a gallery of images. He noticed the empty street corner where the one-legged man used to beg from a gnarled wooden crutch. He noticed the dulling colors of the girls' *áo dàis* and the way some young men looked around and behind them as they walked.

"There," Lanh said one morning outside a shoemaker's corrugated shutter. "You see the pair of sandals on the sidewalk? They are forcing private shops to close, but work goes on inside. Let's go around back. I think we'll find something interesting. Shoot some film here first."

Watanabe was beaming as if he knew what this puzzle was all about. He spoke a few words to the cameraman, who crouched for an angle, aimed his lens obliquely down the block, panned slightly, and zoomed in on the humble sandals. Lanh led them along the street and found a narrow passageway between buildings. It stank of rotting meat and crawled with feral cats, just skin and fur wrapped tightly around their skeletons. A dog barked hoarsely. Through the passage they emerged into a narrow alley and walked back until a delicate *tap-tap* from inside told them they were behind the shoemaker's.

Lanh rapped on the door. The hammering halted in alarm, the way a cricket silences itself near danger. Lanh called as quietly as he could and yet be heard. He called again, "Japanese visitors." Watanabe shrugged, but Lanh gestured for patience and said in English, a bit louder, "I think he will come to try to sell you shoes!"

The door creaked slightly, an eye peaked through the crack, then both eyes appeared with the merchant's common look these days, a tug between anxiety and eagerness. "Hello," Watanabe said in English, which relaxed the craftsman enough to complete the opening, and Lanh leapt into his familiar task of joking, commiserating, lightly bantering until the shoemaker invited them inside.

The smell of leather hung so thickly that it comforted, like a kitchen's soothing blend of deep spices close to dinnertime. The dim light through two cobwebbed windows barely showed the small workbench and its careful array of hammers, awls, knives, needles, and shears. Against a wall stood piles of darkness—leather, Lanh supposed. Strips of plastic twisted among themselves in a corner. In a heap lay pairs of shoes for every layer of society: simple sandals, women's flip-flops with shiny borders, sturdy boots, dress shoes to go with uniforms and suits. The shoemaker was barefoot and shirtless in the close heat. He squatted on the floor to show his visitors how he cut a leather sole from a paper pattern, affixed the insole, sewed the thongs, all the while smiling through the camera at the curious inhabitants of another universe.

"Yes," he explained because Lanh had asked him to state the obvious, "the shoes in front are the signal that there are shoes in back." When he grinned, a gap in his teeth opened wide.

"Will this make trouble?" Watanabe asked later.

"Maybe, although it looks like he's making shoes for officials too. Can you blur his face?"

"I'll tell the office to do it. Anyway, thank you. I never would have noticed the sandals in front if it weren't for your eyes."

"I might not have pointed them out if I hadn't been working for your lens."

Excited contentment should have released him into placid sleep. Instead, the sun came from all directions on Hạ Long Bay, whose wooded islands loomed straight up to bliss. The dazzling day made Lanh shield his eyes. It did not allow secret spaces. His uncle's bright green and red fishing boat putt-putted through the glassy water. His cousins chased each other around the deck, drawing scolds from grownups drinking limeade.

The fine sand of Soi Sim Island warmed their toes. The water cooled them with a graceful touch. The boys climbed from the beach through the harsh scrub onto the highest point above the plunging cliff. Lanh stood looking across the Chinese scroll of landscape. He breathed the air of fragrant salt and *sim*, the fruity smell of rose myrtle. He spread his arms across the highest place of soaring joy that could ever be. His cousins, one by one, posed like divers at the edge, then flew down, arms and hands in wedges, and sliced into the sea, their foam quickly brushed away by a rising breeze. Lanh hesitated to leave this euphoric place, but called by the lot of luck or doom, he dove as well, waking just before he hit the sea.

The pho man was at the door. "What!"

"You are kindly requested," then came a mocking bow, "to appear at twenty-nine Công Lý for a consultation."

"What's at twenty-nine Công Lý?"

"An office."

"What kind of office?"

"An important office."

"All offices think they're important. What's it about?"

"That's all I know. You must go."

"I'm busy."

"I think that's what it might be about."

"What?"

"What you are busy with."

Lanh felt a shudder that he hid quite well.

"You are expected today," said the pho man, who then retreated.

"Are you ever going to make pho again?" Lanh shouted after him. This brought a sly gesture with his hands that said, *How should I know in this age of revolutionary uncertainty?* Or so Lanh translated it for himself.

Number 29 Công Lý turned out to be a tired French villa with thick bougainvillea along a high fence, and an olive-drab guard in a scarred pith helmet in front, an old captured M1 carbine slung across his shoulder. Not a soldier, for sure, but a small man with a big task: to survey and scrutinize and hassle everyone seeking entry. He scowled at Lanh's ID card, which still bore the red-striped yellow flag of a country that—the guard announced in a grating pitch—existed no longer. But since the Provisional Revolutionary Government had not yet replaced these distasteful objects, he could do no more than growl and search his targets with rude alacrity, then wave them in.

Lanh had no idea where to go. So he mounted the broad stairs, entered through the large doorway, and stood in the echoing vestibule looking for someone to ask. Men and women, all in army uniforms, bustled in and out of rooms, back and forth across the lobby, oblivious and preoccupied. He strolled, peering through doors, climbing stairs, asking himself what history this building contained, what tales it was keeping to itself.

"Lanh!" a voice behind startled him, not in a commanding tone but in the warmth of old friendship. He turned and tried to place the face, some apparition from far off, a subtle chord of recognition. The man strode up and embraced Lanh as if they were lost brothers. Lanh pulled back and examined the eyes.

"Liêm? Liêm!"

"Yes, it's me." The man still had the boy's mischievous glint, but with a trace of steel. His face was darker now, not just in hue, also in mystery, as an inviting opening into a cave that lures and conceals.

"Come. There's someone who needs to see you, someone you already know. But first let's compare our lives." *Oh, this is it*, Lanh thought. *This is the man my age I must answer to.* Liêm led him to a bare office filthy with dusty papers strewn across the floor. Oddly, the rat droppings along the walls made Lanh tremble, as if he were visiting his own cell.

Liêm gestured magnanimously for him to take the only chair. Its bamboo bars and protruding nails dug into his legs. Liêm perched on the edge of the empty desk, swept clear of all remnants of purpose, so that he looked slightly downward at his old "comrade," as he called him.

"My co-conspirator!" Liêm cried happily. "All those nights guiding the Japanese! How many French did we help kill? We were patriots. I will ask you later what happened to that Japanese soldier you abandoned, how that came about. But first I will tell you about myself."

"I did not abandon him!" Lanh fired back. "He was hurt. He fell and broke his leg. I moved to help him, but he was injured too badly. He waved me away, he wanted me to run, to save myself. There was nothing I could do to save him."

"So that is your explanation. Later you can say why you led him to a place where he could be killed. Now I will tell my story." *This friendship is like a dead coal that cools to a hard stone.*

The office seemed to grow more stifling as Liêm spun out his tale. With each turning point of sacrifice and suffering for the great cause of Liberation, the room was drained of a little oxygen. With Liêm's every repeated revelation of his sister's capture and rape by the French, with each youthful operation for the Viet Minh, with every bicycle journey down the rugged Hồ Chí Minh Trail, with every bike groaning under ammunition cases, with each one unloaded and parked at a mountain base and its backbreaking load heaved up and over by foot and down to the next depot to pick up another bike, with every sabotage through the twisting tunnels up into the American base, with each bamboo stake sharpened into a punji trap, with every night of fitful sleep and every day of acid hunger, with the firefights that killed his comrades, the years of separation from his parents until they died, the thunder of the B-52s whose bombs left craters as if great beasts had stomped the land, with every chapter—and these were chapters, long and detailed—Lanh felt himself shrinking into his brutal chair. Weakness flowed through his veins. He dared not ask to quench his thirst.

"And on April thirtieth, I stopped to pick up our delegation at Tansonnhut so we could all ride together to our victory." Liêm stood and stretched as if ready to march. "And now you. How have you spent your life?"

Lanh had rehearsed his answer for years. He had inflated episodes, edited out others, embellished here and there, and constructed and revised a worldview that made sense only to himself. It would barely please Thuận, much less this sinewy old friend from the jungle, who was looking down at Lanh's slight paunch, more pronounced as he slumped in the chair. *He can see that I am not even strong. I could not carry half of what he can. I could not walk one tenth the distance, run as far, be as brave.*

The Japanese soldiers, the admitted mistake of the last sniper post, his grandparents' farm, the great gray buffalos he loved to ride, the abortive foray to the Viet Minh, the return to school, the journey to the South, the infatuation with Huế, the mastery of English, the aid work in the Delta, the help for the coup-plotters, the years in prison, the important translations for the *Tribune*, his contempt for the corrupt, his wife and daughters, his decision to stay to keep his roots.

"You forgot Westmoreland," Liêm said when Lanh had finished. "You worked for Westmoreland. We know you did. Why?"

Lanh gave a start. "Who is 'we'?"

"We the Liberators, the true patriots who strip away the lies."

"If I had not interpreted for Westmoreland, Rosie Everett would not have met me, and I would not have been able to help show Americans the faces of misery that they caused."

"Yes, yes, one path leads to another and another. But that was not my question. Why did you work for Westmoreland? Be careful how you answer."

"Is this an interrogation? Have I committed a crime?"

"Lanh, my brother, I am not interrogating you, and I do not know of any crime you may have committed. We are just comparing our lives, the different ways we have taken. You have not asked me why I took the directions that I did—aren't you curious? But I am curious about why you did. Is that so strange when old friends meet after all these years?"

"You said be careful how I answer. Why be careful if this is just a friendly talk?"

"Because friendship is built on honesty, truth."

Lanh pondered for a time, saying nothing, taking his bearings outside the boxes, beyond the definitions. He felt too shackled here in this trap, and so he willed himself to float. He closed his eyes and imagined drifting high above the gridwork of accepted answers, sneering down at them from a righteous altitude.

"All right," Lanh began. "You Liberators and the colonialists—French, Japanese, and American—and the Saigon puppets, you all share one thing." Liêm's eyes widened as if in caution. "No," Lanh replied to the look. "I am not going to be careful. I am going to take you at your word. You want honesty? I am going to be truthful."

There was a slight shake of the head from Liêm, as if all were about to be lost. "I feel guilty facing you," Lanh continued. "All my life I have dreaded this moment. All my life I have wondered what I would say to a fighter who had spent years in the jungle while I had spent years in comfort. My guilt is not my pride. My pride is somewhere else."

"You—" Liêm interrupted, "have no cause for guilt. You do not have to answer to me. I do not condemn everyone who has not taken my path. Even as a boy, I knew you as authentic. You have your history. I want to hear it. I want to hear where your pride is. I am not judging you."

Yes you are, but there is no hiding. "I will exempt you from what I was saying, then. I was saying that all sides have shared one thing. They have not been true to the free spirit of the Vietnamese people. They have built cells. They have forced everyone into the cells. If we're not in this one, then we're in that one. We may move from one to the other from day to night, but we cannot travel outside them. We may liberate ourselves when we retreat into our own homes, but otherwise we are imprisoned in categories made by all of you—by them, not by us. There may be some of us who are comfortable locked in a cell, but I am not one of them, and I think there are many more like me. Perhaps most are secretly free in their thoughts. What is to happen to them now? Like you, I have traveled this country. Unlike you, I have seen a different country. My allegiance is to that country, that country that crosses the boundaries between the labels. My allegiance is not to a piece of yellow cloth with red stripes, not to a piece of blue and red cloth with a gold star. It is to the people, their essence. You finished your journey many years ago. You suffered physically, and you have my respect for your sacrifices. But you also had your pleasure: the comfort of the cell. You didn't want to leave it. You didn't endure the torment of searching. Unlike you, I have not finished my journey. I am still on the road. And I always try to remember that I am just a buffalo boy."

Liêm said nothing. He stared at Lanh. Then he bowed his head slightly in reverence or humility. Or was it sorrow? Lanh stood.

"My friend," he said to Liêm, "if you feel safe with me after hearing this truth, I would like you to meet Thuận and my daughters."

Liêm did not answer. He clasped Lanh by the shoulders. "Now to your appointment." He led the way out of the office, up the staircase to a larger room, also rather bare, with a man in olive drab behind a bigger desk.

"Lanh!" He rose in greeting. "How nice to see you away from that pho stand!"

Lanh returned Minh's pretense with a forthright wince. Liêm disappeared and closed the door behind him. What remained was the vacuum of a friendship suddenly regained and suddenly lost. It swallowed the words that Minh seemed to be speaking. His mouth was moving, but Lanh was not receiving. The face of a boy shimmered: Liêm, tight and loyal.

"Are you listening?" Minh had dropped his façade. "I am telling you important things, and you are off somewhere in a dream?"

The important things were, in no particular order, the predictable indictments: That he had refused to serve the Liberation by evading the simple offer to participate in a great cause by providing information that he gathered in his travels with the American. That he had chosen words to translate against the interests of the people. That he had avoided assisting in his newspaper's monumental exposure of Saigon's machinery of torture and imprisonment—"a critical error," Minh called it. And that he had considered abandoning his country, on the cusp of its Liberation, to flee to America as a deserter and traitor. He must know that the evacuations were kidnappings, especially of children. Further, he now pried into the affairs of the Provisional Revolutionary Government on behalf of another foreign organization, NHK.

After his spate of honesty with his childhood friend, Lanh was in no mood for meekness. But he was thirsty, and there was Minh sipping from a sweating bottle of cold yellow soda. Lanh resisted asking for the favor of something to drink. Minh watched him impassively. Lanh thought of telling Minh that he was playing the textbook character in a cheap interrogation guide—and not playing it with any skill. He considered standing up and walking out, since nobody had told him he was under arrest. He contemplated the tension between integrity and survival. *The road and the path, one after another, might be mined or booby-trapped or ready with an ambush. Who is best to ask? Not the soldier. Not the official. The farmer? The truck driver? The old woman selling lychees? Where are they? Where can I find them?*

"Do you have questions for me?" Lanh asked.

"Do you have answers for me?"

"I have a discussion. Are you interested in a discussion?"

"It is not my job to have a discussion."

"So we're finished here?"

"Not quite." Then Minh said nothing more. Lanh had learned from Rosie and Pen the technique of silence. People couldn't stand silence for very long, and would fill it, often with something more revealing than they had planned—a good trick of interviewing. So, since Minh was trying it, Lanh would as well. They both sat looking at each other, then at the walls and ceiling and floor, sometimes at their hands, leaving their unspoken words to fester.

Minh blinked first. "What you did was awkward for me," he told Lanh. "Or what you didn't do. I made a slightly positive report about you. I almost defended you for refusing to help us. I said that you were more useful uncompromised, that you guided the American into an essential Vietnam, *unvarnished.*" He said the word in English. "You were nobody's agent, so I believed, and would not hesitate to help the American expose the malice of the puppet regime.

"Then, what did you do? You told the police he was going into National Liberation Front territory, and he was stopped."

"No!" Lanh shouted. Minh held up his hand for quiet.

"You made an awkward situation for me. You refused to help him on his torture articles."

"Ridiculous!" Lanh sputtered and stood.

"Sit down. I am not finished. You pressured mothers to give up their begging children. You took them to that Norwegian orphanage, the one that stole Vietnamese children from their parents and sent them away before we could enter this city. You met with the American official in Danang who was tracking the movements of our troops. Your—"

"Enough!" Lanh shouted. He leaned over and shook his fist in Minh's face. Minh did not flinch. "Every word that you have spoken is a lie. You know that, if you are such a good intelligence officer. If you don't know that, then you are a failure and a disgrace to the Liberation."

"Your American's wife, I was about to say, consorted with a spy for the puppet government."

"What? Who?"

"You know perfectly well."

"I know nothing of the kind."

This brought a sneer to Minh's lips. "How often have I heard those words: 'I know nothing.' But Nguyễn Văn Lanh, you are not a stupid man. You know all that and much more."

A new form of fear was poking around Lanh like a rat sniffing for an opening. Fear. Not the fear of the land mine or the mortar. Not the fear of the thief. Not the fear that the bullet with your name on it would find its mark instead of whistling past your ear. Not the very recent fear of your own soldiers beating you or shooting you to crush their way to escape. Those fears were hot. This was a cold fear, and Lanh shivered, which made Minh smile with his lips together.

He then leaned back in his chair behind the desk to observe Lanh's hard breaths. What followed Lanh could barely remember, it was such a rapid, gasping defense, a correction to the record, he kept saying over and over. Truth always buoyed him like clear air. Lies choked him like the buzzing exhaust of a thousand motorbikes in Saigon's streets. He wanted to cough out Minh's fabrications. This putrid office stung his eyes.

Lanh's harangue of objections held no obvious interest for Minh, who broke eye contact, checked his watch, tapped his fingers, swallowed his yellow soda, and then with a wave of his hand interrupted the proceedings as if the defendant's arguments mattered not at all, which of course was the case.

"You're not listening," said Lanh.

"I have a warning for you. In the new order of authority, a journalist must be licensed. You are not licensed. Therefore, until you are approved, any such work is not permitted."

"What does that mean? I am not a journalist."

"But you work as one. For the Japanese."

"I'm just an interpreter."

"Isn't a journalist an interpreter? An interpreter of events? An interpreter of what he sees? You are a journalist. You must be licensed."

"So, how do I get licensed?"

"Licenses are not being issued now."

"What about the reporters for *Nhân Dân*?"

"They came from Hanoi where they are already licensed."

Lanh wished he bragged easily so he could illuminate this dense operative on the advantage of having a fluent press-savvy English speaker "interpret" Vietnam. *I can be an asset, and you are burying me.* The plea would be lost on Minh, a mere functionary keen to execute his orders.

"So I am to resign from NHK?"

"Until you are licensed. In any case, they will not be here very much longer. We are expelling all foreign journalists."

What are you planning to hide? Is there a bloodbath coming? No, it cannot be.

"Wait here," Minh told him. "I need to make an arrangement." The door opened and closed, leaving only the pungent odor of mold in the empty office.

The word *arrangement* would toy with Lanh for the next twenty-four hours, when he was to return to the villa on Công Lý for an appointment with Colonel Võ Đông Giang. Minh had reentered the stifling office with that announcement, delivered as a play of encrypted transparency, hinting at the ominous, blended with false compassion, sliced with the sliver of hope that if all went well, if Lanh acquitted himself properly, then . . .

He dared not say anything in front of the children. In school, they had already heard of the registration of soldiers and other "puppets," the coming rehabilitation into society of "war criminals" in reeducation camps, the "reform study" to last ten days or thirty. The time should rather be measured in years, Lanh figured. After the girls were in bed, he whispered his fears to Thuận, whose iron poise betrayed her desperation, held at bay with the sheer will of dismissal.

"You have done nothing," she said.

"That was exactly what I was accused of—one of the things. Doing nothing. Not spying for them. Not distorting words. Not working on Pen's prisoner series."

"But he wouldn't let you."

"Minh didn't care. Cause and effect have no place in his thinking. If what he does can be considered thinking. He was reciting lines. My fate, apparently, will rest with that Colonel Giang, whose name I know from Pen—the VC head at Camp Davis."

"Will that work for you? That he knew Pen?"

Lanh shrugged despairingly. Once again, as always, his course was being drawn from outside. A great fatigue of powerlessness swept over him, so profound that he spent a dreamless sleep.

In the morning he met Watanabe as usual, checking behind him to see that he wasn't followed by someone gathering evidence of his violation. "They gave me a red light." He shook Watanabe's hand and expressed his sorrow—and his joy at their brief collaboration—then said, "All foreign correspondents will be expelled, I was told." Watanabe's nod lacked surprise, as if to say, the wheel turns as expected.

Lanh killed time by buzzing on his motorbike around his city, by strolling the streets and prowling the alleyways, exploring behind the shuttered shops to find pockets of entrepreneurial resistance. Most tension had drained away. The place he still called Saigon in his head seemed to be finding its footing, testing each step across new ground, touching the limits gingerly. The men his age and younger who were still about wore faces drawn with uncertainty, as well they should, he thought. Loudspeakers blared periodic slogans, new flags and banners blossomed, children began to sport red neckerchiefs, including his own. *No harm done, really. We all have to belong to something.*

Most commerce was gone or hidden, but he managed to find a stall near the market selling cloud-white *bún* with strips of pork on top, which he doused in nuoc mam and marveled at the vibrant flavors, like stunning colors against a gray landscape. He bought a frosty bottle of that yellow soda, raised it all alone in a mock toast to Minh, and took long, large swigs of resentment.

When the hour approached, he rode to 29 Công Lý, locked his scooter to a pole, negotiated his way easily past the officious guard by simply pronouncing the name Võ Đông Giang, and strode inside like an invited guest.

Giang had the high cheekbones and taut face of an ascetic, his sinewy frame accentuated by his baggy olive uniform. He must have been ten or fifteen years older than Lanh, or his guerrilla life had aged him beyond his years. A foul Chinese cigarette dangled from his lips, and he offered another to Lanh from a pack lying on the scarred wooden desk in front of him. Lanh wondered for an instant if he should take one out of courtesy. But no, he said, I don't smoke, thank you.

There followed a curious dialogue, as if between two bruised veterans. Giang had before him a dark green folder of only two or three pages, apparently all he needed on Lanh, or all the new rulers had. He barely glanced at them. Instead, he pierced Lanh's gaze with a stare of interest and, it nearly seemed, some restrained respect.

First, Giang told stories, beginning with the final days at Tansonnhut, when he had instructed his men into the bunker they had dug with boards and knives. The shells came in, he said, a slightly amused smile flickering around his lips, as if tasting a delicious treat after the generations of fasting. "The bombardment began, and I ordered my men to stay down inside. One of them was disobedient. He wanted to see what was happening, so he went up, just outside the entranceway. A shell exploded and tore his arm almost completely off."

Giang gave a smoky laugh as he took a puff. "We bandaged him up and stopped the bleeding, and I told him, 'You're lucky you got hit, because I would have shot you for disobeying my order. But you'll lose your arm, punishment enough.'" The laugh that came from Giang was so delighted that even Lanh joined in. *Why am I liking this man? I seem to trust ruthless honesty, but honest ruthlessness?*

There followed the colonel's long autobiography in the jungles with the Viet Minh; his treks during the American War north to south, south to north, when the Hồ Chí Minh Trail was a jungle path, not yet the highway it became; his assignment in Cuba, where he had learned Spanish; his months in the tunnels of the South, some parts dug out enough to hold small underground concerts by singers smuggled from the North.

The litany of sacrifice made Lanh fidget. Giang stopped his narrative and opened a desk drawer, withdrawing two small glasses and a bottle of deep maroon liqueur, "plum, from Lào Cai," Giang said. He poured a generous share into each glass, pushed one toward Lanh, and raised his for a toast. "To Liberation, at last," he said as he watched Lanh closely. They drank. The sweet burning seemed like a promise.

Giang raised his eyebrows to signal that Lanh's turn had come, and so Lanh decided to leave nothing out, nothing at all, not the dead Japanese soldier, not his easy acquiescence to the Viet Minh commander's dismissal, not his translation work for the Americans—both military and journalistic—not even his soft guilt over staying on the margin of the attempted coup against Diệm, his imprisonment notwithstanding. And, of course, what Giang surely knew already, his parrying Minh's repeated requests for information. He described in detail his journalistic work, first with Rosie, then with her successors, then with Pen, and how he had helped them see, how he had helped Americans see—he hoped. He made sure to mention interpreting for Nguyễn

Thị Hoà, the tortured woman shackled to the stretcher, to which Giang nodded knowingly. Struggling not to sound defensive, Lanh maintained a professional voice to explain Pen's unwillingness to let him risk himself by working on the prisoners series. To Lanh's surprise, Giang nodded slightly in understanding, it appeared.

Otherwise, the interrogator, if that is what Giang was, gave no reaction to the turns of Lanh's life story. It had not included motive. It had not included the plight of not belonging.

"Is that all?" Giang asked, and refilled their glasses with plum liqueur from Lào Cai.

"When Pennyman was stopped before he could get into Liberation Front territory, that was not me. I told no one. I wasn't even sure that's where he was going. I was sorry for him when he was caught. Somebody else must have informed."

With a flick of his hand, Giang brushed away Lanh's concern. "We know," he said. "We think we know who it was, a friend of Pennyman's wife. She did much more than that, and we are dealing with her."

Who? Questions always seemed to bubble up inside Lanh at the wrong times, when an interview was done, when the topic was exhausted, when the details grew tedious. Often he tried to persist, but now he swallowed his curiosity. *Maybe someday, if I meet Pen and Julie again, they'll have a theory.*

"And one more thing: I have a wife and two daughters," Lanh said.

"I also have a wife and two daughters!" Giang exclaimed. "I would have more, but I was away too much.

They are in Hanoi. I have not seen them for a year and a half." He paused, looked far away, then asked, "When did you last see your family?" Behind the colonel's austere façade, no glimpse of wry resentment could be seen, no playful pleasure at the game he'd engineered.

"This morning, of course."

"Of course. You and your family have been fortunate." To which Lanh had no answer. "Imagine if Quốc—you said Quốc?—had accepted you into the Viet Minh. Your path might have been different. Each of us chooses along the way, but the choices are not the same at every junction, depending on where you begin and where you have been."

"Very true."

"True, but not exoneration. Tell me, when Quốc told you that by going back to school you would help your country, did you think he was giving you a command or just advice?"

"I was just a boy, and he was . . ." Lanh couldn't find the right word. "He was a respected leader. I could tell by how the fighters acted with him. So I took his advice as more than a suggestion, perhaps a little less than a command, but a revelation. Yes, a revelation that there are many ways to fight for Vietnam. I felt that if I had insisted on staying with the Viet Minh, I would have disappointed him. For some reason, I didn't want to disappoint him."

At this Giang gave Lanh the deepest nod of understanding so far, and he narrowed his gaze as if contemplating something remarkable. Then he said a stunning thing: "I believe that your Quốc was probably Nguyễn Ái Quốc."

"What?" Lanh nearly shouted. "What? No. Truly?"

"I cannot be certain, but what Quốc said to you I have heard before. It was something Uncle Hồ said often to young boys who wanted to fight: Go back and finish school. And the way his fighters deferred to this Quốc, the way they used the name that he used to call himself—it sounds as if you met him and did not know you had. And have not known all your life until this moment. You see what light the revolution can bring?" And here Giang gave a raspy laugh as he lit another cigarette and again offered one to Lanh.

Lanh spun through childhood and later life, encountering paths that came to him and beckoned musically as he turned away. *Or was I being turned away?* "I met Hồ Chí Minh in the jungle and didn't know it," he said, as if to convince himself. Giang watched him in pleasure. "He determined my direction. Perhaps it was fate," Lanh offered.

"Are you Catholic? Did you come south with all those Catholics?"

"No, Buddhist. My family was Buddhist. I am not religious. Why?"

"You mention fate. That is a prelude to shirking responsibility, to putting it all in God's hands. Or ask forgiveness, isn't that what Christians do? Sin and then ask Jesus to forgive, then sin again and be forgiven, and on and on forever. I learned that in Cuba. I was also raised in a Buddhist family, where I was taught that destiny is impermanent, along with all else in our world."

"Yes," Lanh said, "I remember learning that even karma cannot fully determine this life. The most robust seed will not grow without sunlight and water. In any case, I don't believe any of it, not consciously. I travel on the ground, not in the air."

"What do you believe?"

Now Lanh hesitated. He would sound like a man adrift, not on the ground as he had just claimed. Zealots do not see shades of gray, the builders of boxes do not see any space between them. Yet a neighbor had just been taken away for lying about his army service. Were lies worse than truth now? *I cannot let too many more seconds pass before I answer.*

He began by saying that he was only a buffalo boy, which surely Colonel Giang could appreciate. Giang gave no sign of doing so. Lanh defined his love of what Vietnam could be, free of war, faithful to its essence, blossoming into a future shorn of foreign invaders and corrupters, decent and prosperous and true to a culture both ancient and modern. Lanh tried to stop there, but Giang had a puzzled expression on his face, so he went on. His own search, Lanh explained, his lifetime search, was for his place in these dreams. He had not quite found his place, and so he had drifted—oh, no, he used that word—he had journeyed, journeyed through work that allowed him to see deep into his country and his countrymen, into the soul of Vietnam.

"So you think you found, all by yourself, the soul of Vietnam?" Giang cocked his head in a mocking twist.

"No, no! I've found nothing. I mean, I haven't finished my journey. 'Let the wanderer forget he's wandering.' Do you know the song by Trịnh Công Sơn? 'Let the wanderer forget he's wandering.' That's me. The journey is not about a destination. The journey itself is the goal, every field, every farmer, every market, every tinsmith, every weaver and shoemaker, every child fishing in a pond, every mother loving and every father providing, every Vietnamese raising their eyes. Those and more are the landmarks along the way of the journey."

Giang sighed. He seemed to be weighing something. Then he spoke as if to cut Lanh into a thousand pieces. "You are not on the side of the Revolution, and you are not on the other side. You are confused, and you probably need rehabilitation." Lanh's every muscle hardened. "But I have been given some of the newspaper articles that you helped with. This woman, 'By Rosie Everett,' who wrote so strongly about Agent Orange. That article alone is enough to get me thinking that I should make Agent Orange my cause when I return to Hanoi. It will kill our children yet to be born. We must help them. We must get America to help them. And the tortured woman in the hospital, I will find her and give her a position. The man who set himself on fire, the mother keeping her sick baby to beg in the streets. You did what you said, you showed Americans the results of their imperialism, the crimes of their puppets. You have an eye for injustice, no matter who commits it."

This would be a high compliment in an American newsroom, Lanh figured, but in the euphoric fervor of a new revolution, it could only be dangerous. Indeed, Giang adopted a glare with his final words: "No matter who commits it."

Then Giang concluded their meeting by saying, "As long as you do not practice what you call journalism, you are neither a threat nor an asset. I wish you the strength to survive."

CHAPTER 20

T he monsoons came, so he slept well. His pillow was the whoosh of rain and wind, his pulse the *rat-tat* on tin roofs. The taste of bitter relief in his mouth had finally washed away after Colonel Giang's parting declaration. *Neither a threat nor an asset.* So, after all, there was a space for him between the ready-made boxes. *Neither a threat nor an asset.* Good. He did not want to be either.

But Thuận had shrunk into a posture of defeat. She slumped a little. Some of her fellow teachers had taken the initiative to report for reeducation, which they thought would deter their arrests. Thuận had not. Instead, she lost her job under the forward rush of the Great Liberation.

A household pall overcame Lanh's pains at brightness. Linh no longer embraced her father with her happily curious gaze. Hiền's merry giggle came less often. Lanh announced his sentence from Giang: *I wish you the strength to survive.*

"That I have always had," Lanh told his family, "and since I am not separated from my country, I will be nurtured by my roots in the purity of her soil."

"What purity?" Thuận asked. "I love Vietnam as much as you do, but Vietnam has been lost to us our entire lives, hijacked and kept as a hostage."

"A hostage? To what?"

"To what you yourself have said to me over and over again: to foreign ideologies, colonialism, anti-communism, and now Communism. We should have left. When Pen offered us a way out, we should have taken it. Now where are we?" She said all this while loving Lanh with a beseeching look of adoring sadness.

He began playing his old flute. Tunes from his boyhood came back to him, his fingers finding their way as an aging rider still knows how to make the buffalo start and turn. New songs, love songs, banned political songs he picked out haltingly up in his office loft, no use anymore as an office. The children climbed up with him as he played, hummed along, brought him melodies they wanted him to learn.

The family was running out of the cash carefully hidden in small places around the house. Sometimes they forgot that they had emptied a box or a can or a hollow behind a wall, and were startled when they reached in and found nothing. Thuận began to buy and sell scraps of whatever things she could—mere things, not the care and guidance she had bestowed on her pupils. Strips of discarded tin. Small bunches of overripe bananas. Plastic baskets partly torn. Baseball hats and belts left behind. Broken sunglasses. Lowly things, which folks needed. Lanh continued to play his flute.

Men began to disappear from Lane 342. The pho seller, whose authority had grown larger than the people's derision, rudely searched a house and discovered the treasure of an ancestral lacquer box stuffed with photographs, three of which depicted men in the uniform of the puppet enemy. So went the story that raced along the alley. The man of the house then received an order to attend "reform study," a "humanitarian" alternative to the trial for "national treason" that a less humane government would have logically imposed. The order, which he showed tremulously to neighbors, instructed him to take "enough paper, pens, clothes, mosquito nets, personal effects, food, and money to last ten days." After ten days, he had not returned.

As the pho man patrolled the neighborhood, he kept bypassing Lanh's home, nervously, it seemed to Lanh. He scurried by without a glance, as if to avoid some plague—or was Lanh now a protected deviant? Recalcitrance was a privilege, he knew, but not an occupation.

One morning, on his usual rambling by motorbike around the city, he passed the cathedral where the cyclo driver had set himself ablaze, where crowds had demonstrated their distress against the government before the fall—before the victory. A rain had just let up, and the great brick church was spewing people. Worshippers were congregating in knots outside. The white Madonna seemed to bless them and pity them. In the old days, stands of soft drinks and food would have encircled the plaza, and ambitious tradesmen would have reached out to offer parishioners little crucifixes and rosaries. All had gone nearly unnoticed by Lanh before. Now, their absence made their past presence more obvious.

He gathered some thick, broken branches that lay in the streets, strapped them to his scooter, and rode home. From the desk in his loft, he took his knife, the blade still sharp from the day of his futile murder in Huế. Again, he felt scalded by his furious grief for Vinh. *Why is shame so physical?* He paused and sank into meditation. He calmed his breathing, emptying his thoughts but tracking every breath far down into his toes, his feet and ankles, then calves, then thighs, then abdomen and chest, neck and head, deep and cleansing breaths of the new air of his new life. Into the innocence of emptiness flowed an old memory of a monk's lesson:

A bowl of water is heavy only when you lift it. When you put it down, it is heavy no longer.

He climbed down the ladder and sat cross-legged outside his front door, the oddly shaped pieces of wood by his side, and began to whittle.

This he had not done since boyhood, like his flute. And like his flute, this came as a clear memory archived by fingers and wrists. Before the early afternoon, a crude cross lay on his knee, and he was smoothing it with his blade. By evening, a miniature of a man in a beard and cloak stood upright. By the time darkness overcame Lane 342 and a rain began to sweep along the alley, he had twelve oblong beads in a pile, ready to be strung together. Thuận watched him sympathetically.

In a week, he had perfected a small inventory of trinkets, exquisitely humble, as if by some authentic craftsman in the mountains. When the sun climbed Sunday morning, he rode to the cathedral square and unloaded a board he had prepared, adorned with nails and hooks to hang and display his rosaries. At his feet he spread a faded shawl of Thuận's and lay an artistic array of carved crosses and bearded men in robes. Whoever would ask for Jesus, there he was. If the next person asked for Moses or Peter or John, the figurine was transformed into the blessed character requested. Lanh felt magical, and his patrons felt exalted, he was sure.

He soon became a fixture in the plaza, so much so that he drew the lingering stares of passing police, who seemed uncertain about their mission in this new landscape. After a time, one pair asked for his ID and his explanation, offering Lanh the chance to chat and joke and pass the time until he had them laughing along and ambling off. They wrote down his name, though, and must have sent it up the line far enough to secure him absolution. For they then just stopped to gossip and complain about the foul air of the city, its stealthy commerce, and their distant families in the North unseen in months or years.

"You should play your flute for money," Thuận said one evening. "It's lovely. People need soothing nowadays." Lanh waved her idea away, yet a good idea never quite flies off. It lingers, circling and diving like an enticing irritant. So one weekday morning, Lanh took his flute and the dusty Red Sox hat Rosie had once given him, and parked himself near the central market, now sparse in these early Communist times. He placed his hat upside down on the sidewalk, and began to play, careful to avoid political tunes of the past and just as careful to tease out the nostalgia of timeless yearnings.

People slowed. Some stopped. All listened as if their hearts were breaking. Lanh had salted the hat with several coins, and a few passersby added theirs. Again, policemen bathed him in an uncertain gaze, took his name, and answered when he asked them if they had a favorite tune that he might know to play. From then on they let him be, apparently another gift of absolution from on high.

Music gave him strength, and he grew a little bit daring. He began to play melodies by Trịnh Công Sơn, whose old songs against war—war in any form—had been silenced by the new regime, which could not countenance dismay against a war of liberation, after all. But while Lanh played the notes, the lyrics stayed unsung inside his head, unheard and unimagined by the patrols who swaggered by.

> *The cannons disturb a young child*
> *At midnight a flare shines in the mountains . . .*
> *Each night the native land's eyes stay open wide . . .*
> *Cannons like a chant without a prayer*
> *Children forget to live and anxiously wait*

Musicians find each other, and wanderers cross paths. Over the weeks, the flow of bystanders and listeners eddied into back swirls of players, who emerged one by one to tell Lanh of bygone gigs in dark cafés, even recordings made now and then. A sonorous *đàn tranh* resided silently in an older man's wardrobe, its sixteen strings untuned for years. A two-stringed moon lute danced beneath the fingers of a young fellow eager to play concerts. The son of a farmer claimed to harbor a seasoned rice drum at home and the palms and fingers to mark the time of any tune. A fiddler with a *đàn nhị* asked if he and Lanh could meet sometime and play, perhaps some songs of Trịnh Công Sơn.

So began Lanh's band, just as he would have imagined it, on the simple street without plan or pretense. The fiddler and he made his loft their stage, then others came and joined. Soon Lane 342 was teased by music leaking out of Lanh's house into the alleyway until the musicians themselves stepped into view, drawing the neighborhood together. Even the pho man stood and listened, beating his foot subtly in time.

CHAPTER 21

I n Boston, Pen was interrogated by Rosie. What had he left Lanh with? Enough money? Yes, Pen assured her, 5,000 in green and a camera locked securely in the office safe that should hold him for a long time. And his wife and kids, are they all right? They were okay as far as he knew, no word since the fall. Try to call him. Isn't it risky for him? Don't be ridiculous, he is a man of the people, the NLF are of the people. Hmmm, what people, not people like Lanh, the Communists are not wild fans of independent thinkers.

Rosie screeched at Pen as if he had stuck her with a pin. "Communists! You used the word Communists! That is the epithet of disdain. Didn't you learn anything there?"

"Calm down," Pen said. "I am not going to debate semantics. Let's stick to Lanh. I asked him before I left if he thought there'd be a safe way to send him money or stuff he needed. He shrugged. Who could know? Then he said that maybe by pigeon, someone trustworthy who was coming, who could phone him at home and say he'd brought him medicine. Medicine, that's the code he picked. Not much of a code, but his choice. So I don't think we should call from here. Let's hope that somebody gets there soon, and we can be in touch with him that way."

"I'm worried about him. I've heard nothing."

"Why are you worried? You told him to stay."

"How do you know I told him to stay?"

"He said so. He wrestled with the decision, though not very hard, I think." The phone line went quiet. "Are you there?" Pen asked.

"Yes, I'm here. It was best for him. He would hate the States."

"Perhaps. Probably. Let's hope he hasn't been shipped off for reeducation."

Rosie snarled more eloquently than all the words of scorn she might have mustered at the absurd idea. "Goodbye, Pen."

Through the tight network of Vietnam hacks and do-gooders, word eventually came that a Quaker couple in Ohio had obtained visas. Pen packed an envelope with $200 in crisp twenties, plus a note to Lanh and another to the couple with Lanh's phone number and instructions. Weeks passed, and an envelope with a Cleveland postmark arrived for Pen. He tore it open to find a typed note from the Quakers and a brief letter in close, precise handwriting, signed Nguyễn Văn Lanh.

Dear Pen,

Thank you very much for the medicine. My family needs it. We are doing well. Thuận is buying and selling small items that people want. I have taken up woodcarving, which people near the cathedral like enough to pay a little for. And I am playing the flute again, collecting some coins from generous people who like the music. Maybe my friends and I will form a band. We are all very happy that the war is over. The sandbags are gone from

311

Hồ Chí Minh City, the artillery at night is silent, the people are safe and getting used to the new era. I hope that someday you will be able to return and see that in my heart, I am still a buffalo boy.

At least Lanh was not being "reeducated," as if he ever could be! But the letter struck Pen hard, like a riddle of antonyms: ease and joy and professional prosperity. It told him implicitly what he then saw spelled out in the Quakers' note, that the safe had been stolen, that Thuận had been fired from teaching, and that Lanh had been warned away from journalism. Their note contained only one true revelation: *You will be interested to know officials told Lanh that a friend of your wife's was spying on you for the Saigon regime. Lanh said that might have been how you were prevented from visiting NLF territory. Lanh didn't seem to have any more information, but he was curious to learn who that might have been. We pass it on for whatever it's worth.*

And it was worth an emotional fortune. "Shit!" he shouted to no one, and picked up the phone to call Julie at her studio. "It might have been that tennis teacher," he told her.

"Huh?" She put down her brush.

"The tennis teacher Hạnh? The Quakers say Lanh was told that a friend of yours ratted me out on the way to VC territory. Officials told him she was a spy."

"Oh, no," Julie nearly whispered. "Oh, I'm so sorry, Pen. I had no idea. She was so lovely, really, and her husband, such a cool artist." An awkward beat of silence. "Ah, well, come to think of it, a cartoonist who managed to get things past the censors. I see. I think I see. Her way to secure Dương's accomplishments. But he made people think freely with his cartoons, Pen, really, that's something. She was also my friend, or so I thought. I could say anything to her, and she to me. We hit it off. Maybe she didn't like what she had to do for him." *She passed my secret test—wouldn't interpret for the prisoners. She was scared. Or was that an act?*

"I think she deceived you. Sorry, Jule, it sounds like a phony friendship. You were used."

"That's the simple answer. I'm not so sure. In any case, she and Dương must be in grave danger now. She was so desperate to get out, and I did nothing for her except go through the motions."

"Me neither. She came by the office toward the end, asking me for help. She seemed privileged and terrified all at once. I turned my back on her. Not that I could have done anything. And, frankly, not that I'm sorry for her, knowing this."

"Oh, Pen, that's callous. War forces compromises, you've said so yourself. Who knows how you or I would have behaved?"

"I would not have been a false friend."

"I'm glad you're so upstanding. Now what shall we do with the folder of Dương's cartoons, which we hold for safe-keeping, probably forever?"

Years collapsed and contracted. Julie's portraits of Vietnamese faces were offered for sale at handsome prices in the gallery where she usually displayed. But instead of pleasure, every sale brought her a stab of jealous regret: that she was losing a layer of her life to a stranger, who would possess another stranger. She never offered Mai, of course, but came to guard the other children in Erik's home as well, their faces drawn from the quick photographs Lanh had taken during the street games, children all gone in the plane crash—Robber, Xuân, Binh, and others whose names she'd forgotten. But their merry laughter had not been silenced, their dusty bare feet still slid and danced across the yard. And she was still hobbled by Mai's hugs around her knees.

"I am not going to sell the children—oh, what a terrible way to put it. I am not going to sell their portraits anymore," she told the gallery owner. He was miffed.

As Vietnam opened step by step, Pen and Rosie pigeoned more and more dollars, plus a camera, with travelers whom they trusted to appreciate meeting Lanh. He invariably beguiled them with his earthy insights into his land of metaphors. They would return with admiring accounts and brief notes written in his fine hand. All is well, he would say. Thuận is a little happier since she has grandchildren. He has a band, and now that cafés and restaurants are open, they play three nights a week, traditional Vietnamese music. His religious carvings are still popular. He gives swimming lessons to little kids and is willing to teach English to people who might be in "a position" to learn, a curious choice of words that Pen interpreted—now *he* was the interpreter!—to mean authorized officials or their families.

Pen agitated with his editors to send him there on a reporting trip, but they weaved around the demand. Budgets were tight. Vietnam was not truly open to journalists who didn't want a minder. Maybe later. Maybe someday. Maybe never, was Pen's reading. But then the country that lost the war opened an embassy in Hanoi, and Murphy, the editor on the brink of retirement, pointed to Pen.

"Want to go?" asked his raspy voice on the phone.

"Damned straight!"

"The Vietnamese are being so welcoming to Americans," Murphy growled. "Maybe you can figure out why."

"I guess the victors can be magnanimous."

"Maybe. Check it out. Give us some good copy. Get under the skin of their courtesy. See what they're thinking."

Breathing in Hanoi, beset by a steamy drizzle in August, was as hard as gasping through a soaking blanket. Pen was flustered by beggars and barefoot children selling postcards, more insistent than in Saigon years ago. One little boy peddled copies of Graham Greene's *The Quiet American*. Bicycles and buzzing motorbikes piled with impossibly tall towers of tin boxes and shoes and fruit, seemed tangled together in every intersection. But they miraculously threaded among one another as harmlessly as a loom weaves thread. Women and men in conical hats swayed under bouncing shoulder poles laden by round baskets of bananas and reddish lychees. Women squatting along the curbs beckoned toward their wares. The rhythms of the street brought him a groundswell of nostalgia.

His first night, armed with a list of restaurants from friends who had visited, Pen climbed up steep stairs to a tiny place that served only one dish, *chả cá*, hunks of tender Red River catfish in a circular brazier, charcoal glowing in the center. He picked the morsels out with chopsticks, placed them on heaps of rice noodles, dill, spring onion, and ground peanuts, dipped them in brown sauce, and cruised into a contentment he had not foreseen. Afterwards, in the late evening, he shook off beggars and strolled around the Lake of the Restored Sword, recalled by Lanh so fondly from his boyhood.

Lanh had told Pen the legend one hot afternoon on Lê Lợi Street in Saigon, and Pen could never quite decipher how closely Lanh came, in his own mind, to the line between myth and truth. Myths are important, he remembered Lanh saying; they contain truths. And so now I will tell you one of ours, he had said, a fifteenth-century story of a fisherman named Lê Lợi who pulled up his net one day to find a magical sword, which in his hands for a decade he used to lead an uprising that expelled the Chinese. There in that lake in Hanoi lies the sword, where a giant turtle snatched it from Lê Lợi and restored it to the deep. Pen felt soothed by Lanh's voice meandering through his memories.

He needed Lanh now. His officially assigned interpreter, a woman practically too young to remember the bombing, translated mechanically and superficially, tried to breeze past ordinary folks on the street, and deflected Pen's every probing question as if time were running out. She did nothing to ease the obvious nervousness of people they encountered. She was businesslike, friendly and formal, carefully scripted, politically proper. At least his story on the embassy opening, with the Stars and Stripes raised incongruously over the resurrected city, gave him license to contemplate how fleeting zealotry could be. *Am I also allowed to reflect on the pride and shame I feel about my country? No. I am not permitted self-indulgence in the news columns. Just as well.*

Forced politely through the military museum and the tomb of Hồ Chí Minh, Pen skated on the surface until he flew down to Saigon—he still called it Saigon. After the war, the city's recalcitrance had gone into hibernation. Now it had awakened. A private travel agency provided a laid-back guide, a middle-aged man who drove him to the Củ Chi tunnels, which had been widened to fit hefty American tourists. All the way there and all the way back, the guide's sardonic comments and political jokes filled the car with ir-reverence, sweet and sour.

"After reeducation camp," the guide said, "they ask me join Communist Party. I say no. They say why not? I say I no join gangs, because I know you join gang, you can never leave." He laughed in a high pitch of trust in this American.

Lanh answered the phone. He did not linger in the conversation but named a restaurant and a time. When Pen hung up, he realized something. During all their work together, Lanh had never had him to his home, never intro-duced him to his wife or daughters. But then, too, Pen and Julie had never invited Lanh and his family to the villa, not even for a meal by Nghi, whose dishes would have found no greater admirer in all of Saigon.

The Chinese restaurant was big and loud, a wash of sound drowning out most chance of eavesdropping. From his table, Pen could see the doorway, and he recognized the gangly silhouette, thinner and slightly tilted but still casual-ly loose-jointed. Lanh waved and strode directly to Pen, put out his hand then his arms in an embrace, gracing him with his lopsided smile.

In the tradition of old friendships, the renewal began where it had been suspended, resuming at the same speed. His face, more like worn leather now, still crinkled and beamed and frowned in complete display of every feeling he loaded onto every word. His musical tempo of English, a little halting now, still observed the rhythm and rests of a storyteller. His body still acted out his tales.

News had to be imparted, the mundane and the exceptional: Lanh pulled out black-and-white photos of Thuận and their daughters, their husbands, their assortment of cute kids, all illuminated by his glow. He downplayed his peddler's craft and played up his band. He tried to tell of his bar from "journalism" without self-pity or resentment, waving his hands gracefully in nonchalance. Pen, for his part, dwelled on the tedium of his current reporting job, which could not compare with the exhilarating tension of his years in Vietnam; and he bragged about Julie's success as a portrait artist, begun right here. "But she's still searching," Pen said, "not quite sure how to advance her art. As for me, I feel like I'm treading water, floundering in my work."

"Ah, me too," said Lanh. "But maybe floundering is my purpose. My fate." Then he listed his fates. The flute. The band. The wooden trinkets. The swimming lessons. The English lessons.

"You found people who could study English?"

"One," he said to Pen. "An official. Maybe there will be more. These are all—what's the word? I've forgotten so much of my English. Hobbies?"

"Do you like doing them?

"Of course. I always like doing whatever I am doing. Stay in the present."

"I heard that you wanted to know who the spy was."

Lanh opened a hand as if to let the question float away. "If you wish to tell me. I try not to be very curious about things that might open into minefields. But do you know?"

"We suspect," said Pen. "We think it was Hạnh, her tennis teacher, wife of the cartoonist Dương. Not sure, but likely."

"Is she still here?" Lanh asked.

"I have no idea. We have no idea. We haven't heard from her in the States, and she could probably find us if she's there. She and Dương could find me at the paper anyway."

"So she might be here," said Lanh.

"But you're not going to tell anyone, are you?"

"I have nobody to tell," Lanh said. "I have no official contacts. I live in a no-man's land, as always. Your old pal Võ Đông Giang told me that they thought it was a friend of Julie's, so they probably dealt with the woman long ago."

"And her husband the cartoonist, do you know anything about him?"

"He was famous during the war, but under several names, each for a different newspaper. Then he and his cartoons disappeared, to what hidden or painful or freeing place I don't know."

And what hidden or painful or freeing place have you found? Pen wondered, then let his musing skid away. Old friendships, aside from picking up at speed, take more comfort from the known past than from the uncertain future. So after Lanh ordered dishes with a flourish of expertise, the talk was buoyed by reminiscences. "Remember the ARVN soldiers who were eyeing my camera? And the local commander who gave his troops a lunch break? And the nuoc mam factory? Julie couldn't stand it. I thought she'd never touch it again. But she did go back to it eventually."

"Oh?" Lanh said. "Then I was wrong about her. I put her on the losing side." He stopped for a moment, then said

319

so quietly that the words nearly sank away under the din of the restaurant: "There was Huế."

The two men held a long stare. *Any word about Vinh's wife and kids? Have you found balm for this laceration? I haven't.* Lanh heard Pen's unspoken questions. "His wife wrote to me two years ago. She was going to try to reopen the restaurant, but it sounded more like a wish than a plan. A handful of smoke. Their children are grown. She didn't seem to resent me."

"Us," said Pen.

"What?"

"Resent *us*. I was just as responsible."

"Responsible," Lanh said. "What a thing it is. You can't see it. You can't grab it. You can't hold it, especially in war."

"You can hear it. Whispering at night."

"Look," Lanh answered, "the bowl of water is heavy until you put it down. A Buddhist idea, from a monk long ago. I have trouble doing that."

"Mai," said Pen softly.

"Mai?"

"You remember, Lanh, the adorable little girl at Erik's. Julie wanted—we wanted—to adopt her. She might have saved us from some emptiness, but she was not to be saved." And he cradled his face in his hands. "Sorry. Sorry." Had he looked up, he might have seen a careful look of reproach from his friend.

Should I tell him what I tried to do? Lanh thought. *Should I tell him how I failed her too?* But he veered away. "No need to apologize for sorrow," he said. "Otherwise, we would all have no words in our vocabulary except sorry."

Lanh stayed away from politics, Pen noticed, but he did tell more of Võ Đông Giang's story—the Trail and the tunnels and the Liberation soldier who disobeyed and received his due. For some reason, Giang's intention to shoot the kid if he hadn't been wounded made them both smile at the tough old guy's balls.

"That's why they won," said Pen. "And the tunnels. The tunnels are like a symbol of resolve. Can you imagine the South Vietnamese army or US troops digging tunnels under North Vietnamese bases? Impossible."

Lanh did not take this thread and pull it, so he prevented Pen from seeing what it might unravel. Instead, he spoke of wanderlust unsatisfied. "There is so much of my country I have not seen," he said. "And even where I've been before I have not seen, because I see changes through changing eyes."

"So why not travel?"

"I can't leave the few scraps of work I have here. They are barely enough."

"What about this?" Pen asked. "What if we did a book together? What if I came and traveled with you for a month or two, wherever you wanted to go? I could hire you. You could take pictures, I could write, and we would have a terrific book. I already love seeing Vietnam at peace, without the soldiers and sandbags. It feels uplifting—liberating!" He grinned at his pun.

To read the look on Lanh's face would have taken an artist with Julie's eye. Brightness and shadow played against each other the way spears of sunlight cut shifting patterns on a forest floor. "I'll ask," he said, and pointed upward. He didn't say if he liked the idea, or whether he was afraid of trying only to be refused, kicked away once again.

To Pen's surprise, he was in a taxi headed to Lanh's house. "I will have people for you to meet," Lanh had said with a cryptic grin, and wrote the intricate address: 136D Cách Mạng Tháng Tám Street 8 (Hẻm 342) D.13 Tân Bình District. The driver had scratched his head for a moment, then got it and set off through avenues nearly as busy as in '75.

The alley, strewn with chickens, cats, and children playing the old street games, was barely wide enough for the scratched and dented Citroën cab, which scattered the lane's inhabitants with a rudeness Pen hadn't seen since the days of the ARVN's armored personnel carriers. It braked to a halt in front of a faded green wooden door, and suddenly a smiling Lanh emerged with gestures of welcome.

A serene woman with a touch of gray in her hair, tied back in a bun, was introduced as Thuận. One of the daughters, Linh, put out her hand in greeting but with wary hesitation. A toddler squatted bashfully in a corner. Lanh had Pen climb with him to his loft to see where he had done his work and could look down on the family from "on high," as he put it. Propped up on his desk against the wall, Julie's portrait stood as a reminder, he explained. "It is a reminder of her, and of you, but most of all a reminder of myself, how I would like to imagine myself."

"And how is that?" Pen asked.

"As happy and serious and wise." In light mockery, he copied his own lopsided smile.

"That's what we thought we were then," Pen said. "I don't know about now."

"Now? Even thin strands of suffering long past can be woven into beauty," Lanh said. "You will see," and he checked his watch.

In a brief while, a graceful young woman in a powder blue *áo dài* appeared, smiling shyly. She shook hands with Pen, cast her eyes down in respect, and looked expectantly at Lanh, who said simply, "This is Miss Kim, Võ Tấn Đức's daughter." Pen seemed puzzled. "The man who set himself on fire."

Pen's sob came like a gust of thrill and grief. He spread his arms to ask permission to hug, and Miss Kim moved toward him as he wrapped her as if trying to absorb and relieve all her years of loss.

He scarcely had seconds to ask about her life before another guest came to the door, a woman somewhat older in the austere costume of plain white blouse and black pants, a face he knew from somewhere, he was sure. She strode to him boldly, put out her hand, and declared her hello and her immediate thanks, in a long explanation in Vietnamese, which Lanh translated as gratitude for saving her life.

"Nguyễn Thị Hoà," Lanh explained. "The girl shackled to the stretcher."

Several months had passed when Pen picked up the phone and heard Mandell say that he had just returned from Saigon, had seen Lanh, and had some news. "He got a strong yellow light on the project you two were cooking up. He checked with people and it's a no-go. Sorry, whatever it was. He was very sad about it but seemed resigned, and maybe not surprised. The old guys there have been walled off. Stupid. There's a lot of talent going to waste. And also, he said he has some kind of cancer, he didn't say what. It didn't sound too serious. At least he didn't make it sound that way, but he thought you'd want to know."

Pen typed a letter on flimsy airmail paper and sent it to Lanh's complicated address. He told him that Rosie had died but didn't say that she had taken her own life. He worded his questions carefully, saying nothing about the book idea except, "Sorry about the news, especially about the cancer." What kind? How serious? How's the band, the teaching? No reply arrived.

When Pen heard that travelers were going, he gave them "medicine" and notes to Lanh, but the visitors returned without letters, only sketchy information. He seemed fine, interesting, we went to hear his band. What a great person. Thanks for the introduction.

"Jule, want to go to Saigon?" The line from her studio sounded dead for a moment.

"You're going?"

"For pieces on the flourishing Vietnamese economy. I finally wore them down. They got sick of me badgering them."

"I can't, Pen. You know I've got a big show coming up, and I'm pushing frantically to finish some new drawings to mix in with Vietnam portraits. I can't take off. Sorry."

"We could reconnect. It's still inside us, Vietnam. It hasn't let us go. We could see Lanh, maybe find other people we knew. It's a new chapter."

"Yes, yes, I know. Maybe to lighten my memories. And I could collect more faces."

"Collect faces?" Pen shot back. "Like souvenirs? You've slipped backwards to where you were when you first arrived."

"Oh, that sounds callous. I'm sorry. But that's what I do. Collect. You know what I mean. Collect people's whole stories, beneath the page. I would love to, but I can't. Next time. Will there be a next time? Say hi to Lanh for me."

Hồ Chí Minh City had too many syllables for anybody but the politically orthodox, so Saigon it was. Saigon the heart of the boom, Saigon the jungle of cranes and glass high-rises, Saigon the festivals of bright flowers and banners and *áo dàis*, Saigon the cornucopia of crafts and food and garish lacquerware, of seductive music pouring through the open doors of restaurants.

He had written to Lanh that he was coming, but had the letter been received? He called Lanh's cellphone, which rang and rang and didn't answer. So he gave a taxi driver the address he'd saved on the scrap of paper from Lanh, and soon the sides of Lane 342 were grabbing at the cab as the driver swiveled his head in search of house number 136D.

"Here!" Pen said and pointed to the faded green door.

He knocked. The door was opened slightly by a young girl, wide-eyed, who called over her shoulder, "*Mỹ! Mỹ!*" That word Pen knew very well: *American!* And it made him smile. The house smelled of incense. Thuận came and grasped Pen in a weeping embrace. She led him inside. Many people in the room stared at him.

There, on a low table by a wall, stood Julie's portrait of Lanh, his head cocked, his lopsided smile offering solace. Black ribbons cut diagonally across the upper corners. Smoking joss sticks were stuck in two copper pots on either side. The table was adorned with necklaces of jasmine and bowls heaped with fruit that Lanh had loved.

Pen stood stricken with silence. He and those gathered had no language in common.

ACKNOWLEDGMENTS

I am indebted to Quynh Schafer for checking the manuscript for references to Vietnamese culture, cuisine, and language, and to John Schafer for his translations of Trịnh Công Sơn's lyrics. My thanks also to the reporters who covered the end of the war, especially Arnold R. Isaacs, whose book *Without Honor: Defeat in Vietnam and Cambodia*, vividly described the war's final days and helped provide a basis for my fictionalized depiction here. To him and the many other journalists who have taken risks to report on that war and others, a salute of admiration.